CRITICAL ACCLAIM FOR

Sue Grafton and Kinsey Millhone

A is for Alibi
'Sue Grafton has created a woman we feel we know . . .
Smart, well paced and very funny.'
Newsweek

B is for Burglar
'A woman to identify with . . . a gripping read.'
Punch

C is for Corpse
'C is for classy, multiplex plotting, strong
characterisation and a tough-cookie heroine.'
Time Out

D is for Deadbeat
'D is for deft and diverting.'
Guardian

E is for Evidence
'E is for Excellent, Ms Grafton.'
Sunday Times

F is for Fugitive
'Of the private investigators, Sue Grafton's Kinsey
Millhone is one of the most convincing in operation.'
Independent

G is for Gumshoe
'G is for Grafton, Gumshoe and Good.'
Sunday Telegraph

H is for Homicide
'S is for Super Sleuth in a scorching story.'
Daily Mail

I is for Innocent
'I could also stand for incomparable . . . riveting
throughout, crackling finale.'
Observer

J is for Judgment
'Kinsey Millhone is up there with the giants of the
private eye genre, as magnetic as Marlowe, as
insouciant as Spenser. It's all exhilarating stuff.'
Times Literary Supplement

K is for Killer
'*K is for Killer* is another excellent novel from the
excellent Sue Grafton.'
Daily Mirror

L is for Lawless
'This is Sue Grafton at her best.'
The Spectator

M is for Malice
'M is for marvellous, mesmerising and magnificent.'
Manchester Evening News

O is for Outlaw
'One of the more humane and emphathic sleuths on
the block, Grafton's heroine is also genuinely
believable, full of quirks and all too human
foibles which help the reader identify with her . . .
Absolute top form.'
Time Out

P is for Peril
'Intricate and exciting, with plot turns and twists
mostly unguessable. Grade A entertainment.'
Literary Review

N IS FOR NOOSE

Sue Grafton has become one of the most popular female crime writers, both here and in the US. Born in Kentucky in 1940, the daughter of the mystery writer C.W. Grafton, she began her career as a TV scriptwriter before Kinsey Millhone and the 'alphabet' series took off. Her first novel, *A is for Alibi*, was inspired by Sue's own divorce: '*For months I lay in bed and plotted to kill my ex-husband, but I knew I'd bungle it and get caught so I wrote it in a book instead.*'

Sue freely confesses that Kinsey is her alter ego: 'I think of her as the person I might have been had I not married young and had kids; she is that stripped down piece of my personality.' She writes one book a year and plans to take Kinsey all the way through the alphabet to Z when Kinsey will be forty years old.

Sue Grafton lives in Santa Barbara with her husband Steven Humphrey.

By the same author

KINSEY MILLHONE MYSTERIES
A IS FOR ALIBI
B IS FOR BURGLAR
C IS FOR CORPSE
D IS FOR DEADBEAT
E IS FOR EVIDENCE
F IS FOR FUGITIVE
G IS FOR GUMSHOE
H IS FOR HOMICIDE
I IS FOR INNOCENT
J IS FOR JUDGMENT
K IS FOR KILLER
L IS FOR LAWLESS
M IS FOR MALICE
O IS FOR OUTLAW
P IS FOR PERIL

KEZIAH DANE
THE LOLLY MADONNA WAR

SUE GRAFTON

N

IS FOR NOOSE

PAN BOOKS

First published in the United States of America 1998 by
Henry Holt and Co., Inc., New York

First published in Great Britain 1998 by Macmillan

This edition published 1999 by Pan Books
an imprint of Pan Macmillan Ltd
Pan Macmillan, 20 New Wharf Road, London N1 9RR
Basingstoke and Oxford
Associated companies throughout the world
www.panmacmillan.com

ISBN 0 330 34877 9

15 17 19 18 16 14

A CIP catalogue record for this book is available from
the British Library.

Photypeset by Intype London Limited
Printed and bound in Great Britain by
Mackays of Chatham plc, Chatham, Kent

FOR STEVEN,
who makes my life possible.

The author wishes to acknowledge the invaluable assistance of the following people: Steven Humphrey; Eric S. H. Ching; Shelly Dumas and Sergeant Dick Wood, Inyo County Sheriff's Department; Leon Brune, Inyo County Coroner; Donna Milovich, Spellbinder Books; Robert Failing, M.D.; Dennis Prescott, Supervisor (retired), and Larry Gillespie, Senior Investigator, Santa Barbara County Coroner's Office; Deputy Eric Raney, Commander Bill Crook, and Commander Terry Bunn, Santa Barbara County Sheriff's Department; Captain Ed Aasted, Santa Barbara Police Department; Bruce Bennet; Sheila Millington, Automobile Club of Southern California; Sylvia Stallings; Joe Peus, M.D.; B. J. Seebol; and John Hunt, CompuVision, for saving chapter 22.

N

IS FOR NOOSE

ONE

Sometimes I think about how odd it would be to catch a glimpse of the future, a quick view of events lying in store for us at some undisclosed date. Suppose we could peer through a tiny peep-hole in Time and chance upon a flash of what was coming up in the years ahead. Some moments we saw would make no sense at all and some, I suspect, would frighten us beyond endurance. If we knew what was looming, we'd avoid certain choices, select option B instead of A at the fork in the road: the job, the marriage, the move to a new state, childbirth, the first drink, the elective medical procedure, that long-anticipated ski trip that seemed like such fun until the dark rumble of the avalanche. If we understood the consequences of any given action, we could exercise discretion, thus restructuring our fate. Time, of course, only runs in one direction, and it seems to do so in an orderly progression. Here in the blank and stony present, we're shielded from the knowledge of the dangers that await us, protected from future horrors through blind innocence.

Take the case in point. I was winding my way through the mountains in a cut-rate rental car, heading south on 395 toward the town of Nota Lake, California, where I was going to interview a potential client. The roadway was dry and the view was unobstructed, weather conditions clear. The client's business was unremarkable, at least as far as I could see. I had no idea there was any jeopardy waiting or I'd have done something else.

I'd left Dietz in Carson City, where I'd spent the last two weeks playing nurse/companion while he recovered from surgery. He'd been scheduled for a knee replacement and I'd volunteered to drive him back to Nevada in his snazzy little red Porsche. I make no claims to nurturing, but I'm a practical person and the nine-hour journey seemed the obvious solution to the problem of how to get his car back to his home state. I'm a no-nonsense driver and he knew he could count on me to get us to Carson City without any unnecessary side trips and no irrelevant conversation. He'd been staying in my apartment for the two previous months and since our separation was approaching, we tended to avoid discussing anything personal.

For the record, my last name is Millhone, first name Kinsey. I'm female, twice divorced, seven weeks shy of thirty-six, and reasonably fit. I'm a licensed private detective, currently residing in Santa Teresa, California, to which I'm attached like a tetherball on a very short cord. Occasionally, business will swing me out to other parts of the country, but I'm basically a small-town shamus and likely to remain so for life.

Dietz's surgery, which was scheduled for the first Monday in March, proceeded uneventfully, so we can skip that part. Afterward, I returned to his condo-

minium and toured the premises with interest. I'd been
startled by the place when I first laid eyes on it, as it
was more lavish and much better appointed than my
poor digs back in Santa Teresa. Dietz was a nomad
and I'd never pictured his having much in the way
of material possessions. While I was closeted in a
converted single-car garage (recently remodeled to
accommodate a sleeping loft and a second bathroom
upstairs), Dietz maintained a three-bedroom penthouse
that probably encompassed three thousand square feet
of living space, including a roof patio and garden with
an honest-to-god greenhouse. Granted, the seven-story
building was located in a commercial district, but the
views were astounding and the privacy profound.

I'd been too polite to pry while he was standing right
there beside me, but once he was safely ensconced in
the orthopedic ward at Carson/Tahoe Hospital, I felt
comfortable scrutinizing everything in my immediate
range, which necessitated dragging a chair around and
standing on it in some cases. I checked closets and files
and boxes and papers and drawers, pockets and suit-
cases, feeling equal parts relief and disappointment that
he had nothing in particular to hide. I mean, what's the
point of snooping if you can't uncover something good?
I did have the chance to study a photograph of his ex-
wife, Naomi, who was certainly a lot prettier than he'd
ever indicated. Aside from that, his finances appeared
to be in order, his medicine cabinet contained no sinister
pharmaceutical revelations, and his private correspondence consisted almost entirely of assorted misspelled
letters from his two college-aged sons. Lest you think
I'm intrusive, I can assure you Dietz had searched my

apartment just as thoroughly during the time he was in residence. I know this because I'd left a few booby traps, one of which he'd missed when he was picking open my locked desk drawers. His license might have lapsed, but (most of) his operating skills were still current. Neither of us had ever mentioned his invasion of my privacy, but I vowed I'd do likewise when the opportunity arose. Between working detectives, this is known as professional courtesy. You toss my place and I'll toss yours.

He was out of the hospital by Friday morning of that week. The ensuing recovery involved a lot of sitting around with his knee wrapped in bandages as thick as a bolster. We watched trash television, played gin rummy, and worked a jigsaw puzzle with a picture depicting a roiling nest of earthworms so lifelike I nearly went off my feed. The first three days I did all the cooking, which is to say I made sandwiches, alternating between my famous peanut-butter-and-pickle extravaganza and my much beloved, sliced hot-hard-boiled-egg confection, with tons of Hellmann's mayonnaise and salt. After that, Dietz seemed eager to get back into the kitchen and our menus expanded to include pizza, take-out Chinese, and Campbell's soup—tomato or asparagus, depending on our mood.

By the end of two weeks Dietz could pretty well fend for himself. His stitches were out and he was hobbling around with a cane between bouts of physical therapy. He had a long way to go, but he could drive to his sessions and otherwise seemed able to tend to his own needs. By then, I thought it entirely possible I'd go mad from trailing after him. It was time to hit the road before our togetherness began to chafe. I enjoyed being with him, but I knew my limitations. I kept my farewells perfunctory; lots of airy okay-fine-thanks-a-lot-I'll-see-you-laters. It was my way of minimizing the painful lump in my throat, staving off the embarrassing boo-hoos I thought were best left unexpressed. Don't ask me to reconcile the misery I felt with the nearly giddy sense of relief. Nobody ever said emotions made any sense.

So there I was, barreling down the highway in search of employment and not at all fussy about what kind of work I'd take. I wanted distraction. I wanted money, escape, anything to keep my mind off the subject of Robert Dietz. I'm not good at good-byes. I've suffered way too many in my day and I don't like the sensation. On the other hand, I'm not that good at relationships. Get close to someone and next thing you know, you've given them the power to wound, betray, irritate, abandon you, or bore you senseless. My general policy is to keep my distance, thus avoiding a lot of unruly emotion. In psychiatric circles, there are names for people like me.

I flipped on the car radio, picking up a scratchy station from Los Angeles, three hundred miles to the south. Gradually, I began to tune in to the surrounding landscape. Highway 395 cuts south out of Carson City, through Minden and Gardnerville. Just north of Topaz, I had crossed the state line into eastern California. The backbone of the state is the towering Sierra Nevada Range, the uptilted edge of a huge fault block, gouged out later by a series of glaciers. To my left was Mono Lake, shrinking at the rate of two feet a year, increasingly saline, supporting little in the way of marine life beyond brine shrimp and the attendant feasting of the birds. Somewhere to my right, through a dark green forest of Jeffrey pines, was Yosemite National Park, with its towering peaks and rugged canyons, lakes, and thundering waterfalls. Meadows, powdered now in light snow, were once the bottom of a Pleistocene lake. Later in the spring, these same meadows would be dense with wildflowers. In the higher ranges, the winter snowpack hadn't yet melted, but the passes were open. It was the kind of scenery described as "breathtaking" by those who are easily winded. I'm not a big fan of the outdoors, but even I was sufficiently impressed to murmur "wow" speeding past a scenic vista point at seventy miles an hour.

The prospective client I was traveling to meet was a woman named Selma Newquist, whose husband, I was told, had died sometime within the past few weeks. Dietz had done work for this woman in the past, helping her extricate herself from an unsavory first marriage. I didn't get all the details, but he alluded to the fact that the financial "goods" he'd gotten on the husband had given Selma enough leverage to free herself from the relationship. There'd been a subsequent marriage and it was this second husband whose death had apparently generated questions his wife wanted answered. She'd called to hire Dietz, but since he was temporarily out of commission, he suggested me. Under ordinary circumstances, I doubted Mrs. Newquist would have considered a P.I. from the far side of the state, but my trip home was imminent and I was heading in her direction. As it turned out, my connection to Santa

Teresa was more pertinent than it first appeared. Dietz had vouched for my integrity and, by the same token, he'd assured me that she'd be conscientious about payment for services rendered. It made sense to stop long enough to hear what the woman had to say. If she didn't want to hire me, all I'd be out was a thirty-minute break in the journey.

I reached Nota Lake (pop. 2,356, elevation 4,312) in slightly more than three hours. The town didn't look like much, though the setting was spectacular. Mountains towered on three sides, snow still painting the peaks in thick white against a sky heaped with clouds. On the shady side of the road, I could see leftover patches of snow, ice boulders wedged up against the leafless trees. The air smelled of pine, with an underlying scent that was faintly sweet. The chill vapor I breathed was like sticking my face down in a half-empty gallon of vanilla ice cream, drinking in the sugary perfume. The lake itself was no more than two miles long and a mile across. The surface was glassy, reflecting granite spires and the smattering of white firs and incense cedars that grew on the slopes. I stopped at a service station and picked up a one-page map of the town, which was shaped like a smudge on the eastern edge of Nota Lake.

The prime businesses seemed to be clustered along the main street in a five-block radius. I did a cursory driving tour, counting ten gas stations and twenty-two motels. Nota Lake offered low-end accommodations for the ski crowd at Mammoth Lakes. The town also boasted an equal number of fast-food restaurants, including Burger King, Carl's Jr., Jack in the Box, Kentucky Fried Chicken, Pizza Hut, a Waffle House, an

International House of Pancakes, a House of Donuts, a Sizzler, a Subway, a Taco Bell, and my personal favorite, McDonald's. Additional restaurants of the sit-down variety were divided equally between Mexican, Bar-B-Que, and "Family" dining, which meant lots of screaming toddlers and no hard liquor on the premises.

The address I'd been given was on the outskirts of town, two blocks off the main highway in a cluster of houses that looked like they'd been built by the same developer. The streets in the area were named for various Indian tribes: Shawnee, Iroquois, Cherokee, Modoc, Crow, Chippewa. Selma Newquist lived on a cul-de-sac called Pawnee Way, the house a replica of its neighbors: frame siding, a shake roof, with a screened-in porch on one end and a two-car garage on the other. I parked in the driveway beside a dark Ford sedan. I locked the car from habit, climbed the two porch steps, and rang the bell—*ding dong*—like the local Avon representative. I waited several minutes and then tried again.

The woman who came to the door was in her late forties, with a small compact body, brown eyes, and short dark tousled hair. She was wearing a red-blue-and-yellow plaid blouse over a yellow pleated skirt.

"Hi, I'm Kinsey Millhone. Are you Selma?"

"No, I'm not. I'm her sister-in-law, Phyllis. My husband, Macon, was Tom's younger brother. We live two doors down. Can I help you?"

"I'm supposed to meet with Selma. I should have called first. Is she here?"

"Oh, sorry. I remember now. She's lying down at the moment, but she told me she thought you'd be stopping by. You're that friend of the detective she called in Carson City."

"Exactly," I said. "How's she doing?"

"Selma has her bad days and I'm afraid this is one. Tom passed away six weeks ago today and she called me in tears. I came over as quick as I could. She was shaking and upset. Poor thing looks like she hasn't slept in days. I gave her a Valium."

"I can come back later if you think that's best."

"No, no. I'm sure she's awake and I know she wants to see you. Why don't you come on in?"

"Thanks."

I followed Phyllis across the entrance and down a carpeted hallway to the master bedroom. In passing, I allowed myself a quick glance into doorways on either side of the hall, garnering an impression of wildly over-decorated rooms. In the living room, the drapes and upholstery fabrics were coordinated to match a pink-and-green wallpaper that depicted floral bouquets, connected by loops of pink ribbon. On the coffee table, there was a lavish arrangement of pink silk flowers. The cut-pile wall-to-wall carpeting was pale green and had the strong chemical scent that suggested it had been only recently laid. In the dining room, the furniture was formal, lots of dark glossy wood with what looked like one too many pieces for the available space. There were storm windows in place everywhere and a white film of condensation had gathered between the panes. The smell of cigarette smoke and coffee formed a musky domestic incense.

Phyllis knocked on the door. "Selma, hon? It's Phyllis."

I heard a muffled response and Phyllis opened the door a crack, peering around the frame. "You've got company. Are you decent? It's this lady detective from Carson City."

I started to correct her and then thought better of it. I wasn't from Carson City and I certainly wasn't a lady, but then what difference did it make? Through the opening I caught a brief impression of the woman in the bed; a pile of platinum blond hair framed by the uprights on a four-poster.

Apparently, I'd been invited in because Phyllis stepped back, murmuring to me as I passed, "I have to get on home, but you're welcome to call me if you need anything."

I nodded my thanks as I moved into the bedroom and closed the door behind me. The curtains were closed and the light was subdued. Throw pillows, like boulders, had tumbled onto the carpet. There was a surplus of ruffles, bold multicolored prints covering walls, windows, and puffy custom bedding. The motif seemed to be roses exploding on impact.

I said, "Sorry to disturb you, but Phyllis said it would be okay. I'm Kinsey Millhone."

Selma Newquist, in a faded flannel nightie, pulled herself into a sitting position and straightened the covers, reminding me of an invalid ready to accept a bedtray. I estimated her age on the high side of fifty, judging by the backs of her hands, which were freckled with liver spots and ropy with veins. Her skin tones suggested dark coloring, but her hair was a confection of white-blond curls, like a cloud of cotton candy. At the moment, the entire cone was listing sideways and looked sticky with hair spray. She'd drawn in her eyebrows with a red-brown pencil, but any eyeliner or eye shadow had long since vanished. Through the streaks in her pancake makeup, I could see the blotchy complexion that suggested too much sun exposure. She reached for her cigarettes, groping on the bed table until she had both the cigarette pack and lighter. Her hand trembled slightly as she lit her cigarette. "Why don't you come over here," she said. She gestured toward a chair. "Push that off of there and sit down where I can see you better."

I moved her quilted robe from the chair and placed it on the bed, pulling the chair in close before I took a seat.

She stared at me, puffy-eyed, a thin stream of smoke escaping as she spoke. "I'm sorry you had to see me this way. Ordinarily I'm up and about at this hour, but this has been a hard day."

"I understand," I said. Smoke began to settle over me like the fine spray from someone's sneeze.

"Did Phyllis offer you coffee?"

"Please don't trouble. She's on her way back to her place and I'm fine anyway. I don't want to take any more time than I have to."

She stared at me vaguely. "Doesn't matter," she said. "I don't know if you've ever lost anyone close, but there are days when you feel like you're coming down with the flu. Your whole body aches and your head feels so stuffy you can't think properly. I'm glad to have company. You learn to appreciate any distraction. You can't avoid your feelings, but it helps to have momentary relief." She tended, in speaking, to keep a hand up

13

against her mouth, apparently self-conscious about the discoloration on her two front teeth, which I could now see were markedly gray. Perhaps she'd fallen as a child or taken medication as an infant that tinted the surface with dark. "How do you know Robert Dietz?" she asked.

"I hired him myself a couple of years ago to handle my personal security. Someone threatened my life and Dietz ended up working for me as a bodyguard."

"How's his knee doing? I was sorry to hear he was laid up."

"He'll be fine. He's tough. He's already up and around."

"Did he tell you about Tom?"

"Only that you were recently widowed. That's as much as I know."

"I'll fill you in then, though I'm really not sure where to start. You may think I'm crazy, but I assure you I'm not." She took a puff of her cigarette and sighed a mouthful of smoke. I expected tears in the telling, but the story emerged in a Valium-induced calm. "Tom had a heart attack. He was out on the road . . . about seven miles out of town. This was ten o'clock at night. He must have had sufficient warning to pull over to the side. A CHP officer—a friend of ours, James Tennyson— recognized Tom's truck with the hazard lights on and stopped to see if he needed help. Tom was slumped at the wheel. I'd been to a meeting at church and came home to find two patrol cars sitting in my drive. You knew Tom was a detective with the county sheriff's?"

"I wasn't aware of that."

"I used to worry he'd be killed in the line of duty. I

14

never imagined he'd go like he did." She paused, drawing on her cigarette, using smoke as a form of punctuation.

"It must have been difficult."

"It was awful," she said. Up went the hand again, resting against her mouth as the tears began to well in her eyes. "I still can't think about it. I mean, as far as I know, he never had any symptoms. Or let's put it this way: If he did, he never told me. He did have high blood pressure and the doctor'd been on him to quit smoking and start exercising. You know how men are. He waved it all aside and went right on doing as he pleased." She set the cigarette aside so she could blow her nose. Why do people always peek in their hankies to see what the honking noseblow has just netted them?

"How old was he?"

"Close to retirement. Sixty-three," she said. "But he never took good care of himself. I guess the only time he was ever in shape was in the army and right after, when he went through the academy and was hired on as a deputy. After that, it was all caffeine and junk food during work hours, bourbon when he got home. He wasn't an alcoholic—don't get me wrong—but he did like to have a cocktail at the end of the day. Lately, he wasn't sleeping well. He'd prowl around the house. I'd hear him up at two, three, five in the morning, doing god knows what. His weight had begun to drop in the last few months. The man hardly ate, just smoked and drank coffee and stared out the window at the snow. There were times when I thought he was going to snap, but that might have been my imagination. He really never said a word."

"Sounds like he was under some kind of strain."

"Exactly. That was my thought. Tom was clearly stressed, but I don't know why and it's driving me nuts." She picked up her cigarette and took a deep drag and then tapped the ash off in a ceramic ashtray shaped like a hand. "Anyway, that's why I called Dietz. I feel I'm entitled to know."

"I don't want to sound rude, but does it really make any difference? Whatever it was, it's too late to change, isn't it?"

She glanced away from me briefly. "I've thought of that myself. Sometimes I think I never really knew him at all. We got along well enough and he always provided, but he wasn't the kind of man who felt he should account for himself. His last couple of weeks, he'd be gone sometimes for hours and come back without a word. I didn't ask where he went. I could have, I guess, but there was something about him . . . he would bristle if I pressed him, so I learned to back off. I don't think I should have to wonder for the rest of my life. I don't even know where he was going that night. He told me he was staying home, but something must have come up."

"He didn't leave you a note?"

"Nothing." She placed her cigarette on the ashtray and reached for a compact concealed under her pillow. She opened the lid and checked her face in the mirror. She touched at her front teeth as though to remove a fleck. "I look dreadful," she said.

"Don't worry about it. You look fine."

Her smile was tentative. "I guess there's no point in

being vain. With Tom gone, nobody cares, including me if you want to know the truth."

"Can I ask you a question?"

"Please."

"I don't mean to pry, but were you happily married?"

A little burble of embarrassed laughter escaped as she closed the compact and tucked it back in its hiding place. "I certainly was. I don't know about him. He wasn't one to complain. He more or less took life as it came. I was married before . . . to someone physically abusive. I have a boy from that marriage. His name is Brant."

"Ah. And how old is he?"

"Twenty-five. Brant was ten when I met Tom, so essentially Tom raised him."

"And where is he?"

"Here in Nota Lake. He works for the fire department as a paramedic. He's been staying with me since the funeral though he has a place of his own in town," she said. "I told him I was thinking about hiring someone. It's pointless in his opinion, but I'm sure he'll do whatever he can to help." Her nose reddened briefly, but she seemed to gain control of herself.

"You and Tom were married for, what, fourteen years?"

"Coming up on twelve. After my divorce, I didn't want to rush into anything. We were fine for most of it, but recently things began to change for the worse. I mean, he did what he was supposed to, but his heart wasn't in it. Lately, I felt he was secretive. I don't know, so . . . tight-lipped or something. Why was he out on the highway that night? I mean, what was he doing? What was so precious that he couldn't tell me?"

"Could it have been a case he was working on?"

"It could have been, I suppose." She thought about the possibility while she stubbed out her cigarette. "I mean, it might have been job-related. Tom seldom said a word about work. Other men—some of the deputies—would swap stories in social situations, but not him. He took his job very seriously, almost to a fault."

"Someone in the department must have taken over his workload. Have you talked to them?"

"You say 'department' like it was some kind of big-city place. Nota Lake's the county seat, but that still isn't saying much. There were only two investigators, Tom and his partner, Rafer. I did talk to him—not that I got anything to speak of. He was nice. Rafer's always nice enough on the surface," she said, "but for all of the chit-chat, he managed to say very little."

I studied her for a moment, running the conversation through my bullshit meter to see what would register. Nothing struck me as off but I was having trouble understanding what she wanted. "Do you think there's something suspicious about Tom's death?"

She seemed startled by the question. "Not at all," she said, "but he was brooding about something and I want to know what it was. I know it sounds vague, but it upsets me to think he was withholding something when it clearly bothered him so much. I was a good wife to him and I won't be kept in the dark now he's gone."

"What about his personal effects? Have you been through his things?"

"The coroner returned the items he had on him when

he died, but they were just what you'd expect. His watch, his wallet, the change in his pocket, and his wedding ring."

"What about his desk? Did he have an office here at the house?"

"Well, yes, but I wouldn't even know where to begin with that. His desk is a mess. Papers piled up everywhere. It could be staring me in the face, whatever it is. I can't bring myself to look and I can't bear to let go. That's what I'd like you to do ... see if you can find out what was troubling him."

I hesitated. "I could certainly try. It would help if you could be more specific. You haven't given me much."

Selma's eyes filled with tears. "I've been racking my brain and I have no idea. Please just do *something*. I can't even walk in his den without falling apart."

Oh boy, just what I needed—a job that was not only vague, but felt hopeless as well. I should have bagged it right then, but I didn't, of course. More's the pity as it turned out.

TWO

Toward the end of my visit with her, the Valium seemed to kick in and she rallied. Somehow she managed to pull herself together in a remarkably short period of time. I waited in the living room while she showered and dressed. When she emerged thirty minutes later, she said she was feeling almost like her old self again. I was amazed at the transformation. With her makeup in place, she seemed more confident, though she still tended to speak with a hand lifted to conceal her mouth.

For the next twenty minutes, we discussed business, finally reaching an agreement about how to proceed. It was clear by then that Selma Newquist was capable of holding her own. She reached for the phone and in the space of one call not only booked my accommodation but insisted on a ten percent discount on what was already the off-season rate.

I left Selma's at 2:00, stopping off in town long enough to flesh out my standard junk food diet with some Capt'n Jack's fish and chips and a large Coke. After that, it was time to check into the motel. Obviously, I wouldn't be leaving Nota Lake for another day yet, at the very least. The motel she'd booked was the

Nota Lake Cabins, which consisted of ten rustic cottages set in a wooded area just off the main highway about six miles out of town. Tom's widowed sister, Cecilia Boden, owned and managed the place. When I pulled into the parking lot, I could see that the area was a bit too remote for my taste. I'm a city girl at heart and generally happiest close to restaurants, banks, liquor stores, and movie theaters, preferably bug free. Since Selma was paying, I didn't think I should argue the point, and in truth the rough-hewn log exteriors did look more interesting than the motels in town. Silly me.

Cecilia was on the telephone when I stepped into the office. I pegged her at sixty, as small and shapeless as a girl of ten. She wore a red plaid flannel shirt tucked into dark stiff blue jeans. She had no butt to speak of, just a flat plain in the rear. I was already wishing she'd quit perming the life out of her short cropped hair. I also wondered what would happen if she allowed the natural gray to emerge from under the uniform brown dye with which she'd doused it.

The reception area was compact, a pine-paneled cubbyhole hardly large enough for one small upholstered chair and the rack of pamphlets touting the countless recreational diversions available. A side door marked MANAGER probably led to her private apartment. The reception desk was formed by a twelve-inch writing surface mounted on the lower half of the Dutch door that separated the miniature lobby from the office where I could see the usual equipment: desk, file cabinets, typewriter, cash register, Rolodex, receipt ledger, and the big reservations book she was consulting in response to her caller's inquiry. She seemed ever so faintly annoyed with the questions she was being asked. "I got rooms on the Twenty-fourth, but nothing the day after . . . You want fish cleaning and freezing, try the Elms or the Mountain View . . . Uh-huh . . . I see . . . Well, that's the best I can do . . ." She smiled to herself, enjoying some kind of private joke. "Nope . . . No room service, no weight room, and the sauna's broke . . ."

While I waited for her to finish, I pulled out several pamphlets at random, reading about midweek ski lift and lodging packages closer to Mammoth Lakes and Mammoth Summit. I checked the local calendar of events. I'd missed the big annual trout derby, which had taken place the week before. I was also too late to attend February's big fishing show. Well, dang. I noticed the festivities in April included another fishing show, the trout opener press reception, the official trout opener, and a fish club display, with a Mule Days Celebration and a 30K run coming up in May. It did look like it might be possible to hike, backpack, or mulepack my way into the Eastern Sierras, where I imagined a roving assortment of hungry wildlife lunging and snapping at us as we picked our way down perilously narrow trails with rocks rattling off the mountainside into the yawning abyss.

I looked up to find Cecilia Boden staring at me with a flinty expression. "Yes, ma'am," she said. She kept her hands braced on the Dutch door as if defying me to enter.

I told her who I was and she waved aside my offer of a credit card. Mouth pursed, she said, "Selma said to send her the bill direct. I got two cottages available. You can take your pick." She took a bunch of keys from a hook and opened the lower half of the Dutch door, leaving me to follow as she headed through the front door and down a path packed with cedar chips. The air outside was damp and smelled of loam and pine resin. I could hear the wind moving in the trees and the chattering of squirrels. I left my car where I'd parked it and we proceeded on foot. The narrow lane leading to the cabins was barred by a chain strung between two posts. "I won't have cars back in this part of the camp. The ground gets too tore up when the weather's bad," she said, as if in answer to my question.

"Really," I murmured, for lack of anything better.

"We're close to full up," she remarked. "Unusual for March."

This was small talk in her book and I made appropriate mouth noises in response. Ahead of us, the cabins were spaced about seventy-five feet apart, separated by bare maples and dogwoods, and sufficient Douglas firs to resemble a cut-your-own Christmas tree farm. "Why do they call it Nota Lake? Is that Indian?"

Cecilia shook her head. "Nope. Ancient times, nota was a mark burned into a criminal's skin to brand him a lawbreaker. That way you always knew who the evildoers were. Bunch of desperadoes ended up over in this area; scoundrels deported to this country from England back in the mid-seventeen hundreds. Some reason all of them were branded; killers and thieves, pickpockets, fornicators—the worst of the worst. Once their indenture'd been served, they became free men and disappeared into the west, landing hereabouts. Their descendants went to work for the railroad, doing manual labor along with assorted coolies and coloreds.

Half the people in this town are related to those convicts. Must have been a randy bunch, though where
they found women no one seems to know. Ordered 'em
by mail, if my guess is correct."

We'd reached the first of the cabins and she continued
in much the same tone, her delivery flat and without
much inflection. "This is Willow. I give 'em names
instead of numbers. It's nicer in my opinion." She
inserted her key. "Each one is different. Up to you."

Willow was spacious, a pine-paneled room maybe
twenty feet by twenty with a fireplace made up of big
knobby boulders. The inner hearth was black with soot,
with wood neatly stacked in the grate. The room was
pungent with the scent of countless hardwood fires.
Against one wall was a brass bedstead with a mattress
shaped like a hillock. The quilt was a crazy patch and
looked as if it smelled of mildew. There was a bed table
lamp and a digital alarm clock. The rug was an oval of
braided rags, bleached of all color, thoroughly flattened
by age.

Cecilia opened a door on the left. "This here's the
bath and your hanging closet. We got all the amenities.
Unless you fish," she added, in a small aside to herself.
"Iron, ironing board, coffeemaker, soap."

"Very nice," I said.

"The other cabin's Hemlock. Located over near the
pine grove by the creek. Got a kitchenette, but no fireplace. I can take you back there if you like." For the
most part, she spoke without making eye contact,
addressing remarks to a spot about six feet to my left.

"This is fine. I'll take this one."

"Suit yourself," she said, handing me a key. "Cars

stay in the lot. There's more wood around the side. Watch for black widder spiders if you fetch more logs. Pay phone outside the office. Saves me the hassle of settling up for calls. We got a cafe down the road about fifty yards in that direction. You can't miss it. Breakfast, lunch, and dinner. Open six o'clock in the morning until nine-thirty at night."

"Thanks."

After she left, I waited a suitable interval, allowing her time to reach the office ahead of me. I returned to the parking lot and retrieved my duffel, along with the portable typewriter I'd stashed in the rental car. I'd spent my off-hours at Dietz's catching up on my paper-work. My wardrobe, in the main, consists of blue jeans and turtlenecks, which makes packing a breeze once you toss in the fistful of underpants.

In the cabin again, I set the typewriter by the bed and put my few articles of clothing in a crudely made chest of drawers. I unloaded my shampoo and placed my toothbrush and toothpaste on the edge of the sink, looking around me with satisfaction. Home sweet home, barring the black widders. I tried the toilet, which worked, and then inspected the shower, artfully con-cealed behind a length of white monk's cloth hanging from a metal rod. The shower pan looked clean, but was constructed of the sort of material that made me want to walk on tiptoe. Outings at the community pool in my youth had taught me to be cautious, bare feet still recoiling instinctively from the clots of soggy tissues and rusted bobby pins. There were none here in evidence, but I sensed the ghostly presence of some old-fashioned crud. I could smell the same chlorine tinged with someone else's shampoo. I checked the coffee-maker, but the plug seemed to be missing one prong and there were no complimentary packets of coffee grounds, sugar, or non-dairy coffee whitener. So much for the amenities. I was grateful for the soap.

I returned to the main room and did a quick survey. Under the side window, a wooden table and two chairs had been arranged with an eye to a view of the woods. I hauled out the typewriter and set it up on the tabletop. I'd have to run into town and find a ream of bond and a copy shop. These days, most P.I.s use computers, but I can't seem to get the hang of 'em. With my sturdy Smith-Corona, I don't require an electrical outlet and I don't have to worry about head crashes or lost data. I pulled a chair up to the table and stared out the window at the spindly stand of trees. Even the ever-greens had a threadbare look. Through a lacework of pine needles, I could see a line of fencing that separated Cecilia's property from the one behind. This part of town seemed to be ranchland, mixed with large undeveloped tracts that might have been farmed at one point. I pulled out a tatty legal pad and made myself some notes, mostly doodles if you really want to know.

Essentially, Selma Newquist had hired me to reconstruct the last four to six weeks of her late husband's life on the theory that whatever had troubled him probably took place within that time frame. I don't generally favor spouses spying on one another—especially when one of the parties is dead—but she seemed convinced the answers would give her closure. I had my doubts. Maybe Tom Newquist was simply worried about finances, or brooding about how to occupy his time during his retirement.

I'd agreed to give her a verbal report every two to three days, supplemented by a written account. Selma had demurred at first, saying verbal reports would be perfectly adequate, but I told her I preferred the written, in part to detail whatever information I collected. Productive or not, I wanted her to see what ground I was covering. It was just as important for her to be aware of the information I *couldn't* verify as it was for her to have a record of the facts I picked up along the way. With verbal reports, much of the data gets lost in translation. Most people aren't trained to listen. Given the complexity of our mental processes, the recipient tunes out, blocks, forgets, or misinterprets eighty percent of what's been said. Take any fifteen minutes' worth of conversation and try to reconstruct it later and you'll see what I mean. If the communication has any emotional content whatever, the quality of the information retained degrades even further. A written report was for my benefit, too. Let a week pass and I can hardly remember the difference between Monday and Tuesday, let alone what stops I made and in what order I made them. I've noticed that clients are confident about your abilities until payment comes due and then, suddenly, the total seems outrageous and they stand there wondering exactly what you've done to earn it. It's better to submit an invoice with a chronology attached. I like to cite chapter and verse with all the proper punctuation laid in. If nothing else, it's a demonstration of both your IQ and your writing skills. How can you

trust someone who doesn't bother to spell correctly and/
or can't manage to lay out a simple declarative sentence?

The other issue we'd discussed was the nature of my
fees. As a lone operator, I really didn't have any hard-
and-fast rules about billing, particularly in a case like
this where I was working out of town. Sometimes I
charge a flat fee that includes all my expenses. Sometimes I charge an hourly rate and add expenses on top
of that. Selma had assured me she had money to burn,
but frankly, I felt guilty about eating into Tom's estate.
On the other hand, she'd survived him and I thought
she had a point. Why should she live the rest of her life
wondering if her husband was hiding something from
her? Grief is enough of an affront without additional
regrets about unfinished business. Selma was already
struggling to come to terms with Tom's death. She
needed to know the truth and wanted me to supply it.
Fair enough. I hoped I could provide her with an answer
that would satisfy.

Until I got a sense of how long the job would take,
we'd agreed on four hundred bucks a day. From Dietz,
I'd borrowed a boilerplate contract. I'd penned in the
date and details of what I'd been hired to do and she'd
written me a check for fifteen hundred dollars. I'd run
that by the bank to make sure it cleared before I got
down to business. I'm sorry to confess that while I
sympathize with all the widows, orphans, and under-
dogs in the world, I think it's wise to make sure
sufficient funds are in place before you rush to someone's rescue.

I closed the cabin and locked it, hiked back to my
rental car, and drove the six miles into town. The

highway was sparsely strung with assorted businesses: tractor sales, a car lot, trailer park, country store, and a service station. The fields in between were gold with dried grass and tufted with weeds. The wide sweep of sky had turned from strong blue to gray, a thick haze of white obscuring the mountain tops. Away to the west, a torn pattern of clouds lay without motion. All the near hills were a scruffy red brown, polka-dotted with white. Wind rattled in the trees. I adjusted the heater in the car, flipping on the fan until tropical breezes blew against my legs.

For my stay in Carson City, I'd packed my tweed blazer for dress up and a blue denim jacket for casual wear. Both were too light and insubstantial for this area. I cruised the streets downtown until I spotted a thrift store. I nosed the rental car into a diagonal parking space out front. The window was crowded with kitchenware and minor items of furniture: a bookcase, a footstool, stacks of mismatched dishes, five lamps, a tricycle, a meat grinder, an old Philco radio, and some red Burma-Shave signs bound together with wire. The top one in the pile read DOES YOUR HUSBAND. What, I thought. Does your husband what? Burma-Shave signs had first appeared in the 1920s and many persisted even into my childhood, always with variations of that tricky, bumping lilt. *Does your husband . . . have a beard? . . . Is he really very weird? . . . If he's living in a cave . . . Offer him some . . . Burma-Shave.* Or words to that effect.

The interior of the store smelled like discarded shoes. I made my way down aisles densely crowded with hanging clothes. I could see rack after rack of items that must have been purchased with an eye to function and festivity. Prom gowns, cocktail dresses, women's suits, acrylic sweaters, blouses, and Hawaiian shirts. The woolens seemed dispirited and the cottons were tired, the colors subdued from too many rounds in the wash. Toward the rear, there was a rod sagging under the burden of winter jackets and coats.

I shrugged into a bulky brown leather bomber jacket. The weight of it felt like one of those lead aprons the technician places across your body while taking dental X-rays from the safety of another room. The jacket lining was fleece, minimally matted, and the pockets sported diagonal zippers, one of which was broken. I checked the inside of the collar. The size was a medium, big enough to accommodate a heavy sweater if I needed one. The price tag was pinned to the brown knit ribbing on the cuff. Forty bucks. What a deal. *Does your husband belch and rut? Does he scratch his hairy butt? If you want to see him bathe . . . tame the beast with Burma-Shave.* I tucked the jacket over my arm while I moved up and down the aisles. I found a faded blue flannel shirt and a pair of hiking boots. On my way out, I stopped and untwisted the wire connecting the Burma-Shave signs, reading them one by one.

DOES YOUR HUSBAND

MISBEHAVE?

GRUNT AND GRUMBLE

RANT AND RAVE?

SHOOT THE BRUTE SOME

BURMA-SHAVE.

I smiled to myself. I wasn't half-bad at that stuff. I went out to the street again with my purchases in hand. Let's hear it for the good old days. Lately, Americans have been losing their sense of humor.

I spotted an office supply store across the street. I crossed, stocked up on paper supplies, including a couple of packs of blank index cards. Two doors down, I found a branch of Selma's bank and came out with a wad of twenties in my shoulder bag. I retrieved my car and pulled out, circling the block until I was headed in the right direction. The town already felt familiar, neatly laid out and clean. Main Street was four lanes wide. The buildings on either side were generally one to two stories high, sharing no particular style. The atmosphere was vaguely Western. At each intersection, I caught sight of a wedge of mountains, the snow-capped peaks forming a scrim that ran the length of the town. Traffic was light and I noticed most of the vehicles were practical: pickups and utility vans with ski racks across the tops.

When I arrived back at Selma's, the garage door was open. The parking space on the left was empty. On the right, I spotted a late-model blue pickup truck. As I got out of my car, I noticed a uniformed deputy emerging from a house two doors down. He crossed the two lawns between us, walking in my direction. I waited, assuming this was Tom's younger brother, Macon. At first glance, I couldn't tell how much younger he was. I placed him in his late forties, but his age might have been deceptive. He had dark hair, dark brows, and a pleasant, unremarkable face. He was close to six feet tall, compactly built. He wore a heavy jacket, cropped at the waist to allow ready access to the heavy leather holster on his right hip. The wide belt and the weapon gave him a look of heft and bulk that I'm not sure would have been evident if he'd been stripped of his gear.

"Are you Macon?" I asked.

He offered me his hand and we shook. "That's right. I saw you pull up and thought I'd come on over and introduce myself. You met my wife, Phyllis, a little earlier."

"I'm sorry about your brother."

"Thank you. It's been a rough one, I can tell you," he said. He hooked a thumb toward the house. "Selma's not home. I believe she went off to the market a little while ago. You need in? Door's open most times, but you're welcome to come to our place. It sure beats setting out in the cold."

"I should be fine. I expect she'll be home in a bit and if not, I can find ways to amuse myself. I would like to talk to you sometime in the next day or two."

"Absolutely. No problem. I'll tell you anything you want, though I admit we're baffled as to Selma's purpose. What in the world is she worried about? Phyllis and I can't understand what she wants with a private detective, of all things. With all due respect, it seems ridiculous."

"Maybe you should talk to her about that," I said.

"I can tell you right now what you're going to learn about Tom. He's as decent a fellow as you'd ever hope to meet. Everybody in town looked up to him, including me."

"This may turn out to be a short stay, in that case."

"Where'd Selma put you? Some place nice, I hope."

"Nota Lake Cabins. Cecilia Boden's your sister, as I understand it. You have other siblings?"

Macon shook his head. "Just three of us," he said. "I'm the baby in the family. Tom's three years older than Cecilia and close to fifteen years my senior. I've been trailing after them two ever since I can remember. I ended up in the sheriff's department years after Tom hired on. Like that in school, too. Always following in somebody else's footsteps." His eyes strayed to the street as Selma's car approached and slowed, pulling into the driveway. "Here she is now so I'll leave you two be. You let me know what I can do to help. You can give us a call or come knocking on our door. It's that green house with white trim."

Selma had pulled into the garage by then. She got out of the car. She and Macon greeted each other with an almost imperceptible coolness. While she opened the trunk of her sedan, Macon and I parted company, exchanging the kind of chitchat that signals the end of a conversation. Selma lifted out a brown paper sack of groceries and two cleaner's bags, and slammed the trunk lid down. Under her fur coat, she wore smartly pressed charcoal slacks and a long-sleeved shirt of cherry-colored silk.

As Macon walked back to his house, I moved into the garage. "Let me give you a hand with that," I said, reaching for the bag of groceries, which she relinquished to me.

"I hope you haven't been out here long," she said. "I decided I'd spent enough time feeling sorry for myself. Best to keep busy."

"Whose pickup truck? Was that Tom's?" I asked.

Selma nodded as she unlocked the door leading from the garage into the house. "I had a fellow from the garage tow it the day after he died. The officer who found him took the keys out and left it locked up where it was. I can't bring myself to drive it. I guess eventually I'll sell it or pass it along to Brant." She pressed a button and the garage door descended with a rumble.

"You met Macon, I see."

"He came over to introduce himself," I said as I followed her into the house. "One thing I ought to mention. I'm going to be talking to a lot of people around town and I really don't know yet what approach I'll take. Whatever you hear, just go along with it."

She put her keys back in her purse, moving into the utility room with me close behind. She closed the door after us. "Why not tell the truth?"

"I will where I can, but I gather Tom was a highly respected member of the community. If I start asking about his personal business, nobody's going to say a word. I may try another tack. It won't be far off, but I may bend the facts a bit."

"What about Cecilia? What will you say to her?"

"I don't know yet. I'll think of something."

"She'll fill your ear. She's never really liked me. Whatever Tom's problems, she'll blame me if she can. Same with his brother. Macon was always coming after Tom for something—a loan, advice, good word in the department, you name it. If I hadn't stepped in, he'd have sucked Tom dry. You can do me a favor: Take anything they say with a grain of salt."

The disgruntled are good. They'll tell you anything, I thought.

Once in the kitchen, Selma hung her fur coat on the back of a chair. I watched while she unloaded the groceries and put items away. I would have helped, but she waved aside the offer, saying it was quicker if she did it herself. The kitchen walls were painted bright yellow, the floor a spatter of seamless white-and-yellow linoleum. A chrome-and-yellow-plastic upholstered dinette set filled an alcove with a bump-out window crowded with ... I peered closer ... artificial plants. She indicated a seat across the table from hers as she folded the bag neatly and put it in a rack bulging with other grocery bags.

She moved to the refrigerator and opened the door. "What do you take in your coffee? I've got hazelnut coffee creamer or a little half-and-half." She took out a small carton and gave the pouring spout an experimental sniff. She made a face to herself and set the carton in the sink.

"Black's fine."

"You sure?"

"Really. It's no problem. I'm not particular," I said. I took off my jacket and hung it on the back of my chair while Selma rounded up two coffee mugs, the sugar bowl, and a spoon for herself.

She poured coffee and replaced the glass carafe on the heating element of the coffee machine, heels *tap-tap-tapping* on the floor as she crossed and recrossed the room. Her energy was ever so faintly tinged with nervousness. She sat down again and immediately flicked a small gold Dunhill to light a fresh cigarette. She inhaled deeply. "Where will you begin?"

"I thought I'd start in Tom's den. Maybe the answer's easy, sitting right up on the surface."

THREE

I spent the rest of the afternoon working my way through Tom Newquist's insufferably disorganized home office. I'm going to bypass the tedious list of documents I inspected, the files I sorted, the drawers I emptied, the receipts I scrutinized in search of *some* evidence of his angst. In reporting to Selma, I did (slightly) exaggerate the extent of my efforts so she'd appreciate what fifty bucks an hour was buying in the current market place. In the space of three hours, I managed to go through about half the mess. Up to that point, whatever Tom was fretting about, he'd left precious little in the way of clues.

He was apparently compulsive about saving every scrap of paper, but whatever organizational principle he employed, the accumulation he left behind was chaotic at best. His desk was a jumble of folders, correspondence, bills paid and unpaid, income tax forms, newspaper articles, and case files he was working on. The layers were twelve to fifteen inches deep, some stacks toppling sideways into the adjacent piles. My guess was he knew how to put his hands on just about anything he needed, but the task I faced was daunting.

Maybe he imagined that any minute he'd have the clutter sorted and subdued. Like most disorganized people, he probably thought the confusion was temporary, that he was just on the verge of having all his papers tidied up. Unfortunately, death had taken him by surprise and now the cleanup was mine. I made a mental note to myself to straighten out my underwear the minute I got home. In the bottom drawer of his desk, I found some of his equipment—handcuffs, nightstick, the flashlight he must have carried. Maybe his brother, Macon, would like them. I'd have to remember to ask Selma later.

I went through two big leaf bags of junk, taking it upon myself to throw away paid utility stubs from ten years back. I kept a random sampling in case Selma wanted to sell the house and needed to average her household expenses for prospective buyers. I kept the office door open, conducting an ongoing conversation with Selma in the kitchen while I winnowed and pitched. "I'd like to have a picture of Tom."

"What for?"

"Not sure yet. It just seems like a good idea."

"Take one of those from the wall by the window."

I glanced over my shoulder, spotting several black-and-white photographs of him in various settings. "Right," I said. I set aside the lapful of papers I was sorting and crossed to the closest grouping. In the largest frame, an unsmiling Tom Newquist and the sheriff, Bob Staffer, were pictured together at what looked to be a banquet. There were several couples seated at a table, which was decorated with a handsome centerpiece and the number 2 on a placard in the middle. Staffer had signed the photograph in the lower right-hand corner: "To the best damn detective in the business! As Ever, Bob Staffer." The date was April of the preceding year. I lifted the framed photo from the hook and held it up to the fading light coming in the window.

Tom Newquist was a youthful sixty-three years old with small eyes, a round bland face, and dark thinning hair trimmed close to his head. His expression was one I'd seen on cops ever since time began—neutral, watchful, intelligent. It was a face that gave away nothing of the man within. If you were being interrogated as a suspect, make no mistake about it, this man would ask tough questions and there would be no hint from him about which replies might relieve you of his attention. Make a joke and his smile in response would be thin. Presume on his goodwill and his temper would flash in a surprising display of heat. If you were questioned as a witness, you might see another side of him—careful, compassionate, patient, conscientious. If he was like the other law enforcement officers of my acquaintance, he was capable of being implacable, sarcastic, and relentless, all in the interest of getting at the truth. Regardless of the context, the words "impulsive" and "passionate" would scarcely spring to mind. On a personal level, he might be very different, and part of my job here was determining just what those differences might consist of. I wondered what he'd seen in Selma. She seemed too brassy and emotional for a man skilled at camouflage.

I glanced up to find her standing in the doorway, watching me. Despite the fact that her clothes looked expensive, there was something indescribably cheap about her appearance. Her hair had been bleached to the texture of a doll's wig, and I wondered if up close I could see individual clumps like the plugs of a hair transplant. I held up the picture. "Is this one okay? I'd like to have it cropped and copies made. If I'm backtracking his activities for the past couple of months, the face could trigger something where a name might not."

"All right. I might like to have one myself. That's nice of him."

"He didn't smile much?"

"Not often. Especially in social situations. Around his buddies, he relaxed . . . the other deputies. How's it coming?"

I shrugged. "So far there's nothing but junk." I went back to the masses of paper in front of me. "Too bad you weren't in charge of the bills," I remarked.

"I'm not good with numbers. I hated high school math," she said. And then after a moment, "I'm beginning to feel guilty having you snoop through his things."

"Don't worry about it. I do this for a living. I'm a diagnostician, like a gynecologist when you have your feet in the stirrups and your fanny in the air. My interest isn't personal. I simply look to see what's there."

"He was a good man. I know that."

"I'm sure he was," I said. "This may net us nothing and if so, you'll feel better. You're entitled to peace."

"Do you need help?"

"Not really. At this point, I'm still picking my way through. Anyway, I'm about to wrap it up for this afternoon. I'll come back tomorrow and take another run at it." I jammed a fistful of catalogs and advertising fliers in the trash bag. I glanced up again, aware that she was still standing in the door.

"Could you join me for supper? Brant's going to be working so it would just be the two of us."

"I better not, but thanks. Maybe tomorrow. I have some phone calls to make and then I thought I'd grab a quick bite and make an early night of it. I should finish this in the morning. At some point, we'll have telephone records to go through. That's a big under-taking and I'm saving it for last. We'll sit side by side and see how many phone numbers you can recognize."

"Well," she said, reluctantly, "I'll let you get back to work."

When I had finished for the day, Selma gave me a house key, though she assured me she generally left the doors unlocked. She told me she was often gone, but she wanted me to have the run of the place in her absence. I told her I'd want to look through Tom's personal effects and she had no objections. I didn't want her walking in one day to find me poking through his clothes.

It was fully dark when I left and the streetlights did little to dispel the sense of isolation. The traffic through town was lively. People were going home to dinner, businesses were shutting down. Restaurants were getting busy, the bar doors standing open to release the excess noise and cigarette smoke. A few hardy joggers had hit the sidewalks along with assorted dog owners whose charges were seeking relief against the shrubs.

Once I was out on the highway, I became aware of

the vast tracts of land that bore no evidence of human habitation. By day, the fences and the odd outbuildings created the impression the countryside had been civilized. At night, the mountain ranges were as black as jet and the pale slice of moon scarcely brushed the snowy peaks with silver. The temperature had dropped and I could smell the inky damp of the lake. I felt a flicker of longing to see Santa Teresa with its red-tile roofs, palm trees, and the thundering Pacific.

I slowed when I saw the sign for Nota Lake Cabins. Maybe a crackling fire and a hot shower would cheer me up. I parked my car in the small lot near the motel office. Cecilia Boden had provided a few low-voltage lights along the path to the cabins, small mushroom shapes that cast a circle of dim yellow on the cedar chips. There was a small lighted lamp mounted by the cabin door. I hadn't left any lights on for myself, sensing (perhaps) that the management would frown on such extravagance. I unlocked the door and let myself in, feeling for the light switch. The overhead bulb came on with its flat forty-watt wash of light. I crossed to the bed and clicked on the table lamp, which offered forty watts more. The digital alarm was flashing 12:00 repeatedly, which suggested a minor power outage earlier. I checked my watch and corrected the time to its current state: 6:22.

The room felt drab and chilly. There was a strong smell of old wood fires and moisture seeping through the floorboards from underneath the cabin. I checked the wood in the grate. There was a stack of newspapers close by meant for kindling. Of course, there was no gas starter and I suspected the fire would take more time to light than I had time to enjoy. I went around the room, closing cotton curtains across the windowpanes. Then I peeled off my clothes and stepped into the shower. I'm not one to waste water, but even so, the hot began to diminish before my four minutes were up. I rinsed the last of the shampoo from my hair a split second before the cold water descended full force. This was beginning to feel like a wilderness experience.

Dressed again, I locked the cabin and headed back toward the road, walking briskly along the berm until I reached the restaurant. The Rainbow Cafe was about the size of a double-wide trailer, with a Formica counter with eight stools running down its length and eight red Naugahyde booths arranged along two walls. There was one waitperson (female), one short-order cook (also female), and a boy busperson in evidence. I ordered breakfast for dinner. There's nothing so comforting as scrambled eggs at night; soft cheery yellow, bright with butter, flecked with pepper. I had three strips of crisp bacon, a pile of hash browns sautéed with onion, and two pieces of rye toast, drenched in butter and dripping with jam. I nearly crooned aloud as the flavors blended in my mouth.

On the way back to my cabin, I paused to use the pay phone outside the office. This consisted of an old-fashioned glass-and-metal phone booth missing the original bifold door. I used my credit card to call Dietz. "Hey, babe. How's the patient?" I said when he answered.

"Dandy. How are you?"

"Not bad. Now on retainer."

"In Nota Lake?"

"Where else? Standing in a phone booth in the piney woods," I said.

"How's it going?"

"I'm just getting started so it's hard to tell. I'm assuming Selma talked to you about Tom."

"Only that she thought he had something on his mind. Sounds vague."

"Extremely. Did you ever meet him yourself?"

"Nope. In fact, I haven't even seen her for over fifteen years. How's she holding up?"

"She's in good shape. Upset, as who wouldn't be in her shoes."

"What's the game plan?" he asked.

"The usual. I spent time today going through his desk. Tomorrow I'll start talking to his friends and acquaintances and we'll see what develops. I'll give it until Thursday and then see where we stand. I'd love to be home by the weekend if this job doesn't pan out. How's the knee?"

"Much better. The PT's a bitch, but I'm getting used to it. I miss your sandwiches."

"Liar."

"No, I'm serious. As soon as you finish there, I think you ought to head back in this direction."

"Uh-unh. No thanks. I want to sleep in my own bed. I haven't seen Henry for a month." Henry Pitts was my landlord, eighty-six years old. His would be the cover photo if the AARP ever did a calendar of octogenarian hunks.

"Well, think on it," Dietz said.

"Oh, right. Listen, my Florence Nightingale days are

over. I have a business to run. Anyway, I better go. It's friggin' cold out here."

"I'll let you go then. Take care."

"Same to you," I said.

I put a call through to Henry and caught him on his way out the door. "Where you off to?" I asked.

"I'm on my way to Rosie's. She and William need help with the dinner crowd tonight," he said. Rosie ran the tavern half a block from my apartment. She and Henry's older brother William had been married the previous Thanksgiving and now William was rapidly becoming a restaurateur.

"What about you? Where're you calling from?"

I repeated my tale, filling him in on my current situation. I gave him both Selma's home number and that of the office at the Nota Lake Cabins in case he had to reach me. We continued to chat briefly before he had to go. Once he rang off, I placed a call to Lonnie's office and left a message for Ida Ruth, again giving her my location and Selma's number if she should have to reach me for some reason. I couldn't think of any other way to feel connected. After I hung up, I stuck my hands in my jacket pockets, vainly hoping for shelter from the wind. The notion of spending the evening in the cabin seemed depressing. With only two forty-watt light bulbs for illumination, even reading would be a chore. I pictured myself huddled, squinting, under that damp-looking quilt, spiders creeping from the wood pile the minute I relaxed my vigilance. It was a sorry prospect, given that all I had with me was a book on identifying tire tracks and tread marks.

I crossed to the motel office and peered in through

the glass door. A light was on, but there was no sign of Cecilia. A hand-lettered sign said RING FOR MGR. I let myself in. I bypassed the desk bell and knocked on the door marked MANAGER. After a moment, Cecilia appeared in a pink chenille bathrobe and fluffy pink slippers. "Yes?"

"Hi, Cecilia. Could I have a word with you?"

"Something wrong with the room?"

"Not at all. Everything's fine. More or less. I was wondering if you could spare a few minutes to talk about your brother."

"What about him?"

"Has Selma said anything about why I'm here in Nota Lake?"

"Said she hired you is all. I don't even know what you do for a living."

"Ah. Well, actually, I'm a field investigator with California Fidelity Insurance. Selma's concerned about the liability in Tom's death."

"Liability for what?"

"Good question. Of course, I'm not at liberty to discuss this in any detail. You know, *officially* he wasn't working, but she thinks he might have been pursuing departmental business the night he died. If so, it's always possible she can file a claim." I didn't mention that Tom Newquist wasn't represented by CFI or that the company had fired me approximately eighteen months before. I was prepared to flash the laminated picture ID I still had in my possession. The CFI logo was emblazoned on the front, along with a photograph of me that looked like something the border patrol might keep posted for ready reference.

She stared at me blankly and for one heart-stopping moment I wondered if she was recently retired from some obscure branch of county government. She appeared to be mulling over all the rules and regulations, trying to decide which were in effect on the night in question. I was tempted to embellish, but decided I might be getting in too deep. With lies, it's best to skip across the surface like a dragonfly. The more said at the outset, the more there is to retract later if it turns out you really put your foot in it. She held the door open to admit me. "You better come on in. I don't mind telling you the subject's painful."

"I can imagine it is and I'm sorry to intrude. I met Macon earlier."

"He's useless," she remarked. "No love lost between us. Of course, I never thought of Selma as family either and I'm sure it's ditto from her perspective."

Cecilia Boden's apartment was on a par with my cabin, which is to say, drab, poorly lighted, and faintly shabby. The prime difference was that my place was icy cold where she seemed to keep her room temperature somewhere around "pre-heat." The floor cover was linoleum made to look like wood parquet. She had pine-paneled walls, overstuffed furniture covered with violent-colored crocheted throws. A large television set dominated one corner, with all the furniture oriented in that direction. Cecilia's reading glasses were perched on the arm of the sofa nearest the set. I could see that she was in the process of filling out the crossword puzzle in the local paper. She did this in ballpoint pen without any visible corrections. I revised my estimate of her upwards. I couldn't perform such a feat with a gun to my head.

We took a few minutes to get settled in the living room. While my story sounded plausible, it didn't give me much room to inquire into Tom's character. In any event, why would I imagine Cecilia would have information about what he was doing the night he died? As it turned out, she didn't question my purpose and the longer we chatted, the clearer it became that she was perfectly comfortable discussing Tom and his wife, their marriage, and anything else I cared to ask about.

"Selma says Tom was preoccupied with something in the past few weeks. Do you have any idea what it might have been?"

Cecilia narrowed her eyes at the section of floor she was studying.

"What makes her think there was anything wrong with him?"

"Well, I'm not sure. She said he seemed tense, smoking more than usual, and she thought he was losing weight. She said he slept poorly and disappeared without explanation. I take it this wasn't typical. Did he say anything to you?"

"He didn't confide anything specific," she said, cautiously. "You'll have to talk to Macon about that. They were a lot closer to each other than either one of them was to me."

"But what was your impression? Did you feel he was under some kind of strain?"

"Possibly."

Too bad I wasn't taking notes, what with the wealth of data pouring out. "Did you ever ask him about it?"

"I didn't feel it was my place. That wasn't the nature of our relationship. He went about his business and I went about mine."

"Any *hunches* about what was going on?"

She hesitated for a moment. "I think Tom was unhappy. He never said as much to me, but that's my belief."

I made a sort of *mmm* sound, verbal filler accompanied by what I hoped was a sympathetic look.

She took this for encouragement and launched into her analysis. "Far be it from me to criticize Selma. *He* married her. I didn't. It's possible there was more to her than meets the eye. We'd certainly have to hope so. If you want my opinion, my brother could have done a lot better for himself. Selma's a snob, if you want to know the truth."

This time I murmured, "Really."

Her gaze brushed my face and then drifted off again. "You look like a good judge of character, so I don't feel I'm telling tales out of school when I say this. She has no spiritual foundation even if she does go to church. She's a mite materialistic. She seems to think she can use acquisitions to fill the void in her life, but it won't do."

"For example," I said.

"You saw the new carpet in the living room?"

"Yes, I saw that."

Cecilia shot me a glance filled with satisfaction. "She had that installed about ten days ago. I thought it was in poor taste, doing it so soon, but Selma never asked me. Selma's also confided she's considering having those two front teeth capped, which is not only vain, but completely trivial. Talk about a waste of money. I guess now she's a widder, she can do anything she likes."

What I thought was, what's wrong with vanity? Given the range of human failings, self-absorption is harmless compared to some I could name. Why not do whatever you deem relevant to feeling better about yourself—within reason, of course. If Selma wanted to get her teeth capped, why should Cecilia give a shit? What I said was, "I got the impression she was devoted to Tom."

"As well she should have been. And he to her, I might add. Tom spent his life trying to satisfy the woman. If it wasn't one thing, it was another. First, she had to have a house. Then she wanted something bigger in a better neighborhood. Then they had to join the country club. And on and on it went. Anytime she didn't get what she wanted? Well, she pouted and sulked until he broke down and got it for her. It was pitiful in my opinion. Tom did everything he could, but there wasn't any way to make her happy."

I said, "My goodness." This is the way I talk in situations like this. I could not, for the life of me, think where to go from here. "He was a nice-looking man. I saw a picture of him at the house," I said, vamping.

"He was downright handsome. Why he married Selma was a mystery to me. And that son of hers?" Cecilia pulled her lips together like a drawstring purse. "Brant was a pain in the grits from the first time I ever laid eyes on the boy. He had a mouth on him like a trucker and he was bratty to boot. Back talk and sass? You never heard the like. Did poorly in school, too. Problems with his temper and what they call his impulse control. Of course, Selma thought he was a saint. She wouldn't tolerate a word of criticism regardless of what he did. Poor Tom nearly tore his hair out. I guess he finally managed to get the boy squared away, but it was no thanks to her."

"She mentioned Brant worked as a paramedic. That's a responsible job."

"Well, that's true enough," she conceded grudgingly. "About time he took hold. You can credit Tom for that."

"Do you happen to know where Tom was going that night? I understand he was found somewhere on the outskirts of town."

"A mile north of here."

"He didn't drop in to see you?"

"I wish he had," she said. "I was visiting a friend down in Independence and didn't get back here until shortly after ten fifteen or so. I saw the ambulance pass, but I had no idea it was meant for him."

FOUR

Tuesday morning at nine, I stopped by the offices of the Nota County Coroner. I hadn't slept well the night before. The cabin was poorly insulated and the night air was frigid. I'd moved the thermostat up to 70, but all it did was click off and on ineffectually. I'd crawled into bed wearing my sweats, a turtleneck, and a pair of heavy socks. The mattress was as turgid as a trough of mud. I curled up under a comforter, a quilt, and a wool blanket, with my heavy leather jacket piled on top for the weight. Just about the time I got warm, my bladder announced that it was filled to capacity and required my immediate attention or a bout of bed-wetting would ensue. I tried to ignore the discomfort and then realized I'd never sleep a wink until I'd heeded the message. By the time I got back under the covers, all the ambient heat had been dispelled and I was forced to suffer through the cold again until I drifted off to sleep.

When I woke up at seven, my nose felt like a Popsicle and my breath was visible in puffs against the wan morning light. I showered in tepid water, dried myself shivering, and dressed in haste. Then I dog trotted down the road to the Rainbow Cafe where I stoked up on another breakfast, sucking down orange juice, coffee, sausages, and pancakes saturated with butter and syrup. I told myself I needed all the sugar and fat to refuel my depleted reserves, but the truth was I felt sorry for myself and the food was the simplest form of consolation.

The coroner's office was located on a side street in the heart of the downtown. In Nota County, the coroner is a four-year elected official, who in this case doubled as the funeral director for the county's only mortuary. Nota County is small, less than two thousand square miles, tucked like an afterthought between Inyo and Mono counties. The coroner, Wilton Kirchner III, generally referred to as Trey, had occupied the position for the past ten years. Since there was no requirement for formal training in forensic medicine, all coroner's cases were autopsied by a forensic pathologist under contract to the county.

In the event of a homicide in the county, the Nota County Coroner handles the on-scene investigation, in conjunction with the Sheriff's Department's investigator and an investigator from the Nota County District Attorney's office. The forensic autopsy is then conducted in the "big city" by a pathologist who does several homicide autopsies per month and is called to court numerous times during the year to testify. Since Nota County only has one homicide every two years or so, the coroner prefers that an outside agency provide its expertise, in both autopsy services and testimony.

Kirchner & Sons Mortuary appeared to have been a private residence at one time, probably built in the early twenties with the town growing up around it. The architectural style was Tudor with a façade of pale red brick trimmed in dark-painted timbers. Thin cold sunlight glittered against the leaded glass windows. The surrounding lawns were dormant, the grass as drab and brittle as brown plastic. Only the holly bushes lent any color to the landscape. I could imagine a time when the house might have sat on a sizeable piece of land, but now the property had shrunk and the lots on either side sported commercial establishments: a real estate office and a modest medical complex.

Trey Kirchner came out to the reception area when he heard I was there, extending a hand in greeting as he introduced himself. "Trey Kirchner," he said. "Selma called and said you'd be in here today. Nice to meet you, Miss Millhone. Come on back to my office and let's find out what you need."

Kirchner was in his mid-fifties, tall, broad-shouldered, with a waistline only slightly softer than it might have been ten years before. His hair was a clean gray, parted on the side and trimmed short around his ears. His smile was pleasant, creating concentric creases on either side of his mouth. He wore glasses with large lenses and thin metal frames. The corners of his eyes drooped slightly, somehow creating an expression of immense sympathy. His suit was close-fitting, well pressed, and the dress shirt he wore looked freshly starched. His tie was conservative, but not somber. Altogether, he presented an air of comforting competence. There was something solid about him; a man who, by nature, looked like he could absorb all the sorrow, confusion, and rage generated by death.

I followed him down a long corridor and into his office, which had served as the dining room when the house was first built. The carpet was pale, the wood floors pickled to the color of milk-washed pine. The drapes were beige, silk or shantung, some fabric with a touch of sheen. The mortuary decor leaned to wainscoting, topped with wallpaper murals showing soft mountain landscapes, forests of ever-greens with paths meandering through the woods. This was a watercolor world; pastel skies piled with clouds, the faintest suggestion of a breeze touching the tips of the wallpaper trees. On either side of the corridor at intervals, wide sliding doors had been pushed back to reveal the slumber rooms, empty of inhabitants, bare except for the ranks of gray metal folding chairs and a few potted ferns. The air was cool, underheated, spiced with the scent of carnations though none were in view. Perhaps it was some weird form of mortuary air freshener wafting through the vents. The entire environment seemed geared to somnambulistic calm.

The office we entered seemed designed for the public, not a book, a file, or a piece of paper in sight. I suspected somewhere in the building Trey Kirchner had an office where the real work was done. Somewhere out of sight, too, was the autopsy paraphernalia: cameras, X-ray equipment, stainless steel table, Stryker saw, scalpels, hanging scale. The room where we sat was as bland as a pudding—no smell of formalin, no murky Mason jars filled with snippets of organs—giving no indication of the mechanics of the body's preparation for cremation or burial.

"Have a seat," he said, indicating two matching

upholstered chairs arranged on either side of a small side table. His manner was relaxed, pleasant, friendly, curiously impersonal. "I take it you're here about Tom's death." He reached over and opened the drawer, pulling out a flat manila folder containing a five-page report. "I ran a copy of the autopsy report in case you're interested."

I took the folder. "Thanks. I thought I might have to talk you into this."

He smiled. "It's public record. I could have popped it in the mail and saved you a trip if Selma'd asked for it sooner."

"Tom's death was classified as a coroner's case?"

"Of necessity," he said. "You know he died out on Highway 395 with no witnesses and probably not much warning. He hadn't seen his doctor in close to a year. We figured it was his heart, but you never really know about these things until the post. Could have been an aneurysm. Anyway, Calvin Burkey did the autopsy. He's the forensic pathologist for Nota and Mono counties. Couple of us in attendance. Nothing remarkable showed up. No surprises, nothing unexpected. Tom died of a massive acute myocardial infarction due to severe arteriosclerosis. You'll see it. It's all there. Sections of the coronary artery confirmed ninety-five percent to one hundred percent occlusion. Sixty-three years old. Really, it's amazing he lasted as long as he did."

"Nothing else came to light?"

"In the way of abnormalities? Nope. Liver, gall-bladder, spleen, kidneys were all unremarkable. Lungs looked bad. He'd been smoking all his life, but there was no indication of invasive disease. He'd eaten recently.

According to our report, he'd stopped off at a cafe for a bite of supper. No pills or capsules in his digestive system and the toxin report was clear. What makes you ask?"

"Selma said he'd been losing weight. I wondered if he knew something he wasn't telling her."

"No ma'am. No cancer, if that's what you mean. No tumors, no blood clots, and no hemorrhaging, aside from the myocardium," he said. "Doc said there were signs of a minor heart attack sometime in the past."

I thought about it. "So maybe he knew his days were numbered. That would give him reason to brood."

"Could be," he said. "Tom wasn't in the peak of health, I can assure you of that. The absence of pathology doesn't necessarily mean you feel all that good. I knew him for years and never heard him complain, but he was sixty pounds overweight. Smoked like a chimney, drank like a fish, just to cover both clichés. He was a hell of an investigator, I can tell you that. What's Selma's worry?"

"It's hard to say. I think she feels he was holding out on her, keeping secrets of some kind. She didn't press him for answers so now it's unfinished business and it bothers her a lot."

"And she has no idea what it was?"

"It might not be anything, which is where I come in. Do you have any theories?"

"I don't think you'll turn up anything scandalous. Tom was churchgoing, a good soul. Well liked, well thought-of in the community, generous with his time. If he had any faults, I'd have to say he was straitlaced, too rigid. He saw the world in terms of all black or all white with not a lot in between. I guess he could see the gray, but he never knew what to do with it. He didn't believe in bending the rules, though I've seen him do it from time to time. He was a real straight-ahead guy, but that's good in my opinion. We could use a few more like him. We're going to miss him around here."

"Did you spend any time with him in the past few weeks?"

"Nothing to speak of. Mostly, I saw him in the context of his job. Not surprisingly, the county sheriff's department and the coroner's office are just like that," he said, crossing his fingers. "I'd run into him around town. Played pool with him once. Sucked back a few beers. Bunch of us did a weekend fishing trip last fall, but it's not like we laid around at night baring our souls. Fellow you ought to talk to is his partner, Rafe."

"Selma mentioned him. What's his last name?"

"LaMott."

I sat in the rental car in the Kirchner & Sons parking lot, leafing through Tom Newquist's autopsy report, his death certificate spelling out the particulars of his passing. Age, date of birth, Social Security number, and his usual address; the place and cause of his death and the disposition of his remains. He'd arrived at Nota County Hospital ER as a DOA, autopsied a day later, buried the day after that. On paper, his progression to the grave seemed all too swift, but in truth, once death occurs, the human body is just a big piece of meat quickly going sour. There was something flat and abrupt in the details . . . Tom Newquist deceased . . . his life neatly packaged; beginning, middle, and end. Under the death certificate was a copy of a hand-scrawled note that I gathered had been written by the CHP officer who found him in his truck.

At appx 21 50 $\frac{2}{3}$ Ambulance call to roadside 7.2 mi. out Hiway 395.   Subj in pick-up, removed to side of road.   CRP started @ 22 00.   EMT from Nota Lake taking over @ appx. 22 15. Subj DOA on arrival at Nota Lake ER. Coroner notified.

The notation was signed "J. Tennyson." The autopsy report followed; three typewritten pages detailing the facts as Trey Kirchner had indicated.

I'd been hoping the explanation was obvious, that Tom Newquist was caught in the grip of some terminal disease, his preoccupation as simple as an intimation of his mortality. This was not the case. If Selma's perceptions were correct and he was brooding about something, the subject wasn't an immediate threat to his health or well-being. It was always possible he'd been experiencing heart problems—angina pain, arrhythmia, shortness of breath on exertion. If so, he might have been weighing the severity of his symptoms against the consequences of consulting his physician. Tom Newquist might have seen enough death to view the process philosophically. He might have been more fearful of medical intervention than the possibility of dying.

I set the folder on the seat beside me and started the car. I wasn't sure where to go next, but I suspected the logical move would be to talk to Tom's partner,

Rafer LaMott. I checked my map of Nota Lake and spotted the sheriff's substation, which was part of the Civic Center on Benoit about six blocks west. The sun had been climbing through a thin layer of clouds. The air was chilly, but there was something lovely about the light. Along the main thoroughfare, the buildings were constructed of stucco and wood with corrugated metal roofs: gas stations, a drugstore, a sporting goods shop, and hair salon. Rimming the town was the untouched beauty of distant mountains. The digital thermometer on the bank sign showed that it was 42 degrees.

I parked across the street from the Nota Lake Civic Center, which also included the police station, the county courthouse, and assorted community services. The complex of administrative offices was housed in a building that had once been an elementary school. I know this because the words "Nota Lake Grammar School" were carved in block letters on the architrave. I could have sworn I could still see the faint imprint of construction paper witches and pumpkins where they'd been affixed to the windows with cellophane tape, the ghosts of Halloweens past. Personally, I hated grade school, having been cursed with a curious combination of timidity and rebellion. School was a minefield of unwritten rules that everyone but me seemed to sense and accept. My parents had died in a car crash when I was five, so school felt like a continuation of the same villainy and betrayal. I was inclined to upchuck without provocation, which didn't endear me to the janitor or classmates sitting in my vicinity. I can still remember the sensation of recently erupted hot juices collecting in my lap while students on either side of me flocked away in distaste. Far from experiencing shame, I felt a sly satisfaction, the power of the victim wreaking digestive revenge. I'd be sent down to the school nurse where I could lie on a cot until my Aunt Gin came to fetch me. Often at lunchtime ... (before I learned to barf at will) ... I'd beg to go home, swearing to look both ways when I was crossing the street, promising not to talk to strangers even if they offered sweets. My teachers rebuffed every plaintive request, so I was doomed to remain; fearful and anxious, undersized, fighting back tears. By the time I was eight, I learned to quit asking. I simply left when it suited me and suffered the consequences later. What were they going to do, shoot me down in cold blood?

The entrance to the Civic Center opened into a wide corridor that served as a lobby, currently undergoing renovations. File cabinets and storage units had been moved into the uncarpeted space. The walls were lined with panels of some unidentified wood. The ceiling was a low gridwork of acoustical tiles. Portions of the hallway were marked off with traffic cones strung together with tape, hand-lettered signs pointing to the current locations of several displaced departments.

I found the sheriff's substation, which was small and consisted of several interconnecting offices that looked like the "Before" photos in a magazine spread. Fluourescent lighting did little to improve the ambience, which was made up of a hodgepodge of technical manuals, wall plaques, glossy paneling, office machines, wire baskets, and notices taped to all the flat surfaces. The civilian clerk was a woman in her thirties who wore running shoes, jeans, and an M.I.T. sweatshirt over a white turtleneck. Her name tag identified her as Margaret Brine. She had chopped-off black hair, oval glasses with black frames, and a dusting of freckles under her powder and blush. Her teeth were big and square with visible spaces between.

I took out a business card and placed it on the counter. "I wonder if I might talk to Rafer LaMott."

She picked up my card, giving it a cursory look. "Will he know what this is about?"

"The coroner suggested I talk to him about Tom Newquist."

Her gaze lifted to mine. "Just a minute," she said. She disappeared through a door in the rear that I assumed led into other offices. I could hear a murmur, and moments later Rafer LaMott appeared, shrugging himself into a charcoal brown sport coat. He was an African American in his forties, probably six feet tall, with a caramel complexion, closely cropped black hair, and startling hazel eyes. His mustache was sparse, and he was otherwise clean-shaven. The lines in his forehead resembled parallel seams in a fine-grained leather. The sports coat he wore over black gabardine pants looked like cashmere. His shirt was pale beige, his tie a mild brown with a pattern of black paperclips arranged in diagonal lines up and down the length.

He had my card in his hand, reading out the information in a slightly cocky tone. "Kinsey Millhone, P.I. from Santa Teresa, California. What can I help you with?"

I could feel a prickly sensation at the back of my neck. His expression was non-committal. Technically, he wasn't rude, but he certainly wasn't friendly and I sensed from his manner he was not going to be much help. I tried a public smile, nothing with any sincerity or warmth. "Selma Newquist hired me. She has some questions about Tom."

He regarded me briefly and then moved through the gate at one end of the counter. "I have to be some place, but you can follow me out. What questions?"

I had no choice but to trot along beside him as he headed down the hall toward a rear entrance. "She says he was upset about something. She wants to know what it was."

He pushed the door open and passed through, picking up his pace in a manner that suggested mounting agitation. I caught the door as it swung shut and passed through right after him. I had to two-step to keep up. He pulled his car keys from his pocket as he descended the steps. He walked briskly across the parking lot and slowed when he reached a nondescript, white compact car, which he proceeded to unlock. As he opened the car door, he turned to look at me. "Listen, here's the truth and no disrespect intended. Selma was always trying to pry into Tom's business, always pressing him for something just in case the poor guy had a fleeting thought of his own. The woman comes equipped with emotional radar, forever scanning her environment, trying to pick up matters of no concern to her. Repeat that and I'll deny it so you can save your breath."

"I have no intention of repeating it. I appreciate your candor—"

"Then you can appreciate this," he said. "Tom never said a word against her, but I can tell you from experience, she's exhausting to be around. Tom was a good guy, but now that he's gone, it's a relief not to have to see her. My wife and I never really wanted to spend time with Selma. We socialized when we had to out of our affection for him. If that sounds spiteful, I'm sorry, but that's the bottom line. My best advice to you is leave the man in peace. He's barely cold in his grave and she's trying to dig him up again."

"Could he have been worried about a case?"

He glanced away from me then with a quick smile of disbelief that I'd pursued the point. I could see him rein himself in, struggling to be patient in hopes of getting rid of me. "He had as many as ten, fifteen files on his desk when he died. And no, you can't see them so don't even ask."

"But nothing particularly distressing?"

"I'm afraid I can't tell you what distressed Tom and what didn't."

"Who's taken over his workload?"

"I took some files. A new guy just hired on and he's taking the rest. None of that information is for public consumption. I don't intend to compromise any ongoing investigation to satisfy Selma's morbid curiosity so you can bag that idea."

"Do you think Tom had personal problems he didn't want her to know?"

"Ask somebody else. I don't want to say anything more about Tom."

"What's the big deal? If you'd give me some help, I'd be out of here," I said.

By way of an answer, he got into the car and pulled the door shut. He turned the key in the ignition, pressing a button in the console. The car window slid down with a mild whir. When he spoke again, his tone was more pleasant. "Hey, this may sound rude, but do yourself a favor and let it drop, okay? Selma's a narcissist. She thinks everything's about her."

"And this isn't?"

He pressed the button again and the window slid back into place. End of subject. End of Q&A. He put the car in reverse and backed out of the space, taking off with a little chirp as he threw the gear into first. I could only stare after him. Belatedly, I sensed a stinging heat rise in my face. I raised a hand to my cheek as though I'd been slapped.

FIVE

I got in my car and headed back to Selma's, still completely unenlightened. I couldn't tell if Rafer knew something or if he was simply annoyed at Selma's hiring a private detective. Oddly enough, I found his rudeness more inspirational than daunting. Tom had died without much warning, out on the highway with no opportunity to clean up his business. For the moment, I was operating on the assumption that Selma's intuition was correct.

I left my car out in front and crossed the lawn to the porch. Selma'd left a note taped to the door saying she'd be over at the church until noon. I tried the door, which was unlocked, so I didn't need the key she'd given me the night before. I let myself in, calling a hello as I entered in case Brant was on the premises. There was no call in response, though several lights in the house were on. I took a few minutes to move through the empty rooms. The house was one story and most of the living space was laid out on one floor. Just off the kitchen, I found a set of stairs leading down to the basement.

I flipped on the light and descended halfway, peering

over the rail. I could see woodworking equipment, a washer and dryer, a hot-water heater, and various odds and ends of furniture, including a portable barbecue and lawn chairs. A half-open door on the far wall led to the furnace room. There appeared to be ample storage. I'd nose around later, going through the cardboard boxes and built-in cabinets.

I returned to Tom's office and sat down at his desk, wondering what secrets he might have kept from view. What I was looking for—if, indeed, there was any-thing—didn't have to be related to Tom's work. It could have been anything: drink, drugs, pornography, gam-bling, an affair, an affinity for young boys, a tendency to cross-dress. Most of us have something we'd prefer to keep to ourselves. Or maybe there was nothing. I didn't like to admit it, but Rafer's attitude toward Selma was already having an effect. I'd resisted his view, but a small touch of doubt was beginning to stir.

I abandoned Tom's desk, feeling restless and bored. So far, I hadn't turned up one significant scrap of paper. Maybe Selma was nuts and I was wasting my time. I went out to the kitchen and poured myself a glass of water. I opened the refrigerator and stared at the con-tents while I pretended to quench my thirst. I closed the refrigerator door and checked the pantry. All the stuff she'd brought back from the store looked alarming; artificial and imitation products of the Miracle Whip variety. There was a plate of what looked like raisin-oatmeal cookies on the counter, with a note that said "Help yourself." I ate several. I left the glass in the drainboard and wandered into the hall. The phone seemed to ring every fifteen minutes, but I let the machine pick up messages. Selma was much in demand, but it was all charity-related work—the church bazaar, a fund-raising auction for the new Sunday school wing.

I turned my attention to the master bedroom. Tom's clothes were still hanging in his half of the closet. I began to go through his pockets. I checked the top shelf, his shoe boxes, dresser drawers, his change caddy. I found a loaded Colt .357 Magnum in one bed table drawer, but there was nothing else of importance. The remaining content of the drawer was that embarrassing assortment of junk everyone seems to keep somewhere: ticket stubs, match books, expired credit cards, shoe-laces. No dirty magazines, no sex toys. I looked under the bed, slid a hand along under the mattress, peeked behind picture frames, tapped with a knuckle across the walls in the closet, pulled up a corner of the rug, looking for hidden panels in the floor.

In the master bath, I checked the medicine cabinet, the linen closet, and the hamper. Nothing leaped out at me. Nothing seemed out of place. For a while, in despair, I stretched out on the master bedroom floor, breathing in carpet fumes and wondering how soon I could decently quit.

I went back into the den, where I finished going through the remaining junk on his shelves. Aside from feeling virtuous for cleaning out his desk drawers, I'd acquired absolutely no insights about Tom Newquist's life. I checked his credit card receipts for the past twelve months, but neither his Visa nor his MasterCard showed anything unusual. Most activity on the card could easily be matched to his desk calendar. For instance, a series of hotel and restaurant charges the previous February were related to a seminar he'd attended in Redding, California. The man was systematic. I gave him points for that. Any work-related charges to his telephone bill were later invoiced to his work and reimbursed accordingly. He didn't pad his account by so much as a penny. There was no pattern of outlandish expenses and nothing to suggest any significant or unexplained outlay of cash.

I heard a car pull into the drive. If this was Selma coming in, I'd tell her I was quitting so she wouldn't waste any more of Tom's hard-earned money. The front door opened and closed. I called a "Hello" and waited for a response. "Selma, is that you?" I waited again. "The Booger Man?"

This time I got a manly "Yo!" in response, and Selma's son, Brant, appeared in the doorway. He was wearing a red knit cap, a red sweatsuit, and pristine white leather Reeboks, with a white towel wrapped around his neck. Brant, at twenty-five, was the kind of kid matronly housewives in the supermarket turned around and checked out in passing. He had dark hair and fierce brows over serious brown eyes. His complexion was flawless. His jaw was boxy, his cheeks as honed as if his face had been molded and shaped in clay first and then carved out of flesh. His mouth was fleshy and his color was good; a strong winter tan overlaid with the ruddy burn of snow glare and wind. His posture was impeccable: square shoulders, flat stomach, skinny through the hips. If I were younger, I might have whimpered at the sight of him. As it is, I tend to disqualify any guy that much younger than me, especially in the course of work. I've had to learn the hard way (as it were) not to mix pleasure with business.

"My mom's not here yet?" he asked, pulling the towel from around his neck. He removed his knit cap at the same time and I could see that his hair was curling slightly with the sweaty dampness of his workout. His smile showed straight white teeth.

"Should be any minute. I'm Kinsey. Are you Brant?"

"Yes ma'am. I'm sorry. I should have introduced myself." I shook hands with him across the littered expanse of his father's desk. His palm was an odd gray. When he saw that I noticed, he smiled sheepishly. "That's from weightlifting gloves. I just came from the gym," he said. "I saw the car out front and figured you were here. How's it going so far?"

"Well enough, I guess."

"I better let you get back to it. Mom comes, tell her I'm in the shower."

"Sure thing."

"See you in a bit," he said.

Selma got home at 12:15. I heard the garage door grumble up and then down. Within minutes, she'd let herself in the door that led from the garage into the kitchen. Soon afterward, I could hear the clattering of dishes, the refrigerator door opening and shutting, then the chink of flatware. She appeared in the den doorway, wearing a cotton pinafore-style apron over slacks and a matching sweater. "I'm making chicken salad sand-wiches if you'd like to join us. You met Brant?"

"I did. Chicken salad sounds great. You need help?"

"No, no, but come on out and we can talk while I finish up."

I followed her to the kitchen where I washed my hands. "You know what I haven't come across yet is Tom's notebook. Didn't he take field notes when he was working an investigation?"

Surprised, Selma turned from the counter where she was putting together sandwiches. "Absolutely. It was a little loose-leaf notebook with a black leather cover, about the size of an index card, maybe a little bigger, but not much more than that. It must be around here some place. He always had it with him." She began to cut sandwiches in half, placing them on a platter with sprigs of parsley around the edge. Every time I buy parsley, it turns to slime. "Are you sure it's not there?" she asked.

"I haven't come across it. I checked his desk drawers and his coat pockets."

"What about his truck? Sometimes he left it in the glove compartment or the side pocket."

"Good suggestion. I should have thought of that myself."

I opened the connecting door and moved into the garage. I skirted Selma's car and opened the door to the pickup on the driver's side. The interior smelled heavily of cigarette smoke. The ashtray bulged with cigarette butts buried in a shallow bed of ash. The glove compartment was tidy, bearing only a batch of road maps, the owner's manual, registration, proof of insurance, and gasoline receipts. I looked in the side pockets in both doors, looked behind the visors, leaned over and scanned the space under the bucket seats. I checked the area behind the seats, but there was only a small tool kit for emergencies. Aside from that, the interior revealed nothing. I slammed the driver's side door shut, glancing idly along the garage shelves in passing. I don't know what I thought I'd see, but there was no little black notebook within range.

I returned to the kitchen. "Scratch that," I said. "Any other ideas?"

"I'll have a look myself later on today. He could have left the notebook at work, though he seldom did that. I'll call Rafer and ask him."

"Won't he claim the notes are department property?"

"Oh, I'm sure not," she said. "He told me he'd do anything he could to help. He was Tom's best friend, you know."

But not yours, I thought. "One thing I'm curious about," I said tentatively. "The night he died . . . if he'd had any warning . . . he could have called for help if he'd had a radio. Why no CB in his truck? Why no pager? I know a lot of guys in law enforcement who have radios installed in their personal vehicles."

"Oh, I know. He meant to do that, but hadn't gotten around to it. He was always busy. I couldn't get him to take the time to drop it off and get it done. That's the sort of thing you tend to remember when there's no way to deal with it."

Brant reappeared, wearing the blue uniform that identified him as an emergency medical technician for the local ambulance service. B. NEWQUIST was embroidered on the left. His skin radiated the scent of soap and his hair was now shower-damp and smelled of Ivory shampoo. I allowed myself one small inaudible whine of the sort only heard by dogs; neither Brant nor his mother seemed to pick up on it. I sat at the kitchen table, just across from him, politely eating my sandwich while I listened to them chat. Midway through lunch, the telephone rang again. Selma got up. "You two go ahead. I'll pick that up in Tom's den."

Brant finished his sandwich without saying much and I realized it was going to be my job to initiate conversation.

"I take it Tom adopted you."

"When I was thirteen," Brant said. "My . . . I guess you'd call him a birth father . . . hadn't been in touch for years, since my mom and him divorced. When she married Tom, he petitioned the court. I'd consider him my real dad whether he adopted me or not."

"You must have had a good relationship."

He reached for the plate of cookies on the counter and we took turns eating them while we continued our conversation. "The last couple of years we did. Before that, we didn't get along all that great. Mom's always been easygoing, but Tom was strict. He'd been in the army and he came down real hard on the side of obeying rules. He encouraged me to get involved with Boy Scouts—which I hated—karate, and track, stuff like that. I wasn't used to having restrictions laid on me so I fought back at first. I guess I did just about anything I could think of to challenge his authority. Eventually he shaped up," he said, smiling slightly.

"How long have you been a paramedic?"

"Three years. Before that, I didn't do much of anything. Went to school for a while, though I wasn't any great shakes as a student back then."

"Did Tom talk to you about his cases?"

"Sometimes. Not lately."

"Any idea why?"

Brant shrugged. "Maybe what he was working on wasn't that interesting."

"What about the last six weeks or so?"

"He didn't mention anything in particular."

"What about his field notes? Have you seen those?"

A frown crossed his face. "His field notes?"

"The notes he kept—"

Brant interrupted. "I know what field notes are, but I don't understand the question. His are missing?"

"I think so. Or put it this way, I haven't been able to lay hands on his notebook."

"That's weird. When it wasn't in his pocket, he kept it in his desk drawer or his truck. All his old notes, he bound up in rubber bands and stored in boxes in the basement. Have you asked his partner? Might be at the office."

"I talked to Rafer once but I didn't ask about the notebook because at that point, I hadn't even thought to look."

"Can't help you on that one. I'll keep an eye out around here."

After lunch, both Selma and Brant took off. Brant had errands to run before he reported for work and Selma was involved in her endless series of volunteer positions. She'd posted a calendar on the refrigerator and the squares were filled with scribbles for most days of the week. A silence settled on the house and I felt a mild ripple of anxiety climb my frame. I was running out of things to do. I went back to the den and pulled the phone book out of Tom's top drawer. Given the size of the town, the directory was no bigger than a magazine. I looked up James Tennyson, the CHP officer who'd found Tom that night. There was only one Tennyson, a James W., listed on Iroquois Drive in this same development. I checked my city map, grabbed my jacket and my handbag, and headed out to the car.

Iroquois Drive was a winding roadway lined with two-story houses and an abundance of evergreens. Residents were apparently encouraged to keep their garage doors closed. Backyards in this section were fully fenced or surrounded by hedges and I could see swing sets and jungle gyms as well as above-ground swimming pools, still covered for the winter. The Tennysons lived at the end of the street in a yellow stucco house with dark green shutters and a dark green roof. I parked out in front, snagging the morning paper from the lawn as I passed. I pushed the doorbell, but heard no reassuring *ding dong* inside. I waited a few minutes and then tried a modest knock.

The door was opened by a young woman in jeans with a sleeping baby propped against her shoulder. The child might have been six months old; sparse golden curls, flushed cheeks, flannel sleepers with feet, and a big diapered butt.

"Mrs. Tennyson?"

"That's right."

"My name is Kinsey Millhone. I was hoping to have a word with your husband. I take it he's the one who works for the CHP."

"That's right."

"Is he at work?"

"No, he's here. He works nights and sleeps late. That's why the doorbell's turned off. You want to come in and wait? I just heard him banging around so it shouldn't be long."

"If you don't mind." I held up the newspaper. "I brought this in. I trust it's yours."

"Oh, thanks. I don't even bother until he's up. The baby gets into it and tears the whole thing to pieces if I'm not looking. Cat does the same thing. Sits there and bites on it just daring me to get mad."

She moved aside to admit me and I stepped into the entrance. Like Selma's, this house seemed overheated, but I may have been reacting to the contrast with the outside cold. She closed the door behind me. "By the way, I'm Jo. Your name's Kimmy?"

"Kinsey," I corrected. "It was my mother's maiden name."

"That's cute," she said, flashing me a smile. "This is Brittainy. Poor baby. We call her Bugsy for some reason. Don't know how that got started, but she'll never live it down." Jo Tennyson was trim, with a ponytail and bangs, her hair a slightly darker version of her daughter's. She couldn't have been much more than twenty-one and may have become a mother before she could legally drink. The baby never stirred as we proceeded to the kitchen. Jo put the newspaper on the kitchen table, indicating a seat. She moved around the room, setting up her husband's breakfast one-handed while the baby slept on. I watched with fascination as she opened a fresh cereal box, shook some of the contents in a bowl, and fetched a spoon from the drawer, which she closed with one hip. She retrieved the milk carton from the refrigerator, poured coffee into three mugs, and pushed one in my direction. "You're not in sales, I hope."

I shook my head and then murmured a thank you for the coffee, which smelled great. "I'm a private investigator. I have some questions for your husband about Tom Newquist's death."

"Oh, sorry. I didn't realize it was business or I could have called him first thing. He's just fooling around. He likes to take his time in the morning because the rest of his day's so hectic. Let me see where he's at. If you want any more coffee, help yourself. I'll be right back."

During her absence, I took the opportunity to engage in a little sit-down observation. The house was untidy—I'd seen that in passing—but the kitchen was particularly disorganized. Counters were cluttered, the cabinet doors hung open, the sink piled with dishes from the last several meals. I thought the vinyl floor tile was gray with a dark mottled pattern, but on closer inspection it turned out to be white overlaid with an assortment of sooty footprints. I straightened up as she returned.

"He'll be right here. I didn't peg you for a detective. Are you local?"

"I'm from Santa Teresa."

"I didn't think you looked familiar. You should talk to Tom's wife. She lives in this subdivision, over in that direction about six blocks, on Pawnee. The snooty street we call it."

"She's the one who hired me. You know her?"

"Uh-unh. We go to the same church. She's in charge of the altar flowers and I help when I can. She's really good-hearted. She's the one who gave Bugsy her little christening dress. Here's James. I'll leave the two of you alone so you can talk."

I got to my feet as he entered the kitchen. James Tennyson was fair-haired, clean-cut, and slender, the kind of earnest young man you want assisting you on the highway when your fan belt goes funny or your rear tire's blown. He was dressed in civilian clothes: jeans, a sweatshirt, and a pair of sheepskin slippers. "James Tennyson. Nice to meet you."

"Kinsey Millhone," I said as the two of us shook hands. "I'm sorry to bother you at home, but I was over at the Newquists and it seemed so close. I saw your name on a report I picked up from the coroner and looked you up in the book."

"Not a problem. Sit down."

"Thanks. Go ahead with your breakfast. I didn't mean to intrude."

He smiled. "I guess I will if you don't mind. What can I do for you?"

While James ate his cereal, I laid out Selma's concerns. "I take it you knew him personally?"

"Yeah, I knew Tom. Mean, we weren't real good friends ... him and Selma were older and ran with a different crowd ... but everybody in Nota Lake knew Tom. I tell you, his death shook me. I know he's kind of old, but he was like a fixture around here."

"Can you tell me how you found him? I know he had a heart attack. I'm just trying to get a feel for what happened."

"Well, this was ... what ... five, six weeks ago ... and really nothing unusual. I was cruising 395 when I spotted this vehicle off to the side of the road. Hazard lights were on and the engine was running so I pulled in behind. I recognized Tom's pickup. You know he lives here in the neighborhood so I see the truck all the time. At first I thought he might be having engine problems or something like that. Both the doors were locked, but once I got close I could see him slumped over. I tapped on the window, thinking he'd pulled over and fell asleep at the wheel. I figured the heater was running because the windshield was covered with condensation, windows all cloudy."

"How'd you get in?"

"Well, the window on the driver's side was open a crack. I had a wire in my car and popped the lock up with that. I could see he's in trouble. He looked awful, his eyes open, muck in the corners of his mouth."

"Was he still alive at that point?"

"I'm pretty sure he was gone, but I did what I could. I tell you my hands were shaking so bad, I couldn't make 'em do right. I nearly busted the window and would have if I hadn't managed to snag the lock when I did. I hauled him down out of the truck onto the side of the road and did CPR right there. I couldn't pick up a heartbeat. His skin was cool to the touch, or at least it seemed like that to me. It was freezing outside and even with the heater turned on, temperature inside the truck had dropped. You know how it does. I radioed for help . . . got an ambulance out there as fast as I could, but there was nothing for it. Doc in ER declared him dead on arrival."

"You think he knew what was happening and pulled over to the side?"

"That'd be my guess. He must have had some kind of chest pain, maybe shortness of breath."

"Did you happen to see Tom's notebook? Black leather, about this big?"

He thought back for a moment, shaking his head slowly. "No ma'am. I don't believe so. Of course, I wasn't looking for it. It was in his truck for sure?"

"Well, no, but Selma says he kept it with him and it hasn't turned up yet. I thought maybe you spotted it and turned it into the department."

"I'da probably done that if I'd seen it. I wouldn't want my notes circulating. A lot of it looks like gibberish, but you need 'em when you type up your reports and if you're called on to testify in court. Wasn't among his personal items? The coroner's office would've returned all his clothes and anything he had on him. You know, his watch, contents of his pockets, and like that."

"I asked Selma the same thing and she hasn't seen it. Anyway, we'll keep looking. I appreciate your time. If anything comes to mind, you can reach me through her."

"I can't imagine there's anything to investigate about him. You couldn't meet a nicer fellow. He's the best. A good man and a good cop."

"So I gather."

I went back to the motel. I couldn't face another minute of sitting in Tom's den. For all we knew, Tom might have been suffering from a chemical depression. We'd been assuming his problem was situational, but it might not have been. *My* problem was situational. I was home-sick and wanted out.

I let myself into the cabin, noting with approval that the room had been done up. The bed was made and the bathroom had been scrubbed, the toilet paper left with a point folded in the first sheet. I sat down at the table and rolled a piece of paper in my Smith-Corona. I began to type out an account of the last day's activities. Selma Newquist was just going to have to make her peace with Tom's passing. Death always leaves unfinished business in its wake, mysteries beyond fathoming, countless unanswered questions amid the detritus of life. All the stories are forgotten, the memories lost. Hire anyone you want and you're still never going to find out what a human being is made of. I could sit here and type 'til I was blue in the face. Tom Newquist was gone and I suspected no one would ever know what his final moments had been.

SIX

I found myself that night in a place called Tiny's Tavern, one of those shit-kicking bars so many small towns seem to spawn. Cecilia had indicated this was a popular hangout for off-duty law enforcement and I was there trolling as much as anything. I was also avoiding the cabin, with its frigid inside temperatures and depressive lighting. Tiny's had rough plank walls, sawdust on the floor, and a bar with a brass footrail that stretched the length of the room. As in an old Western saloon, there was a long mirror behind the bar with a glittering double image of all the liquor bottles on display. The place was gray with cigarette smoke. The air was over-heated and smelled of spilled beer, faulty plumbing, failed deodorant, and cheap cologne. The jukebox was gaudy green and yellow with tubes of bubbles running up the sides and stocked with a strange mix of gospel tunes interspersed with country music, the latter dominant. Occasionally, a couple would clomp around mechanically on the ten-by-ten dance floor while the other patrons looked on, calling out encouragement in terms I thought rude.

I wasn't sure about the unspoken assumptions in a

place like this. A woman alone might look like an easy mark for any guy on the loose. For a week night, there seemed to be a fair number of unattached fellows in the place, but after an hour on the premises no one seemed to take any particular notice of me. So much for my fantasy of being accosted by cads. I perched on a barstool, sipping bad beer and shelling peanuts from a brass bowl that might have enjoyed a previous life as a spittoon. There was something satisfactory about tossing shells on the floor, though sometimes I ate the shells too, figuring the fiber was healthy in a diet like mine, burdened as it is with all that cholesterol and fat.

The bartender was a guy in his twenties with a shaved head, a dark mustache and beard, and a tattoo of a scorpion on the back of his right hand. I flirted with him mildly just to occupy my time. He seemed to understand there was no serious chance of a wild sexual encounter in his immediate future. I put some quarters in the jukebox. I chatted with the waitress named Alice, who had bright orange hair. I made trips to the ladies' room. I practised a little balancing trick with a fork and a burnt match. If there were any off-duty cops on the premises, I realized I wouldn't recognize them in their off-duty clothes.

At ten, Macon Newquist came in. He was in uniform, moving through the bar at a leisurely pace, checking the crowd for drunks, minors, and any other form of trouble in the making. He spoke to me in passing, but didn't seem inclined to make small talk. Shortly after he left, my idleness paid off when I spotted the civilian clerk from the sheriff's substation. I couldn't for the life of me remember her name. She came in as a part of a foursome with a fellow I assumed to be her husband and another couple, all of them roughly the same age. The four were dressed in a combination of cowboy and ski attire: boots, jeans, Western-cut shirts, down parkas, ski mittens, and knit caps. They found an empty table on the far side of the room. I stared at the clerk with her dark hair cropped short above her ears, dark brown eyes glinting behind her small oval glasses. The other woman was auburn-haired, top-heavy, and pretty, probably plagued with unwanted suggestions about breast-reduction surgery. The clerk's hubby held a consultation and then headed in my direction, pausing at the far end of the bar where he ordered a pitcher of beer and four oversized mugs. In the meantime, the women shed their jackets, took up their purses, and left the table, heading toward the ladies' room. I signaled for another beer just to hold my place and then made a beeline for the facilities myself. My path intersected theirs and the three of us reached the door at just about the same time. I slowed my pace and allowed the two of them to enter first.

The clerk was saying, "Oh, honey. Billie's taken up with that trashy fellow from the video store. You know the one with the attitude? I don't know what she sees in him unless it's you-know-what. I told her she ought to think a little more of herself . . ."

The two continued to talk as they passed through the door and into the first two out of three toilet stalls. I entered the third and eavesdropped my tiny heart out while the three of us peed in a merry chorus. What the hell was her name? She and her companion discussed Billie's son, Seb, who suffered from genital warts so persistent his penis looked like a pink fleshy pickle according to someone named Candy who'd dumped him forthwith. Three toilets were flushed in succession and we reassembled at the sinks so we could wash our hands. The other woman skipped her personal cleanliness and moved on to the ritual of combing her hair and adjusting her makeup. I was tempted to point out the sign on the wall, urging us to curb the spread of disease, but I realized the warning was intended for tavern employees. Apparently, the rest of us were at liberty to contaminate anyone we touched. I tried to set a good example, lathering like a surgeon on the brink of an operation, but the woman didn't follow suit.

Miraculously, just then, my brain supplied the clerk's name in a satisfying mental burp. I caught her eye in the mirror and flashed her a smile as she was pulling out a paper towel so she could dry her hands. "Aren't you Margaret?"

She looked at me blankly and then said "Oh hi" without warmth. I couldn't tell if she'd forgotten me, or remembered and simply didn't want to be engaged in conversation. Probably the latter. She crumpled the paper towel and pushed it down in the wastebasket.

"Kinsey Millhone," I prompted, as if she'd recently inquired. "We met this morning at the office when I was talking to Detective LaMott." I held out my hand and she was too polite to decline a handshake.

She said, "Nice seeing you again."

"I thought I recognized you the minute you came in, but I couldn't remember where I knew you from." I turned and gave a little wave to the other woman.

"Hi. How are you? Kinsey Millhone," I said. "And you're . . .?"

She seemed to hesitate, glancing at Margaret. "Earlene." She held her hand out and I had no choice but to take it, germs and all.

"My best friend," Margaret interjected.

"Well, isn't that nice," I said. Earlene's handshake consisted of laying her fingers passively across mine. It was like having a half pound of cooked linguini placed in your palm for safekeeping. She had a round pretty face with a button nose and plump lips, a mutant body that was all breasts, with diminishing hips and legs that petered out into tiny feet. She flicked another look at Margaret, clearly picking up on her lack of enthusiasm. I was acting like a salesperson, forcing chitchat to gain a foothold in the conversation. Telemarketers use this device all the time, as if the rest of us don't know what their phony friendliness is all about.

Margaret wasn't fooled. She tucked her bag up against her body and gripped it closely with her arm. "I don't know what you said to Rafer, but he was ticked off all day and I was the one had to take the flak."

"Really? I'm sorry to hear that. I didn't mean to set him off."

"Everything sets him off since Tom passed away. They worked together for years, long before I hired on."

"I can see why he'd be upset." I was making myself sick with all this conciliatory bullshit, though it seemed to be having the desired effect.

Margaret rolled her eyes. "He'll get over it, I guess,

but I wouldn't advise you to cross paths with him if you can help it."

"I'll avoid him if possible, but I'm only in town for another couple of days and I'm not sure where else to get information."

I was hoping this would prompt an offer of assistance, but Margaret didn't seem to care. She stood there without a word, forcing me to blunder on. "Why don't I just tell you what I need and maybe you can help. Honestly, I'm not looking for any dirt on Tom Newquist. That's not my intention. I've heard he's a great guy and everybody seems real sorry that he's gone."

"Well, that's true," she said, grudgingly.

"I wasn't sure what to make of your boss. I mean, I could tell he was aggravated, but I couldn't figure out what I'd done."

"It's not you in particular. Rafer says Selma's the one stirring up trouble. Says he's sick and tired of her meddling in Tom's affairs."

"It's hardly meddling," I said. "She was married to the man and has a legitimate concern."

"About what?"

"She told me Tom was worried about something. He slept badly. He brooded. She kept hoping he'd confide in her, but he never said a word. She wanted to ask him, but she couldn't bring herself to do it. You know how it is. You've got a subject you want to talk about and you keep trying to find the perfect time to do it. I guess he was prickly and she was reluctant to irritate him. At any rate, before she could broach the subject, he dropped dead, so now she's stuck."

"That still doesn't entitle her to mess around in Tom's business."

"Of course not, but she's troubled by the possibility he died with some burden. She's heartsick she didn't barge in when she had the chance. That's why she's hired me."

"Good luck," Margaret said in a tone that really meant she hoped I'd fall in a hole.

"I don't think my chances are good, but I don't blame her for trying. She's hoping to make amends. What's wrong with that? In her place, you'd do the same thing, wouldn't you?"

Margaret said, "Well." I could see she was having trouble marshaling an argument. She was good at put-downs; not so good when it came to defending her position. I was feeling damp from the effort of telling the truth. Lies are always easier because the only thing you risk is getting caught. Once you stoop to the truth, you're screwed because if the other person isn't buying, you've got nothing left to sell.

Earlene was watching us like a spectator at a tennis match. Her bright blue eyes darted with interest between my face and Margaret's. I really couldn't tell whose side she was on, but I decided to pull her in. "What do you think, Earlene? What would you do in Selma's place?"

"Same thing, I guess. I can see your point." She flicked a look at Margaret. "You said yourself Tom was a bear the last few weeks before he passed." She looked back at me, hooking a thumb in Margaret's direction. "She thought he was going through the change. You know, moody and short-tempered . . ."

"*Earlene.*"

"Well, it's the truth."

"Of course, it's true, but that doesn't mean it bears repeating in the ladies' room." This from the woman discussing someone's genital warts.

"Do you have any idea what was bothering him?" I asked.

Margaret was indignant. "I most certainly do not. And I have to tell you I think she'd be better off letting sleeping dogs lie. If he'd wanted her to know, he'd have told her, so it's really none of her concern. Even if he was crabby and hard to get along with, that's hardly a crime."

"But who'd know? Who should I be talking to if not Rafer?"

Earlene raised her hand. "Wouldn't hurt to ask Hatch."

"Would you butt out?" Margaret snapped.

"Who's Hatch?" I asked Earlene.

"Hatch's her husband. He's sitting right out there," she said, pointing toward the bar.

Margaret snorted. "He won't help and I give you odds Wayne won't either. Wayne hasn't worked for Tom in years so what's he know about anything?"

"Hatch worked for Tom?" I said to Margaret.

"Uh-unh. Both him and Wayne are sheriff's deputies, only Wayne covers Whirly Township and Hatch is working days down here."

"It couldn't do any harm," I said.

Margaret thought about it and then frowned. "I don't guess I can stop you, but it's a waste of time if you ask me."

The three of us left the ladies' room together.

"I'll grab my beer and be right back," I said.

I hustled my butt over to the bar to get my things. I figured in my absence Margaret could go to work on her husband, thus advancing my case. I grabbed my beer mug and jacket and moved over to their table, watching as Hatch dutifully scrounged up an extra chair from a table nearby. I went through another round of introductions, trying to seem winsome as I shook hands with both men. "Winsome" is not a quality I normally project. "Did Margaret tell you what I was up to?"

Hatch said, "Yes ma'am." He was a big rangy man with a thatch of blond hair shorn close along the sides. His face was bony, all jaw and cheekbones, with a big bumpy nose. His ears stuck out like handles on a vase.

Earlene's husband, Wayne, took a swig of beer and put the mug down with a tap. He was dark-haired with a receding hairline, the hair itself cut short and combed forward. He had the pretty-boy handsomeness of a small-time thug. He didn't seem to like me. He avoided my eyes, his attention diverting to other parts of the room. Once in a while he tuned into the conversation, but he made it plain he didn't like the idea of discussing Tom with anyone.

Hatch at least *seemed* friendly, so I focused on him. "I understand you knew Tom."

"Everybody knew Tom," he said.

"Can you tell me a little bit about him?"

Hatch regarded me uneasily, shaking his head. "You're not going to get me to say anything bad about the man."

"Absolutely not. I'm hoping to get a sense of who he

was. I never met him myself so I'm operating in the dark. How long did you know him?"

"Little over fifteen years, since way before I joined the sheriff's department. I'd moved up here from Barstow and first thing you know, someone broke into my apartment and took my stereo. Tom was the one showed up when I dialed 9-1-1."

"What was he like?"

"With regard to what?"

"Anything. Was he smart? Was he funny? Was he a hang-loose kind of guy?"

Hatch tilted his head, allowing one shoulder to creep up toward his ear. "I'd say Tom was a good cop, first, last, and always. You just about couldn't separate the man from the job. He was smart, for sure, and he played by the book."

"Someone who didn't bend the rules," I said, repeating the coroner's comment.

"Yeah, right. You know, little things, he might try to give a guy a break, but high-ticket crime, he was a strictly law-and-order type. All this victim stuff you see nowadays cut no ice with him. He believed you're accountable and there's no two ways about it. He took a hard line on that and I think he was right. Small town like this, somebody breaks the law, you might have dated their sister or they lived down the street from you way back when. In Tom's mind, it wasn't personal. He wasn't mean or anything like that. Business was just business and you had to respect him for his attitude."

"Can you give me an example?"

"I can't think of one offhand. What about you,

Wayne? You know what I'm saying. What's the kind of thing Tom did?"

Wayne shook his head. "Hey, Hatch. This is your party. By me."

Hatch scratched at his chin, pulling at the flesh underneath. "Well now, here's one I remember and this is pretty typical I'd say. We had this good ol' boy named Sonny Gelson. Remember him, hon? This was maybe five, six years ago, I guess. He used to live over by Winona in a big old falling-down house." He didn't wait for a response, but I could see Margaret nod as her husband went on. "His wife shot 'im one night by mistake. She thought he was an intruder and pumped a big hole in his chest. About six months before, she'd reported a prowler and Sonny got her a Smith & Wesson. So one night he's out of town and she's home by herself. She hears someone in the downstairs hall, pulls the gun out of a drawer, and pops the guy as he comes in. Problem was the gun misfired and blew up in her hand. Sonny'd packed the reload himself and I guess he'd done it wrong, or that's what it looked like at any rate. Bullet still exited the gun and hit him smack in the chest. I think he died before Judy could even dial 9–1–1. Meantime, Judy's got a hand full of fragments and she's bleeding all over everywhere. See, but now here's the point. Tom got it in his head that this's premeditated murder. He's convinced the whole thing's a setup. So here's Judy Gelson crying her heart out for her terrible mistake. She swears she didn't know it was him. The whole town's up in arms. Everybody out there protesting. DA was going to let her plead out and let it go at that. I doubt she'd have served time because her record was clean. Save the county a ton of money, plus a lot of bad press. Tom just kept digging and pretty soon he comes up with this hefty insurance policy. Turns out Judy had a lover and the two of 'em concocted this plan to get rid of her husband, take the money, and run. She's the one jimmied the cartridge with an overload of fast powder so she'd look like an innocent victim of circumstance herself. Tom's the one nailed her and he'd went *steady* with her once upon a time. She's homecoming queen in high school and they nearly run off together the night of the senior prom. Cut no ice with him and that's the point I'm trying to make."

"What happened to Judy Gelson?"

"She's doing twenty-five to life somewhere. Lover dropped out of sight. In fact, nobody ever figured out who he was. Maybe somebody local with a lot to lose. Tom was always workin' that one, trying to get a line on the guy. It bugged him to see a fellow get away with anything."

"He liked to work old cases?"

"Everybody does. Always the chance you'll crack one and make a name for yourself. Anyway, it's more than that; it's putting paid to an account. 'Closure' they call it nowadays, but it amounts to the same thing."

I glanced at Margaret, saying, "That's all Selma wants."

Hatch shook his head at the mention of her name. "Well, now Selma. She's something else. I wouldn't want to say anything bad about her. Tom was crazy about her, worshiped the ground she walked on, and that's no lie."

Margaret chimed in. "The rest of us find Selma pretty hard to take."

"How so?"

"Oh, you know, she's easily offended, imagines slights where there's none intended. Tom tried his best to reassure her, but it was never enough. You'd run into the two of 'em out in public and he'd always make sure she was included in the conversation, didn't he?" she said, turning to Earlene for confirmation. "I think he knew people didn't like her and he wanted her to look good."

"That's right. He'd sit there and draw her out . . . get her to talking like anybody gave a shit. Everybody liked him and hadn't any use for her."

"So in a way, her insecurity was justified," I said.

Earlene laughed. "Sure, but if she wasn't so self-centered, people might like her better. Selma's convinced the sun rises and sets in her own hineybumper and she had Tom convinced of it, too. He used to jump every time she snapped her fingers. On top of that she's a social climber, acting like she's so much better than the rest of us. In a town this size, we all tend to socialize. You know, go to the same church, join the same country club. Selma has to be there, right out in front. The woman's tireless, I'll give her that. Ask her to do anything and she's got it done just like that."

Earlene's husband, Wayne, had caught my eye more than once in the course of her recital. I thought he was irritated that she was talking to me. Given the fact that Wayne had worked with Tom, I suspected he didn't like his wife being so free with her opinions. He seemed guarded, remote, his eyes pinned on the table while the other three exchanged anecdotes. I couldn't get a fix on the source of his disaffinity. Maybe Rafer'd had a chat with him and made it clear he didn't want any of his deputies to cooperate with me. Or maybe his attitude reflected the habitual reluctance of a cop to share information, even at the level of gossip and personal opinion.

I caught his attention. "What about you, Wayne? Anything you'd care to add?"

He smiled, but more to himself than at me. "Ask me, them three are doing pretty good."

"You agree with their assessment?"

"Basically, I don't see Tom's marriage as any of our business. What him and Selma worked out is between them."

Earlene tossed a crumpled paper napkin in his direction. "You old sourpuss," she said.

"You're not going to get me to respond," he replied airily.

"Oh, loosen up. Honest to Pete. You never liked Selma any better than the rest of us so why not admit it?"

"Say what you want. You're not going to draw me into this."

"Let him be," I said. I was suddenly feeling tired. The combination of tension and smoke-filled air was giving me a headache. I'd asked for general information and that's what I'd received. It was clear no one was going to offer up much more than that. "I think I'll head on back to the motel," I said.

"Don't go away mad. Just go away," Wayne said, smiling.

"Very funny. Ha ha," Earlene said to him.

"We'd best be off, too," Margaret said, glancing at her watch. "Oh, geez. I have to be at work at eight and look what time it is. Eleven forty-five."

Earlene reached for her jacket. "I didn't realize it was that late and we still have to drop you off at your place."

"We can walk. It's not far," Margaret said.

"Don't be silly. It's no trouble. It's right on our way."

The four of them began to gather their belongings, shrugging into their parkas, scraping chairs back as they rose.

"Catch you later," I said.

Various good-bye remarks were made, the yada-yada-yada of superficial social exchange. I watched them depart, and then returned to the bar where I settled my tab. Alice, the orange-haired waitress, was just taking a break. She pulled up a stool beside me and lit a cigarette. Her eyes were rimmed in black eyeliner and she had a fringe of thick dark lashes that had to be false; bright coral lipstick, a swathe of blusher on each cheek. "You a cop?"

"I'm a private investigator."

"Well, that explains," she said, blowing smoke to one side. "I heard you're asking around about Tom Newquist."

"Word travels fast."

"Oh, sure. Town this small there's not much to talk about," she said. "You're barking up the wrong tree with that bunch you were talking to. They're all law enforcement, loyal to their own. You're not going to get anyone to say a bad word about Tom."

"So I discover. You have something to add?"

"Well, I don't know what's been said. I knew him from in here. I knew her somewhat better. I used to run into the two of them at church on occasion."

"I gather she wasn't popular. At least from what I've heard."

"I try not to judge others, but it's hard not to have *some* opinion. Everybody's down on Selma and it seems unfair. I just wish she'd quit worrying about those silly teeth of hers." Alice put a hand to her mouth. "Have you noticed her doing this? Half the time I can hardly hear what's she saying because she's so busy trying to cover up her mouth. Anyway, Tom was great. Don't get me wrong . . . I grant you Selma's abrasive . . . but you know what? He got to look good by comparison. He wasn't confrontational. Tom'd never dream of getting in your face about anything. And why should he? He had Selma to do that. She'd take on anyone. Know what I mean? Let her be the bitch. She's the one takes all the heat. She does the work of the relationship while he gets to be Mr. Good-Guy, Mr. Nice-As-Pie. You see what I'm saying?"

"Absolutely."

"It might have suited them fine, but it doesn't seem right to hold her entirely accountable. I know her type; she's a pussy cat at heart. He could have pinned her ears back. He could have raised a big stink and she'd have backed right off. He didn't have the gumption so why's that her fault? Seems like the blame should attach equally."

"Interesting," I said.

"Well, you know, it's just my reaction. I get sick and tired of hearing everyone trash Selma. Maybe I'm just like her and it cuts too close. Couples come to these agreements about who does what. I'm not saying they sit down and discuss it, but you can see my point. One might be quiet, the other talkative. Or maybe one's outgoing where the other one's shy. Tom was passive—pure and simple—so why blame her for taking over? You'd have done it yourself."

"Selma says he was very preoccupied in the last few weeks. Any idea what it was?"

She paused to consider, drawing on her cigarette. "I never thought much about it, but now you mention it, he didn't seem like himself. Tell you what I'll do. Let me ask around and see if anybody knows anything. It's not like people around here are dishonest or even secretive, but they protect their own."

"You're telling me," I said. I took out a business card and jotted down my home number in Santa Teresa and the motel where I was staying.

Alice smiled. "Cecilia Boden. Now there's a piece of work. If that motel gets to you, you can always come to my place. I got plenty of room."

I smiled in return. "Thanks for your help."

I headed out into the night air. The temperature had dropped and I could see my breath. After the clouds of smoke in the bar, I wondered if I was simply exhaling the accumulation. The parking lot was only half full and the lighting just dim enough to generate uneasiness. I took a moment to scan the area. There was no one in sight, though the line of pine trees on the perimeter could have hidden anyone. I shifted my car keys to my right hand and hunched my handbag over my left shoulder as I moved to the rental car and let myself in.

I slid under the wheel, slammed the car door, and locked it as quickly as possible, listening to the locks flip down with a feeling of satisfaction. The windshield was milky with condensation and I wiped myself a clear patch with my bare hand. I turned the key in the ignition, suddenly alerted by the sullen grinding that indicated a low charge on the battery. I tried again and the engine turned over reluctantly. There was a series of misses and then the engine died. I sat there, projecting a mental movie in which I'd be forced to return to the bar, whistle up assistance, and finally crawl into bed at some absurd hour after god knows what inconvenience.

I caught a flash of headlights in the lane behind me and checked the source in my rearview mirror. A dark panel truck was passing at a slow rate of speed. The driver, in a black ski mask, turned to stare at me. The eye holes in the knit mask were rimmed with white and the opening for the mouth was thickly bordered with red. The driver and I locked eyes, our gazes meeting in the oblong reflection of the rearview mirror. I could feel my skin prickle, the pores puckering with fear. I thought *male*. I thought *white*. But I could have been wrong on both counts.

SEVEN

I could hear the crunch of gravel, a dull popping like distant gunfire. The truck slowed and finally came to a halt. I could hear the engine idling against the still night air. I realized I was holding my breath. I wasn't sure what I'd do if the driver got out and approached my car. After an interminable thirty seconds, the truck moved on while I followed its reflection in my rearview mirror. There was no lettering on the side so I didn't think the vehicle was used for commercial purposes. I turned my head, watching as the panel truck reached the end of the aisle and took a left. There was something unpleasant about being the subject of such scrutiny.

I tried starting my car again. "Come *on*," I said. The engine seemed, if anything, a little less energetic. The panel truck was now passing from right to left along the lane in front of me, the two of us separated by the intervening cars, parked nose to nose with mine. I could see the driver lean forward, the masked face now tilted in my direction. It was the blankness that unnerved me, the shapeless headgear wiping out all features except the eyes and mouth, which stood out in startling relief. Terrorists and bank robbers wore masks like this, not ordinary citizens concerned about frostbite. The panel truck stopped. The black ski mask was fully turned in my direction, the prolonged look intense. I could see that both the eye holes and the mouth hole had been narrowed by big white yarn stitches, with no attempt to disguise the modification. The driver extended a gloved right hand, index finger pointing at me like the barrel of a gun. Two imaginary bullets were fired at me, complete with recoil. I flipped him the bird in return. This brief digital exchange was charged with aggression on his part and defiance on mine. The driver seemed to stiffen and I wondered if I should have kept my snappy metacarpal retort to myself. In Los Angeles, freeway shootings have been motivated by less. For the first time, I worried he might have a real weapon somewhere down by his feet.

I pumped the gas with my foot and turned the key again, uttering a low urgent sound. Miraculously, the engine coughed to life. I put the car in neutral and applied pressure on the accelerator, flipping on the headlights while I gunned the engine. The arrow on the voltage indicator leaned repeatedly to the right. I flicked my attention to the panel truck, which was just turning out of the lot at the far end. I released the emergency brake and put the car in reverse.

I backed out of the slot, shifted gears, and swung the car into the lane heading in the opposite direction, peering through the dark to see what had happened to the panel truck. I could hear my heart thudding in my head, as if fear had forced the hapless organ up between my ears. I reached the marked exit and eased forward, searching the streets beyond for signs that the panel truck was rounding the block. The street was empty as far as I could see. I patted myself on the chest, a calming gesture designed to comfort and reassure. Nothing had actually happened. Maybe the driver was mistaken, thinking I was an acquaintance and then realizing his error. Someone passing in a panel truck had turned and looked at me, firing symbolically with a pointed index finger and a wiggle of his thumb. I didn't think the incident would make the national news.

It wasn't until I was midway through town that I caught a glimpse of the truck falling into line half a block back. I could see now that one headlight was sitting slightly askew, the beam directed downward, like someone with one crossed eye. I checked in all directions, but I could see no other traffic and no pedestrians. At this late hour, the town of Nota Lake was deserted, stores locked for the night with only an occasional cold interior light aglow. Even the gas station was shut down and cloaked in darkness. The streetlights washed the empty sidewalks with the chilliest of illumination. Stoplights winked silently from green to red and then to green again.

Was this a problem or was it not? I considered my options. My gas gauge showed half a tank. I had plenty of gas to get back to the motel, but I didn't like the idea of someone following me and I didn't want to try to outrun my pursuer if it came to that. Highway 395, leading out to the Nota Lake Cabins, represented one long continuous stretch of darkened road. The few businesses along the highway would be closed for the night, which meant my vulnerability would increase as the countryside around me became less populated. I glanced in the rearview mirror. The panel truck still hung half a block back, matching my speed, a sedate twenty miles an hour. I could feel myself shuddering from some internal chill. I turned on the heater. I was desperate to get warm, desperate for the sight of another human being. Didn't people walk their dogs? Didn't parents dash out for a quart of milk or a croupy child's cough medicine? How about a jogger I could flag down on sight? I wanted the driver of the panel truck to see that I had help.

I turned left at the next street and drove on for three blocks, eyes pinned to the rearview mirror. Within seconds, the panel truck came around the corner behind me and took up its surveillance. I continued west for six blocks and then turned left again. This street paralleled Main, though it was narrower and darker, a quiet residential neighborhood with no houselights showing. Ordinarily, I keep a gun in my briefcase, which is tucked into the well behind the VW's backseat. But this car was a rental and when I'd left Santa Teresa, I was with Dietz. Why did I need a weapon? The only jeopardy I imagined was living in close quarters with an invalid. Given my nature, what scared me was the possibility of emotional claustrophobia, not physical danger.

I was checking the rearview mirror compulsively every couple of seconds. The panel truck was still there, with one headlight focused on the street and one on me. I've taken enough self-defense classes to know that women, by nature, have trouble assessing personal peril. If followed on a darkened street, many of us don't know when to take evasive action. We keep waiting for a sign that our instincts are correct. We're reluctant to make a fuss, just in case we're mistaken about the trouble we're in. We're more concerned about the possibility of embarrassing the guy behind us, preferring to do nothing until we're sure he really means to attack. Ask a woman to scream for help and what you get is a pathetic squeak with no force behind it and no power to dissuade. Oddly, I found myself suffering the same mind-set. Maybe the guy in the panel truck was simply on his way home and I happened to be taking the very path he intended to take all along. Uh-hun, uh-hun. On the other hand, if the driver in the truck was trying to psych me out, I didn't want to give him the satisfaction of any overt reaction.

I refused to speed up. I refused to play tag. I turned left again, driving at a measured rate as the blocks rolled by. Ahead of me, close to the intersection, was the Nota Lake Civic Center with the sheriff's headquarters. Next door was the fire department and next door to that was the police station. I could see the outside lights showing, though I wasn't sure the place was even open this close to midnight. I coasted to a stop and idled the engine with my headlights on. The panel truck rolled up even with my car and the driver turned, as before, to stare. I could have sworn there was a smile showing through the red-rimmed knit mouth. The driver made no other move and, after a tense moment, he drove on. I checked the rear license plate, but it was covered with tape and no identifying numbers showed. The truck began to speed up, turned left at the intersection, and disappeared from sight. I felt my insides turning luminous as adrenaline poured through me.

I waited a full five minutes, though it felt like for

ever. I studied the street on all sides, craning my head to scan the area behind, lest someone approach on foot. I was afraid to shut down my engine, worried I wouldn't be able to get the car started again. I squeezed my hands between my knees, trying to warm my icy fingers. The feeling of apprehension was as palpable as a fever, racking my frame. I caught a glimpse of headlights behind me again and when I checked the rearview mirror, I saw a vehicle come slowly around the corner. I made a sound in my throat and leaned on the horn. A howling blare filled the night. The second vehicle eased up beside me and I could see now that it was James Tennyson, the CHP officer, in his patrol car. He recognized my face and rolled down the window on the driver's side. "You okay?" he mouthed.

I pressed a button on the console and opened the window on the passenger side of my car.

"Something I can help you with?" he asked.

"Someone's been following me. I didn't know what else to do, but come here and honk."

"Hang on," he said. He spotted a parking place across the street and pulled his patrol car over to the stretch of empty curb. He left his vehicle running while he crossed the street. He walked around to my side of the car and hunkered so we could talk face-to-face. "What's the story?"

I explained the situation, trying not to distort or exaggerate. I wasn't sure how to convince him of the alarm I'd felt, but he seemed to accept my account without any attempt to dismiss my panic as foolish or unwarranted. He was in his twenties by my guess and I suspected I'd seen more in the way of personal combat than he had. Still, he was a cop in uniform and the sight of him was reassuring. He was earnest, polite, with that fair unlined face and all the innocence of youth.

"Well, I can see where that'd worry you. It seems creepy to me, too," he said. "Might have been a guy sitting in the bar. Sometimes the fellows around here get kind of weird when they drink. Sounds like he was waiting for you to come out to the parking lot."

"I thought so, too."

"You didn't notice anybody in Tiny's staring at you?"

"Not at all," I said.

"Well, he probably didn't mean any harm, even if he scared you some."

"What about the truck? There couldn't be that many black panel trucks in a town this size."

"I haven't seen it, but I've been cruising the highway south of town. I was passing the intersection when I caught a glimpse of your headlights so I doubled back. Thought you might be having car trouble, but I wasn't sure." He tilted his head in the direction of the police station. "They're locked up for the night. You want me to see you home? I'd be happy to."

"Please," I said.

He escorted me the six miles to the motel, driving ahead of me so I could keep my gaze fixed on the sight of his patrol car. There was no sign of the panel truck. Once at the Nota Lake Cabins, we parked side by side and he walked me to the cabin, waiting while I unlocked the door and flipped on the light inside. I intended to check the premises, but he held out an arm like the captain of the grade school safety patrol. "Let me do this."

"Great. It's all yours," I said.

I make no big deal about these things. I'm a strong, independent woman, not an idiot. I know when it's time to turn the task over to a cop; someone with a gun, a nightstick, a pair of handcuffs, and a paycheck. He did a cursory inspection while I followed close on his heels, feeling like a cartoon character with slightly quaking knees. If a mouse had jumped out, I'd have shrieked like a fool.

He glanced in the closet, behind the bathroom door. He moved the shower curtain aside, got down on his hands and knees and looked under the bed. He didn't seem any more impressed with the place than I'd been. "Never been inside one of these before. I believe I'd take a pass if it came right down to it. Doesn't Ms. Boden believe in heat?"

"I guess not."

He got to his feet and brushed the soot from his knees. "What kind of money does she get for this?"

"Thirty bucks a night."

"That much?" He shook his head with amazement. He made sure the windows were secured. While I waited in the cabin, he made a circuit of the place outside, using his flashlight beam to cut through the dark. He came back to the door. "Looks clear to me."

"Let's hope."

He let his gaze settle on my face. "I can take you somewhere else if you'd prefer. We got motels in the heart of town if you think you'd feel safer. You'd be warmer, too."

I considered it briefly. I was both keyed up and exhausted. Moving at this hour would be a pain in the ass. "This is fine," I said. "I didn't see any sign of the truck on the way out. Maybe it was just a practical joke."

"I wouldn't count on that. World's full of freaks. You don't want to take something like this lightly. You might want to talk to the police in the morning and file a report. Wouldn't hurt to lay the groundwork in case something comes up again."

"Good point. I'll do that."

"You have a flashlight? Why don't you take this tonight and you can return it to me in the morning. I got another in the car. You'll feel better if you have a weapon."

I took the flashlight, hefting the substantial weight of it in my hand. You could really hurt somebody if you whacked 'em up the side of the head. I'd seen scalps laid wide open when the edge hit just right. I felt like asking for his nightstick and his radio, but I didn't want to leave him denuded of equipment.

I held up the flashlight. "Thanks. I'll drop it off to you first thing."

"No hurry."

Once he was gone, I locked the door and then went through the cabin carefully, doing just as he'd done. I made sure the windows were locked, looked under every piece of furniture, in closets, behind curtains. I turned the lights out and let my eyes adjust to the dark, then moved from window to window, eyeing the exterior. The black wasn't absolute. There was a moon up there somewhere, bathing the surrounding woods in a silvery glow. The trunks of the birches and the sycamores shone as pale as ice. The evergreens were dense, shapeless, and compelling against the night landscape. I should have gone to another motel. I regretted the isolation, wishing that I could find myself safely ensconced in one of the big chains—a Hyatt or a Marriott, one with hundreds of identical rooms and numerous in-house security. In my current situation, I had no phone and no immediate neighbors. The rental car was parked at least a hundred yards away, not readily available if I should have to make a hasty exit.

I leaned my forehead against the glass. From out on the highway, I could catch flashes of light as an occasional car sped by, but none seemed to slow and none turned into the motel parking area. Times like this, I longed for a husband or a dog, but I never could decide which would be more trouble in the long run. At least husbands don't bark and tend to start off paper trained.

I remained fully dressed and brushed my teeth in the dark, barely letting the water run as I washed my face. Frequently, I paused, listening to the silence. I took my shoes off, but kept them by the side of the bed within easy reach. I crawled under the covers and propped myself against the pillows, flashlight in hand. Twice, I got up and looked out the windows, but there was nothing to see and eventually I felt calm return.

I didn't sleep well, but in early morning light, I felt better.

I was blessed with a full three minutes of hot water before the pipes began to clank. I walked out to the highway into a morning filled with icy sunlight and air clear as glass. I could smell loam and pine needles. There was no sign of the panel truck. Nobody in a ski mask paused to stare at me. I had breakfast at the Rainbow, taking a certain comfort at the mundane nature of the place. I watched the short-order cook, a young black girl working with remarkable efficiency and concentration.

Afterward, I returned to Selma's.

Her sister-in-law, Phyllis, was in the kitchen. The two of them were working at the breakfast table, which was covered with paperwork. File folders were spread out, lists of names on legal pads with removable tags attached. I gathered they were determining the seating for some country club event, arguing about who to seat by whom for maximum entertainment and minimum conflict.

"Nawp. I wouldn't do that," Phyllis said. "The fellows like each other, but the women don't speak. Don't you remember that business between Ann Carol and Joanna?"

"They're not still mad about that, are they?"

"Sure are."

"Unbelievable."

"Well, trust me. You seat them together, you got a war on your hands. I've seen Joanna throw one of those hard dinner rolls at Ann Carol. She bonked her right in the eye and raised a welt this big."

Selma paused to light a cigarette while she studied the chart. "How about put her at Table 13?"

Phyllis made a rueful face. "I guess that'd do. I mean, it's dull, but not bad. At least Ann Carol wouldn't be subject to an attack by flying yeast bread."

Selma looked up at me. "Morning, Kinsey. What's on your plate today? Are you about finished in there?"

"Almost," I said. I glanced at Phyllis, wondering if this was a subject to be discussed in front of her.

Selma caught my hesitation. "That's fine. Go ahead. You don't have to worry about her. She knows all this."

"I'm drawing a blank. I don't doubt your story. I'm sure Tom was worried about something. Other people have told me he didn't seem like himself. I just can't find any indication of what was troubling him. Really, I'm no better informed now than when I started. It's frustrating."

I could see the disappointment settle across Selma's face.

"It's only been two days," she murmured. Phyllis was frowning slightly, straightening a pile of papers on the table in front of her. I hoped she had something to offer, but she said nothing so I went on.

"Well, that's true," I said. "And there's always the chance something will pop up unexpectedly, but so far there's nothing. I just thought you should know. I can give you a rundown when you have a minute."

"I guess you can only do your best," Selma said. "Coffee's hot if you want some. I left you a mug alongside that little pitcher of milk over there."

I crossed to the coffeemaker and poured myself a cup, taking a quick whiff of the milk before adding it to my coffee. I debated whether to mention the business with the panel truck, but I couldn't see the point. The two of them were already back at work and I didn't want to have to deal with their concern or their speculation. I might net myself a little sympathy, but to what end?

"See you in a bit," I said. The two didn't lift their heads. I shrugged to myself and moved into the den.

I stood in the doorway while I sipped my coffee, staring at the disarray that still littered the room. I'd been working my way through the mess in an orderly fashion, but the result seemed fragmented. Many jobs were half done and those I'd completed hadn't netted me anything in the way of hard data. I'd simply proceeded on the assumption that if Tom Newquist was up to something he had to have left a trace of it somewhere. There were numerous odd lots of paperwork I wasn't sure how to classify. I'd piled much of it on the desk in an arrangement invisible to the naked eye. I was down to the dregs and it was hard to know just where to go from here. I'd lost all enthusiasm for the project, which felt dirty and pointless. I did have six banker's boxes stacked along one wall. Those contained the files that I'd labeled and grouped: previous income tax forms, warranties, insurance policies, property valuations, various utility stubs, telephone bills, and credit card receipts. Still no sign of his field notes, but he might have left them at the station. I made a mental note to check with Rafer on that.

I set my mug on an empty bookshelf, folded together a fresh banker's box, and began to clear Tom's desk. I placed papers in the box with no particular intention except to tidy the space. I was here as an investigator, not as char in residence. Once I cleared the desk, I felt better. For one thing, I could see now that his blotter was covered with scribbles: doodles, telephone numbers, what looked like case numbers, cartoon dogs and cats in various poses, appointments, names and addresses, drawings of cars with flames shooting from the tailpipes. Some of the numerals had been cast in three dimensions, a technique I employed sometimes while I was talking on the phone. Some items of information were boxed in pen; some were outlined and shaded in strokes of different thicknesses. I pored over the whole of it as though it were hieroglyphic, then panned across the surface item by item. The drawings were much like the ones sixth-grade boys seemed to favor in my elementary days—daggers and blood and guns firing fat bullets at somebody's cartoon head. The only repeat item was a length of thick rope fashioned into a hangman's noose. He'd drawn two of those; one with an X'd-out phone number in the center, the second with a series of numbers followed by a question mark. In one corner of the blotter was a hand-drawn calendar for the month of February, the numbers neatly filled in. I did a quick check of the calendar and realized the numbers didn't correspond to February of this year. The first fell on a Sunday, and the last two Saturdays of the month had been X'd out. I paused long enough to make a detailed list of all the telephone and case numbers.

Intrigued, I retrieved the file of telephone records from the past six months, hoping for a match. I was temporarily sidetracked when I spotted seven calls to the 805 area code, which covers Santa Teresa County, as well as Perdido County to the south and San Luis Obispo County to the north of us. One number I recognized as the Perdido County Sheriff's Department. There were six calls to another number spaced roughly two weeks apart. The most recent of these was late January, a few days before his death. On impulse, I picked up the phone and dialed the number. After three rings, a machine clicked on, a woman's voice giving the standard: "Sorry I'm not here right now to receive your call, but if you'll leave your name, number, and a message, I'll be happy to get back to you as soon as I can. Take as long as you need and remember, wait for the beep." Her voice was throaty and mature, but that was the extent of the information I gleaned. I waited for the beep and then thought better of a message, quietly replacing the handset without saying a word. Maybe she was a friend of Selma's. I'd have to ask when I had the chance.

I made a note of the number and went back to work. I tried comparing the numbers on the phone bills with the numbers on the blotter and that netted me a hit. It looked as if someone—I assumed Tom—had completed a call to the number I'd seen X'd out in the center of one noose, though that number had been noted without the 805 area code attached. I tried the number myself and the call was picked up by a live human being. "Gramercy. How may I direct your call?"

"Gramercy?"

"Yes ma'am."

"This is the Gramercy Hotel in downtown Santa Teresa?"

"That's correct."

"Sorry. Wrong number."

I depressed the plunger and disconnected. Well, that was odd. The Gramercy Hotel was a fleabag establishment down on lower State Street. Why would the

Newquists call them? I circled the number in my notes, adding a question mark, and then I went back to my survey of telephone bills. I could find no other number that seemed significant on the face of it. I placed another banker's box on the desk top and continued packing.

At ten, I paused to stretch my legs and did a few squats. I still had the lower cabinets to unload, two of which were enclosed by wide doors spanning the width of the bookshelves. I decided to get the worst of it over with. I got down on my hands and knees and began to pull boxes out of the lefthand side. The storage space was so commodious I had to insert my head and shoulders to reach the far corners. I heaved two boxes into view and then sat there on the floor, going through the contents.

At the top of the second box, I came across two blue big-ring loose-leaf binders that looked promising. Apparently, Tom had photocopies of the bulk of the reports in the sheriff's department case books. This was the log of unsolved crimes kept on active status, though many were years old, copies yellowing. These were the cases detectives reworked any time new information came to light or additional leads came in. I leafed through with interest. This was Nota County crime from the year 1935 to the present. Even reading between the lines, there wasn't much attention paid to the rights of the defendant in the early cases. The notion of "victim's rights" would have seemed a curious concept in 1942. In those days, the victim had the right to redress in a court of law. These days, a trial isn't about guilt or innocence. It's a battle of wits in which competing attorneys, like intellectual gladiators, test their use of rhetoric. The mark of a good defense attorney is his ability to take any given set of facts and recast them in such a light that, *presto change-o*, as if by magic, what appeared to be absolute is turned into a frame-up or some elaborate conspiracy on the part of the police or government. Suddenly, the perpetrator becomes the victim and the deceased is all but forgotten in the process.

"Kinsey?"

I jumped.

Phyllis was standing in the doorway.

"Shit, you scared me," I said. "I didn't hear you come in."

"I'm sorry. I'm just on my way home. Can I talk to you for a minute?"

"Sure. Come on in."

"In private," she added, and then turned on her heel.

EIGHT

I scrambled to my feet and followed her down the hall. Behind us, I could hear Selma chatting with someone on the phone. When we reached the front door, Phyllis opened it and moved out onto the porch. I hesitated and then joined her, stepping to one side as she pulled the door shut behind us. The cold hit like a blast. The sky had turned hazy, with heavy gray clouds sliding down the mountains in the distance. I crossed my arms and kept my feet close together, trying to preserve body heat against the onslaught of nippy weather.

The outfit Phyllis sported was thin cotton and looked more appropriate for a summer barbecue. She wore abbreviated tennis socks, little pom-poms resting on the backs of her walking shoes. No coat or jacket. She spoke in a low tone as if Selma might be hovering on the far side of the door. "There's something I thought I better mention while I had the chance."

"Aren't you cold?" I asked. There she stood with her bare arms in a skimpy cotton blouse, her skirt blowing against her bare legs. I was wearing a long-sleeved turtleneck and jeans and I was still on the verge of lockjaw trying to keep my teeth from chattering.

She made a careless gesture, brushing aside the bitter chill. "I'm used to it. Doesn't bother me. This will only take a minute. I should have said something sooner, but I haven't had the chance."

For mid-March, her face seemed remarkably tanned. I had to guess it was from skiing, given that the rest of her was pale. Her face was nicely creased, lines radiating from the corners of her eyes, lines bracketing her mouth. Her nose was long and straight, her teeth very white and even. She looked like the perfect person to have with you when you were down; pleasant and capable without being too earnest.

Out in the yard, a stiff breeze ruffled through the dead grass. I clamped my mouth shut, trying to keep from whining like a dog. I could feel my eyes water from the cold. Soon my nose would start running and me with no hankie. I sniffed, trying to postpone the moment I'd have to use my shirt sleeve. I focused on Phyllis, already chatting away.

"You know Macon joined the sheriff's department because of Tom. The two fellows were always close—despite the difference in their ages—and of course when Tom married Selma, we wished him all the best."

"Aren't there any other jobs in this town? Everyone I've met is in law enforcement."

Phyllis smiled. "We all know each other. We tend to hang out together, like a social club."

"I guess so," I said, mentally begging her to hurry since I was freezing my ass off.

"Tom was a wonderful man. I think you'll find that out when you start asking around."

"So everybody says. In fact, most people seem to prefer him to her," I said.

"Oh, Selma has her good points. Not everybody likes her, but she's all right. I wouldn't say we're friends ... in fact, we're not even that close, which may seem surprising given the fact we live two doors away ... but you can see somebody's weaknesses and still like them for their better qualities."

"Absolutely," I said. This was hardly an endorsement, but I understood what she was saying. I felt like making that rolling hand gesture that says *Come on, come on.*

"Selma'd been complaining to me for months about Tom. I guess it's the same thing she told you. Well, in September ... this was about six months ago ... Tom and Macon went to a gun show in Los Angeles and I tagged along. Selma wasn't really interested—she had some big event that weekend—so she didn't come with us. Anyway, I happened to see Tom with this *woman* and I remember thinking, uh oh. Know what I mean? Just something about the way they had their heads bent together didn't look right to me. Let's put it this way. This gal was interested. I could tell by the way she looked at him."

I felt a flash of irritation. I couldn't believe she was telling me this. "Phyllis, I wish you'd mentioned this before *now.* I've been in there slogging through that bullshit and what I hear you saying is that Tom's 'problem' didn't have anything to do with paperwork."

"Well, that's just it. I don't really know. I asked Macon about the woman and he said she was a sheriff's investigator over on the coast. Perdido, I believe, though

119

I could be wrong about that. Anyway, Macon said he'd seen her with Tom on a couple of occasions. He told me to keep my mouth shut and that's what I did, but I felt awful. Selma was planning this big anniversary party at the country club and I kept thinking if Tom was . . . well, you know . . . if he was *involved* with someone, Selma was going to end up looking like a fool. Honestly, what's humiliating when your husband's having an affair is realizing everybody in the whole town knows about it but you. I don't know if you've ever had the experience yourself—"

"So you told her," I suggested, trying to jump her like a game of checkers. I did conclude from her comments that Macon had subjected her to the very humiliations she was so worried about for Selma.

Phyllis made a face. "Well, no, I didn't. I never worked up my nerve. I hate to defy Macon because he turns into such a bear, but I was debating with myself. I adored Tom and I couldn't decide how much I owed Selma as a sister-in-law. I mean, sometimes friendship takes precedence regardless. On the other hand, you don't always do someone a favor telling something like that. In some ways, it's hostile. That's just the way I see it. At any rate, the next thing I knew, Tom had passed away and Selma was beside herself. I've felt terrible ever since. If I'd told her what I suspected, she could have confronted him right then and put a stop to it."

"You know for a fact he was having an affair?"

"Well, no. That's the point. I thought Selma should be warned, but I didn't have any *proof*. That's why I was so reluctant to speak up. Macon felt like it was none of our business, and with him breathing down my neck I was caught between a rock and hard place."

"Why tell me now?"

"This was the first opportunity I had. When I was listening to you in there, I realized how frustrating this must be from your perspective. I mean, you might turn up evidence if you knew where to look. If he was scr— misbehaving, so to speak—he had to leave *some* trace, unless he's smarter than most men."

The front door burst open and Selma popped her head out. "*There* you are. I thought the two of you'd gone off and left me. What's this all about?"

"We were just jawing," Phyllis said, without missing a beat. "I was on my way home and she was nice enough to walk me out."

"Would you look at her? She's frozen. Let the poor thing come in here and get thawed out, for Pete's sake!"

Gratefully, I scurried into the house while the two of them discussed another work session the next morning. I headed for the kitchen where I washed my hands. I should have considered another woman in the mix. It might explain why Tom's buddies were being so protective of him. It might also explain the six 805 calls to the unidentified woman whose message I'd picked up from her answering machine.

A few minutes later, Selma came in, agitated. "Well, if that doesn't take the cake. I cannot believe it. She was just telling me about a dinner party coming up in the neighborhood, but have I been invited? Of course not," she was saying. "Now I'm a widow, I've been dropped like a hot potato. I know Tom's friends . . . the fellows . . . would include me, but you know how women are; they feel threatened at the thought of a single woman on the loose. When Tom was alive, we were part of a crowd that went everywhere. Cocktail parties, dinners, dances at the club. We were always included in the social scene, but in the weeks since he died I haven't left the house. The first couple of days, of course, everybody pitched in. Casseroles and promises. That's how I think of it. Now, I sit here night after night and the phone hardly rings except for things like this. Scut work, I call it. Good old Selma's always up for a committee. I do and I do. I really knock myself out and what's the point? The women are all too happy to pass off responsibility. Saves them the effort, if you know what I mean."

"But Selma, it's only been six weeks. Maybe people are trying to show their respects, giving you time to grieve."

"I'm sure that's their version," she said tartly.

I made some reply, hoping to get her off the subject. Her view was distorted and I wondered what would happen if she could see herself as others saw her. It was her very grandiosity that offended, not her insecurities. Selma seemed to be unaware of how transparent she was, oblivious to the disdain with which she was regarded for her snobbery.

She seemed to shake off her mood. "Enough of this pity party. It won't change anything. Can I fix you a bite of lunch? I'm heating some soup and I can make us some grilled cheese sandwiches."

"Sounds great," I said. Already I felt guilty accepting her hospitality when I'd sat around listening to other people's withering assessments. I'd told myself it was part of the information I was gathering, but I could have protested the venom with which such opinions had been delivered. By now familiar with the kitchen, I opened the cupboard door and took down soup bowls and plates. "Will Brant be joining us?"

"I doubt it. He's still in his room, probably dead to the world. He goes to the gym three days a week, so he likes to sleep in on the mornings between. Let me go check." She disappeared briefly and returned shaking her head. "He'll be right out," she said. "Why don't you tell me what you've found out so far."

I took out an extra plate and bowl, then opened the silverware drawer and took out soup spoons. While she heated the soup and grilled sandwiches, I filled her in on activities to date, giving her a verbal report of where I'd been and who I'd talked to. My efforts sounded feeble in the telling. Because of what Phyllis had told me, I now had a new avenue to explore, but I was unwilling to mention it when I was only dealing with suspicions. Selma had never even *suggested* the possibility of another woman, and I wasn't going to introduce the subject unless I found some reason to do so.

Brant appeared just as we were sitting down to eat. He was wearing jeans and cowboy boots, his snug white T-shirt emphasizing the effectiveness of his workouts. Selma ladled soup into bowls and cut the sandwiches in half, putting one on each plate.

We began to eat in the kind of silence I found mildly unsettling. "What made you decide to become a paramedic?" I asked.

I had caught Brant with his mouth full. He smiled, embarrassed, signaling the delay while he tucked half the food in his cheek. "I had a couple of friends in the fire department so I took a six-month course. Bandages and driving. I think Tom was hoping I'd join the sheriff's department, but I couldn't see myself doing that. I enjoy what I do. You know, it's always something."

I nodded, still eating. "Is the job what you expected?"

"Sure. Only more fun," he said.

I might have asked him more, but I could see him glance at his watch. He wolfed down the last of his sandwich and crumpled his paper napkin. He pushed back from the table, picking up his half-empty bowl and his plate. He stood at the sink and drank a few mouthfuls of soup before he rinsed his bowl and set it in the dishwasher.

Selma gestured. "I'll get that."

"I got it," he said as he added his sandwich plate. I heard his spoon *chink* in the silverware container just before he snapped the dishwasher shut. He gave his mother's cheek a quick buss. "Will you be here a while?"

"I've got a meeting at the church. What about you?"

"I think I'll drive on down to Independence and see Sherry."

"Will you be back tonight?"

"I wouldn't count on it," he said.

"You drive carefully."

"Twenty-five whole miles. I think I can handle it." He snagged the four remaining cookies from the plate, placing one in his mouth with a grin. "Better make more cookies. This was a short batch," he said. "See you later."

*

Selma left the house after lunch so I didn't have the chance to broach the subject that was beginning to tug at me—a quick trip to Santa Teresa to pick up my car. I'd had the rental for over three weeks and the cost was mounting daily. I'd never imagined an extended stay in Nota Lake so my current wardrobe was limited. I longed to sleep in my own bed even for one night. The issue of the female sheriff's investigator I could dig into once I got home. Anything else of interest here could wait 'til I got back to Nota Lake.

Meanwhile, it was time to have a chat with the Nota Lake Police Department. Given the new lead, I couldn't see how last night's incident could be tied to my investigation, but I thought I should do the smart thing and report it anyway. I left a note for Selma, shrugged on my leather jacket, took my shoulder bag, and headed off.

The Nota Lake Police Department was housed in a plain one-story building with a stucco exterior, a granite entryway, and two wide granite steps. The windows and the plate glass door were framed in aluminum. An arrow under a stick figure in a wheelchair indicated an accessible entrance somewhere to the left. The bushes along the front had been trimmed to window height and from the flagpole both the American and the State of California flags were snapping in the breeze. Six radio antennae had been erected on the roof like a series of upright fishing poles. As with the Nota Lake Fire Department, located next door, this was generic architecture, a strictly functional facility. No tax dollars had been needlessly squandered here.

The interior was consistent with its no-frills decor,

strongly reminiscent of the sheriff's headquarters two doors down: a lowered ceiling of fluorescent panels and acoustical tile, metal file cabinets, wood-grained laminate counters. On the desks, I could see the backs of the two computer monitors and attendant CPUs from which countless electrical cords sprouted like airborne roots.

The desk officer was M. Corbet, a fellow in his forties with a smooth round face, thinning hair, and a tendency to wheeze. "Thiss iss asthma in case you're thinking I'm contagious," he said. "Cold air gets to me and this dry heat doesn't help. Excuse me a second." He had a small inhaler that he placed in his lips, sucking deeply of the mist that would open up his bronchi. He set the inhaler aside with a shake of his head. "Thiss-iss the damndest thing. Never had a problem in my life until a couple years back. Turns out I'm allergic to house dust, animal hair, pollen, and mold. What's a fella supposed to do? Quit breathing altogether is the only cure I know."

"That's a tough one," I said.

"Doctor tells me it's more and more people developing allergies. Says he has this one patient reacts to inside air. Synthetics, chemicals, microbes coming through the heating vents. Poor woman has to tote around an oxygen trolley everywhere she goes. Passes out and falls down the minute she encounters any alien pathogens. Thankfully, I'm not yet as bad off as her, though the chief had to take me off active duty and put me on desk. Anyway, that's my story. Now what can I help you with?"

I gave him my business card, hoping to establish my credibility before I launched into a description of the events involving the driver of the panel truck. Officer Corbet was polite, but I could tell just by looking at him that the issue of someone in a ski mask staring at me real hard wasn't going to qualify as a major case for the Crimes Against Persons unit, which probably consisted solely of him. Lungs awhistle, he took my report, printing the particulars in block letters on the proper form. He placed his hands on the counter, tapping with his fingers as if he was playing a little tune. "I do know someone with a truck like that."

"You do?" I said, surprised.

"Yes ma'am. Sounds like Ercell Riccardi. He lives right around the corner about three doors down. Keeps his truck parked in the drive. I'm surprised you didn't see it on your way over here."

"I didn't come from that direction. I turned right off of Main."

"Well, you might want to have a look. Ercell leaves it sit out any time it's not in use."

"With keys in the ignition?"

"Yes ma'am. It's not like Nota Lake is the auto-theft capital of the world. I think he started doing it maybe five, six years back. We had us a rash of break-ins, bunch of kids busting into cars, smashing windows, taking tape decks, going joyriding. Ercell got tired of replacing the stereo so he 'give up and give in' is how he puts it. Last time his truck was broke into he didn't even bother to file a claim. Said it was driving his rates up and to hell with the whole thing. Now he leaves the truck open, keys in the ignition, and a note on the dash saying, 'Please put back in the drive when you're done.'"

"So people take his truck any time they like?"

"Doesn't happen that often. Occasionally, somebody borrys it, but they always put it back. It's a point of honor with folks and Ercell's a lot happier."

The telephone began to ring and Officer Corbet straightened up. "Anyway, if you think the truck was Ercell's, just give us a call and we'll talk to him. It's not something he'd do, but anybody could have hopped in his vehicle and followed you."

"I'll take a look."

Out on the street again, I shoved my hands in my jacket pockets and headed for the corner. As soon as I turned onto Lone Star, I saw the black panel truck. I approached it with caution, wondering if there were any way I could link this truck to the one I'd seen. I circled the vehicle, leaning close to the headlights. Impossible in daylight to see if the beams were askew. I moved around to the rear and ran a finger across the license plate, scrutinizing the surface where I could see faint traces of adhesive. I stood up and turned to study the house itself. A man was stationed at the window, looking out at me. He stared, scowling. I reversed my steps and returned to my parking spot.

When I reached the rental car, Macon Newquist was waiting, his black-and-white vehicle parked behind mine at the curb. He glanced up at me, catching my eye with a smile. "Hi. How are you? I figured this was your car. How's it going?"

I smiled. "Fine. For a minute, I thought you were giving me a ticket."

"Don't worry about that. In this town, we tend to reserve tickets for people passing through." He crossed his arms and leaned a hip against the side of the rental. "I hope this doesn't seem out of line, but Phyllis mentioned that business about the gun show. I guess she passed along her opinion about the gal Tom was talking to."

I felt my reaction time slow and I calculated my response. Phyllis must have felt guilty about telling me and blabbed the minute she got home. I thought I better cover so I shrugged it aside. "She said something in passing. I really didn't pay that much attention."

"I didn't want you to get the wrong impression."

"No problem."

"Because she attached more to it than was warranted."

"Ah."

"Don't get me wrong. You don't know the ladies in this town. Nothing escapes their notice and when it turns out to be nothing, they make it into something else. The woman Tom was talking to, that was strictly professional."

"Not surprising. Everybody tells me he was good at his job. You know her name?"

"I don't. I never heard it myself. She's a sheriff's investigator. I do know that much because I asked him about it later."

"You happen to know what county?"

He scratched at his chin. "Not offhand. Could be Kern, San Benito, I forget what he said. I could see Phyllis put the hairy eye-ball on the two of them and I didn't want you to be misled. Last thing Selma needs is some kind of gossip about him. All she has is her memories and once those are tainted, what's she got left?"

"I couldn't agree more. Trust me, I'd never be irresponsible about something like that."

"That's good. I'm glad to hear that. People don't like the notion you're using up Tom's money on a wild-goose chase. So what's your timetable on this?"

"That remains to be seen. If you have any ideas, I hope you'll let me know."

Macon shook his head. "I wish I could help, but I realize I'm the wrong one to ask. I know I offered, but this is one of those circumstances where I'm not going to be objective. People admired Tom and I'm not just saying that because I admired him myself. If there was something tacky in his life . . . well, people aren't going to want to know that about him. You take somebody like Margaret's husband. I believe you talked to him at Tiny's. Hatch was a protégé of Tom's, and the other fellow, Wayne, was somebody Tom rescued from a bad foster care situation. See what I mean? You can't run around asking those fellows what Tom was *like*. They don't take to it that well. They'll be polite, but it's not going to sit right."

"I appreciate the warning."

"I wouldn't call it a warning. I don't want to give you the wrong impression. It's just human nature to want to protect the people we care about. All I'm saying is, let's not be hasty and cause trouble for no reason."

"I wouldn't dream of it."

NINE

I went back to the motel, making a brief detour into the Rainbow Cafe, where I picked up a pack of chips and a can of Pepsi. I was eating for comfort, but I couldn't help myself. I hadn't jogged for three weeks and I could feel my ass getting larger with every bite I ate. The young black woman who handled the griddle had paused to follow the weather channel on a small color television at the end of the counter. She was trim and attractive with loopy corkscrew curls jutting out around her head. I saw a frown cross her face when she saw what was coming up. "Hey now. I'm sick of this. Whatever happened to spring?" she asked of no one in particular.

Out in the Pacific, the radar showed the same clustered pattern of color as a CAT scan of the brain, areas of storm activity represented in shades of blue, green, and red. I was hoping to hit the road for home before the bad weather reached the area. March was unpredictable, and a heavy snowstorm could force the mountain passes to close. Nota Lake was technically located out of the reach of such blockades, but the rental car had no chains and I had scant experience driving in hazardous conditions.

Back in the cabin, I finished typing up my notes, translating all the pointless activity into the officious-sounding language of a written report. What ended up on paper didn't add up to anything because I'd neatly omitted the as-yet-unidentified female sheriff's investigator, who may or may not have been interested in Tom Newquist and he in her. San Benito or Kern County, yeah, right, Macon.

At two, I decided to make a trip to the copy shop in town. I locked the cabin behind me and headed for my car. Cecilia must have been peering out the office window because the minute I walked by, she rapped on the glass and made a beckoning motion. She came to the door, holding a piece of paper aloft. Cecilia was so small she must have been forced to buy her clothes in the children's department. Today's outfit consisted of a long red sweatshirt with a teddy bear appliquéd on the front worn over white leggings, with a pair of enormous jogging shoes. Her legs looked as spindly as a colt's, complete with knobby knees. "You had a telephone call. Alice wants you to get in touch. I took the number this time, but in future, she ought to try reaching you at Selma's. I run a motel here, not an answering service."

Her aggrieved tone was irritating and inspired a matching complaint. "Oh, hey, now that I've got you, do you think I could get some heat? The cabin's almost unliveable, close to freezing," I said.

An expression of annoyance flashed across her face. "March first is the cutoff date for heating oil out here. I can't just whistle up delivery because a couple of short-term visitors to the area make a minor fuss." Her tone suggested she'd been beleaguered with grumbles the better part of the day.

"Well, do what you can. I'd hate to have to complain to Selma when she's footing the bill."

Cecilia gave the door a little bang as she withdrew. Good luck to me, getting any other messages. I crossed to the pay phone and stood there, searching for change in the bottom of my handbag. I found a little cache of coins tucked in one corner along with assorted hairs and a ratty tissue. I dropped some money in the slot and dialed. Alice picked up on the fourth ring just about the time I expected her machine to kick in. "Hello?"

"Hello, Alice? Kinsey Millhone. I got your message. Are you at work or home?"

"Home. I'm not due at Tiny's until four. I was in the process of setting my hair. Hang on a sec while I get the curlers out on this side. Ah, better. Nothing like a set of bristles sticking in your ear. Listen, this might not be helpful, but I thought I'd pass it along. The waitress who works counter over at the Rainbow is a good friend of mine. Her name's Nancy. I mentioned Tom and told her what you were up to. She says he came in that night about eight-thirty and left just before closing. You can talk to her yourself if you want."

"Is she the black girl?"

"Nuhn-uhn. That's Barrett, Rafer LaMott's daughter. Nancy doubles as a cashier. Brown hair, forties. I'm sure you've seen her in there because she's seen you."

"What else did she say? Was he alone or with someone?"

"I asked that myself and she says he was alone, at

least as far as she could see. Said he had a cheeseburger and fries, drank some coffee, played some tunes on the jukebox, paid his ticket, and left about nine-thirty, just as she was closing out the register. Like I said, it might not mean anything, but she said she'd never known him to come in at that hour. You know the night he was found, he was out on 395, but he was heading toward the mountains instead of home to his place."

"I remember that," I said. "The coroner mentioned his having eaten a meal. According to Selma, he was in for the night. He didn't even leave a note. By the time she got back from church, he was DOA at the local emergency room. Maybe he got a phone call and went to meet someone."

"Or maybe he just got hungry, hon. Selma's the type who'd make him eat veggies and brown rice. He could have sneaked out for something decent." She laughed at herself. "I always said the food out there would kill you. I'll bet his arteries seized up from all the fat he took in."

"At least we know where he was in the hour just before he died."

"Well, that's hardly news. Nancy says the coroner covered the same ground. Anyways, I told you it wouldn't count for much. I guess that about says it for my detective career."

"You never know. Oh, one more thing as long as I have you on the line. You ever hear rumors about Tom and any other woman?"

She barked out a laugh. "Tom? You gotta be kidding. He was stuffy about sex. Lot of guys, you can tell just by looking they got a problem around dominance. Assgrabbers and pinchers, fellows telling dirty jokes and gawking at your boobs. They wouldn't mind a quick bounce on the front seat of their pickups, but believe me, romance is the fartherest thing from their minds. Tom was always pleasant. I've never known him to flirt and I never heard him make any kind of off-color remark. What makes you ask?"

"I thought he might have been at the Rainbow for a rendezvous."

"Oh, a *rahndez-vous*. That's rich. Listen, if you're fooling around in this town, you'd best meet somewhere else unless you want everyone to know. Why take the risk? If his sister'd showed up, she'd have spotted him first thing. Cecilia's not that fond of Selma, but she'd have told on him anyway. That's how people around here operate. Anything you find out is fair game."

"I take it word's gone out about me."

"You bet."

"What's the consensus? Anybody seem upset?"

"Oh, grumbles here and there. You're picking up notice, but nothing serious that I've heard. Town this size, everybody has an opinion about something— especially fresh blood like yours. Some of the guys were wondering if you're married. I guess they noticed no wedding ring."

"Actually, I took my ring off to have the diamond reset."

"Bullshit."

"No, really. My husband's *huge*. He's always pumped up on steroids so he's touchy as all get out. He'd tear the head off anyone who ever laid a hand on me."

She laughed. "I bet you've never been married a day in your life."

"Alice, you would be surprised."

As predicted, the weather was turning nasty as the front moved in. The morning had been clear, the temperatures in the fifties, but by early afternoon, a thick mass of clouds had accumulated to the north. The sky changed from blue to a uniform white, then to a misty-looking dark gray, which made the day seem as gloomy as a solar eclipse. All the mountain peaks had been erased and the air became dense with a fine, biting spray.

Here's what I did with my afternoon. I drove into town and went to the copy shop, where I made copies of my typewritten report and several cropped five-by-seven photocopy enlargements made of the head shot of Tom Newquist. I dropped the original photograph and the original of my report in Selma's mailbox, drove six blocks over, and left the flashlight inside the storm door on James Tennyson's front porch. And I still had hours to kill before I could decently retire.

In the meantime, I was bored and I wanted to get warm. Nota Lake didn't have a movie theater. Nota Lake didn't have a public library or a bowling alley that I could spot. I went to the lone bookstore and wandered up and down the aisles. The place was small but attractive, and the stock was more than adequate. I picked up two paperbacks, returned to the cabin, crawled under a pile of blankets, and read to my heart's content.

At six, I hunched into my jacket and walked over to the Rainbow through an odd mix of blowing sleet and buffeting rain. I ate a BLT on wheat toast and then chatted idly with Nancy while she rang up my bill. I already knew what she had to say, but I quizzed her nonetheless, making sure Alice had reported accurately. At 6:35, I went back to the cabin, finished the first book, tossed that aside, and reached for the next. At ten o'clock, exhausted from a hard day's work, I got up, brushed my teeth, washed my face, and climbed back in bed, where I fell promptly asleep.

A sound filtered into the tarry dream I was having. I labored upward, slow swimming, my body weighted with dark images and all the leaden drama of sleep. I felt glued to the bed. My eyes opened and I listened, not even sure where I was. Nota Lake crept back into my consciousness, the cabin so cold I might as well have slept outside. What had I heard? I turned my head with great effort. According to the clock, it was 4:14, still pitch black. The tiny scrape of metal on metal . . . not the sound of a key . . . possibly a pick being worked into the door lock. Fear shot through me like a bottle rocket, lighting my insides with a shower of adrenaline. I flung the covers aside. I was still fully dressed, but the chill in the cabin was numbing to both my face and my hands. I swung my legs over the side of the bed, felt for my shoes, and shoved my feet in without bothering to tie the laces.

I stood where I was, tuned now to the silence. Even in the depths of the country with minimal light pollution, I realized the dark wasn't absolute. I could see the blocks of six lighter gray squares that were the windows on three sides. I glanced back at the bed, empty white sheets advertising my departure. Hastily, I arranged the pillows to form a plump body shape, which I covered with my blankets. This always fooled the bad guys. I eased over to the door, trying to pick up the scratchings of my intruder over the pounding of my heart. I felt along the door jamb. There was no security chain so once the lock was jimmied, there was nothing else between me and my night visitor. The cabin, though dark, was beginning to define itself. I surveyed the details in memory, looking for a weapon somewhere among the homely furnishings. Bed, chair, soap, table, shower curtain. On my side of the door, I kept my fingers on the thumblock to prevent its turning. Maybe the guy would assume his skills were rusty or the lock was stiff. On the other side of the door, I could hear a faint chunking across wood chips as my visitor retreated in search of some other means of ingress. I tiptoed to the table and picked up a wooden chair. I returned to the door and eased the top rail under the knob, jamming the legs against the floor. It wouldn't hold for long, but it might slow him down. I took a brief moment to bend down and tie my shoes, unwilling to risk the sound of my laces clicking across the expanse of bare wooden floor. I could hear faint sounds outside as the intruder patiently circled the cabin.

Were the windows locked? I couldn't recall. I moved from window to window, feeling for the shape of the latches. All of them seemed to be secured. A slight parting of the curtains allowed me a thin slice of the exterior. I could see dense Christmas tree shapes, a series of evergreens that dotted the landscape. No traffic on the highway. No lights in neighboring cabins. To the left, I caught movement as someone disappeared around the side of the cabin toward the rear.

I crossed the room in silence, entering the darker confines of the bathroom. I felt for the shower curtain, hanging by a series of rings from a round metal rod. I let my fingers explore the brackets, which were screwed into the wall on either side of the shower stall. Carefully, I lifted the rod from the slots, sliding the curtain off, ring by ring. Once in hand, I realized the rod was useless, too light, too easily bent. I needed a weapon, but what did I have? I glanced at the frosted glass of the bathroom window, which appeared infinitesimally paler than the dark of the wall surrounding it. Framed in the center was the intruder's head and shoulders. He cupped his hands to the glass to afford himself a better look. It must have been frustrating to discover the dark was too dense to penetrate. I stood without moving though I could see his movements outside. A snippet of sound, perhaps the faint scrape of a clawhammer being eased into crack between the frame and the glass.

Feverishly, I reviewed the items in the cabin, hoping to remember something I could use as a weapon. Toilet paper, rug, clothes hangers, ironing board. Iron. I set the curtain rod aside, taking care not to make a sound. I moved to the closet, feeling through the dark until my fingers encountered the ironing board. I raised up on tiptoe and lifted the iron from the shelf above, shielding the contours with my hand so as to avoid banging into anything. I searched for the end of the plug, holding the prongs while I unwrapped the cord. Blindly, I felt for the outlet near the sink, inserted the prongs, and slid the heat lever on the iron as far to the right as it would go. I set the iron upright on the counter. I glanced back at the window. The head-and-shoulders silhouette was no longer visible.

I eased my way across the room to the door, where I leaned closer and pressed my ear to the lock, trying not to disturb the chair. I could hear the key pick slide in again. I could hear the tiny torque wrench join its mate as the two rods of metal crept across the tumblers. Behind me, I could hear a ticking from the bathroom as the iron picked up heat. I'd rammed the setting up to LINEN, a fabric known to wrinkle more easily than human flesh. I longed to feel the weight of the iron in my hand, but I didn't dare yank the plug from the socket just yet. I could feel pain in my chest where the rubbery muscle of my heart slapped the wooden pales of my rib cage. I'd picked many a lock myself and I was well acquainted with the patience required for the task. I'd never known anyone who could use a lockpick wearing gloves, so the chances were he was using his bare hands. From the depths of the lock, I fancied I could hear the pick ease across the tumblers and lift them one by one.

I placed my right hand lightly on the knob. I could feel it turn under my fingers. With the chair still in place, I did a quick tiptoe dance across the room to the bath. I could feel heat radiating from the iron as I pulled the plug from the socket. I wrapped my fingers around the handle and returned to the door, taking up my vigil. My night visitor was now in the process of easing the door open, probably fearful of creaks that might alert me to his presence. I stared at the doorframe, willing him to appear. He pushed. The chair began to inch forward. As stealthily as a spider, his fingers crept around the frame. I lunged, iron extended. I thought my timing was good, but he was quicker than I expected. I made contact, but not before he'd kicked the door in. The chair catapulted past me. I could smell the harsh chemical scent of scorched wool. I pressed the iron into him again and sensed burning flesh this time. He uttered a harsh expletive—not a word but a yelp.

At the same time, he swung and his fist caught me in the face. I staggered backward, off balance. The iron flew out of my hand and clattered heavily across the floor. He was fast. Before I knew what was happening, he'd kicked my feet out from under me. I went down. He had my arm racked up behind me, his knee planted squarely in the middle of my back. His weight made breathing problematic and I knew within minutes I'd black out if he didn't ease up. I couldn't fill my lungs with sufficient air to make a sound. Any movement was excruciating. I could smell stress sweat, but I wasn't sure if it was his or mine.

Now you see? This is precisely the kind of moment I was talking about. There I was, face down on Cecilia Boden's bad braided rug, immobilized by a fellow threatening serious bodily harm. Had I foreseen this sorry development the day I left Carson City, I'd have done something else . . . dumped the rental car and flown home, bypassing the notion of employment in Nota Lake. But how was I to know?

Meanwhile, the thug and I were at a temporary impasse while he decided what kind of punishment to inflict. This guy was going to hurt me, there was no doubt of that. He hadn't expected resistance and he was pissed off that I'd put up even so puny a fight as I had. He was supercharged, juiced up on rage, his breathing labored and hoarse. I tried to relax and, at the same time, steal myself for the inevitable. I waited for a bash on the back of the head. I prayed that a pocketknife or semiautomatic didn't appear on his list of preferred weapons. If he yanked my head back, he could slit my throat with one quick swipe of a blade. Time hung suspended in a manner that was almost liberating.

I'm not a big fan of torture. I've always understood that in situations of extreme duress—offered the choice between, say, a hot poker in the eyeball or betraying a friend—I'd rat out my pal. This is one more reason to keep others at a distance, since I clearly can't be trusted to keep a confidence. Under the current circumstances, I surely would have begged for mercy if I'd been capable of speech.

Hostility energizes. Once unleashed, anger is addicting and the high, while bitter, is irresistible. He half-lifted himself away from me and slammed his knee into my rib cage, knocking the breath out of me. He grabbed the index finger of my right hand and in one swift motion snapped it sideways, dislocating the finger at what I later learned was the proximal interphalangeal joint. The sound was like the hollow pop of a raw carrot being snapped in two. I heard myself emit a note of anguish, high pitched and ragged as he reached for the next finger and popped the knuckle sideways in its socket. I could sense that both fingers protruded now in an unnatural relationship to the rest of my hand. He delivered a kick and then I heard his heavy breathing as he stood staring down at me. I closed my eyes, fearful of provoking further attack.

I kept my face down against the rug, sucking in the odor of damp cotton fiber saturated with soot, feeling absurdly grateful when he didn't kick me again. He crossed the cabin in haste. I heard the door bang shut behind him and then the sound of his muffled footsteps as they faded away. In due course, at a distance, I heard a car engine start. I was alive. I was hurt. Time to move, I thought.

I rolled over on my back, cradling my right arm. I could feel my hands tremble and I was making noises in my throat. I'd broken out in a sweat, so much heat coursing through my body that I thought I'd throw up. At the same time, I began to shake. A stress-induced personality had separated herself from the rest of me and hovered in the air so that she could comment on the situation without having to participate in my pain and humiliation.

You really should get help, she suggested. *The injuries won't kill you, but the shock well could. Remember the symptoms? Pulse and breathing become faster. Blood pressure drops. Weakness, lethargy, a little clamminess? Does that ring a bell here?*

I was laboring to breathe, struggling to keep my wits about me while my vision brightened and narrowed. It had been a long time since I'd been hurt and I'd nearly forgotten how it felt to be consumed by suffering. I knew he could have killed me, so I should have been happy this was the worst he'd conjured up. What exhilaration he must have felt. I had been brought low and my attempts at self-defense seemed pathetic in retrospect.

I held my hand against my chest protectively while I eased onto my side and from there to my knees. I pushed upward with left elbow, supporting myself clumsily as I struggled to my feet. I was mewing like a kitten. Tears stung my eyes. I felt abased by the ease with which I'd been felled. I was nothing, a worm he could have crushed underfoot. My cockiness had left me and now belonged to him. I pictured him grinning, even laughing aloud as he sped down the highway. He would shake his fist in the air with joy, reliving my subjugation in much the same way I would in the days to come.

I turned on the overhead light and looked down at my hand. Both my index finger and my insult finger jutted out at thirty-degree angles. I really couldn't feel much, but the sight of it was sickening. I found my bag near the bed. I picked up my jacket and laid it across my shoulders like a shawl. Oddly, the cabin wasn't that disordered. The iron had been flung into the far corner of the room. The wooden chair had been knocked over and the braided rug was askew. Tidy little bun that I am, I righted the chair and flopped the rug back into place, picked the iron up and returned it to the top closet shelf, cord dangling. Now I had only myself to accommodate.

I locked the cabin with effort, using the unaccustomed left hand. I headed toward the motel office. The night was cold and a soft whirl of snow whispered against my face. I drank deeply of the cold, refreshed by the dampness in the air. Out near the road, I could see the glow of the motel vacancy sign, a red neon beacon issuing its invitation to passing motorists. There was no traffic on the highway. None of the other cabins showed any signs of life. Through the office window, I could see a table lamp aglow. I went in. I leaned against the doorframe while I knocked on Cecilia's door. Long minutes passed. Finally, the door opened a crack and Cecilia peered out.

I could hear the mounting roar of a fainting spell rising around my ears. I longed to sit down and put my head down between my knees. I took a deep breath, shaking my head in hopes of clearing it.

Still squinting, she tied the sash of her pink chenille robe as she emerged. "What's this about?" she said, crossly. "What's the matter with you?"

I held up my hand. "I need help."

TEN

Cecilia dialed 9–1–1 and reported the break-in and the subsequent attack. The dispatcher said he'd send an ambulance, but Cecilia assured him she could get me to the hospital in the time it would take the paramedics to arrive. She threw on her sweats, a coat, and running shoes, and put me in her ancient Oldsmobile. To give her credit, she seemed properly concerned about my injury, patting me occasionally and saying things like, "You hang on now. You'll be fine. We're almost there. It's just down the road." She drove with exaggerated care, both hands on the steering wheel, chin lifted so she could see over the rim. Her speed never exceeded forty miles an hour and she solved the problem of which lane to drive in by keeping half the car in each.

I no longer felt pain. Some natural anesthesia had flooded through my system and I was woozy with its effect. I leaned my head back against the seat. She studied me anxiously, no doubt worried I'd barf on the hard-to-clean upholstery fabric.

"You're dead white," she said. She depressed the window control, opening the window halfway so that a wide stream of icy air whipped against my face. The highway was glossy with moisture, snow blowing across the road in diagonal lines. At this hour of the night, there was a comforting silence across the landscape. So far, the snow wasn't sticking, but I could see a powdering of white on tree trunks, an airy accumulation in the dead and weedy fields.

The hospital was long and low, a one-story structure that stretched in a straight line like some endless medical motel. The exterior was a mix of brick and stucco, with a roof of three-tab asphalt shingle. The parking area near the ambulance entrance was virtually deserted. The emergency room was empty, though the few brave souls on duty roused themselves and appeared in due course, one of them a clerk whose name tag read L. LIPPINCOTT. I was guessing *Lucille, Louise, Lillian, Lula*.

Ms. Lippincott's gaze flicked away from the bristling bouquet of digits. "How did you fall?"

"I didn't. I was assaulted," I said and then proceeded to give her an abbreviated account of the attack.

Her facial expression shifted from distaste to skepticism, as though there must be portions of the story I'd neglected to tell. Perhaps she fantasized some bizarre form of self-abuse or S&M practices too nasty to relate.

I sat in a small upholstered chair, reciting my personal data—name, home address, insurance carrier—while she entered the information into her computer. She was in her sixties, a heavy-boned woman with graying hair arranged in perfect wavelets. Her face looked like half the air had leaked out, leaving soft pouches and seams. She wore a nursy-looking pantsuit of waffle-patterned white polyester with large shoulder pads and big white buttons down the front. "Where'd Cecilia disappear to? Wasn't she the one brought you in?"

"I think she's gone off to find a restroom. She was sitting right out there," I said, indicating the waiting area. A new-found talent allowed me to point in two directions simultaneously—index and insult fingers going north-west, ring finger and pinkie steering east-north-east. I tried to avoid the sight, but it was hard to resist.

She made a photocopy of my insurance card, which she set to one side. She entered a print command and documents were generated, none of which I was able to sign with my bunged-up right hand. She made a note to that effect, indicating my acceptance of financial responsibility. She assembled a plastic bracelet bearing my name and hospital ID number and affixed that to my wrist with a device resembling a hole punch.

Chart in hand, she accompanied me through a doorway and showed me a seat in an examining room about the size of a jail cell. She stuck my chart in a slot mounted on the door before she left. "Someone'll be right with you."

The place looked like every other emergency room I'd ever been exposed to: beige speckled floor glossy with wax, making it easy to remove blood and other body fluids; acoustical tile on the ceiling, the better to dampen all the anguished cries and screams. The prevailing smell of rubbing alcohol made me think about needles and I desperately needed to lie down that instant. I set my jacket aside and crawled up on the examining table, where I lay on the crackling paper and stared at the ceiling. I wasn't doing well. I was shivering.

The lights seemed unnaturally bright and the room oscillated. I laid my left arm across my eyes and tried to think about something nice, like sex.

I could hear a low conversation in the corridor and someone came in, picking up my chart from the door. "Miss Millhone?" I heard the click of a ballpoint pen and I opened my eyes.

The ER nurse was black, her name tag identifying her as V. LaMott. She had to be Rafer LaMott's wife, mother to the young woman working as a short-order cook over at the Rainbow Cafe. Was theirs the only African American family in Nota Lake? Like her daughter, V. LaMott was trim, her skin the color of tobacco. Her hair was cropped close, her face devoid of makeup. "I'm Mrs. LaMott. You've met my husband, I believe."

"We spoke briefly."

"Let's see the hand."

I held it up. Something about her mention of Rafer made me think he'd confessed to her fully about his rudeness to me. She looked like the kind of woman who'd have given him a hard time about that. I hoped.

I kept my face averted while she completed her inspection. I could feel myself tense up, but she was careful to make only gingerly contact. There was apparently no nurse's aide on duty so she checked my vital signs herself. She took my temperature with an electronic thermometer that gave nearly instant results and then she held my left arm against her body as she pumped up the blood pressure cuff and took a reading. Her hands were warm while mine felt bloodless. She made notes on my chart.

"What's the *V* stand for?" I asked.

"Victoria. You can call me Vicky if you like. We're not formal around here. Are you on any medication?"

"Birth control pills."

"Any allergies?"

"Not that I know of."

"Have you had a tetanus shot in the last ten years?"

My mind went blank. "I can't remember."

"Let's get that over with," she said.

I could feel the panic mount. "I mean, it's really not necessary. It's not a problem. I have two dislocated fingers, but the skin wasn't broken. See? No cuts, no puncture wounds. I didn't step on a nail."

"I'll be right back."

I felt my heart sink. In my weakened condition, I hadn't thought to lie. I could have told her anything about my medical history. She'd never know the difference and it was my lookout. Lockjaw, big deal. This was all too much. I'm phobic about needles, which is to say I sometimes faint at the very idea of injections and become giddy at the sight of a *S-Y-R-I-N-G-E.* I've been known to pass out when *other* people get shots. In traveling, I would never go to a country that required immunizations. Who wants to spend time in an area where smallpox and cholera still run rampant among the citizens?

What I hate most in the world are those obscene newscasts where there's sudden minicam coverage of wailing children being stabbed with hypodermics in their sweet, plump little arms. Their expressions of betrayal are enough to make you sick. I could feel the sweat breaking out on my palms. Even lying down I was worried I'd lose consciousness.

She came back in a flash, holding the you-know-what on a little plastic tray like a snack. In my only hope of control, I persuaded her to stick me in the hip instead of my upper arm, though lowering my blue jeans was a trick with one hand.

"I don't like it either," she said. "Shots scare me silly. Here we go."

Stoically, I bore the discomfort, which truly wasn't as bad as I remembered it. Maybe I was maturing. Ha ha ha, she said.

"Shit."

"Sorry. I know it stings."

"It's not that. I just remembered. My last tetanus shot was three years ago. I took a bullet in the arm and they gave me one then."

"Oh, well," she said. She inserted the syringe into a device labeled "sharps" and neatly snapped off the needle, like I might snatch it away and stick myself with it six more times for fun. Ever the professional, I took advantage of the opportunity to quiz her about the Newquists while we waited for the doctor. "I gather Rafer and Tom were good friends," I said, for openers.

"That's right."

"Did the four of you spend much time together?" The answer seemed slow in coming so I offered a prompt. "You might as well be honest. I've heard it all by now. Nobody likes Selma."

Vicky smiled. "We spent time together when we had to. There were occasions when we couldn't avoid her so we made the best of it. Rafer didn't want to make a scene, nor did I for that matter, I swear to god, she once said to me—these are her exact words—'I'd have invited you over, but I thought you'd be more comfortable with your own kind.' I had to bite my tongue. What I wanted to say is 'I sure wouldn't want to hang out with a bunch of white trash like you.' And just to complicate matters, our daughter, Barrett, was going out with her son."

"She must have loved that."

"She could hardly object. She was always so busy acting like she wasn't prejudiced. What a joke. If it wasn't so pitiful it'd have cracked me up. The woman has no education and no intelligence to speak of. Rafer and I both graduated from U.C.L.A. He's got a degree in criminology . . . this was before he applied for the position with the sheriff's department. I've got a B.A. in nursing and an R.N. on top of that."

"Selma knew the kids were dating?"

"Oh, sure. They went steady for years. Tom was crazy about Barrett. I know he felt she was a good influence on Brant."

"Does Brant have a problem?"

"Basically, he's a good person. He was just screwed up back then, like a lot of kids that age. I don't think he ever did drugs, but he drank quite a bit and rebelled every chance he had."

"Why'd they break up?"

"You'd have to ask Barrett. I try not to mess in her business. You want my assessment, I think Brant was too needy and dependent for someone like her. He tended to be all mopey and clinging. This was years ago, of course. He was twenty, at that point. She was just out of high school and didn't seem that interested in getting serious."

Her comments were cut short when the doctor came in. Dr. Price was in his late twenties, thin and boyish, with bright blue eyes, big ears, dark auburn hair, and a pale freckled complexion. I could still see the indentation on his cheek where he'd bunched up his pillow to sleep. I pictured the entire ER staff napping on little cots somewhere. He wore surgical greens and a white lab coat, stethoscope coiled in his pocket like a pet snake. I wondered how he'd ended up at a hospital as small as this. I hoped it wasn't because he was at the bottom of his med school class. He took one look at my fingers and said, "Oh wow! Keen!" I liked his enthusiasm.

We had a chat about my assailant and the job he'd done. He studied my jaw. "He must have clipped you good," he said.

"That's right. I'd forgotten about that. How's it look?"

"Like you put eye shadow in the wrong place. Any other abrasions or contusions? That's doctor talk," he said. "Means little hurt places on your body."

"He kicked me twice in the ribs."

"Let's take a look," he said, pulling up my shirt.

My ribcage on the right side was swiftly turning purple. He listened to my lungs to make sure a rib hadn't been thrust into them on impact. He palpated my right arm, wrist, hand, and fingers, and then proceeded to deliver a quick course on joints, ligaments, tendons, and exactly what happens when someone wrenches them asunder. We trooped into the other room where a rumpled-looking technician took X-rays of both my chest and my hand. I returned to the table and lay down again, feeling thoroughly air-conditioned as the room spun.

When the film had been developed, he invited me into the corridor where he tucked the various views onto the lighted screen. Vicky joined us. We stood there, the three of us, and studied the results. I felt like a colleague called in for consultation on a troublesome case. My ribs were bruised, but not cracked, likely to be sore for days, but requiring no further medical attention. Roentgenographically speaking, the two pesky fingers were completely screwed. I could see that no bones were broken, though Dr. Price did point out two small chips he said my body would reabsorb.

I went back to the table where I reclined again with relief. My butt was still smarting from the sting of the tetanus, so I hardly noticed when the doctor, with a merry whistle, stuck me repeatedly in the joints on both fingers. I'd ceased to care by then. Whatever they did, I was too grossed out to notice. While I stared at the wall, the doctor maneuvered my digits back into their original upright position. He left the room briefly. When I finally dared to look at my hand, I saw that the injured fingers were now fat and reddened. While the fingers would now bend, the knuckles were swollen as though with sudden rheumatoid arthritis. I placed my mouth against the hot, numb flesh like a mother gauging a baby's fever with her lips.

Dr. Price returned with (1) a roll of adhesive tape, (2) a packet of gauze, and (3) a metal splint that looked like a bent Popsicle stick, for which my insurance company would ultimately be charged somewhere in the neighborhood of five hundred dollars. He taped the two fingers together and then affixed them to the ring finger with another wrapping of tape, all supported by the splint. I could sense my premiums going up. Medical insurance is only valid if the benefits are never used. Otherwise, you're rewarded with a cancellation notice or a hefty increase in rates.

I could hear another conference in the hallway and a deputy appeared outside the examining room door. He chatted with Dr. Price and then the doctor departed, leaving me alone with him. This was a fellow I hadn't seen before; a tall skinny kid with a long face, dark hair, dark ragged eyebrows that met in the middle, and shiny metal braces on his teeth. Well, I was filled with confidence.

"Ms. Millhone, I'm Deputy Carey Badger. I understand you had a problem. Can you tell me what happened?"

I said, "Sure," and went through my sad tale of woe again.

With his left hand, he jotted the information in a small spiral-bound notebook, his eyes never leaving my face. His pencil was the size you'd use on a bridge tally, small and thin, the point looking blunt. He might have been a waiter making a little memo to himself . . . tuna on wheat toast, hold the mayo. "Any idea who this fellow was?" he asked.

"Not a clue."

"What about height and weight? Can you give me an estimate?"

"I'd say close to six feet and he must have outweighed

me by a good sixty pounds. I'm one eighteen, which would put him at a hundred and seventy-five or one eighty minimum."

"Anything else? Scars, moles, tattoos?"

"It was pitch black. He wore a ski mask and heavy clothing so I didn't see much of anything. Night before, the same guy followed me out of Tiny's parking lot. I couldn't swear on a stack of Bibles, but I can't believe two different fellows would come after me like that. The first time, he drove a black panel truck with no plate numbers visible. I reported it this morning to the Nota Lake Police."

"Can you tell me anything else about him?"

"He smelled strongly of sweat."

He turned the page, still writing, and then frowned at his notes. "What'd he do the first encounter? Did he accost you on that occasion?"

"He stared and did this," I said, making a little shooting gesture with my left hand. "It doesn't sound like much, but it was meant to intimidate me and it did."

"He didn't talk to you either time?"

"Not a word."

"What about the vehicle he was driving? Was it the same one last night?"

"I didn't see. He must have parked out by the road and walked back to the cabin where I was staying."

"So he must have known which one it was, unless this was random breaking and entering."

I looked at him with interest. "That's true. I hadn't thought of that. I wonder how he found out which cabin I was in. I woke while he was picking the lock.

When that didn't work, he tried the window in the bathroom. After that, he went to work on the door again."

"And after he dislocated your fingers, he took off?"

"Correct. I could hear a car start in the distance, but I have no idea what kind it was. At that point I was focused on pulling myself together to get help."

Deputy Badger made an additional note for himself and then tucked his little book in his pocket with the pencil in the coil of wire. "I guess that's it then. I'll pass this information on to the deputy works days."

There was conversation outside the door and Rafer LaMott appeared. He shook hands with the deputy, who soon excused himself and disappeared down the hall. I could see Rafer's wife out at the nurse's station, her body language suggesting that she was well aware of his presence. I wondered if she'd called him herself. He looked freshly showered and shaved, natty in a pair of tan corduroy trousers and a soft red cashmere vest with a dress shirt under it. His expression was neutral. He put his hands in his pockets, leaning casually against the wall. He looked like an ad in a menswear catalog. "Cecilia was tired so I told her to go on home. As soon as you're finished here, I'll take you anywhere you want."

ELEVEN

It was six A.M. by the time Rafer finally put me in the front seat of his car. The offer of a ride was as close to an apology as I was likely to get. No doubt his true motivation was to quiz me about the current state of my investigation, but I really didn't care. The sun was not officially up and the early morning air was curiously gloomy. I was at a loss where to have him deliver me. I couldn't bear the idea of being in the cabin by myself. I didn't think Selma would be up at this hour and I couldn't believe Cecilia would welcome my further company. As if reading my mind, Rafer said, "Where to?"

"I guess you better drop me at the Rainbow. I can hang out there until I figure out what to do next."

"I'd like to check the cabin. I've got a print tech from Independence coming up at seven, as soon as he gets in. Maybe we'll get lucky and find out your intruder left his prints."

"Perform an exorcism while you're at it. I don't expect a good night's sleep until I'm out of there."

He glanced over at me. "You thinking about going home?"

"I've been thinking about that ever since I arrived."

He was silent for a while, turning his attention to the road. The town was beginning to come to life. Cars passed us, headlights almost unnecessary as the sky began to alter in gradients from steel gray to dove. At one of the intersections, a restaurant called Elmo's was ablaze with light, patrons visible through the windows. I could see heads bent over breakfast plates. A waitress moved from table to table with a coffeepot in each hand, offering refills. Out on the sidewalk, two women in sweatsuits were absorbed in conversation as they jogged. They arrived at the corner as the light turned red and began to run in place. We moved forward again.

Rafer finally spoke up. "Last time I had anything to do with a P.I. guy claimed to be working a missing-persons case. I went to quite a bit of trouble to follow up, taking two days of my time to track his fellow down in another state. Turns out the P.I. lied to me. He was trying to collect on a bad debt. I was pissed."

"I don't blame you," I said. I began to rack my brain, trying to remember if I'd lied to him myself.

"You have a theory about last night's attack?"

"I'm assuming this was the same guy who followed me from Tiny's," I said.

His gaze returned to the road. "I heard about that. Corbet made sure we got a copy of the report. I passed it on to the CHP so they could keep an eye out as well. Anything missing?"

"I didn't even bother to look. I was too busy taking care of this," I said, lifting my hand. "Anyway, I doubt the motive was theft. I think the point was to discourage my investigation."

"Why?"

"You tell me. I guess he feels protective of Tom Newquist. That's the best I can do."

"I'm not convinced this has anything to do with Tom."

"And I can't prove it does so where does that leave us?"

"You could be mistaken, you know. You're single and you're attractive. That makes you a natural target—"

"For what? This wasn't sexually motivated. It was plain old assault and battery. The guy wanted to cause me great bodily harm."

"What else?"

"What else, what? There's nothing else," I said. "Here's a question for you: Where's Tom's notebook? It's missing. No one's seen it since he died."

He shot me a look and then shook his head blankly. I could see him casting back in his mind. "I'm trying to remember when I last saw it. He usually kept it some-where close, but I know it's not in his desk drawers because we cleaned those out."

"The CHP officer doesn't remember seeing it in the truck. It didn't occur to him to look for it, but it does seem odd. I know it must irritate you that I'm pursuing the point—"

"Look. I was out of line on that. I get huffy about Selma. It has nothing to do with you."

I could feel the distance between us easing. There's nothing as disarming as a concession of that sort. "It may not be relevant in any event," I said. "What's the procedure on reports? Wouldn't most of his notes have already been written up and submitted?"

"Possibly. He kept his own copies of every report in the particular file he was working. The originals are sent to the records section down in Independence. Reports are submitted at regular intervals. Newer officers seem to be better organized about this stuff. Old timers like me and Tom tend to do things when we get around to it."

"Would there be any way to work backward by checking to see what reports were missing?"

"I don't know how you'd do that and it wouldn't tell you much. You'd have no way of knowing where he'd been and who he'd talked to, let alone the content of conversations. It's not uncommon to have a file with a couple of reports missing... especially if he was working a case and hadn't typed up his notes yet. Besides, all notes wouldn't be incorporated, just the information he judged relevant. You might scribble down a lot of stuff that wouldn't amount to a hill of beans when you get right down to it."

"Suppose he was developing information on a case of his?"

"He probably was. It also might have been a case someone else had worked that he was reworking for some reason."

"Such as?"

Rafer shrugged. "He might have picked up a new lead. Occasionally, there's a case in the works where the information is sensitive... might be an informant in another state, or something to do with Internal Affairs."

"My point exactly. I mean, what if Tom was privy to something he didn't know how to handle."

"He'd have told me. We talked about everything."

"Suppose it concerned you?"

He made a little move that indicated agitation. "Let's get off this, okay? I'm not saying we can't talk about this further, but let me think about it some."

"One more thing. And don't get all testy on me. Just tell me what you think. Is there any possibility Tom might have been involved with another woman?"

"No."

I laughed. "Try to keep your answer to twenty-five words or less," I said. "Why not?"

"He was a deeply moral man."

"Well, couldn't that explain his brooding? A man with no conscience wouldn't be at war with himself."

"Objection, your honor. Purely speculative."

"But Rafer, something was troubling him. Selma's not the only one who saw that. I don't know if it was personal or professional, but from what I gather, he was truly distressed."

We pulled into the parking area between the Rainbow Cafe and the Nota Lake Cabins. Rafer put the car in park and then opened his door. "Come on. I'll buy you breakfast. I got a daughter works here."

I struggled with the handle and then gave up. I sat while he walked around the car and opened the door on my side. He even offered a helping hand as I emerged. "Thanks. I can see this is going to be a pain."

"It'll be good for you," he said. "Force you to deal with your dependency issues."

"I don't have dependency issues," I said stoutly.

He smiled in response.

He held the cafe door open and I entered ahead of him. The place was bustling, all men, clearly the stopping-off place of early risers, ranchers, cops, and laborers on their way to work. The interior was, as usual, overheated, and smelled of coffee, bacon, sausages, maple syrup, and cigarettes. The brown-haired waitress, Nancy, was taking an order from a table full of fellows in overalls while Barrett, behind the counter, was focused on a griddle spread with pancakes and omelettes in the making. Rafer took the lead and found us an empty booth. As we passed the intervening tables, I could see we were attracting any number of stares. I was guessing the jungle drums had already spread the news about my assailant.

"How'd you end up in Nota Lake?" I asked, as we slid into the seats.

"I started out as a dispatcher for the L.A.P.D., working on my degree at night. Once I graduated, I applied to the academy. I was hired on at San Bernardino, eventually assigned to robbery detail, but when Barrett was born, Vicky started bugging me to leave LA. She was working as an ER nurse at Queen of Angels, and hated the commute. Even on two salaries, we couldn't afford to buy a house in any of the areas we liked. I heard about an opening in the sheriff's department up here. Vick and I drove up one weekend and fell in love with the place. That's been twenty-three years. Tom was already here. He grew up in Bakersfield."

Two tables over, I caught sight of Macon with his gaze fixed on me. He leaned forward, making some comment. The man with him made one of those casual turns, pretending to glance idly around the room when he was really taking aim at me. I picked up a menu, pretending I didn't notice him pretending not to notice me. Margaret's husband, Hatch.

"You know what you want?" Rafer asked. "I do the works myself. I keep trying to reform, but I can't resist."

"I'm with you," I said. "Your daughter's name is Barrett?"

"That was Vick's idea. I'm not sure where she got it, but it seems to fit. The job is temporary, by the way. She's applied to med school. She wants to be a shrink. This allows her to live at home and save her money 'til she goes."

"Where'd she do her undergraduate work? U.C.L.A.?"

"Where else?" he said, smiling. "What about you?"

"I hated school," I said. "I made it through high school by the hair of my chinny-chin-chin, but that's as far as I went. Well, I guess I did three semesters of junior college, but I hated that, too."

"How so? You seem smart."

"I'm too rebellious," I said. "I graduated from police academy, but that was more like boot camp than academia."

"You're a cop?"

"I was. I was rebellious about that, too."

Nancy appeared with a coffee pot in hand. She was in her forties, hair pulled back in a smooth chignon over which she wore a net. She had large brown eyes, a beauty mark high on her right cheek, and the sort of body men seem to have trouble keeping their hands off. She wore a T-shirt, generously cut slacks, and brown oxfords with an inch-thick crêpe sole. "You're out early," she remarked to Rafer. We both pushed our mugs in her direction and she filled them.

"You met Kinsey?"

"Not formally, but I know who she is. I'm Nancy. You talked to Alice about me."

"How are you," I said. "I'd shake hands if I could."

"Yeah, I heard about that. Cecilia stopped by when we were opening the place. She says you took quite a hit. I can see your jaw turning blue."

I put a hand to the place. "I keep forgetting about that. It must look terrific."

"Gives you character," she said. She glanced at Rafer. "What's for breakfast?"

He looked back at the menu. "Well, let's see. I'm trying to keep my cholesterol up so I think I'll have the blueberry pancakes, sausage, couple of scrambled eggs, and coffee."

"Make that two," I said.

"You want orange juice?"

"Oh sure. What the heck?" he said.

"Back in a flash," she said.

I saw Rafer's gaze flicker to the window. "Excuse me. I see Alex. I'll take him on back to the cabin and get him started."

I had to use two hands to hold my coffee mug, given that three fingers on my right hand were taped together like an oven mitt. The doctor had told me I could remove the tape after a day or two, as long as it felt comfortable. He'd given me four painkillers, neatly sealed in a small white envelope. I remembered a similar envelope from my childhood church-going days, when my nickel or dime offering was placed in the collection plate. The plate itself was wood, passed from hand to hand until it reached an usher at the end of the pew. I'd been kicked out of any number of Sunday school classes for reasons I've repressed, but my Aunt Gin, feeling huffy on my behalf, decided I was entitled to go to proper church services. I suppose her intention was to expose me to spiritual admonition. Mostly what I learned was how hard it is to do an accurate visual count of organ pipes.

I glanced out the window, watching Rafer cross the parking pad, heading toward the cabin in the company of a young man carrying a black case, like a doctor's bag. I took a physical inventory, noting the sore ribs on my right side. I didn't think my jaw was swollen, but it was clearly bruised. No teeth missing or loose. I could feel a knot on my butt the size of a silver dollar and I knew from experience it would itch like a son of a bitch for weeks on end.

"Miss Millhone, can I talk to you?"

I looked up. James Tennyson was standing at the table in his tan CHP uniform, complete with all its creaking paraphernalia: nightstick, flashlight, keys, holster, gun, bullets.

"Sure. Have a seat."

He put a hand against his holster, securing his gun as he slid into the booth. I thought he was ill at ease, but I didn't know him well enough to be certain. "I saw Rafer step away from the table and figured you might have a few minutes."

"This is fine. Nice to see you. You got your flashlight back?"

"Yes ma'am. I appreciate your returning it. Jo found

it inside the storm door when she went out to get the paper." He pointed at my hand. "I just heard about the fellow coming after you last night. You all right?"

"More or less."

"He meant business."

"I'll survive," I said.

"The reason I came over . . . I didn't even think about this until yesterday. The night Tom died? I was cruising along 395 when I spotted his truck . . . you know, with the hazard lights on. At first, I didn't realize it was him because he was still some distance away, but I intended to stop and see if there was anything I could do. Anyway, there was a woman walking along the road, heading toward town."

"A woman?"

"Yes ma'am. I'm almost sure."

"And she was facing you?"

"That's right, but she veered off about then. This was shortly before I passed so I didn't get a good look at her, just a fleeting impression. She was bundled up pretty good. If it hadn't been for Tom and trying to get help for him, I'd have cruised back in her direction in case she needed help."

"Is it unusual to see someone walking out there?"

"Yes ma'am. At least, I thought it was at the time. This was miles from anywhere and there's very little in the way of houses out there, except for one subdivision. She could have been out for a jog, but she didn't seem dressed for that, and in the dark? I doubt it. Anyway, it struck me as odd. I guess in my mind I was thinking she might have got mad at her boyfriend and taken off on foot. I didn't see another vehicle so I don't think it was a flat tire or anything like that."

"And this was no one you knew?"

"I really couldn't say. It was nobody I recognized under the circumstance. Like I said, I didn't think much about it and later it slipped my mind entirely. I don't even know what made me think of it. Just the fact that you asked."

I thought about it for a moment. "How far away was she from the truck when you saw her?"

"It couldn't have been a quarter of a mile because I could see Tom's hazard lights blinking in the distance."

"Do you think she was *with* him?"

"I suppose it's possible," he said. "If he was having chest pains, she might have been on her way to find help."

"Why not flag you down?"

"Beats me. I don't know what to make of it," he said.

"I'd like to see the spot where Tom's truck was parked," I said. "Could you maybe take me out there later?"

"Sure, I'd be happy to, but the place isn't hard to find. It's maybe a mile in that direction. You look for a couple big boulders near a pine with the top sheared off. Thing was struck by lightning in a big storm last year. Just keep an eye out. You can't miss it. It's on the right-hand side."

"Thanks."

He glanced toward one of the tables near the front of the cafe. "My breakfast is here. You have any more questions, give me a call."

I watched him move away. Hatch and Macon stood together near the cash register, waiting for Nancy to take their money. My conversation with James hadn't gone unnoticed, though both men made a big display of their disinterest. Rafer returned, entering the cafe without the technician, whom I assumed was busy at the cabin with his little brushes and powders. Rafer eased into the seat, saying, "Sorry about that. I told him we'd join him as soon as we finished here."

When we reached the cabin after breakfast, the door was standing open. I could see smudges of powder along the outside edges of the sills. Rafer introduced me to the fingerprint technician, who rolled a set of my prints for elimination purposes. Later, he'd ink a set of Cecilia's prints, along with the prints of any cleaning or mainten-ance workers. He could have saved himself the trouble. The cabin yielded nothing in the way of evidence: no useful prints on the window glass, nothing on the hard-ware, no footprints in the damp earth leading to or from the cabin.

The interior seemed dank, the bed still lumpy with the pillows I'd tucked under the pile of blankets. The place was drab. It was cold. The digital clock was blinking, which meant there'd been another power failure. The adrenaline had seeped slowly out of me like gray water down a clogged drain. I felt like crap. A rivulet of revulsion trickled over me and I was embar-rassed anew at the inadequacies of my attempt to defend myself. Anxiety whispered at the base of my spine, a feathery reminder of how vulnerable I was. A memory burbled up. I was five years old again, bruised and bloodied after the wreck that killed my parents. I'd forgotten the physical pain because the wrenching emotional loss had always taken precedence.

While Rafer and the tech conferred outside, talking in low tones, I hauled out my duffel and began to pack my things. I went into the bathroom, gathered up my toiletries, and tossed them in the bottom of the bag. I didn't hear Rafer come in, but I was suddenly aware of him standing in the doorway. "You're taking off?" he asked.

"I'd be crazy to stay here."

"I agree with you on that, but I didn't think you were finished with your investigation."

"That remains to be seen."

His gaze rested on me with concern. "You want to talk?"

I looked up at him. "About what? This is a simple job to me, not some moral imperative. I'm getting paid for a piece of work. I guess I have my limits on that score."

"You're going to quit?"

"I didn't say that. I'll talk to Selma first and then we'll see where we go from here."

"Look, I can see you're upset. I'd offer you protection, but I don't have a deputy to spare. We operate on a shoestring—"

"I appreciate the sentiment. I'll let you know what I decide."

"It wouldn't hurt to have help. You know anybody who could pitch in on personal security?"

"Oh, please. Absolutely not. I wouldn't do that. This

is strictly my problem and I'll handle it," I said. "Trust me, I'm not being pig-headed or proud. I hired a body-guard once before, but this is different."

"How so?"

"If that guy meant to kill me, he'd have done it last night."

"Listen, I've been beat up in my day and I know what it can do to you. Screws your head up. You lose your confidence. It's like riding a horse—"

"No, it's not! I've been beaten up before—" I raised a hand, stopping myself with a shake of my head. "Sorry. I didn't meant to snap at you. I know you mean well, but this is mine to deal with. I'm fine. I just don't want to spend another minute in this godforsaken place."

"Well," he said, infusing the single syllable with skepticism. He paused, silent, hands in his pockets, rocking back on his heels. I zipped the duffel, picked up my jacket and my handbag, looking around the cabin. The table was still littered with my papers and I'd forgotten about the Smith-Corona, still sitting in its place with the lid half closed. I snapped the cover into place and stuffed papers in a manila envelope that I shoved into an outer pocket of the duffel. Using my left hand, I lifted the typewriter case. "Thanks for the ride and thanks for breakfast."

"I have to get on in to work, but you let me know if there's anything I can do to help."

"You can carry this," I said, passing him the type-writer. He did me one better, carrying both the duffel and the Smith-Corona as he escorted me to the car. I waited until he'd pulled away and then I headed for the office and stuck my head in the door. There was no sign of Cecilia. The usual table lamp was still on, but her door was shut and I imagined her catching up on the sleep she'd lost taking me to the emergency room. I got into my car and pulled out of the parking lot, turning left onto 395.

I kept an eye on the odometer, clocking off a mile and then began to look for the spot where Tom's truck had been parked the night he died. As Tennyson indicated, it wasn't hard to find. Two massive boulders and a towering pine tree with the top missing. I could see the raw white inner wood where the lightning had slashed away at the trunk.

I eased over onto the berm and parked. I got out of the car, draping my heavy leather jacket across my shoulders. There was no traffic at this hour and the morning air was silent. The sky was massed with dark gray, the mountains obscured by mist. Snow had begun to fall; big lacy flakes that settled on my face like a series of kisses. For a moment, I leaned my head back and let the snow touch my tongue.

There was, of course, no remaining trace of vehicles having been parked here six weeks before. If the truck, Tennyson's patrol car, and the ambulance had chewed up the soil and gravel along the shoulder, nature had come afterward and smoothed away any suggestion of events. I did a grid search, my gaze fixed on the barren ground as I walked a linear pattern. I imagined Tom in his pickup, the pain like a knife wedged between his shoulder blades. Nausea, clamminess, the chill sweat of Death forcing him to concentrate. For the time being, I set aside the image of the woman walking down the road. For all I knew, she was a figment of James Tennyson's imagination, some piece of misdirection designed to throw me off. In any investigation, you have to be careful about accepting information without a touch of skepticism. I wasn't sure of his motivation. Maybe, as implied, he was just a genuinely helpful guy who took his job seriously and wanted to apprise me of his recollection. What interested me here was the possibility that Tom had dropped his notebook out the window, or that he'd somehow destroyed the contents in the final moments of his life.

I covered every inch of ground within a radius of a hundred feet. There was no notebook, no pages fluttering in the breeze, no confetti of torn paper, no nook or cranny into which such detritus might have been secreted. I kicked over rocks and dead leaves, set aside fallen branches and dug into crusty patches of snow. It was hard to believe Tom had dragged himself out here to take care of such business. I was operating on the assumption that his field notes were sensitive and that he'd made some effort to secure the confidentiality of the contents. Then again, perhaps not. The notes might not have been relevant.

I returned to my car and turned the key in the ignition, not without struggle. The tape on my right hand made everything slightly awkward and I suspected that the compensatory effort over the next couple of days was going to wear me down. While the injury wasn't major, it was annoying and inconvenient, a constant reminder that I'd suffered at someone's hands. I did a U-turn onto the highway and headed back to Selma's. By ten A.M., I was on the road for home.

TWELVE

Shortly after leaving Nota Lake, I'd thought I caught a glimpse of a county sheriff's cruiser keeping me company from half a mile back. The car was too far away to identify the driver, but the effect was to make me feel I was being ushered across the county line. I kept my eye on the rearview mirror, but the black-and-white maintained a discreet distance. When we reached the junction of 395 and 168, a road sign indicated that it was five miles to Whirly Township, seven miles to Rudd. The patrol car turned off. Whether the escort was deliberate or coincidental, I couldn't be sure. Nor could I determine whether the intention was benign or belligerent. Earlene's husband, Wayne, was the deputy who worked in Whirly Township, so maybe it was only him on his way to work.

After that, the desert landscape sped by in a monotonous repetition of scrub-covered low hills, and I spent the rest of the journey in a haze of road-induced hypnosis. The intervening towns were few—Big Pine, Independence, Lone Pine, Cartago, Olancha—unexpected small enclaves that consisted primarily of gas stations, wooden cottages, coffee shops, perhaps a pizza restaurant or a Frosty Freeze, sometimes still boarded over for the winter. In most towns, there seemed to be more buildings abandoned than were currently in use. The structures were low wood fronts with a Western or Victorian feel to them. In some areas, the commercial businesses seemed to be devoted almost entirely to propane sales and service. An occasional feed store would be tucked in among the cottonwoods and pines. I passed one of those plain motel-style brown-and-yellow churches that made you suspect it would be depressing to believe whatever these people believed.

Between townships, the empty stretches of wilderness picked up. The air felt clear, warming as the road descended from the higher elevations. The snow had disappeared, soft flakes turning into an even softer rain. What should have been a clear, unobstructed view was subdivided by the march of power lines, telephone poles, and oil derricks—the cost of doing business in an otherwise pristine countryside. Out of the raw hills to my left I could see the occasional cinder cone and the dark craggy outcroppings of lava from ancient volcanic activity. Rocks dotted the landscape: green, red, brown, and cream. The area was undercut by two major fault lines—the San Andreas and the Garlock—that in 1872 had generated one of the largest earthquakes in Californian history.

Gradually, I let my thoughts drift back to events I'd left behind. I'd spent an hour at Selma's before I'd departed Nota Lake. So far, given my four days' work, I'd earned a thousand dollars of the fifteen hundred she'd paid me in advance. That meant that I would owe *her* money if I decided to quit . . . which I confess had crossed my mind. My medical insurance would cover the expenses incurred in behalf of my bunged-up hand. She'd been properly upset by what had happened and we'd gone through the predictable litany of horror and remorse. "I feel sick. This is my fault. I got you into this," she'd said.

"Don't be silly, Selma. It isn't *your* fault. If nothing else it gives credence to your hunch about Tom's 'secret,' if you want to call it that."

"But I never dreamed it'd be dangerous."

"Life is dangerous," I said. I was feeling oddly impatient, ready to move on to the job at hand. "Look, we can sit here and commiserate, but I'd much prefer to use the time constructively. I've got a big pile of phone bills. Let's sit down together and see how many numbers you recognize. Any that seem unfamiliar, I can check from Santa Teresa."

Which is what we'd done, eliminating slightly more than three-quarters of the calls listed for the past ten months. Many were Selma's, related to her church work, charity events, and assorted friendships outside the 619 area code. Some of the remaining numbers she'd recognized as business calls, a fact confirmed by judicious use of Tom's Rolodex. I'd placed the entire file of last year's phone bills in my duffel and then I'd gone down to the basement to take a look at the storage boxes I'd seen previously. There, in the dry, overheated space that smelled of ticking furnace and hot paper, a curious order prevailed.

Despite the fact that both Tom's desk and his den upstairs were an ungodly mess, Tom Newquist was systematic, at least where work was concerned. On a shelf to my left was a series of cardboard boxes where he'd placed bundles of field notes going back twenty-five years, including his days at the academy. Once a notebook had been filled, his method was to remove the six-hole lined pages, apply a wrapper showing the inclusive dates, and then secure them with a rubber band. Many times several bundles of notes pertained to the same case and those tended to be packed in separate manila envelopes, again labeled and dated. I could walk my fingers back through his investigations, year after year, without gaps or interruptions. Occasionally, on the outside of an envelope he'd penned a note indicating that a call or teletype had come through regarding the particulars of a case. He would then type an update and include a copy with his notes, indicating the agency making the call, the nature of the inquiry, and the details of his response. He was clearly prepared to substantiate his findings with court testimony where required, on every investigation he'd done since he'd been in Nota Lake. The last of the bundled notes were dated the previous April. Missing were notes from May and June of last year until the time of his death. I had to assume the missing notebook covered the previous ten months. There was no other gap in his records of that magnitude.

I went back upstairs, through the kitchen, and into the garage, where I searched the truck again—more thoroughly than I had the first time around. I even eased onto one shoulder so I could shine a flashlight up under the seats, thinking Tom might have secured his note-book in the springs. There was no sign of it, so essentially I was back to square one. My only conso-lation was knowing I'd left no stone unturned—as far as I could tell. Clearly, I'd overlooked *something* or I'd have his notes in hand.

The rain increased as I drove south. At Rosamond, I found a McDonald's and stopped to use the restroom. I picked up a big cola, a large order of fries, and a QP with cheese. I downed a painkiller while I was at it. Twelve minutes later, I was on the road again. The closer I came to Los Angeles, the more my spirits lifted. I hadn't even realized how depressed I was until my mood began to improve. The rain became my companion, the windshield wipers keeping a steady rhythm as the highway sizzled under my tires. I turned on the radio and let the drone of bad music fill the car.

When I reached Highway 5, I turned north as far as the junction with Highway 126, where I cut west again through Fillmore and Santa Paula. Here the landscape was made up of citrus and avocado groves, the roadway populated with produce stands, beyond which tracts of houses stretched out as far as the eye could see. Route 126 spilled into 101 and I nearly whimpered aloud at the sight of the Pacific. I rolled the window down and tilted my head sideways, letting raindrops blow on my face. The scent of the ocean was dense and sweet. The surf made its relentless approach and retreat, soft pounding at the shoreline, where occasional sea birds race-walked along the hard-packed sand. The water was silken, endless reams of gray taffeta—churning lace at the edge. I'm not fond of mountains, in part because I have so little interest in winter sports, especially those requiring costly equipment. I avoid activities associated with speed, cold, and heights, and any that involve the danger of falling down and breaking significant body parts. As fun as it all sounds, it's never appealed to me. The ocean is another matter, and while I can spend brief periods in land-locked locations, I'm never as happy as I am when close to deep water. Please understand, I don't go *in* the water because there are all manner of biting, stinging, tentacled, pincered, slimy things down there, but I like to *look* at the water and spend time in its immense, ever-changing presence. For one thing, I find it therapeutic to consider all the creatures not devouring me at any given moment.

Thus cheered, I powered through the final few miles into Santa Teresa. I took the Cabana off-ramp and turned left, passing the bird refuge on my right and shortly thereafter, the volleyball courts on the sand at East Beach. By that time, I'd been on the road for five hours, so focused on home that my foot felt as if it was welded to the accelerator. I was exhausted. My neck was stiff. My mouth tasted like hot metal. My bruised fingers were deadened by drugs yet somehow managed to throb with pain. Also, my butt hurt along with everything else.

My neighborhood looked the same, a short residential street a block from the beach: palms, tall pines, wire fences, crooked sidewalks where tree roots had buckled the concrete. Most houses were stucco with aging red-tile roofs. An occasional condominium appeared between single-family dwellings. I found a parking spot across the street from my apartment, once a single-car garage, now a two-story hideaway attached by a sunporch to the house where my landlord lives. This month marked the fifth anniversary of my tenancy and I treasure the space I've come to think of as mine.

It took me two trips to unload the rental car, passing in and out of Henry's squeaking gate. I made a pile on the small covered porch, unlocked the front door, left the typewriter by the desk, went back for my duffel, and hauled it up the spiral stairs. I stripped off my clothes, removed the bandages from my hand, and treated myself to a long hot shower wherein I washed my hair, did a left-handed leg shave, and sang a medley of show tunes with half the lyrics consisting of *dah-dah-dah*. The luxury of being clean and warm was almost more than I could bear. I skipped my flossing for once, did a left-handed toothbrushing, and annointed myself with an inexpensive drugstore cologne that smelled like lilies of the valley. I put on a fresh turtle-neck, a fresh pair of jeans, clean socks, Reeboks, and a touch of lipstick. I checked my reflection in the bath-room mirror. Nah, that looked dumb. I rubbed off the lipstick on a piece of toilet paper and pronounced myself whole. After that, all I had to do was spend approxi-mately twenty minutes trying to get my fingers splinted and retaped. This was going to be ob-*noxious*.

I ducked out my door and splashed across the patio in the rain. Henry's garden was just coming to life again. The weather in Santa Teresa is moderate all year long, but we do enjoy a nearly indiscernible spring in which green shoots nudge through the hard ground as they do every place else. Henry had begun to clear the flower beds where his annuals and a few tomato plants would eventually go. I could smell the wet walkways, bark mulch, and the few narcissus that must have opened in the rain. It was quarter to five and the day was gloomy with approaching twilight, the light a mild gray from the rain clouds overhead.

I peered through the window in Henry's back door while I rapped on the glass. Lights were on and there was evidence he was in the midst of a cooking project. For many years, Henry Pitts earned his living as a commercial baker and now that he's retired, he still loves to cook. He's lean-faced, tanned, and long-legged, a gent with snowy white hair, blue eyes, a beaky nose, and all of his own teeth. At eighty-six, he's blessed with intelligence, high spirits, and prodigious energy. He came into the kitchen from the hallway carrying a stack of the small white terrycloth towels he uses when he cooks. He usually has one tucked in his belt, another resting on his shoulder, and a third that occasionally serves as an oven mitt. He was wearing a navy T-shirt and white shorts, covered by a big baker's apron that extended past his knees. He set the towels on the counter and hurried to unlock the door, his face wreathed in smiles.

"Well, Kinsey. I didn't expect you back today. Come on in. What happened to your hand?"

"Long story. In a minute, I'll give you the abbreviated version."

He stepped aside and I entered, giving him a hug as I passed. On the counter I could see a tall Mason jar of flour, a shorter jar of sugar, two sticks of butter, a tin of baking powder, a carton of eggs, and a bowl of Granny Smith apples; pie tin, rolling pin, grater.

"Something smells wonderful. What's cooking?"

Henry smiled. "A surprise for Rosie's birthday. I've got a noodle pudding in the oven. This is a Hungarian dish I hope you won't ask me to pronounce. I'm also making her a Hungarian apple pie."

"Which birthday?"

"She won't say. Last I heard, she was claiming sixty-six, but I think she's been shaving points for years. She has to be seventy. You'll be joining us, I hope."

"I wouldn't miss it," I said. "I'll have to sneak out and find a gift. What time?"

"I'm not going over 'til six. Sit, sit, sit and I'll fix a pot of tea."

He settled me in his rocking chair and put the kettle on for tea while we filled each other in on events during the weeks I'd been gone. In no particular order, we went through the usual exchange of information: the trip, Dietz's surgery, news from the home front. I laid out the job as succinctly as I could, including the nature of the investigation, the players, and the attack the night before, a process that allowed me to listen to myself. "I have a couple of leads to check. Apparently, Tom was in touch with a local sheriff's investigator, though, at this point, I'm not sure if the contact was personal or professional. The way I heard it, they had their heads bent together and the woman's manner was noticeably flirtatious. Strictly rumor, of course, but it's worth looking into."

"And if that doesn't pan out?"

"Then I'm stumped."

While I finished my tea, Henry put together the pie crust and began to peel and grate apples for the filling. I washed my cup and saucer and set them in his dish rack. "I better whiz out and find a present. Are you dressing for the party?"

"I'm wearing long pants," he said. "I may rustle up a sports coat. You look fine as you are."

As it turned out, Rosie's entire restaurant had been given over to her birthday party. This tacky neighborhood tavern has always been my favorite. In the olden days (five years ago), it was often empty except for a couple of local drunks who showed up daily when it opened and generally had to be carried home. In the past few years, for reasons unknown, the place has become a hangout for various sports teams whose trophies now grace every available surface. Rosie, never famous for her good humor, has nonetheless tolerated this band of testosterone-intoxicated rowdies with unusual restraint. That night, the ruffians were out in full force and in the spirit of the occasion had decorated the restaurant with crêpe paper streamers, helium balloons, and hand-lettered banners that read WAY TO GO ROSIE! There was a huge bouquet of flowers, a keg of bad beer, a stack of pizza boxes, and an enormous birthday cake. Cigarette smoke filled the air, lending the room the soft, hazy glow of an old tintype. The sportsers had seeded the jukebox with high-decibel hits from the 1960s and they'd pushed all the tables back so they could do the twist and the Watusi. Rosie looked on with an indulgent smile. Someone had given her a cone-shaped hat covered with glitter, a strand of elastic under her chin, and a feather sticking out the top. She wore the usual muumuu, this one hot pink with a three-inch ruffle around the low-cut neck. William looked dapper in a dark three-piece suit, white dress shirt, and a navy tie with red polka dots, but there was no sign of anyone else from the neighborhood. Henry and I sat to one side—he in jeans and a denim sports coat, I in jeans and my good tweed blazer—like spectators at a dance contest. I'd spent the better part of an hour at a department store downtown, finally selecting a red silk chemise I thought would tickle her fancy.

We ducked out at ten and scurried home through the rain.

I locked the door behind me and moved through the apartment, marveling at the whole of it: the porthole window in the front door, walls of polished teak and oak, cubbyholes of storage tucked into all the nooks and crannies. I had a sofa bed built into the bay window for guests, two canvas director's chairs, bookshelves, my desk. Up the spiral stairs, in addition to the closet built into one wall, I had pegs for hanging clothes, a double-bed mattress laid on a platform with drawers built into it, and a second bathroom with a sunken tub and a window looking out toward the ocean. I felt as if I were living on a houseboat, adrift on some river, snug and efficient, warm, blessed with light. I was so thrilled to be home I could hardly bear to go to bed. I crawled, naked, under a pile of quilts and listened to the rain tapping on the Plexiglas skylight. I felt absurdly possessive—my pillow, my blanket, my secret hideaway, my home.

The next thing I knew, it was six A.M. I hadn't set my alarm, but I woke automatically, reverting to habit. I tuned into the sound of rain, bypassed the thought of jogging, and went back to sleep again. I roused myself at eight and went through my usual morning ablutions. I had breakfast, read the paper, and then set the typewriter case on the desk top. I paused, making a quick trip upstairs where I retrieved my notes from the duffel. My first chore of the morning would be to return the rental car. That done, I'd take a cab to the office, where I'd put in an appearance and catch up with the latest lawyerly gossip. I still hadn't decided whether to work from the office or home. I'd either stay where I was or bum a ride home from someone at Kingman and Ives.

In the meantime, I thought I'd get my typewriter set up and begin the painful hunt-and-peck addition to my progress report. It wasn't until I opened the typewriter case that I saw what I'd missed in the process of packing to leave Nota Lake. Someone had taken the middle two rows of typewriter keys and twisted the metal into a hopeless clot. Some of the keys had been broken off and some were simply bent sideways like my fingers. I sat down and stared with a sense of bafflement. What was going on?

THIRTEEN

I decided to skip the office and concentrate on running down the few leads I had. In my heart of hearts, I knew perfectly well the trashing of my typewriter had taken place in Nota Lake before I'd left. Nonetheless, the discovery was disconcerting and tainted my sense of security and well-being. Annoyed, I opened my bottom desk drawer and took out the Yellow Pages, flicked through to TYPEWRITERS-REPAIRING, and made calls until I found someone equipped to handle my vintage Smith-Corona. I made a note of the address and told the shop owner I'd be there within the hour.

I took out my notes and found the local numbers I'd cribbed from the surface of Tom Newquist's blotter. When I'd dialed the one number from Tom's den, the call had been picked up by an answering machine. I was operating on the assumption that the woman I'd heard was the same female sheriff's investigator Phyllis claimed she'd seen flirting with Tom. If I could have a talk with her, it might go a long way toward cleaning up my questions. I punched in the number. Once again a machine picked up and the same throaty-voiced woman told me what I could do with myself at the sound of the beep. I left my name, my home and office numbers, and a brief message indicating that I'd like to talk to her about Tom Newquist. Next, I called the Perdido Sheriff's Department, saying: "I wonder if you could help me. I'm trying to get in touch with a sheriff's investigator, a woman. I believe she's in her forties or fifties. I don't have her name, but I think she's employed by the Perdido County Sheriff's Department. Does any of this ring a bell?"

"What division?"

"That's the point. I'm not sure."

The fellow on the phone laughed. "Lady, we've got maybe half a dozen female officers fit that description. You're going to have to be more specific."

"Ah. I was afraid of that," I said. "Well, I guess I'll have to do my homework. Thanks anyway."

"You're entirely welcome."

I sat there, mentally chewing on my pencil. What to do, what to do. I dialed Phyllis Newquist's number in Nota Lake and naturally got an answering machine into which I entrusted the following: "Hi, Phyllis. This is Kinsey. I wonder if you could give me the name of the female sheriff's investigator Tom was in touch with down here. I've got a home telephone number, but it would help if you could find out what her name is. That way, I can try her at work and maybe speed things along. Otherwise, I'm stuck waiting for this woman to call back." Again, I left both my home and office numbers and moved down my mental list.

The second number I'd picked up from Tom's blotter was for the Gramercy Hotel. I thought that one deserved my personal attention. I tucked Tom's photograph in my handbag, grabbed my jacket and an umbrella, and headed out into the rain. My fingers, though bruised and swollen, were not throbbing with pain and for that I was grateful. I used my left hand where I could, fumbling with car keys, transferring items from one hand to the other. The simplest transactions were consequently slowed since the splint on my right hand forced me to proceed by awkward degrees. I made a second trip for the typewriter, which I placed on the front seat.

I dropped off the typewriter, extracting a promise from the repair guy to get it back to me as soon as possible. I returned the rental to the agency's downtown office, completed the financial transactions, and then took a cab back to my apartment. I picked up my car, which—after a series of groans and stutters—finally coughed to life. Progress at last.

I drove into downtown Santa Teresa and left my car in a nearby public parking garage. Umbrella tilted against the rain, I walked one block over and one block down. The Gramercy Hotel was a chunky three-story structure on lower State Street, a residential establishment favored by the homeless when their monthly checks came in. The stucco building was painted the sweet green of a crème de menthe frappé and featured a covered entrance large enough to accommodate six huddled smokers seeking shelter from the rain. A marquee across the front spelled out the hotel rates.

SGL RMS $9.95.   DBL RMS $13.95
DAILY*WEEKLY*MONTHLY
RATES ALSO AVAILABLE ON REQUEST.

A fellow using a plastic garbage bag as a rain cloak greeted me rheumy-eyed as he moved his feet to allow me passage into the lobby. I lowered my umbrella, trying not to stab any of those assembled for their morning libations. It seemed early for package liquor, but maybe that was fruit juice being passed in the brown paper bag.

The hotel must have been considered elegant once upon a time. The floor was green marble with a crooked path of newspapers laid end to end to soak up all the rainy footsteps that criss-crossed the lobby. In places, where the soggy papers had been picked up, I could see that the newsprint had left reverse images of the head-lines and text. Six ornate pilasters divided the gloomy space into sections, each of which sported a blocky green plastic couch. To all appearances, the clientele was discouraged from spending time lounging about on the furniture as a hand-printed sign offered the fol-lowing admonishments:

NO SMOKING

NO SPITTING

NO LOITERING

NO SOLICITING

NO DRINKING ON THE PREMISES

NO FIGHTING

NO PEEING IN THE PLANTERS

Which just about summed up my personal code. I approached the long front desk, located beneath an archway decorated with white plaster scrolls and orna-mental vegetation. The fellow behind the marble counter was leaning forward on his elbows, clearly interested in my intentions. This felt like one more fool's errand, but it was truly the only thing I could think to do at this point.

"I'd like to talk to the manager. Is he here?"

"I guess that's me. I'm Dave Estes. And your name?"

"Kinsey Millhone." I took out my business card and passed it across to him.

He read it with serious attention to each word. He was in his thirties, a cheerful-looking fellow with an open countenance, glasses, a crooked smile, slight over-bite, and a hairline that had receded to reveal a long sloping forehead like an expanse of empty seashore when the tide is out. What hair he had was a medium brown and cropped close to his head. He wore a brown jumpsuit with many zippered pockets, like an auto mechanic's. The sleeves were rolled up to reveal muscular forearms.

"What can I help you with?"

I placed the photograph of Tom Newquist on the counter in front of him. "I'm wondering if you happen to have seen this man. He's an investigator for the Nota County Sheriff's Department. His name is Tom—"

"Hold on, hold on," he cut in. He held a hand up to silence me, motioning me to wait a moment, during which time he made the kind of face that precedes a sneeze. He closed his eyes, screwed up his nose, and opened his mouth, panting. His expression cleared and he pointed at me. "Newquist. Tom Newquist."

I was astonished. "That's right. You know him?"

"Well, no, I don't know him, but he was in here."

"When was this?"

"Oh, I'd say June of last year. Probably the first week. I'd say the Fifth if forced to guess."

I was so unprepared for the verification, I couldn't think what to ask next.

Estes was looking at me. "Did something happen to him?"

"He died of a heart attack a few weeks back."

"Hey, too bad. Sorry to hear that. He didn't seem that old."

"He wasn't, but I don't think he took very good care of himself. Can you tell me what brought him in here?"

"Oh, sure. He was looking for some guy who'd just been released from jail. We seem to get a lot of fellows here in that situation. Don't ask me why. Classy place like this. Word must go out that we got good rates, clean rooms, and won't tolerate a lot of nonsense."

"Do you remember the name of the man he was looking for?"

"That's an easy one to remember for other reasons, but I like to test myself anyway. Hang on." He went through the same procedure, face screwed up to show how hard he was working. He paused in his efforts. "You're probably wondering how I do this. I took a course in mnemonics, the art of improving the memory. I spend a lot of time by myself, especially at night when I'm on desk duty. Trick is you come up with these devices, you know—aids and associations—that help fix an item in the mind."

"That's great. I'm impressed."

"Reason I remember the time frame for your Newquist's visit is I started my study just about the time he came in. He was my first practice case. So the name

Newquist? No problem. *New* because the fellow was new to me, right? *Quist* as in question or query. New fellow came in with a question, hence *Newquist*."

"That's good," I said. "What about his first name?"

Estes smiled. "You told me that. I'd forgotten it myself."

"And the other guy? The one he was inquiring about?"

"What did I come up with for that? Let's see. It had something to do with dentists. Oh, yes. His last name was Toth? That's *tooth* with an O missing. That was a good one because the fellow had a tooth missing so it all tied together. His first name was Alfie. Dentists connect to doctors. And like at the doctor's, you say 'Ahh' when they stick in that tongue depressor in your mouth? First name began with *A*. So mentally, I go through all the *A* names I can think of. Allen, Arnold, Avery, Alfie. And there you have it."

"So Tom Newquist was here on business."

"That's correct. Trouble is, he missed him. Toth'd been here two weeks, but he moved out June One, shortly before this detective of yours came in."

"Do you have any idea why he was looking for Toth?"

"Said he was developing a lead on a case he was working. I remember that because it was just like the movies. You know, Clint Eastwood comes in, flashing a badge and real serious. All I know is Newquist never had the chance to talk to him because Toth was gone by then."

"Did he leave a forwarding address?"

"Well, no, but I have his ex-wife's address, under

'nearest relative not living with you.' That's so we got someone to call if a guy trashes the room or drops dead. It's a hassle trying to figure out what to do with a dead body."

"I can imagine," I said. "Is there any way I could get the ex-wife's name and address?"

"Sure. No problem. This's not confidential information as far as I'm concerned. People check in, I tell 'em the hotel files are open to the authorities. Cops come in asking to see records. I don't insist on a subpoena. That'd be obstruction of justice, in my opinion."

"I'm sure the police appreciate your attitude, but don't the hotel guests object?"

Dave Estes shrugged. "I guess the day I get sued, we'll change the policy. You know, another fellow came in, too. Plainclothes detective. This was earlier, maybe June One. I wasn't working that day or I'd have filed it away in the old noggin," he said with a tap to his temple. "I told Peck he better take the same course I did, but so far I haven't managed to talk him into it."

"Too bad," I said. "So who was this other detective who came in?"

"Can't help you there and that's my point. If Peck took this course, he could recall in detail. Since he didn't; no dice. The slate's blank. End of episode."

"Could I talk to Peck myself?"

"You could, but I can tell you exactly what he's going to say. He remembers this investigator came in—had a warrant and all, but Toth wasn't on the premises. In fact, he checked out later that day so maybe he was worried about the law catching up with him. Detective called back the next morning and Peck gave him the address and telephone number of Toth's ex-wife, same as I would."

"Did you tell Tom Newquist about the other detective?"

"Same way I'm telling you. I figured it must have been a cop he knew."

"What about Toth's ex? Did you tell him how to get in touch with her?"

"Sure did. The woman had a regular parade coming through the door."

"Hasn't anybody suggested you shouldn't be quite so free passing out information?"

"Lady, I'm not the guardian of public safety. Some cop comes in looking for information, I don't want to get in his way."

"What about the warrant? Was that local?"

"Can't answer that. Peck doesn't pay attention to these items the same way I do. He's got the right idea—we're here to cooperate. Place like this, you want the cops on your team. Fight breaks out, you want action when you hit 9–1–1."

"Not to mention help with all the bodies afterward."

"Now you're getting it."

"Could we just back up a minute and see if I got this straight? Alfie Toth was here two weeks, from sometime in the middle of May."

"Right."

"Then a plainclothes detective came in with a warrant for his arrest. Alfie heard about it and, not surprisingly, checked out later that day. The detective called back and Peck told him how to get in touch with Alfie Toth's ex-wife."

"Sure. Peck figured that's where Toth went," Estes said.

"Then around June Fifth, Tom Newquist came in and you passed the same information along to him."

"Hey, I don't show favorites, is my motto. That's why I'm giving it to you. Why say yes to one and no to someone else is the way I look at it."

"You haven't given me anything yet," I said.

He reached for a piece of scratch paper and jotted down a woman's name, address, and telephone number, apparently off the top of his head. He passed it across the counter.

I took the paper, noting at a glance the Perdido address. "Sounds like Alfie Toth was suddenly very popular."

"Yep."

"And you have no idea why?"

"Nope."

"What's Peck's first name?"

"Leland."

"Is he in the phone book if I need to talk to him?"

Estes shook his head. "Number's unlisted. Now *that* I wouldn't give out without getting his permission."

I thought about it for a moment, but couldn't think what other ground I should cover. I could always check with him later if something else occurred to me. "Well. Thanks for the help. You've been very generous and I appreciate that." I reached for my umbrella, shifting my handbag from my right shoulder to my left so I could manage both.

"Don't you want to hear the rest of it?"

I hesitated. "What rest?"

"The guy's dead. Murdered. Some backpacker found his body up near Ten Pines couple months ago. January Thirteen. Reason I remember is it's my great-aunt's birthday. Death. Birth. Doesn't take a wizard to make that connection. I got it locked right in here."

I stared at him, remembering a brief mention of it in the paper. "*That* was Alfie Toth?"

"Yep. Coroner figured he'd been dead six, seven months—since right about the time everybody came looking for him—including the fellow with the warrant and your Tom Newquist. Somebody must have caught up with him. Too bad Peck's never bothered to develop his skills. He might've been the state's star witness."

"To what?"

"Whatever comes up."

I sat in my car, trying to figure out what this meant. Everybody had wanted to talk to Alfie Toth until he turned up dead. I'd have to search back issues of the local newspaper, but as nearly as I remembered, there was precious little information. Decomposed remains had been found in a remote area of the Los Padres National Forest, but I hadn't registered the name. There was no mention of cause of death, but the presumption was of foul play. The police had been stingy with the details, but perhaps they'd told the papers everything they knew. I hadn't been aware of any other reference to the matter and I'd thought no more of it. The Angeles and Los Padres national forests are both dumping grounds for homicide victims, whose corpses one imagines littering the hiking trails like bags of garbage.

I dutifully fired up the VW and drove the eight blocks to the public library, where I turned up the relevant paragraph in a copy of the *Santa Teresa Dispatch* for January 15.

BODY FOUND IN LOS PADRES
THAT OF TRANSIENT

The decomposed remains discovered by a hiker in the Los Padres National Forest January 13 have been identified as a transient, Alfred Toth, 45, according to the Santa Teresa County Sheriff's Department. The body was found Monday in the rugged countryside five miles east of Manzanita Mountain. Detectives identified Toth through dental work after linking the body to a missing-persons report filed by his ex-wife, Perdido resident Olga Toth. The case is being investigated as a homicide. Anyone with information is asked to call Detective Clay Boyd at the Sheriff's Department.

I found a pay phone outside the building, scrounged a couple of coins from the bottom of my handbag, dialed the Santa Teresa County Sheriff's Department, and asked for Detective Boyd.

"Boyd." The tone was flat, professional, all business. All he'd done so far was give me his name and already I knew he wasn't going to be my best friend.

"Hi, my name is Kinsey Millhone," I said, trying not to sound too chirpy. "I'm a local private investigator working on a case that may connect to the death of Alfie Toth."

Pause. "In what way?"

"Well, I'm not sure yet. I'm not asking for confidential information, but could you give me an update? The last mention in the paper was back in January."

Pause. This was like talking to someone on a time delay. I could have sworn he was taking notes. "What's the nature of your interest?"

"Ah. Well, that's tricky to explain. I'm working for the wife—I guess I should make that the widow—of a sheriff's investigator up in Nota Lake. Tom Newquist. Did you know him by any chance?"

"Name doesn't sound familiar."

"He drove down last June to talk to Alfie Toth, but by the time he reached the Gramercy, Toth had moved out. They might have connected later—I'm not sure about that yet—but I'm assuming this was part of an ongoing investigation."

"Uh-unh."

"Do you have any record of Newquist's contacting your department?"

"Hang on." He sounded resigned, a man who couldn't be accused later of thwarting the public's right to know.

He put me on hold. I listened to the mild hissing that signals one's entrance into telephone hyperspace. I sent up a little prayer of thanks that I wasn't being subjected to polka music or John Philip Sousa. Some companies patch you into news broadcasts with the volume pitched too low and you sit there wondering if you're flunking some bizarre hearing test.

Detective Boyd clicked back in. He apparently had the file open on the desk in front of him as I could hear him flipping pages. "You still there," he asked idly.

"I'm here."

"Tom Newquist didn't get in touch with us when he was here, but I do show we've been in communication with Nota Lake."

I said, "Really. I wonder why he didn't let you know he was coming down."

"Gosh, I don't know. That's a stumper," he said blandly.

"If he'd gotten in touch, would there be a note of it?"

"Yes ma'am."

I could see how this was going to go. I was on a fishing expedition and Detective Boyd was responding only to direct questions. Anything I didn't ask, he wasn't going to volunteer. Somehow I had to snag his interest and inspire his cooperation. "Why don't I tell you my problem," I said conversationally. "His widow's convinced her husband was deeply troubled about something."

"Uh-unh."

I could feel my frustration mount. How could this man be so pleasant and so completely obtuse at the same time? I switched gears. "Was Alfie Toth wanted for some crime at the time of his death?"

"Not that I'm aware of. He'd just finished serving time on a conviction for petty theft."

"The desk clerk at the Gramercy says a plainclothes detective came in with a warrant for his arrest."

"Wasn't one of ours."

"You don't show any outstanding warrants?"

"No ma'am, I don't."

"But there must have been *some* connection or Tom Newquist wouldn't have bothered to drive all the way down here."

"I'll tell you what. If this is just a question of satisfying Mrs. Newquist's curiosity, I can't see any reason to share information. Why don't you talk to Nota Lake and see what they have to say. That'd be your best bet."

"Are you telling me you *have* information?"

"I'm telling you I'm not going to reveal the substance of an ongoing investigation to any yahoo who asks. You have knowledge of the facts—something new to contribute—we'd be happy to have you come in."

"Has there been a resolution to the case?"

"Not so far."

"The newspapers indicated that this was being investigated as a homicide."

"That's correct."

"Do you have a suspect?"

"Not at this time. I wouldn't say that, no."

"Any leads?"

"None that I'm willing to tell you about," he said. "You want to make a trip out here, I could maybe have you talk to the watch commander, but as far as giving out information by phone, it ain't gonna fly. I don't mean to cast aspersions, but you could be anyone . . . a journalist."

"God forbid," I said. "Surely you don't think I'm anyone that low."

I could hear him smile. At least he was enjoying

himself. He seemed to think about it briefly and then he said, "Let's try this. Why don't you give me your number and if anything comes up I'm at liberty to pass along, I'll be in touch."

"You're entirely too kind."

Detective Boyd laughed. "Have a good day."

FOURTEEN

Olga Toth opened the door to her Perdido condominium wearing a bright yellow outfit that consisted of form-fitting tights and a stretchy cotton tunic, cinched at the waist with a wide white bejeweled plastic belt. The fabric clung to her body like a bandage that couldn't quite conceal the damage time had inflicted on her sixty-year-old flesh. Her knee-high boots looked to be size elevens, white vinyl alligator with a fancy pattern of stitchwork across the instep. She'd had some work done on her face, probably collagen injections given the plumpness of her lips and the slightly lumpy appearance of her cheeks. Her hair was a dry-looking platinum blond, her brown eyes heavily lined, with a startling set of eyebrows drawn in above. I could smell the vermouth on her breath before she said a word.

I'd driven the thirty miles to Perdido in the midst of a drizzling rain, that sort of fine spray that required the constant flip-flop of windshield wipers and the fiercest of concentration. The roadway was slick, the blacktop glistening with a deceptive sheen of water that made driving hazardous. Under ordinary circumstances, I might have delayed the trip for another hour or two, but I was worried the cops would somehow manage to warn Alfie's ex-wife of my interest, urging her to keep her mouth shut if I knocked on her door.

The address I'd been given was just off the beach, a ten-unit complex of two-story frame townhouses within view of the Pacific. Olga's was on the second floor with an exterior stairway and a small sheltered entrance lined with potted plants. The woman who answered the door bell was older than I'd expected and her smile revealed a dazzling array of caps.

"Mrs. Toth?"

She said, "Yes?" Her tone conveyed a natural optimism, as though, having sent in all the forms, having held on to the matching numbers that established her eligibility, she might open the door to someone bearing the keys to her new car or, better yet, that oversized check for several million bucks.

I showed her my card. "Could I talk to you about your ex-husband?"

"Which one?"

"Alfie Toth."

Her smile faded with disappointment, as though there were better ex-husbands to inquire about among her many. "Honey, I'm sorry to be the one to tell you, but he's deceased so if you're here about his unpaid bills, the line forms at the rear."

"This is something else. May I come in?"

"You're not here to serve process," she asked, cautiously.

"Not at all. Honest."

"Because I'm warning you, I put a notice in the paper

203

the day we separated saying I'm not responsible for debts other than my own."

"Your record's clean as far as I'm concerned."

She studied me, considering, and then stepped back. "No funny business," she warned.

"I'm never funny," I said.

I followed her through the small foyer, watching as she retrieved a martini glass from a small console table. "I was just having a drink in case you're interested."

"I'm fine for now, but thanks."

We entered a living room done entirely in white; trampled-looking, white nylon cut-pile carpeting, white nylon sheers, white leatherette couches, and a white vinyl chair. There was only one lamp turned on and the light coming through the curtains had been subdued by the rain. The room felt damp to me. The glass-and-chrome coffee table bore a large arrangement of white lilies, a pitcher of martini's, several issues of *Architectural Digest*, and a recent issue of *Modern Maturity*. Her eye fell on the latter about the same time mine did. She leaned forward impatiently. "That belongs to a friend. I really hate those things. The minute you turn fifty, the AARP starts hounding you for membership. Not that I'm anywhere close to retirement age," she assured me. She poured herself another drink, adding olives she plucked from a small bowl nearby. She licked her fingertips with enthusiasm. "Olives are the best part," she remarked. Her nails, I noticed, were very long and pink, thick enough to suggest acrylics or poorly done silk overlays.

"What sort of work do you do?" I asked.

She motioned me into a seat at one end of the couch

while she settled at the other end, her arm stretched out along the back. "I'm a cosmetologist and if you don't mind my saying so—"

I held up a hand. "Don't give me beauty tips. I can't handle 'em."

She laughed, an earthy guttural sound that set her breasts ajiggle. "Never hurts to try. You ever get interested in a makeover, you can give me a buzz. I could do wonders with that mop of yours. Now what's this about Alfie? I thought all his problems were over and done with, the poor guy."

I filled her in on the nature of the job I'd been hired to do, thinking that as a widow, she might appreciate Selma Newquist's concern about her husband's mental state in the weeks before he died.

"I remember the name Newquist. He was the one called me a couple weeks after Alfie took off. Said it was important, but it really wasn't urgent, as far as I could tell. I told him Alfie was still around some place and I'd be happy to go looking for him if he'd give me a day or two."

"How long was Alfie here?"

"Two days, maybe three. I don't let any ex of mine stay longer than that. Otherwise, you have fellows camping on your doorstep every time you turn around. They all want the same thing." She lifted her right hand, ticking off the items as she mentioned them. "They want sex, want their laundry done, and a few bucks in their pocket before you send 'em on their way."

"What made Alfie leave the Gramercy?"

"I got the impression he was nervous. I noticed he was jumpy, but he never said why. Alfie was always restless, but I'd say he was looking for a place to hole up. I think he was hoping for the chance to set up permanent residence here, but I wasn't having any. I tried to discourage any long-range plans of his. He was a sweet man, the sweetest. He was twenty years younger than me though you never would have guessed. We were married for eight years. Of course, he was in and out of jail for most of it which is why we lasted as long as we did."

"What was he in jail for?"

She waved the question away. "It was never anything big—bad checks, or petty thievery, or public drunkenness. Sometimes he did worse, which is how he ended up in prison. Nothing violent. No crimes against persons. His problem was he couldn't figure out how to outsmart the system. It wasn't in his nature, so what could you do? You couldn't fault him for being dumb. He was just born that way. He tended to fall into bad company, always taking up with some loser with a harebrained scheme. He was easily dominated. Anybody could lead poor Alfie around by the nose. It all sounded good to him. That's how innocent he was. Most of it ended in disaster, but he never seemed to learn. You had to love that about him. He was good-looking, too, in a goofy sort of way. What he did, he did well, and the rest you might as well write off as a dead loss."

"What was it he did well?"

"He was great in the sack. The man was hung like a donkey and he could fuck all day."

"Ah. And how did you two meet?"

"We met in a bar. This was when I was still doing the singles scene, though I've about given that up. I don't know about you, but these days, I stick to the personal ads. It's a lot more fun. Are you single? You look single."

"Well, I am, but it seems to suit me."

"Oh, I know what you mean. I don't mind living on my own. I have no problem with that. I prefer it, to tell the truth. I just don't know how else to get *laid*."

"You run ads for sex?"

"Well, you don't come right out and say so. That'd be dumb," she remarked. "There's a hundred cute ways to put it. 'Party-Hearty,' 'Girls Just Want to Have Fun,' 'Passionate at Heart Seeks Same.' Use the right termin- ology and guys get the point."

"But doesn't that make you nervous?"

"What?" she said, her big eyes fixed on me blankly.

"You know, picking up a bed partner through a news- paper ad."

"How else are you going to get 'em? I'm not pro- miscuous by any stretch, but I've got your normal appetite for these things. Three, four times a week, I get the itch to go lookin' for love." She shimmied in her seat, snapping her fingers to indicate the joys of the bump-and-grind single life, something I'd obviously missed. "Anyway, at the time I met Alfie, I was still cruising the clubs which, believe me, in Perdido really limits your range, not to mention your choices. Looking at Alf, I never guessed his talents would be so impressive. The man never got tired—just kept banging away. I mean, in some ways, it was fortunate he spent so much time in jail." She paused to sip her martini, lifting her eyebrows appreciatively.

I made some bland comment, wondering what might

constitute a proper response to these revelations. "So he was here less than a week last June," I said, trying to steer her back onto neutral ground.

She set the glass on the table. "Something like that. Couldn't have been long, because I met the fellow I'm currently balling at the end of May. Lester didn't take kindly to the idea of Alfie's sleeping on my couch. Men get territorial, especially once they start jumping your bones."

"Where'd he go when he left?"

"Your guess is as good as mine. Last time I saw him he was gathering up his things. Next thing I know, they're asking about his bridgework, trying to identify his body from the crowns on his molars. This was the middle of January so he'd been gone six months."

"Do you think something frightened him into leaving when he did?"

"I didn't think so at the time, but that could have been the case. The cops seemed to think he'd been killed shortly after he took off."

"How'd they pinpoint the time?"

"I asked the same thing, but they wouldn't give me any details."

"Did you identify his body?"

"What was left of it. I'd reported him missing, oh I'd say early September. His parole officer had somehow tracked down my address and telephone number and he was in a tiff because Alfie hadn't been reporting. There he was chewing me out. I told him what he could do with it."

"Why'd you wait so long to call the cops?"

"Don't be silly. Somebody spends as much time as

Alfie did on the wrong side of the law, you don't call the cops just because he hasn't showed his face in two months. He was usually missing, as far as I was concerned. In jail or out of town, on the road . . . who the hell knows? I finally filed a report, but the cops didn't take it seriously until the body showed up at Ten Pines."

"Did the police have a theory about what happened to him?"

She shook her head. "I'll tell you this. He wasn't killed for his money because the man was stone broke."

"You never told me why Newquist was looking for Alfie in the first place."

"That was in regard to a homicide in Nota County. He'd heard Alfie was friends with a fellow whose body was found back in March of last year. I guess they had reason to believe the two were traveling together around the time of this man's death."

"Alfie was a suspect?"

"Oh, honey, the cops will never say that. They think you'll be more cooperative if they tell you they're looking for a potential witness to a crime. In this case, probably true. Alfie was a sissy. He was scared to death of violence. He'd never kill anyone and I'd swear to that on a stack of Bibles."

"How did Tom Newquist find out Alfie was here?"

"The fellow at the hotel told him."

"I mean, in Santa Teresa."

"Oh. I don't know. He never said a word about that. He might have run the name through the computer. Alfie'd just done a little jail time so he'd have popped right up."

"What about the victim? Did Newquist give you the name of the other man?"

"He didn't have to. I knew him through Alfie. Fellow by the name of Ritter. He and Alfie met in prison. This was six years ago at Chino. I forget what Alfie was doing time for at that point, something stupid. Ritter was vicious, a real son of a bitch, but he protected Alfie's backside and they hung around together after they got out. Alfie wanted Ritter to stay here as well, but I said absolutely not. Ritter was a convicted rapist."

"'Ritter,' was the first name or last?"

"Last. His first name was something fruity, maybe Percival. Everybody called him Pinkie."

"What was Alfie's reaction when he heard about Ritter's death?"

"I never had the chance to tell him. I looked all over town for him, but by then he was gone and I figured he took off. As it turns out, he was probably dead within days, at least according to the cops."

"I take it he was good about keeping in touch?"

"The man never went a week without calling to borrow money. He referred to it as his stud fee, but that was just a joke between us. Alfie was proud."

"I'm sure he was," I said.

"I really miss the guy. I mean, Lester's okay, but he can be prissy about certain sexual practices. He's opposed to anything south of the border, if you know what I mean."

"You don't think Lester had anything to do with Alfie's death? He might have been jealous."

"I'm sure he would have been if he'd known, but I never said a word. I told him Alfie was camping out on

210

my couch, but he had no idea we were screwing like bunny rabbits every chance we got. Bend over to tie your shoe, Alfie'd be right on you, the big dumb lug."

"And no one else called or came around looking for him?"

"I was off at work most days so I don't really know what Alfie did with himself, except drink, play the ponies, and watch the soaps on TV. He liked to shop. He dressed sharp so that's where a lot of his money went. Why the credit card companies kept sending him plastic is beyond my comprehension. He filed bankruptcy twice. Anyway, he might have had friends. He usually did. Like I said, he was a sweet guy. You know, horny, but kind."

"He sounds like a nice man," I murmured, hoping God wouldn't strike me dead.

"Well, he was. He wasn't quarrelsome or hard to get along with. He never got in bar fights or said a cross word to anyone. He was just a big dumb Joe with a hard-on," she said, voice wavering. "Seems like, any more, people don't get killed for a reason. It's just something that happens. Alfie was a bumpkin and he didn't always show good sense. Someone could have killed him for the fun of it."

I drove back to Santa Teresa, trying not to think much about the information I'd gleaned. I let thoughts wash over me without trying to put them in order or make any sense of them. I was getting closer to something. I just wasn't sure what it was. One thing seemed certain:

Tom Newquist was on the same track and maybe what he'd found caused him untold distress.

I reached my apartment shortly after three o'clock. The rain had passed for the moment, but the sky was darkly overcast and the streets were still wet. I bypassed the puddles, my furled umbrella tucked under my arm, moving through the gate with a sense of relief at being home. I unlocked my door and flipped on the lights. By then, my hand was beginning to ache mildly and I was tired of coping with the splint. I shed my jacket, went into the kitchenette for water, and took some pain medication. I perched on a stool and removed the gauze wrap from my fingers. I tossed the splint but left the tape in place. The gesture was symbolic, but it cheered me up.

I checked the answering machine, which showed one message. I pressed Replay and heard Tom's contact at the sheriff's department, who'd left me one sentence. "Colleen Sellers here, home until five if you're still interested."

I tried her number. She picked up quickly, almost as though she'd been waiting for the call. Her "Hello" was careful. No infusion of warmth or friendliness.

"This is Kinsey Millhone, returning your call," I said. "Is this Colleen?"

"Yes. Your message said you wanted to get in touch with me regarding Tom Newquist."

"That's right. I appreciate your getting back to me. Actually, this is awkward. I'm assuming you've heard that he passed away." I hate the phrase *passed away* when what you really mean is *died*, but I thought I should practise a little delicacy.

"So I heard."

That was as much as she gave me so I was forced to plunge right on. "Well, the reason I called . . . I'm a private investigator here in town . . ."

"I know who you are. I checked it out."

"Well, good. That saves me an explanation. Anyway, for reasons too complicated to go into, I've been hired by his widow to see if I can find out what was going on the last two months of his life."

"Why?"

"Why?"

"Why is it too complicated to go into?"

"Is there any way we can do this in person?" I asked.

There was a momentary pause, during which I heard an intake of breath that led me to believe she was smoking. "We could meet someplace," she said.

"That would be good. You live in Perdido? I'd be happy to drive down, if you like, or . . ."

"I live in Santa Teresa, not that far from you."

"That's great. Much better. You just let me know when and where."

Again, the pause while she processed. "How about the kiddy park across from Emile's in five minutes."

"See you there," I said, but she was gone by then.

I spotted her from a distance, sitting on one of the swings in a yellow slicker with the hood up. She had swiveled the seat sideways, the chains forming a twisted X at chest height. When she lifted her feet, the chains came unwound, swiveling her feet first in one direction and then another. She tipped back, holding herself in position with her toes. She pushed off. I watched her straighten her legs in a pumping motion that boosted her higher and higher. I thought my approach would interrupt her play, but she continued swinging, her expression somber, her gaze fixed on me.

"Watch this!" she said and at the height of her forward arc she let herself fly out of the swing. She sailed briefly and then landed in the sand, feet together, her arms raised above her head as though as the end of a dismount.

"Bravo."

"Can you do that?"

"Sure."

"Let's see."

Geez, the things I'll do in the line of duty, I thought. I'm a shameless suck-up when it comes to information. I took her place on the swing, backing up as she had until I was standing on tiptoe. I pushed off, holding on to the chains. I leaned back as I straightened my legs and then pumped back, leaning forward, continuing in a rocking motion as the trajectory of the swing increased. I went higher and higher. At the top of the swing, I released myself and flew forward as she had. I couldn't quite stick the landing and was forced to take a tiny side step for balance.

"Not bad. It takes practice," she said charitably. "Why don't we walk? You got your bumbershoot?"

"It's not raining."

She pushed her hood back and looked up. "It will before long. Here. You can share mine."

She put up her umbrella, a wide black canopy above our heads as we walked. The two of us held the shank, forced to walk shoulder to shoulder. Up close, she smelled of cigarettes, but she didn't ever light one in my presence. I placed her in her late forties, with a square face, oversized glasses set in square red frames, and shoulder-length blond hair. Her eyes were a warm brown, her wide mouth pushing into a series of creases when she smiled. She was large-boned and tall with a shoe size that probably compelled her to shop out of catalogs.

"You don't work today?" I asked.

"I'm taking a leave of absence."

"Mind if I ask why?"

"You can ask anything you want. Believe me, I'm experienced at avoiding answers when the questions don't suit. I turn fifty this coming June. I'm not worried about aging, but it does make you take a long hard look at your life. Suddenly, things don't make sense. I don't know what I'm doing or why I'm doing it."

"You have family in town?"

"Not any more. I grew up in Indiana, right outside Evansville. My parents are both gone . . . my dad since 1976, my mom just last year. I had two brothers and a sister. One of my brothers, the one who lived here, was diagnosed with a rare form of leukemia and he was dead in six months. My other brother was killed in a boating accident when he was twelve. My sister died in her early twenties of a botched abortion. It's a very strange sensation to be out on the front lines alone."

"You have any kids?"

She shook her head. "Nope, and that's another thing I question. I mean, it's way too late now, but I wonder about that. Not that I ever wanted children. I know myself well enough to know I'd be a lousy mom, but at this stage of my life, I wonder if I should have done it differently. What about you? You have kids?"

"No. I've been married and divorced twice, both times in my twenties. At that point, I wasn't ready to have children. I wasn't even ready for marriage, but how did I know? My current lifestyle seems to preclude domesticity so it's just as well."

"Know what I regret? I wish now I'd listened more closely to family stories. Or maybe I wish I had someone to pass 'em on to. All that verbal history out the window. I worry about what's going to happen to the family photograph albums once I'm gone. They'll be thrown in the garbage . . . all those aunts and uncles down the tubes. Junk stores, you can sometimes buy them, old black-and-white snapshots with the crinkly edges. The white-frame house, the vegetable garden with the sagging wire fence, the family dog, looking solemn," she said. Her voice dropped away and then she changed the subject briskly. "What'd you do to your hand?"

"A fellow dislocated my fingers. You should have seen them . . . pointing sideways. Made me sick," I said.

We strolled on for a bit. To the right of us, a low wall separated the sidewalk from the sand on the far side. There must have been two hundred yards of beach before the surf kicked in; all of this looking drab in current weather conditions. "How are we doing so far?" I asked.

"In what respect?"

"I assume you're sizing me up, trying to figure out how much you want to tell."

"Yes, I am," she said. "Tom confided in me and I take that seriously. I mean, even if he's dead, why would I betray his trust?"

"That's up to you. Maybe this is unfinished business and you have an opportunity to see it through for him."

"This is not about Tom. This is about his wife," she said.

"You could look at it that way."

"Why should I help her?"

"Simple compassion. She's entitled to peace of mind."

"Aren't we all?" she said. "I never met the woman and probably wouldn't like her even if I did, so I don't give a shit about her peace of mind."

"What about your own?"

"That's my concern."

That was as much as I got out of her. By the time we'd walked as far as the wharf, the rain was beginning to pick up again. "I think I'll peel off here. I'm a block down in that direction. If you decide you have more to tell me, why don't you get in touch."

"I'll think about that."

"I could use the help," I said.

I trotted toward home under a steadily increasing drizzle that matted my hair. What was it with these people? What a bunch of anal-retentives. I decided it was time to quit horsing around. I ducked into the apartment long enough to run a towel through my hair, grab my handbag and umbrella, and lock up again. I retrieved my car and drove the ten blocks to Santa Teresa Hospital.

FIFTEEN

I caught Dr. Yee on his way to the parking lot. I'd left the VW in a ninety-minute spot at the curb across from the hospital emergency room and I was circling the building, intending to enter by way of the main lobby. Dr. Yee had emerged from a side door and was preparing to cross the street to the parking garage. I called his name and he turned. I waved and he waited until I'd reached his side.

Santa Teresa County still utilizes a sheriff-coroner system, in which the sheriff, as an elected official, is also in charge of the coroner's office. The actual autopsy work is done by various forensic pathologists under contract to the county, working in conjunction with the coroner's investigators. Steven Yee was in his forties, a third-generation Chinese American, with a passion for French cooking.

"You looking for me?" He was easily six feet tall, slender and handsome, with a smooth round face. His hair was a straight glossy black streaked with exotic bands of white that he wore combed straight back.

"I'm glad I caught you. Are you on your way home?

I need about fifteen minutes of your time, if you can spare it."

He glanced at his watch. "I'm not due at the restaurant for another hour," he said.

"I heard about that. You have a second career."

He smiled with pleasure, shrugging modestly. "Well, the money's not great, but I make enough here. It's restful to chop leeks instead of . . . other things."

"At least you're skilled with a boning knife," I said.

He laughed. "Believe me, nobody trims meat as meticulously as I do. You ought to come in some night. I'll treat you to a meal that'll make you weep for the pure pleasure."

"I could use that," I said. "You know me and Quarter Pounders with cheese."

"So what's up? Is this work?"

"I'm looking for information about a man named Alfie Toth. Are you familiar with the case?"

"Should be. I did the post," he said. He hooked a thumb in the direction of the building. "Come on back to my office. I'll show you what we have."

"This is great," I said happily, as I followed him. "I understand Toth's death may be related to a suspected homicide in Nota Lake. One of the sheriff's investigators there was working on the case when he died of a heart attack a few weeks back. His name was Tom Newquist. Did he get in touch with you?"

"I know the name, but he didn't contact me directly. I spoke to the Nota Lake coroner by phone and he mentioned him. What's your connection? Is this an insurance claim?"

"I don't work for CF these days. I've got an office in Lonnie Kingman's law firm on Capillo."

"What happened to CF?"

"They fired my sorry butt, which is fine with me," I said. "It was time for a change so now I'm doing mostly freelance work. Newquist's widow hired me. She says her husband was stressed out and she wants me to find out why. Nota Lake law enforcement's been very tight-lipped on the subject and the cops here aren't much better."

"I'll bet."

When we reached the elevator, he punched the Down button and we chatted idly of other matters as we descended into the bowels of the building.

Dr. Yee's office was a small bare box down the hall from the morgue. The ante-room was lined with beige filing cabinets, the office itself barely large enough for his big rolltop desk, his swivel chair, and a plain wooden chair for guests. His medical books had been moved to the shelves of a freestanding bookcase and the top of his desk was now reserved for a neat row of French cookbooks, trussed on either side by a large jar of murky formalin in which floated something I didn't care to inspect. He was using a gel breast implant as a paperweight, securing a pile of loose notes. "Hang on a second and I'll pull the file," he said. "Have a seat."

The chair was stacked with medical journals so I perched on the edge, grateful Dr. Yee was willing to trust me. Dr. Yee was never careless with information, but he wasn't as paranoid as the police detectives. He returned with a file folder and a manila envelope and took his seat in the swivel chair, tossing both on the desk beside me.

"Are those the photographs? Can I see?"

"Sure, but they won't tell you much." He reached for the envelope and extracted a set of color photographs, eight-by-ten prints showing various views of the scene where Alfie Toth had been found. The terrain was clearly rugged: boulders, chaparral, an ancient live oak. "Toth was identified through his skeletal remains, largely dental work. Percy Ritter's body in Nota Lake was found in much the same circumstances; same MO and a similar remote locale. In both cases, it took a while before anyone stumbled across the remains."

I paused, staring at one close-up view with perplexity, not quite sure what I was looking at; probably the lower half of Alfie Toth's body crumpled on the ground. The pelvic bones appeared to be still joined, but the femur, tibia, and fibulas were tangled together in a heap, like bleached kindling. The haphazard skeletal assortment looked like a Halloween decoration badly in need of assembly.

Dr. Yee was saying, "Ritter's mummified body was found fully clothed with various personal items in his pockets . . . expired California driver's license, credit cards. Identification was confirmed by his fingerprints, which had to be reconstituted. Must have been dry out there because bacterial growth and putrefaction are halted when the body moisture diminishes below fifty percent. Ritter's flesh was as stiff as leather, but Kirchner managed to retrieve all but the right-hand thumb and ring finger. Ritter'd had his prints in the system since 1972. What a bad ass. Real scum."

"I didn't know you could salvage prints like that."

He shrugged. "You sometimes have to sever the fingers first. To rehydrate, you can soak 'em in a three percent lye solution or a one percent solution of Eastman Kodak Photo-Flo 200 for a day or two. Another method is to use successive alcohol solutions, starting at ninety percent and gradually decreasing. With Ritter, the first presumption was of suicide, though Kirchner said he had big doubts and the county sheriff did, too. Keep in mind, there wasn't any suicide note at the scene, but there was also no environmental disorder and no signs of trauma on the body. No fractured hyoid to suggest cervical compression, no evidence of knife wounds, skull fractures, gunshot—"

"In other words, no signs of foul play."

"Right. Which is not to say he couldn't have been subdued in some way. Same thing with Toth, except there was no personal ID. Sheriff's department went back through months' worth of missing-persons reports, contacting relatives. They made the initial match that way."

"So what are we looking at?" I asked, turning the photograph so he could see.

"To all appearances, both guys tied a rope around a boulder, put a noose around their necks, pushed the rock through the Y of a tree limb, and hung themselves. It wasn't until later that the similarities came to light."

I stared at him. "That's odd." I glanced down at a photograph, in which I could now see the crisscross of rope circling the circumference of a rock about the size of a large watermelon. Toth's torso and extremities had separated, falling in a tumble on one side of the tree while the upper half of his body, pulled by the weight of the boulder, had fallen on the other still attached by the length of rope.

"Nothing remarkable about the rope, in case you're wondering. Garden variety clothes line available at any supermarket or hardware store," he said. Dr. Yee watched my face. "Not to be racist about it, but the method's more compatible with an Asian sensibility. Some dude out in Nota County, how'd it even occur to him? And then a second one here? I mean, it's possible Toth heard about his pal's alleged suicide and imitated his methodology, but even so, it seems off. As far as I know, the Nota Lake cops kept the specifics to themselves. That was information only shared between agencies."

"Really. If Alfie Toth wanted to kill himself, you'd think he'd blow his brains out; something simple and straightforward, more in keeping with his lifestyle."

Dr. Yee shifted back in his chair with a squeak. "A more plausible explanation is that both victims were killed by the same party. The reason the cops are so paranoid is to avoid all the kooks and the copycats. Someone ups and confesses, you don't want anyone other than the killer in possession of the details. So far the papers haven't gotten wind of it. They know a body was found here, but that's about the extent of it. I'm not sure reporters have put two and two together with the deceased in Nota Lake. That didn't get any play here."

"What's the estimated time of death for Ritter?"

"Oh, he'd been there five years from Kirchner's estimate. A gasoline receipt among his effects was dated

April 1981. Gas station attendant remembers the two of them."

"Quite a gap between deaths," I said. "Have you ever run across a methodology like this?"

"Only in a textbook. That's what makes it curious. Take a look at this." He reached backward and pulled a thin oversized volume from the bottom shelf. "Tomio Watanabe's *Atlas of Legal Medicine*. This was first published in 'sixty-eight, printed in Japan, so it's hard to find these days." He flipped the pages open to a section on hangings and turned the book so I could see. The photographs were of Japanese suicide victims, apparently supplied by various police headquarters and medical examiners' offices in Japan. One young woman had wedged her neck in the V of a tree, which effectively compressed her carotid and vertebral arteries. Another woman had made a double loop of long rope, which she wound around her neck and then put her feet through, achieving strangulation by ligature. In the method Dr. Yee'd referred to, a man tied a rope around a stone, which he placed on a chair. He'd wrapped the same rope around his neck, sat with his back to the chair back, and then tilted the chair forward so the stone rolled off the seat and strangled him. I studied the photographs on adjoining pages, which depicted in graphic detail the ingenuity employed by human beings in extinguishing their lives. In every case, I was looking at the face of despair. I stared at the floor for a moment, running the scenario through my head like a piece of film. "There's no way two men on opposite sides of California would have independently devised the same method."

"Probably not," he said. "Though, given the fact

they were friends, it's possible they overheard someone describe the technique. If you're intent on suicide, the beauty of it is once you topple the boulder through the fork in the tree, there's no way back. Also, death is reasonably quick; not instantaneous, but you'd lose consciousness within a minute or less."

"And these are the only two deaths of this kind that you know of?"

"That's right. I don't think this is serial, but the two have to be connected."

"How'd you hear about Ritter's death?"

"Through Newquist. He'd known about Ritter since his body was discovered back in March of this past year. When a backpacker came across Toth, he reported it to the local sheriff's department and they contacted Nota Lake because of the similar MO."

"Isn't there a chance Toth killed his friend Ritter, hoping to make it look like suicide instead of murder, and then ended up killing himself the same way? There'd be a certain irony in that."

"It's possible," he said dubiously, "but what's your picture? Toth commits a murder and five years pass before he finds himself overwhelmed with guilt?"

"Doesn't make much sense, does it?" I said, in response to his tone. "I talked to his ex-wife and from what she said, he wasn't behaving like a man who was terminally depressed." I checked my watch. It was close to 4:45. "Anyway, I better let you go. I appreciate the information. This has been a big help."

"My pleasure."

*

When I got home at five o'clock, Henry's kitchen lights were on and I found him sitting at his kitchen table with a file box in front of him. I tapped on the glass and he motioned me in. "Help yourself to a cup of tea. I just made a pot."

"Thanks." I took a clean mug from the dish rack and poured myself a cup of tea, then sat at the kitchen table watching Henry work.

"These are rebate coupons. A new passion of mine in case you're wondering," he said. Henry had always been enthusiastic about saving money, sitting down daily with the local paper to clip and sort coupons in preparation for his shopping trips.

"Can I help?"

"You can file while I cut," he said. He passed me a pile of proof of purchase seals, which I could see were separated according to the company offering to refund a portion of the price. He was saying, "Short's Drugs has started a Receipt Savers Rebate Club, which allows you to collect your rebates and send them in all at once. There's no point in trying to get fifty cents back when it costs you nearly thirty-five cents for stamps."

"I can't believe the time you put in on this," I remarked as I filed. Over-the-counter diet remedies, detergent, soap, mouthwash.

"Some are products I use anyway so who can resist? Look at this one. Free toothpaste. Makes your smile extra white it says."

"Your smile's already white."

"Suppose I end up preferring the taste of this one. There's no harm in trying something new," he said. "Here's one for shampoo. You get one free if you buy before April First. Only one per customer and I've got mine already, so I kept this for you if you're interested."

"Thanks. You do this in addition to the store coupons?"

"Well, yes, but this takes a lot more patience. Sometimes it takes as long as two to three months, but then you get a nice big check. Fifteen bucks once. Like found money. You'd be surprised how quickly it adds up."

"I'll bet." I took a sip of my tea.

Henry passed me another ragged pile of clippings. "When you finish that batch, you can start on these."

"I don't mean to sound petty," I said, bringing the conversation around to my concerns, "but honestly, Rosie paid more attention to those rowdies than she did to us last night. It didn't hurt my feelings so much as piss me off."

Henry seemed to smile to himself. "Aren't you overstating your case?"

"Well, it may be too strong a term, but you get my point. Henry, how much children's aspirin do you take these days? I counted fifteen of these."

"I donate the extras to charity. Speaking of pain relievers, how's your hand?"

"Good. Much better. It hardly hurts," I said. "I take it Rosie's attitude doesn't bother you."

"Rosie's Rosie. She's never going to change. If it bugs you, tell her. Don't complain to me."

"Oh right. I see. You want me to take the point."

"Battle of the Titans. I'd like to see that," he remarked.

*

At six, I left Henry's, stopping by my apartment to pick up my umbrella and a jacket. Once again, the rain had eased off, but the cold saturated the air, making me grateful to step into the tavern. Rosie's was quiet, the air scented with the pungent smell of cauliflower, onions, garlic, bacon, and simmering beef. There were two patrons sitting in a booth, but I could see they'd been served. The occasional clink of flatware on china was the only sound I heard.

Rosie was sitting at the bar by herself, absorbed in the evening paper, which was open in front of her. A small television set was turned on at the far end of the bar, the sound muted. There was no sign of William and I realized if I was going to catch her, this would be my only chance. I could feel my heart thump. My bravery seldom extends to interactions of this kind. I pulled out the stool next to hers and perched. "Something smells good."

"Lot of somethings," she said. "I got William fixing deep-fried cauliflower with sour cream sauce. Also hot pickled beef, and beef tongue with tomato sauce."

"My favorite," I said dryly.

Behind us, the door opened and a foursome came in, admitting a rush of cold air before the door banged shut again. Rosie eased down off her stool and moved across the room to greet them, playing hostess for once. The door opened again and Colleen Sellers was suddenly standing in the entrance. What was *she* doing here? So much for my confrontation with Rosie. Maybe Colleen had decided to give me some help.

*

"I don't even know what I'm doing here," she said, glumly. Her blond hair drooped with the damp and her glasses had fogged over from the heat in the place.

"Talking about Tom."

"I guess."

"You want to tell me the rest of it?"

"There's nothing much to tell."

We were seated in the back booth I usually claim as my own. I'd poured her a glass of wine that was now sitting in front of her untouched. She removed her glasses, holding them by the frames while she pulled a paper napkin from the dispenser and cleaned the lenses in a way that made me worry she was scratching them. Without the glasses, she looked vulnerable, the misery palpable in the air between us.

"When did you first meet him?"

"At a conference up in Redding a year ago. He was there by himself. I never did meet his wife. She didn't like to come with him, or at least that's what I heard. I gathered she was a bit of a pain in the ass. Not that he ever admitted it, but other people said as much. I don't know what her gig was. He always spoke of her like she was some kind of goddess." She pushed her hair back from her face and tucked it behind her ears in a style that wasn't flattering. She put on her glasses again and I could see smears on the lenses.

"Did you meet by chance or by design?"

Colleen rolled her eyes and a weary smile played around her mouth. "I can see where you're headed, but okay . . . I'll bite. I knew he was going to be there and I looked him up. How's that?"

I smiled back at her. "You want to tell it your way?"

"I'd appreciate that," she said dryly. "Until the conference in Redding, I only dealt with him by phone. He sounded terrific so naturally, I wanted to meet him in person. We hit it off right away, chatting about various cases we'd worked, at least the interesting ones. You know how it is, trading professional tales. We got talking department politics, his experiences versus mine, the usual stuff."

"I don't mean to sound accusatory, but someone seemed to think the two of you were very chummy."

"Chummy?"

"That you were flirtatious. I'm just telling you what I heard."

"There's no law against flirting. Tom was a doll. I never knew a man yet who couldn't use a little boost to his ego, especially at our age. My god. Who the hell's telling you this stuff? Someone trying to make trouble, I can tell you that."

"How well did you know him?"

"I only saw him twice. No, correction. I saw him three times. It was all work at first, starting with the case he was on."

"What case was that?"

"County sheriff up in Nota Lake found an apparent suicide in the desert, an ex-con named Ritter, who'd hung himself from a branch of a California white oak. Identification was confirmed through his fingerprints and Tom tracked him back as far as his release from Chino in the spring of 'eighty-one. Ritter had family in this area; Perdido to be precise. He talked to them by phone and they told him Ritter'd been traveling with a pal."

"Alfie Toth," I supplied. I was curious to hear her version, but I didn't want her to think I was completely ignorant of the facts.

"How'd you hear about him?" she asked.

"Hey, I have my sources just like you have yours. I know Tom drove down here in June to look for him."

"That's right. I was the one got a line on the guy. Toth had been arrested here on a minor charge. I called Tom and he said he'd be down within a day. This was mid-April. I told him I'd be happy to make the contact, but he preferred doing it himself. I guess he got caught up in work and it was June by the time he made it down here. By then, Toth was gone."

"So Tom never talked to him?"

"Not that I know of. As it turned out, Toth's body was the one found in January of this year. The minute the ID was made, I called Tom. The MO was the same for both Ritter and Toth and that was worrisome. The two deaths had to be related, but it was tough to determine what the motivation might have been."

"From what I hear, the murders were separated by a five-year time gap. You have a theory about that?"

I could see her mouth pull down and she wagged her head to convey her ambivalence. "This was one time when Tom and I didn't agree on anything. It could have been a double-cross ... you know, a bank heist or burglary with Ritter and his sidekick betraying an accomplice. Fellow catches up with them and kills Ritter on the spot. Then it takes another five years to hunt down his pal, Toth."

"What was Tom's idea?"

"Well, he thought Toth might have been a witness to

Ritter's murder. Something happens in the mountains and Pinkie Ritter dies. Toth manages to get away and eventually the killer catches up with him."

I said, "Or maybe Alvin Toth killed Ritter and someone else came along and avenged Ritter's death."

She smiled briefly. "As a matter of fact, I suggested that myself, but Tom was convinced the perpetrator was the same in both cases."

I thought about Dr. Yee's assessment, which was the same as Tom's. "It would help if I knew how to get in touch with Ritter's family."

"I can give you the phone number. I don't have it with me, but I could call you later if you like."

"That'd be great. One other thing. I know this is none of my business, but were you in love with Tom? Because that's what I'm picking up, reading between the lines," I said.

Her body language altered and I could see her debate with herself about how much to reveal. "Tom was loyal as a dog, completely devoted to his wife, which he let me know right off the bat. Ain't that always the way? All the good men are married."

"So they say."

"But I'll tell you something. We had real chemistry between us. It's the first time I ever understood the term *soul mate*. You know what I mean? We were soul mates. No kidding. It was like finding myself in this other guise ... my spiritual counterpart ... and that was heady stuff. We'd be in a room together with five or six hundred other people and I always knew where he was. It was like tentacles stretching all the way across the auditorium. I wouldn't even have to look for him. The bond was that strong. There wasn't anything I couldn't say to him. And laugh? God, we laughed."

"You go to bed with him?" I asked, casually.

A blush began to saturate Colleen's cheeks. "No, but I would have. Hell, I was so crazy about him I broached the subject myself. I was shameless. I was wanton. I'd have taken him on any basis ... just to be with him once." She shook her head. "He wouldn't do it, and you know why? He was honorable. Decent. Can you imagine the gall of it in this day and age? Tom was an honorable man. He made a promise to be faithful and he meant it. That's one of the things I admired most about him."

"Maybe it's just as well. He wouldn't have been good at deceit even if he'd been willing to try."

"So I've told myself."

"You miss him," I said.

"I've cried every day since I heard about his death. I never even had the chance to say goodbye to him."

"It must be tough."

"Awful. It's just awful. I miss him more than I missed my own mother when she died. So maybe if I'd slept with him, I'd have had to kill myself or something. Maybe the loss and the pain would have been impossible to bear."

"You might have had less respect for him if he'd given in."

"That's a risk I'd have taken, given half a chance."

"At any rate, I'm sorry for your pain."

"No sorrier than I am. I'm never going to find another guy like him. So what can you do? You soldier on. At least his wife has the luxury to mourn in public. Is she taking it hard?"

"That's why she hired me, trying to find relief."

Colleen looked away from me casually, trying to conceal her interest. "What's she like?"

I thought for a moment, trying to be fair. "Generous with her time. Terribly insecure. Efficient. She smokes. Sort of hard-looking, platinum blond hair teased out to here. She has slightly gaudy taste and she's crazy about her son, Brant. This was Tom's stepson."

"Do you like her? Is she nice?"

"People claim she's neurotic, but I do like the woman. A few don't, but that's true of all of us. There's always someone who thinks we're dogshit."

"Did she love him?"

"Very much, I'd say. It was probably a good marriage . . . maybe not perfect, but it worked. She doesn't like the idea of his dying with unfinished business."

"Back to that," she said.

"I'd do the same for you if you hired me to find answers."

Colleen's gaze came back to mine. "You thought it was me. That we were having an affair."

"It crossed my mind."

"If I'd had an affair with him, would you have told his wife the truth?"

"No. What purpose would it serve?"

"Right." She was silent for a moment.

"Do you know why Tom was so distressed?" I asked.

"I might."

"Why so protective?"

"It's not up to me to ease her mind," she said. "Who's easing mine?"

I held my hands up in surrender. "I'm just asking the question. You have to do as you see fit."

"I have to go," she said abruptly, gathering up her coat. "I'll call you later with the phone number for Ritter's daughter."

I held a finger up. "Hang on. I just remembered. I have something for you if you're interested." I reached into the outer zippered compartment of my shoulder bag and pulled out one of the black-and-white photographs of Tom at the April banquet. "I had these done up in case I needed 'em. You might like to have something to remember him by."

She took the picture without comment, a slight smile playing across her mouth as she studied it.

I said, "I never met him myself, but I thought it captured him."

She looked up at me with tears rimming her eyes. "Thank you."

SIXTEEN

When I returned from my run the next morning, there was a message from Colleen Sellers on my answering machine, giving me the name and Perdido address of a woman named Dolores Ruggles, one of Pinkie Ritter's daughters. As this represented the only lead I had, I gassed up the VW and headed south on 101 as soon as I was showered and dressed.

On my left, I could see fields under cultivation, the newly planted rows secured by layers of plastic sheeting as slick and gray as ice. Steep hills, rough with low-growing vegetation, began to crowd up against the highway. On my right, the bleak Pacific Ocean thundered against the shore. Surfers in black wetsuits waited on rocking boards like a scattered flock of sea birds. The rains had moved on, but the sky was still white with a ceiling of sluggish clouds and the air was thick with the mingled scents of brine and recent precipitation. Snow would be falling in the high Sierras near Nota Lake.

I took the Leeward off-ramp and made two left turns, crossing over the freeway again in search of the street where Dolores Ruggles lived. The neighborhood was a

warren of low stucco structures, narrow streets inter-
secting one another repeatedly. The house was a plain
box, sitting in a plain treeless yard with scarcely a bush
or a tuft of grass to break up the monotonous flat look
of the place. The porch consisted of a slab of concrete
with one step leading up to the front door and a small
cap of roofing to protect you as you rang the bell, which
I did. The door was veneer with long sharp splinters of
wood missing from the bottom edge. It looked like a
dog had been chewing on the threshold.

The man who opened the door was drying his hands
on a towel tucked into the waist of his trousers. He
was easily in his sixties, maybe five-foot-eight, with a
coarsely lined face and a thinning head of gray-white
hair the color of wood ash. His eyes were hazel, his
brows a tangle of wiry black and gray. "Keep your shirt
on," he said, irritably.

"Sorry. I thought the bell was broken. I wasn't even
sure anyone was home. I'm looking for Dolores
Ruggles."

"Who the hell are you?"

I handed him my card, watching his lips move while
he read my name. "I'm a private investigator," I said.

"I can see that. It says right here. Now we got that
established, what do you want with Dolores? She's busy
at the moment and doesn't want to be disturbed."

"I need some information. Maybe you can help me
and we can spare her the imposition. I'm here about
her father."

"The little shithead was murdered."

"I'm aware of that."

"Then what's it to you?"

"I'm trying to find out what happened."

"What difference does it make? The man is D-E-A-D dead and not soon enough to suit my taste. I've spent years coping with all the damage he did."

"Could I come in?"

He stared at me. "Help yourself," he said abruptly and turned on his heel, leaving me to follow. I scurried after him, taking a quick mental photograph as we passed through the living room. Not to sound sexist, but the room looked as if it had been designed by a man. The floors were bare hardwood, stained dark. I noted a tired couch and a sagging upholstered chair, both shrouded by heavy woven Indian-print rugs. I thought the coffee table was antiqued, but I could see as I passed the only patina was dust. The walls were lined with books: upright, sideways, slanting, stacked, packed two deep on some shelves, three deep on others. The accumulation of magazines, newspapers, junk mail, and catalogs suggested a suffocating indifference to tidiness.

"I'm doing dishes out here," he said, as he moved into the kitchen. "Grab a towel and you can pitch in. You might as well be useful as long as you're picking my brain. By the way, I'm Homer, Dolores's husband. Mr. Ruggles to you."

His tone had shifted from outright rudeness to something gruff, but not unpleasant. I could see he'd been rather good-looking in his day; not wildly handsome, but something better—a man with a certain amount of character and an appealing air. His skin was darkly tanned and heavily speckled with sun damage, as if he'd spent all his life toiling in the fields. His shirt was an earth brown with an elaborately embroidered yoke done in threads of gold and black. He wore cowboy boots that I suspected were intended to add a couple of inches to his height.

By the time I reached the kitchen, he'd turned on the water again and he was already back at work, washing plates and glassware. "Towel's in there," he said, nodding at the drawer to his immediate left. I took out a clean dish towel and reached for a plate still hot from the rinse water. "You can stack those on the kitchen table. I'll put 'em up when we're done."

I glanced at the table. "Uhm, Mr. Ruggles, the table needs to be wiped. Do you have a sponge?"

Homer turned and gave me a look. "This is a telling trait of yours, isn't it?"

"Oh, sure," I said.

"Skip the Mr. Ruggles bit. It sounds absurd."

"Yes, sir."

That netted me half a smile. He wrung out the cloth and tossed it in my direction with a shake of his head. I wiped off the table top, setting several items aside: newspaper; salt-and-pepper shakers shaped like the Wolf and Little Red Riding Hood; a clutch of pill bottles with Dolores's name plastered on them, along with various warning labels. Whatever she was taking, she was supposed to avoid alcohol, excessive exposure to sunlight, and the operation of heavy machinery. I wondered if this referred to cars, tractors, or Amtrak locomotives. When I'd finished, I handed him the rag and then picked up the dish towel and resumed wiping the plate.

"So what's the deal?" he said belatedly. "What's your

interest in Pinkie Ritter? Nice girl like you should be ashamed."

"I didn't know anything about him until yesterday. I've been tracking down a friend of his, who may have been . . . Could we just skip this part? It's almost too tricky to explain."

"You're talking Alfie Toth."

"Thank you. That's right. Everybody seems to know about him."

"Yeah, well, Alfie was a birdbrain. Women thought he was attractive, but I couldn't see it myself. How can you think some guy's handsome when you know he's dim? To my way of thinking, it spoils the whole effect. I think he hung out with my father-in-law for protection, which just goes to show you how dumb he was."

"You knew Alfie was dead?"

"You bet. The police told us about it when his body turned up. They came around asking the same question you probably want answered, which is what's the connection and who did what to whom? I'll give you the same answer I gave them. I don't know."

"What's the story on Pinkie? I take it you didn't think much of him."

"That's a gross understatement. I really hated his guts. Whoever killed Pinkie saved me life in prison. Pinkie had six kids—three sons and three daughters— and mistreated every one of them from the day they were born 'til they got big enough to fight back. Nowadays there's all this talk of abuse, but Pinkie did the real thing. He punched them, burned them, made 'em drink vinegar and hot sauce for talking back to him. He locked them in closets, set them out in the cold. He screwed 'em, starved 'em, threatened them. He hit 'em with belts, boards, metal pipes, sticks, hairbrushes, fists. Pinkie was the meanest son of a bitch I ever met and that's goin' some."

"Didn't anybody intervene?"

"People tried. Lot of people blew the whistle on him. Trick was trying to prove it. Teachers, guidance counselors, next-door neighbors. Sometimes Children's Services managed to take the kids away from him and foster them out. Judge always gave 'em back." He shook his head. "Pinkie knew how the game was played. He kept a clean house—the kids saw to that—and he did like to cook—that was his specialty. It's what he did for a living when he wasn't breaking their heads or breaking the law. Social workers came around and everything looked fine. Kids knew better than to open their mouths. Dolores says she can remember the six of them lined up in the living room, answering questions just as nice as you please. Pinkie wouldn't be in the room, but he was always somewhere close. Kids knew better than to rat on him or they'd be dead by dark. They'd stand there and lie. Said social workers knew, but couldn't get anything on him without their assistance. Only thing saved 'em was his getting thrown in jail."

"What about his wife? Where was she all this time?"

"Dolores thinks he killed her though it couldn't be proved. He claims she ran off with some barfly and was never heard from again. Dolores says she remembers as a kid waking up in the dead of night. Pinkie was out in the woods behind the house with a power saw. Lantern on the ground throwing these big shadows up against the trees. Moths fluttering around the light. She still has nightmares about that. She was the baby in the family, six years old at the time. I think the oldest was fifteen. She went out there next day. The ground was all turned, probably to hide the blood. She still remembers the smell—like a package of chicken when it's gone funny and has to be thrown out. Mom was never seen nor heard from again."

"Pinkie sounds like a very nasty piece of work."

"The worst."

"So anybody could have killed him, including one of his kids. Is that what you're saying?"

"That would cover it," he said. "Of course, by the time he died, they were out from under his control. The rest of the kids had scattered to hell and gone. Couple of 'em still in California, though we don't see 'em all that much." Homer finished the last dish and turned the water off. I continued drying silverware while he put away the clean plates.

"When did you see him last?"

"Five years ago in March. The minute he got out of Chino, he headed straight up here, arrived on the Twenty-fifth and stayed a week."

"Good memory," I remarked.

"The cops asked me about that so I looked it up. How I pinpointed the date is I withdrew five hundred bucks from a bank account the day Pinkie left. I counted backward from that and the date stuck in my mind. Anything else you want to quiz me about?"

"I didn't mean to interrupt. Go on."

"Dolores was the only kid of his still living in the area so naturally, he felt she owed him room and board for as long as he liked."

"She agreed to that?"

"Of course."

"Didn't you object?"

"I did, but that was an argument I couldn't win. She felt guilty. She's a hell of a gal and what she's endured, believe me, you don't want to know—but the upshot is, she's anxious to please, easily manipulated—especially when it came to him. She wanted that man's love. Don't ask me to explain, given what she suffered. He was still Daddy to her and she couldn't turn him away. He was just like he always was: demanding, critical. He refused to lift a finger, expecting her to wait on him hand and foot. I finally got fed up and told him to clear out. Pinkie says, 'Fine, no problem. I won't stay where I'm not wanted. To hell with you,' he says. He was sore as a boil and feeling much put upon, but I was damned if I'd back down."

"Toth was with him at the time?"

"Off and on. I think Alfie's ex-wife lived in town somewhere. He mooched off her when he wasn't here mooching off us."

"And the two left together?"

"As far as I know. At least, that was the plan."

"And where were they headed?"

"Los Angeles. You piece it together later and it turns out they stole a car in Los Angeles and drove up to Lake Tahoe."

"What about Pinkie's parole officer? Wasn't he supposed to report in?"

"Hey, you're talking a career criminal. Following the rules wasn't exactly his strong suit. Who the hell knows how he got away with it? Same with Toth."

"You think someone could have been after them?"

"I wouldn't know," he said. "Pinkie didn't act like he was worried. Why? You think someone might have been trailing them?"

"It's possible," I said.

"Yeah, well it's also possible Pinkie overstepped his bounds for once. He was one of those little guys, chip on his shoulder and feisty as all get out. I can't say that about Alfie. He seemed harmless. Pinkie's another matter. Whoever killed Pinkie should get a medal, in my opinion. And don't quote me. Dolores gets upset if she hears me talkin' like that. I notice I'm doing all the talking."

"I appreciate that."

"This is good. I appreciate your appreciation. Now it's your turn. What's a private investigator doing in the middle of a homicide investigation? Last I heard they didn't have a suspect so you can't be working for the public defender's office."

Given his cooperation, I thought he was entitled to an explanation. I filled him in on the situation, beginning with Selma Newquist and ending with Colleen Sellers. The only thing I omitted were details of the two killings. He didn't seem curious about specifics and I wouldn't have revealed the information for all the money in the world. In the meantime, on an almost subliminal level, I could hear an odd series of voices from another room. At first, I thought the sound was coming from a radio, or television set, but the phrases were repeated, the tone lifeless and mechanical. Homer heard it, too, and his gaze caught mine. He tilted his head in the direction of the short hallway that seemed to lead into a back bedroom. "Dolores's back there. You want to talk to her?"

"If you think it's okay."

"She can handle it," he said. "Give me a second and I'll tell her what's going on. She might have something to add."

He moved down the hall to the door, tapping once before he entered. As he eased through the opening, I felt a moment's unease. Here I was in a strange house in the company of a man I'd never laid eyes on before. I had taken him at face value, trusting him on instinct though I wasn't sure why. Really, I only had his word for it that Dolores was in the other room. I had one of those flash fantasies of him emerging from the bedroom with a butcher knife in hand. Fortunately, life, even for a private eye, is seldom this interesting. The door opened again and Homer motioned me in.

At first sight, I thought Dolores Ruggles couldn't have been a day over twenty-five. Later, I found out that she was twenty-eight, which still seemed too young to be married to a man Homer's age. Slim, petite, she sat at a workbench in a room filled with Barbie dolls. Floor to ceiling, wall to wall, dressed in an astonishing array of styles, these bland plastic women were decked out in miniature sun dresses, evening clothes, suits, furs, shorts, capes, pedal pushers, bathing suits, baby doll pajamas, sheaths—each outfit complete with appropriate accessories. There was a whole row of Barbie brides, though I'd never thought of her as married. The row below showed twenty Barbies uniformed as flight attendants and nurses, which must have represented the entire gambit of career options available to her. Some of the dolls were still in their boxes and some were freestanding, affixed to round plastic mounts. There was a row of seated Barbies—black, Hispanic, blonde, brunette—their long perfect legs extended like a chorus line, all shoeless, their unblemished limbs ending in nearly pointed toes. Their arms were long and impossibly smooth. Their necks must have contained extra vertebrae to support the weight of their tousled manes of hair. I confess I found myself at a loss for words. Homer leaned against the open door, watching for my reaction.

I could tell something was expected of me so I said, "Amazing," in what I hoped was a properly respectful tone.

Homer laughed. "I thought you'd like that. I don't know a woman alive who can resist a room full of dolls."

I said, "Ah."

Dolores glanced at me shyly. She had a doll in her lap, not a Barbie to all appearances, but some other type. With a little hammer and an X-acto knife, she was cutting open its stomach. There was a box of identical little plastic girls, sexless, unmarred, standing close together with their chests pierced in a pattern of holes like those old-fashioned radio speakers. Beside them, there was a box of little girls' heads, eyes demurely closed, a smile turning up the corners of each set of perfect lips. "Chatty Cathys," she said. "It's a new hobby. I fix their voices so they can talk again."

"That's great."

Homer said, "I'll leave you girls to your own devices. You have a lot you want to talk about."

He closed me into the room with her, as pleased with himself as a parent introducing two new best friends to each other. Clearly, he hadn't guessed my unfortunate history with surrogate children. My first, a Betsy Wetsy, if she'd survived, would have had to enter therapy at some point in her life. At age six, I thought it was a bore to be constantly feeding her those tiny bottles of water and it annoyed me no end every time she peed in my lap. Once I figured out it was the water, I quit feeding her altogether and then I used her as the pedestrian I ran over with my trike. This was my definition of motherly love and probably explains why I'm not a parent today.

"How many Barbies do you have?" I asked, feigning enthusiasm for the little proto-women.

"A little over two thousand. That's the star of my collection, a number one Barbie still in her original package. The seal's been broken, but she's in near-mint condition. I'm afraid to tell you what I paid," she said. Her speech was uninflected, her manner without affect. She made little eye contact, addressing most of her comments to the doll as she worked. "Homer's always been very supportive."

"I can see that," I said.

"I'm a bit of a purist. A lot of collectors are interested in others in the line—you know, Francie, Tuttie and Todd, Jamie, Skipper, Christie, Cara, Casey, Buffy. I never cared for them myself. And certainly not Ken. Did you have a Barbie as a kid?"

"I can't say I did," I said. I picked one up and examined her. "She looks like she's suffering from some sort of eating disorder, doesn't she? What prompted you to get into Chatty Cathys? That seems far afield for a Barbie purist."

"Most of the Chatties aren't mine. I'm repairing them for a friend who runs a business doing this. It's not as far-fetched as it seems. Chatty Cathy was introduced in 1960, the year after Barbie. Chatty Cathy was more realistic—freckles, buck teeth, little pot belly—this in addition to her ability to speak. Even with Barbie, 1967 to 1973 is known as the Talking Era, which includes the Twist 'n' Turn dolls. Few people realize that."

"I know I didn't," I said. "What's that thing?"

"That's the little three-inch vinyl record of Cathy's sayings. When you pull the string, it activates a spring that makes that little rubber belt drive the turntable. The early versions of the doll had eleven sayings, but that was increased to eighteen. Odd thing about Chatties is that no two look alike. Of course, they were mass-produced, but they all seem to be different. It's almost creepy in some ways. Anyway, I'm sure you didn't drive all the way down here to talk about dolls. You're interested in my father."

"Homer filled me in, but I'd like to hear your version. I understand he and Alfie Toth spent some time with you just after they were released from Chino."

"That's right. Pops was feeling sorry for himself because none of the other kids wanted anything to do with him. He tried to spend a night with my brother, Clint—he lives down in Inglewood by the L.A. airport. Clint's still bitter about Pops. He refused to let him in, but he told him he could sleep in the toolshed if he wanted to. Pops was furious, of course, so he left in a huff, but not before he broke into Clint's house. Him and Alfie waited 'til Clint was gone, stole his cash, and busted up all his furniture."

"That must have been a big hit. Did Clint report it to the police?"

Dolores seemed startled, the first real reaction I'd seen. "Why would he do that?"

"I've heard there was a plainclothes detective trying to serve a warrant against Toth around the time of his death. I'm wondering if it dated back to that same incident."

Dolores shook her head. "I'm sure not. Clint would never do a thing like that. He might not want Pops in his house, but he'd never snitch on him. It's odd, but when my sister Mame called—this was just about a year ago—to say they'd found his body, I started laughing so hard I peed my pants. Homer had to call the doctor when it turned out I couldn't quit. Doctor gave me a shot to calm me down. He said it was hysteria, but it was actually relief. We hadn't heard from him for five years by then so I guess I was waiting for the other shoe to drop."

"Why do you think he went from Clint's to Lake Tahoe?"

"My sister lives up there. Or one of them, at any rate. Not in Lake Tahoe exactly, but that vicinity."

"Really? I've been curious what prompted him to travel in that direction."

"I don't think Mame's husband was any happier to see him than Homer was."

"How long was he with her?"

"A week or so. Mame told me later him and Alfie

went off to go fishing and that's the last anyone ever saw Pops as far as I know."

"Do you think I could talk to her? I'm sure the police have covered this ground, but it would be helpful to me."

"Oh, sure. She isn't hard to find. She works as a clerk in the sheriff's department up there."

"Up there where?"

"Nota Lake. Her name is Margaret, but everybody in the family calls her Mame."

SEVENTEEN

When I got home, Henry was in the backyard, kneeling in the flower bed. I crossed the lawn, pausing to watch him at work. He was aware of my presence, but seemed content with the quiet. He wore a white T-shirt and farmer's pants with padded knees. His feet were bare, long, and bony, the high arches very white against the faded grass. The air was sweet and mild. Even with the noon sun directly overhead, the temperature was moderate. I could already see crocuses and hyacinths coming up in clusters beside the garage. I sat down on a wooden lawn chair while he turned the soil with a hand trowel. The earth was soft and damp, worms recoiling from the intrusion when his efforts disturbed them. His rose bushes were barren sticks, bristling with thorns, the occasional leaf bud suggesting that spring was on its way. The lawn, which had been dormant much of the winter, was beginning to waken with the encouragement of recent rains. I could see a haze of green where the new blades were beginning to push up through the brown. "People tend to associate autumn with death, but spring always seems a lot closer to me," he remarked.

"Why's that?"

"There's no deep philosophical significance. Somehow in my history, a lot of people I love have ended up dying this time of year. Maybe they yearn to look out the window and see new leaves on the trees. It's a time of hope and that might be enough if you're on your way out; allows you to let go, knowing the world is moving on as it always has."

"I have to go back to Nota Lake," I said.

"When?"

"Sometime next week. I'd like to hang out here long enough to get my hand back in working order."

"Why go at all?"

"I have to talk to someone."

"Can't you do that by phone?"

"It's too easy for people to tell lies on the phone. I like to see faces," I said. I was silent, listening to the homely chucking of his trowel in the dirt. I pulled my legs up and wrapped my arms around my knees. "Remember in the old days when we talked about vibes?"

I could see Henry smile. "You have bad vibes?"

"The worst." I held up my right hand and tried flexing the fingers, which were still so swollen and stiff I could barely make a fist.

"Don't go. You don't have anything to prove."

"Of course I do, Henry. I'm a girl. We're always having to prove something."

"Like what?"

"That we're tough. That we're as good as the guys, which I'm happy to report is not that hard."

"If it's true, why do you have to prove it?"

"Comes with the turf. Just because we believe it, doesn't mean guys do."

"Who cares about men? Don't be macha."

"I can't help it. Anyway, this isn't about pride. This is about mental health. I can't afford to let some guy intimidate me like that. Trust me, somewhere up in Nota Lake he's laughing his ass off, thinking he's run me out of town."

"The Code of the West. A girl's gotta do what a girl's gotta do."

"It feels bad. The whole thing. I don't remember feeling this much dread. That son of a bitch *hurt* me. I hate giving him the opportunity to do it again."

"At least your tetanus shot's up to date."

"Yeah, and my butt still hurts. I got a knot on my hip the size of a hard-boiled egg."

"So what worries you?"

"What worries me is I got my fingers dislocated before I knew jack-shit. Now that I'm getting closer, what's the guy going to do? You think he'll go down without trying to take me with him?"

"Phone's ringing," he remarked.

"God, Henry. How can you hear that? You're eighty-six years old."

"Three rings."

I was off the chair and halfway across the yard by then. I left my door open and caught the phone on the fly, just as the machine kicked in. I pressed STOP, effectively cutting off the message. "Hello, hello, hello."

"Kinsey, is that you? I thought this was your machine."

"Hi, Selma. You lucked out. I was out in the yard."

"I'm sorry to have to bother you."

"Not a problem. What's up?"

"Someone's been searching Tom's study. I know this sounds odd, but I'm sure someone came in here and moved the items on his desk. It's not like the room was trashed, but something's off. I can't see that anything's missing and I don't know how I'd prove it even if there was."

"How'd they get in?"

She hesitated. "I was only gone for an hour, maybe slightly more. I hardly ever lock the door for short periods like that."

"What makes you so sure someone was there?"

"I can't explain. I'd been sitting in Tom's den earlier, before I went out. I was feeling depressed and it seemed like a comfort just to sit in his chair. You know how it is when you think about things. You're aware of your surroundings because your gaze tends to wander while your mind is elsewhere. I guess I was realizing how much work you'd done. Anyway, when I got home, I set my handbag on the kitchen table and went back to the car. I'd picked up some boxes to finish packing Tom's books. The minute I walked into his den I could see the difference."

"You haven't had any visitors?"

"Oh, please. You know how people have been treating me. I might as well hang out a sign . . . 'Town siren. Straying husbands apply here.'"

"What about Brant? How do you know he wasn't in there looking for something on Tom's desk?"

"I asked him, but he was at Sherry's until a few

minutes ago. I had him check the perimeter, but there's no sign of forced entry."

"Who'd bother to force entrance with all the doors unlocked?" I said. "Can Brant tell if anything's missing?"

"He's in the same boat I'm in. It's certainly nothing obvious, if it's anything at all. Whoever it was seemed to work with great care. It was only coincidental that I'd been in there this morning or I don't think I'd have noticed. Do you think I should call the sheriff's office?"

"Yeah, you better do that," I said. "Later, if it turns out something's been stolen, you can follow up."

"That's what Brant said." There was a tiny pause while she changed tacks, her voice assuming a faintly injured tone. "I must say, I've been upset about your lack of communication. I've been waiting to hear from you."

"Sorry, but I haven't had the chance. I was going to call you in a bit," I said. I noticed how defensive I sounded in response to her reproof.

"Now that I have you on the line, could you tell me what's happening? I assume you're still working even if you haven't kept in touch."

"Of course." I controlled my desire to bristle and I filled her in on my activities the past day and a half, sidestepping the personal aspects of Tom's relationship with Colleen Sellers. Telling a partial truth is much harder than an outright lie. Here I was, trying to protect her, while she was chiding me for neglect. Talk about ungrateful. I was tempted to tell all, but I repressed the urge. I kept my tone of voice professional, while my inner kid hollered *Up yours*. "Tom came down here in

June as part of an investigation. Do you remember the occasion? He was probably gone overnight."

"Yes," she said, slowly. "It was two days. What's the relevance?"

"There was a homicide down here Tom felt was connected to some skeletal remains found in Nota County last spring."

"I know the case you're referring to. He didn't say much about it, but I know it bothered him. What about it?"

"Well, if we're talking about an active homicide investigation, I don't have the authority. I'm a private investigator, which is the equivalent of doing freelance research. I can't, even on your say-so, stick my nose into police business."

"I don't see why not. Surely, there's no law against asking questions."

"I *have* asked questions and I'm telling you what I found. Tom was stressed out about matters that had nothing to do with you."

"Why didn't he tell me what it was, if that's true?"

"You were the one who said he played things close to his chest, especially when it came to work."

"Well yes, but if this is strictly professional, then why would someone go to all the trouble to search the house?"

"Maybe the department needed his notes or his files or a telephone number or a missing report. It could be anything," I said, rattling off the possibilities as quickly as they occurred to me.

"Why didn't they call and ask?"

"How do I know? Maybe they were in a hurry and

you weren't home," I said, exasperated. It all sounded lame, but she was backing me into corners and it was annoying me no end.

"Kinsey, I am paying you to get to the bottom of this. If I'd known you weren't going to help, I could have used that fifteen hundred dollars to get my teeth capped."

"I'm doing what I can! What do you want from me?" I said.

"Well, you needn't take *that* attitude. A week ago, you were cooperative. Now all I'm hearing are excuses."

I had to bite my tongue. I had to talk in very distinct, clipped syllables to keep from screaming at her. I took a deep breath. "Look, I have one lead left. As soon as I get up there, I'll be happy to check it out, but if this is sheriff's department business, then it's out of my hands."

There was one of those silences that sounded like it contained an exclamation point. "If you don't want to finish the job, why don't you come right out and say so?"

"I'm not saying that."

"Then when are you coming back?"

"I'm not sure yet. Next week. Maybe Tuesday."

"Next *week*?" she said. "What's wrong with today? If you got in your car now, you could be here in six hours."

"What's the big hurry? This has been going on for weeks."

"Well, for one thing, you still owe me five hundred dollars' worth of work. For that kind of money, I would think you'd want to get here as soon as possible."

"Selma, I'm not going to sit here and argue about this. I'll do what I can."

"Wonderful. What time shall I expect you?"

"I have no idea."

"Surely, you can give me *some* idea when you might arrive. I have other obligations. I'll be gone all day tomorrow. I go to ten o'clock service and then spend some time with my cousin down in Big Pine. I can't sit around waiting for you to show up any time it suits. Besides, if you're coming, I'll need to make arrangements."

"I'll call when I get there, but I'm not going to stay at the Nota Lake Cabins. I hate that place and I won't be put in that position. It's too remote and it's dangerous."

"Fine," she said, promptly. "You can stay here at the house with me."

"I wouldn't dream of imposing. I'll find another motel so there won't be any inconvenience for either one of us."

"It's no inconvenience. I could use the company. Brant thinks it's high time he moved back to his place. He's already in the process of packing up. The guest room is always ready. I insist. I'll have supper waiting and no arguments about that, please."

"We'll talk about it when I get there," I said, trying to conceal my irritation. I was rapidly reassessing my opinion of the woman, ready to cast my vote with her legions of detractors. This was a side of her I hadn't seen before and I was churning with indignation. Of course, I noticed I'd already started revising my mental timetable, preparing to hit the road as soon as possible. Having consented, in effect, I now found myself wanting to get it over with. I shortened the fare-thee-wells, trying to get her off the phone while I could.

The minute I replaced the receiver, I picked it up again and placed a call to Colleen Sellers. While the interminable ringing of her line went on, I could feel my impatience mount. "Come on, come on. Be there . . ."

"Hello?"

"Colleen, it's Kinsey here."

"What can I do for you?"

She didn't sound that thrilled to hear from me, but I was through pussy-footing around. "I just spent thirty minutes with Pinkie Ritter's daughter Dolores and her husband. Turns out Pinkie has another daughter in Nota Lake, which is why he and Alfie went up there in the first place."

"And?"

"This is someone I've met, a woman named Margaret who works for the sheriff's department as a clerk. I'm going to have to go back up there and talk to her again, but I can't go without knowing what I'm up against."

"Why call me? I can't help."

"Yes, you can . . ."

"Kinsey, I don't know anything about this and frankly, I'm annoyed you keep pressing the point."

"Well, *frankly*, I guess I'll just have to risk your irritation. What's the matter with you, Colleen?"

"Does it ever occur to you that I might find this painful? I mean, I'm sorry as hell for Selma, but she's not the only one who's suffered a loss. I was in love with him, too, and I don't appreciate your constantly picking at the wound."

"Oh, really. Well, it's interesting that you should say

so because you want to know what I think is going on? I think it pisses you off that you never had any power or any control in that relationship. Tom may have taken the moral high ground, acting from his lofty-sounding principles, but the fact is he left you with nothing and this is your payback."

"That's not true."

"Try again," I said.

"What's to pay back? He never did anything to me."

"Tom was a tease. He was willing to flirt, but he was quick to draw lines you couldn't cross. He could afford to enjoy your attention because it didn't cost him a thing. He accepted the tribute without taking any risks, which meant he got to feel virtuous while you were left like a kid with your nose pressed to the glass. You could see what you wanted, but you weren't allowed to touch. And now you're thinking that's the best you'll ever have, which is *really* bullshit because you didn't have anything. All this talk about pain is an attempt to sanctify a big, fat, emotional zero." I knew I was only ragging on her because Selma had ragged on me, but it felt good nonetheless. Later, I'd feel guilty for being such a bitch, but for now it seemed like the only way to get what I wanted.

She was silent for a moment. I could hear the intake of cigarette smoke, followed by the exhale of her breath. "Maybe."

"Maybe, my ass. It's the truth," I said. "Everybody sees him as noble, but I think he was supremely egotistical. How honorable was he when he never had the courage to tell his wife?"

"Tell her what?"

"That he was tempted to be unfaithful because of his attraction to you. He didn't act on his feelings, but it's no bloody wonder she ended up feeling insecure. And what did it net you? You're still hung up on him and you may never get yourself off the hook."

"Look, you really don't know what you're talking about so let's skip all the homegrown psychology. Tell me what you want and get it over with."

"You have to level with me."

"Why?"

"Because my life may depend on it," I snapped. "Come on, Colleen. You're a professional. You know better. You sit there doling out little tidbits of information, hanging on to the crumbs because it's all you have. This is serious damn shit. If Tom were in your position, do you think he'd withhold information in a situation like this?"

She inhaled again. "Probably not." Grudgingly.

"Then let's get on with it. If you know what's going on, for god's sake, let's have it."

She seemed to hesitate. "Tom was facing a moral crisis. I was the easy part, but I wasn't all of it."

"What do you mean, you were the easy part?"

"I'm not sure how to explain. I think he could do the right thing with me and it was a comfort to him. That situation made sense while the other problem he was facing was more complicated."

"You're just guessing at this or do you know for a fact?"

"Well, Tom never came out and said so, but he did allude to the issue. Something about not knowing how to reconcile his head and his gut."

"In regard to what?"

"He felt responsible for Toth's murder."

"He felt *responsible*? How come?"

"A breach of confidentiality."

"As in what? I don't get it."

"Toth's whereabouts," she said. "I gave him the address and phone number of the Gramercy. Tom thought someone used the information to track Toth down and kill him. It was driving him crazy to think the man might have died because of his carelessness."

I felt myself blinking at the phone, trying to make sense of what she'd said. "But Selma tells me Tom was always tight-lipped. That was one of her complaints. He never talked about anything, especially when it came to his work."

"It wasn't *talk* at all. He thought someone took an unauthorized look at his notes."

"But his notebook is missing."

"Well, it wasn't back then."

"Who did he suspect? Did he ever mention a name?"

"Someone he worked with. And that's my guess, by the way, not something he said to me directly. Why else would it bother him if it wasn't someone betraying the department?"

I felt myself grow still. I flashed on the officers I'd met in Nota Lake: Rafer LaMott; Tom's brother Macon; Hatch Brine; James Tennyson; Earlene's husband, Wayne. Even Deputy Carey Badger who'd taken my report on the night of the assault. The list seemed to go on and on and all of them were connected with the Nota Lake Sheriff's Department or the CHP. At the back of my mind, I'd been flirting with a possibility I'd scarcely dared to admit. What I'd been harboring was the suspicion that my attacker had been trained at a police academy. I'd been resisting the notion, but I could feel it begin to take root in my imagination. He'd taken me down with an efficiency I'd been taught once upon a time myself. Whether he was currently employed in some branch of law enforcement, I couldn't be sure, but the very idea left me feeling cold. "Are you telling me one of Tom's colleagues was involved in a double homicide?"

"I think that was his suspicion and it was tearing him apart. Again, this wasn't something he said. This is my best guess."

This time I was silent for a moment. "I should have seen that. How stupid of me. Shit."

"What will you do now?"

"Beats the hell out of me. What would you suggest?"

"Why not talk to someone in Internal Affairs?"

"And say what? I'm certainly willing to give them anything I have, but at this point, it's all speculation, isn't it?"

"Well, yes. I guess that's one reason I didn't call myself. I've got nothing concrete. Maybe if you talk to Pinkie's daughter up there, it will clarify the situation."

"Meanwhile alerting the guy that I'm breathing down his neck," I said.

"But you can't do this on your own."

"Who'm I gonna call? The Nota Lake Sheriff's Department?"

"I'm not sure I'd do that," she said, laughing for once.

"Yeah, well if I figure it out, I'll let you know," I

said. "Any other comments or advice while we're on the subject?"

She thought about it briefly. "Well, one thing . . . though you may have already thought about this. It must have been general knowledge Tom was working on this case, so once he dropped dead, the guy must have thought he was home free."

"And now I come along. Bad break," I said. "Of course, the guy can't be sure how much information Tom passed to his superiors."

"Exactly. If it's not in his reports, it might still be in circulation somewhere, especially with his notes gone. You'd better hope you get to 'em before someone else does."

"Maybe the guy already has them in his possession."

"Then why's he afraid of you? You're only dangerous if you have the notes," she said.

I thought about the search of Tom's den. "You're right."

"I'd proceed with care."

"Trust me," I said. "One more question while I have you on the line. Were you ever in Nota Lake yourself?"

"Are you kidding? Tom was too nervous to see me there."

I replaced the receiver, distracted. My anxiety level was rising ominously, like a toilet on the verge of overflowing. The fear was like something damp and heavy sinking into my bones. I have a thing about authority figures, specifically police officers in uniform, probably dating from that first encounter while I was trapped in the wreckage of my parents' VW at the age of five. I can still remember the horror and the relief of being rescued by those big guys with their guns and night-sticks. Still, the sense of jeopardy and pain also attached to that image. At five, I wasn't capable of separating the two. In terms of confusion and loss, what I'd experienced was irrevocably bound up with the sight of men in uniform. As a child, I'd been taught the police were my pals, people to turn to if you were lost or afraid. At the same time, I knew police had the power to put you in jail, which made them fearful to contemplate if you were sometimes as "bad" as I was. In retrospect, I can see that I'd applied to the police academy, in part, to ally myself with the very folks I feared. Being on the side of the law was, no doubt, my attempt to cope with that old anxiety. Most of the officers I'd known since had been decent, caring people, which made it all the more alarming to think that one might have crossed the line. I couldn't think when anything had frightened me quite as much as the idea of going up against this guy, but what could I do? If I quit this one, then what? The next time I got scared, was I going to quit that job, too?

I went up the spiral stairs and dutifully started shoving items in my duffel.

EIGHTEEN

The ocean was white with fog, the horizon fading into milk a hundred yards offshore. The sun behind clouds created a harsh, nearly blinding light. Colors seemed flattened by the haze, which lent a chill to the air. A quick check of the weather channel before I'd departed showed heavy precipitation in the area of California where I was headed and within the first twenty-five miles, I could already begin to sense the shift.

I took Highway 126 through Santa Paula and Fillmore until I ran into Highway 5, where I doglegged over to Highway 14. I drove through canyon country—balding, brown hills, tufted with chapparel, as wrinkled and hairy as elephants. Power lines marched across the folds of the earth while the highway spun six lanes of concrete through the cuts and crevices. Residential developments had sprung up everywhere, the ridges dotted with tract houses so that the natural rock formations looked strangely out of place. There was evidence of construction still in progress—earth movers, concrete mixers, temporary equipment yards enclosed in wire fencing in which heavy machinery was being housed for the duration. An occasional Porta-Potty occupied the wide aisle between lanes of the freeway. The land was the color of dry dirt and dried grass. Trees were few and didn't seem to assert much of a presence out here.

By the time I'd passed Edwards Air Force Base, driving in a straight line north, the sky was gray. The clouds collected in ascending layers that blocked out the fading sun overhead. The drizzle that began to fall looked more like a fine vapor sheeting through the air. Misty-looking communities appeared in the distance, flat and small, laid out in a grid, like an outpost on the moon. Closer to the road, there would be an occasional outbuilding, left over from god knows what decade. The desert, while unforgiving, nevertheless tolerates man-made structures, which remain—lopsided, with broken windows, roofs collapsing—long after the inhabitants have died or moved on. I could see the entire expanse of rain-swept plains to the rim of hushed buff-colored mountains. The telephone poles, extending into the horizon ahead of me, could have served as a lesson in perspective. Behind the barren, pointed hills, rugged granite out-croppings grew darker as the rain increased. Gradually, the road moved into the foothills. The mountains beyond them were imposing. Nothing marred the featureless, pale surface—no trees, no grass, no mark of human passage. At higher elevations, I could see vegetation where low-hanging clouds provided sufficient moisture to support growth.

I'd tucked my semiautomatic in the duffel. The gun experts, Dietz among them, were quick to scoff at the little Davis, but it was a handgun I knew and it felt far more familiar to me than the Heckler and Koch, a more recent acquisition. Given the condition of my bunged-up fingers, I doubted I'd be capable of pulling the trigger in any event, but the gun was a comfort in my current apprehensive state.

Little by little, I was giving up my initial irritation with Selma. As with anything else, once a process is under way, there's no point in railing against the Fates. I regretted that I hadn't had time to contact Leland Peck, the clerk at the Gramercy Hotel. I'd taken his co-worker's word that he had nothing to report. Any good investigator knows better. I should have taken the trouble to look him up so I could quiz him about his recollections of the plainclothes detective with the warrant for Toth's arrest.

In the meantime, secure in my ignorance of events to come, I thought idly of the night ahead. I truly hate being a guest in someone's home. The bed seldom suits me. The blankets are usually skimpy. The pillows are flat or made out of hard rubber that smells of half-deflated basketballs. The toilet refuses to flush fully or the handle gets stuck or the paper runs out so that you're forced to search all the cabinets looking for the ever so cunningly hidden supply. Worst of all, you have to "make nice" at all hours. I don't want someone across the table from me while I'm eating my breakfast. I don't want to share the newspaper and I don't want to talk to anyone at the end of the day. If I were interested in that shit, I'd be married again by now and put a permanent end to all the peace and quiet.

By the time I arrived in Nota Lake at 6:45, night had settled on the landscape and the weather was truly nasty. The drizzle had intensified into a stinging sleet. My windshield wipers labored, collecting slush in an arc that nearly filled my windshield. My guess was the people of Nota Lake, like others in perpetually cold climates, had strategies for coping with the shifting character of snow. From my limited experience, the freezing rain seemed extremely hazardous, making the roadway as slick as a skating rink. In moments, I could feel the vehicle slide sideways and I slowed to a snail's pace. At the road's edge, the dead grass had stiffened, collecting feathery drifts of whirling snow. Selma had bullied me into having supper with her. I'm easily influenced in food matters, having been conditioned these past years by Rosie's culinary imperiousness. When ordered about by any woman with a certain autocratic tone, I do as I'm told, largely helpless to resist.

I parked out in front of Selma's, snagged my duffel, and hurried to the front porch, head bent, shoulders hunched as though to avoid the combination of blowing rain and biting snow. I knocked politely, shifting impatiently from foot to foot until she opened the door. We exchanged the customary chitchat as I stepped into the foyer and dried my feet on a rag rug. I shrugged off my leather jacket and eased out of my shoes, conscious of the pristine carpet. The house was toasty warm, hazy from the cigarette smoke sealed into the winterproofed rooms. I shivered with belated relief at being out of the cold. I padded after Selma, who showed me to the guest room. "Take whatever time you need to freshen up and get settled. I cleared some space in the closet and emptied a drawer for your things. I'll be out in the kitchen putting the finishing touches on supper. You know your way around, but don't hesitate to holler if you need anything."

"Thanks."

Once the door closed behind me, I surveyed the room with dismay. The carpet here was hot pink, a cut-pile cotton shag. There was a four-poster bed with a canopy and a puffy, quilted spread of pink-and-white checked gingham. The same fabric continued in the dust ruffle and ruffled pillow shams, stacked three deep. A collection of six quilted teddy bears was grouped together in a window seat. The wallpaper was pink-and-white stripes with a floral border across the top. There was an old-fashioned vanity table with a padded seat and a pink-and-white ruffled skirt. Everything was trimmed in oversized white rickrack. The guest bath was an extension of this jaunty decorative theme, complete with a crocheted cozy for the extra roll of toilet paper. The room smelled as though it had been closed up for some time and the heat here seemed more intense than in the rest of the house. I could feel myself start to hyperventilate with the craving for fresh air.

I crossed to the window, like a hot prowl thief trying to escape. I managed to inch up the sash, only to be faced with a seriously constructed double-glazed storm window. I worked at the latches until I loosened all of them. I gave the storm window a push and it fell promptly out of the frame and dropped into the bushes below. *Oops.* I stuck my head through the gap and let the blessed sleet blow across my face. The storm window had landed just beyond my grasp so I left it where it was, resting in the junipers. I lowered the sash again and adjusted the ruffled curtains so the missing storm window wasn't evident. At least, at bedtime, I could sleep in a properly refrigerated atmosphere.

Selma had urged me to freshen up and I used her advice to stall my return to the kitchen. I peed, washed my hands, and brushed my teeth, happy to occupy my time with these homely ablutions. I stood in the bathroom and stared at myself in the mirror, wondering if I'd ever develop an interest in the painful process of plucking my eyebrows. Not likely. My jaw was still bruised and I paused to admire the ever-changing hue. Then I stood in the bedroom and did a quick visual scan. I removed my handgun from the duffel and hid it between the mattress and the box springs near the head of the bed. This would fool no one, but it would allow me to keep the gun close. I didn't think it would be wise to pack a rod in this town, especially without the proper permit. Finally, there was nothing for it but to take a deep breath and present myself at the supper table.

Selma seemed subdued. Her attitude surprised me, given the fact that she'd gotten her way. I was back in Nota Lake, staying at her house, which was the last thing I wanted. "I kept everything simple. I hope you don't mind," she said.

"This is fine," I said.

She took a moment to stub out her cigarette, blowing the final stream of smoke to one side. This, for a smoker, constitutes etiquette. We pulled out our chairs and took seats at the kitchen table.

Given my usual diet, a home-cooked meal of any kind is an extraordinary treat. Or so I thought before I was faced with the one she'd prepared. This was the menu: iced tea with Sweet 'N Low already mixed in, a green Jell-O square with fruit cocktail and an internal ribbon of Miracle Whip, iceberg lettuce with bottled dressing the color of a sunset. For the main course, instant mashed potatoes with margarine and a stout slice of meatloaf, swimming in diluted cream of mushroom soup. As I ate, my fork exposed a couple of pockets of dried mashed potato flakes. The meatloaf was strongly reminiscent of something served at the Perdido County Jail, where there was an entire (much-dreaded) punishment referred to as being "on meatloaf." On meatloaf means an inmate is placed on a diet of meatloaf and two slices of squishy white bread twice a day, with only drinking water from the faucet. The meatloaf, a six-inch patty made of turkey, kidney beans, and other protein-rich filler, is served on something nominally known as gravy. Every third day the law mandates that the inmate has to be served three square meals for one day, then back to meatloaf. By comparison to Selma's version, a simple QP with cheese came off looking like a gourmet feast. Especially since I knew for a fact she didn't feed Brant this way.

Selma was quiet throughout the meal and I didn't have much to contribute. I felt like one of those married couples you see out in restaurants—not looking at each other, not bothering to say a word. The minute we'd finished eating, she lit up another cigarette so I wouldn't miss a minute of the tars and noxious gases wafting across the table. "Would you like coffee or dessert? I have a nice coconut cream pie in the freezer. It won't take a minute to thaw. I can pop it in the microwave."

"Golly, I'm full. This was great."

"Are you cold? I saw you shiver. I can turn the heat up if you like."

"No, no. Really. I'm toasty warm. This was wonderful."

She tapped her cigarette ash on the edge of her plate. "I didn't ask you about your fingers."

I held up my right hand. "They're a little stiff yet, but better."

"Well, that's good. Now that you're back, what's the plan?"

"I was just thinking about that," I said. "I'm not sure what to make of this and I don't want it going any further, but I think I have a line on what was bothering Tom."

"Really?"

"After we spoke this morning, I made another phone call. Without going into any detail . . ." I paused. "I'm not even sure how to tell you this. It seems awkward."

"For heaven's sake. Just say it."

"It looks like Tom suspected a fellow officer in that double homicide he was investigating."

Selma looked at me, blinking, while she absorbed the information. She took a deep drag of her cigarette and blew out a sharp stream of smoke. "I don't believe it."

"I know it sounds incredible, but stop and think about it for a minute. Tom was trying to establish the link between the two victims, right?"

"Yes."

"Well, apparently he believed one of his colleagues lifted Alfie Toth's address from his field notes. Toth was murdered shortly afterward. Toth was always on the move, but he'd just gotten out of jail and he was living temporarily in a fleabag hotel. This was the first time anyone had managed to pin him down to one location.

No one else in Nota Lake knew where Alfie Toth was hanging out except him."

"What makes you so sure? He might have mentioned it to someone. Or someone else might have come up with the information independently," she said.

"You're right about that. The point is, Tom must have gone crazy thinking he played a role in Alfie's death. Worse yet, suspecting someone in the department had a hand in it."

"But you don't really *know*," she said. "This is just a guess on your part."

"How are we ever going to *know* anything unless someone 'fesses up? And that seems unlikely. I mean, so far this 'someone' has gotten away with it."

"Who told you this?"

"Don't worry about that. It was someone with the sheriff's department. A confidential source."

"Confidential, my foot. You're making a serious allegation."

"You think I don't know that? Of course I am," I said. "Look, I don't like the idea any better than you do. That's why I came back, to pin it down."

"And if you can't?"

"Then, frankly, I'm out of ideas. There is one possibility. Pinkie Ritter's daughter, Margaret . . ."

Selma frowned. "That's right. I'd forgotten their relationship. The connection seems odd, what with her working for Tom."

"Nota Lake's a small town. The woman has to work somewhere, so why not the sheriff's department? Everybody else seems to work there," I pointed out.

"Why didn't she speak up when you were here before?"

"I didn't know about Ritter until yesterday."

"I think you better talk to Rafer."

"I think it's best to keep him out of this for now." I caught the odd look that crossed her face. "What?"

She hesitated. "I ran into him this afternoon and told him you'd be back this evening."

I felt my eyes roll in despair and I longed to bang my head on the table top just one time for emphasis. "I wish you'd kept quiet. It's hard enough as it is. Everybody here knows everybody else's business."

She waved aside my objection like a pesky horsefly sailing through the smoke-filled air. "Don't be silly. He was Tom's best friend. What will you do?"

"I'll talk to Margaret tonight and see what she knows," I said. "After that, my only option is to go back to Santa Teresa and confer with the sheriff's department there."

"And tell them what? You don't have much."

"I don't have *anything*," I said. "Unless something develops, I'm at a dead loss."

"I see. Then I suppose that's it." Selma stubbed out her cigarette and got up without another word. She began to clear the dinner dishes, moving from the table to the sink.

"Let me help you with that," I said, getting up to assist.

"Don't trouble." Her tone of voice was frosty, her manner withdrawn.

I began to gather up plates and silverware, moving to the sink where she was already scraping leftover

Jell-O into the garbage disposal. She ran water across a plate, opened the door to the dishwasher, and placed it in the lower rack. The silence was uncomfortable and the clattering of plates contained a note of agitation.

"Is something on your mind?" I asked.

"I hope I didn't make a mistake in hiring you."

I glanced at her sharply. "I never offered you a guarantee. No responsible P.I. could make a promise like that. Sometimes the information simply isn't there," I said.

"That's not what I meant."

"Then what were you referring to?"

"I never even asked you for references."

"A little late at this point. You want to talk to some of my past employers, I'll make up a list."

She was silent again. I was having trouble tracking the change in her demeanor. Maybe she thought I was giving up. "I'm not saying I'll quit," I said.

"I understand. You're saying you're out of your league."

"You want to go up against the cops? Personally, I've got more sense."

She banged a plate down so hard it broke down the middle into two equal pieces. "My husband *died*."

"I know that. I'm sorry."

"No, you're not. Nobody gives a shit what I've gone through."

"Selma, you hired me to do this and I'm doing it. Yes, I'm out of my league. So was Tom, for that matter. Look what happened to him. It fuckin' broke his heart."

She stood at the sink, letting the hot water run while her shoulders shook. Tears coursed along her cheeks. I stood there for a moment, wondering what to do. It seemed clear she'd go on weeping until I acted sincerely moved. I patted her awkwardly, making little murmurings. I pictured Tom doing much the same thing in his life, probably in this very spot. Water gurgled down the drain while the tears poured down her face. Finally, I couldn't stand it. I reached over and turned off the water. Live through enough droughts, you hate to see the waste. Where originally her grief had seemed genuine, I now suspected the emotion was being hauled out for effect. At long last, with much blowing and peeking at her nose products, she pulled herself together. We finished up the dishes and Selma retreated to her room, emerging shortly afterward in her nightie and robe, intending to make herself a glass of hot milk and get in bed. I fled the house as soon as it was decently possible. Nothing like being around a self-appointed invalid to make you feel hard-hearted.

Margaret and Hatch lived close to the center of town on Second Street. I'd called from Selma's before I left the house. I'd scarcely identified myself when she cut in, saying, "Dolores said you came to see her. What's this about?"

In light of her father's murder, the answer seemed obvious. "I'm trying to figure out what happened to your father," I said. "I wondered if it'd be possible to talk to you tonight. Is this a bad time for you?"

She'd seemed nonplussed at my request, conceding with reluctance. I couldn't understand her attitude, but I wrote it off to my imagination. After all, the subject had to be upsetting, especially in light of his past abusiveness. Twice she put a palm across the mouthpiece and conferred with someone in the background. My assumption was that it was Hatch, but she made no specific reference to him.

The drive over was uneventful, despite the treacherous roads and the continuous sleet. There was no accumulation of snow so far, but the pavement was glistening and my tires tended to sing every time I hit a slippery patch. I had to use the brakes judiciously, pumping gently from half a block back when I saw the stoplights ahead of me change. Paranoid as I was at that point, I did note the close proximity of the Brine's house to the parking lot at Tiny's Tavern where I'd been accosted. Once Wayne and Earlene dropped the Brines off at home, Hatch could easily have doubled back. I found myself scouring the streets for sight of a black panel truck, but of course saw nothing.

I entered a tract of brick ranch houses maybe fifteen years old, judging from the maturity of the landscaping. Tree trunks were now sturdy, maybe eight inches in diameter, and the foundation plantings had long ago crept over the windowsills. I slowed when I spotted the house number. The Brines had two cars and a pickup truck parked in or near the drive. I found a parking spot two doors down and sat at the curb wondering if there was a party in progress. I turned in my seat and studied the house. There were dim lights in front, brighter lights around the side and toward the portion of the rear that I could see from my vantage point. This was Saturday night. She hadn't mentioned a Tupperware party or Bible study, nor had she suggested I come at some other time. Maybe they were having friends in to watch a little network television. I debated with myself. I didn't like the idea of walking into a social gathering, especially since I could always talk to her tomorrow. On the other hand, she'd said I could come and meeting with her tonight would delay my return to Selma's. I still had a key to her place and the plan was for me to let myself in the front door whenever I got back that night. The car became noticeably colder the longer I sat. The neighborhood was quiet with little traffic and no one visible on foot. Someone peeking out the windows would think I'd come to case the joint.

I got out of the car and locked the doors. The side-walks must have been warmer than the streets. Snowflakes melted instantly, leaving shallow pools in lieu of icy patches. The trees in the yard were some deciduous variety, caught by surprise with tiny green buds in sight. March in this area must have been a constant series of nature pranks. I knocked on the door, hoping I wasn't walking in on a naughty lingerie party. Maybe that's why she'd invited me, in hopes I'd purchase a drawerful of underpants to replace all my tatty ones.

Margaret opened the door wearing blue jeans and a thick, red sweater with a Nordic design across the front; snowflakes and reindeer. She wore clunky calf-high suede boots with a sheepskin lining that must have felt warm on a night like this. With her black hair and oval glasses, she looked like a teenager hired to babysit. "Hi. Come on in."

"Thanks. I hope I'm not interrupting. I saw cars in the drive."

"Hatch's poker night. The boys are in the den," she said, hooking a thumb toward the rear. "I'm on kitchen detail. We can talk out there."

Like Selma's house, this one smelled as if it had been sealed for the winter, the rubber gaskets on the storm windows insuring the accumulation of smoke and cooking smells. The wall-to-wall carpet was a burnt orange high-low, the walls in the living room painted a shade of café au lait. The eight-foot sofa was a chocolate brown with two black canvas butterfly chairs arranged on either side of the coffee table. "You didn't have any trouble finding the place?" she asked.

"Not at all," I said. "You prefer Margaret or Mame? I know Dolores refers to you as Mame."

"Either one is fine. Suit yourself."

I followed her to the kitchen at the end of the hall. She was in the process of preparing food, platters of cold cuts on the long wood-grained Formica counter. There were bowls of chips, two containers of some kind of dip made with sour cream, and a mixture of nuts and Chex cereals tossed with butter and garlic powder. I know this because all the ingredients were still in plain view. "If you'll help me move these snacks to the dining room, we can get 'em out of the way and we can talk."

"Sure thing."

She picked up two bowls and shoved the swinging door open with a hip, holding it for me while I moved through with the tray of sliced cheeses and processed meats. Of course, it was all so unwholesome I was immediately hungry, but my appetite didn't last long. Through an archway to my left, I saw Hatch and his five buddies sitting on metal folding chairs at the poker table in the den. There were countless beer bottles and beer mugs in evidence, cigarettes, ashtrays, poker chips, dollar bills, coins, bowls of peanuts. To a man, the entire gathering turned to look at me. I recognized Wayne, James Tennyson and Brant; the other two fellows I'd never seen before. Hatch made a comment and James laughed. Brant raised his hand in greeting. Margaret paid little attention to the lot of them, but the chill from the room was unmistakable.

I placed bowls on the table and moved back to the kitchen, trying to behave as though unaffected by their presence. Here's the truth about my life. Just about any jeopardy I encounter in adulthood I experienced first in elementary school. Guys making private jokes have struck me as sinister since I was forced to pass the sixth-grade boys every morning on my way to "kinney garden." Even then, I knew no good could come of such assemblages and I avoid them where possible.

I picked up a platter from the kitchen counter and intercepted Margaret as she reached the swinging door. "Why don't I pass these to you and you can put them on the table," I said, feigning helpfulness. In truth, I couldn't bear subjecting myself to that collective stare.

She took the platter without comment, holding the door open with her hip. "You might want to open a couple more beers. There's some on the bottom shelf of the refrigerator out on the utility porch."

I found six bottles of beer and the beer flip and made myself useful removing caps. Once we'd assembled the eats, Margaret pulled the swinging door shut and sighed with relief. "Lucky they don't play more than once a month," she said. "I told Hatch they should rotate, but he likes to have 'em here. Usually Earlene tags along with Wayne and helps me set up, but she's coming down with a cold and I told her to stay home. Shit . . . excuse my language . . . I forgot to put out the paper plates. I'll be right back." She snatched up a giant package of flimsy paper plates and moved toward the dining room. "You want anything to eat, you can help yourself," she said. As I was still burping meatloaf, I thought it wise to decline.

She came back to the kitchen and tossed the cellophane packaging in the trash, then turned and leaned against the counter, crossing her arms in front. "What can I help you with?" The question suggested cooperation, but her manner was all business.

"I'm just wondering what you can tell me about his last visit. I'm assuming he and Alfie Toth came to the area to see you that spring."

"That's right," she said. As though to distract herself, she began to screw lids on the pickle jars, stowing mustard and mayonnaise back in the refrigerator. "I hope you don't think this is disrespectful, but my father was a loser and we all knew that. Truthfully, I was happiest when he was in jail. He always seemed to cause trouble."

"Was he a problem on this visit?"

"Of course. Mostly chasing women. Like any woman here was that hard up," she said.

"From what little I know, I never pictured him as a ladies' man."

"He wasn't, but he'd just gotten out of jail and he was itching to get laid. He'd be at Tiny's at four, the minute the doors opened. Once he started drinking, he'd hit on anyone who crossed his path. He thought he was irresistible and he'd be angry and combative when his ham-handed flirtations didn't net him what he wanted."

"Anybody in particular?"

Margaret shrugged. "A waitress at the Rainbow and one at Tiny's. Alice, the one with red hair."

"I know her," I said.

"That's all he talked about, how horny he was. *Poontang*, he called it. I was embarrassed. I mean, what kind of talk is that coming from your dad? He couldn't have been more obnoxious. He got in fights. He borrowed money. He dinged the truck. People around here won't tolerate behavior like that. It drove Hatch insane so, of course, the two of us were fighting. Hatch wanted them out of here and I can't say I blamed him. What are you going to do though, your own dad? I could hardly ask him to leave. He'd been here less than a week."

"So what finally happened?"

"We sent him and Alfie off on a fishing trip. Anything to get them out from underfoot for a couple of days. Hatch lent 'em a couple of fishing rods he never did get back. He was p.o.'d about that. Anyway, I don't know what happened, but something must have gone wrong. Next morning, Alfie showed up and said they'd decided to take off and he'd come for their things."

"Where was your father?"

"Alfie told us Daddy was waiting for him and he had to get a move on or Pinkie'd be furious with him. I didn't think anything about it. I mean, it did sound like him. He was always trying to get Alfie to fetch and carry for him."

"Did Tom know all this?"

"I told him in March when Daddy's remains turned up. Once the body was identified, Tom notified me and I passed the news on to the rest of the family. Before that, as far as I knew, Dad was fine."

"Didn't it strike you as odd that no one in the family ever heard from him once he supposedly left here?"

"Why should it? Bad news travels fast. We always figured if something happened to him, someone would be in touch. Police or a hospital. He always carried ID. Besides, we heard from Alfie now and then. I guess the two of them split up, or that's the impression he gave."

"Why did he call?"

Margaret shrugged. "Beats me. Just to see how we were doing is what he said."

"Did he ever ask about your dad?"

"Well, yes, but it wasn't like he really wanted to get in touch. You know how it is. How's your dad? . . . What do you hear from him? . . . And that sort of thing."

"So he was wondering if Pinkie ever showed up again. Is that it?"

"I guess. Finally, he stopped calling and we lost touch with him."

"Maybe he realized Pinkie wasn't ever going to put in an appearance."

"That's what Tom said. He thought Daddy might have been murdered the very day Alfie left, though there was never any way to prove it. One thing they found was a gas receipt he'd tucked in his pocket. That was dated the day before. Him and Alfie filled up the tank on their way to the lake. You think Alfie knew something?"

"Almost certainly," I said.

"Maybe the two of them quarreled."

"It's always possible," I said. "Judging from his behavior, he was either trying to create the impression that Pinkie was alive, or he really wasn't sure himself. The last time you saw him . . . when he stopped by to pick up their belongings . . . did he seem okay to you?"

"Like what?"

"He wasn't nervous or in a hurry?"

"He was in a hurry for sure, but no more than he'd be with Daddy waiting."

"Any signs he'd been in a scuffle?"

"Nothing that I noticed. There wasn't any dirt or scratches."

"How did they plan to travel? Bus, train, plane? Hitchhiking?"

"They must have gone by bus. I mean, that was my assumption because the truck was left over at the Greyhound station. Hatch spotted it in the parking lot later that same day," she said.

NINETEEN

By the time I left Margaret's, it was close to nine-thirty. I unlocked the VW and slid under the wheel, sticking the key in the ignition. A car approached and as it pulled up alongside, I could see that it was Macon, driving a black-and-white. Even through the car window I could tell he was better dressed for the cold than I was. I was wearing my brown leather bomber jacket, but was short the gloves, scarf, and cap. I rolled down my window. His car idled, static from the radio filling the air. The temperature had dropped. I blew on my fingers briefly and then turned the key in the ignition, firing up the VW just to get the engine warm. I adjusted the heat, which in a VW consists of moving one lever from OFF to ON. "What's up?" I asked.

"I'm on tonight anyway so I thought I might as well follow you home. I talked to Selma a little while ago and she told me what was going on. I'm glad you came back. She was worried you'd abandon ship."

"Believe me, I was tempted. I'd rather be at home," I said.

"I remember this Pinkie Ritter business. Ornery son of a gun. Was Margaret any help?"

"About what you'd expect," I said, evading the issue. "I'm heading over to Tiny's. She says he hustled one of the waitresses so I'll see what she says. It might not mean anything, but I could pick up additional information. Maybe a jealous husband or a boyfriend was dealing out paybacks. You have any other suggestions?"

"Not offhand. You seem to be doing pretty good," Macon said, but he didn't sound convinced. "Why don't you let me ask around and see what I can find out. Seems like the fewer people who know what you're after the better."

"My sentiments exactly. Anyway, I better get a move on before I freeze."

Macon glanced at his watch. "How long will this take?"

"Not that long. Thirty minutes at best. I'm not even sure Alice works Saturdays. I'm assuming she does."

"Why don't I follow you as far as the parking lot? I can swing back at ten and follow you to Selma's. If the woman isn't working, have a Coke or something until I show up."

"I'd appreciate that. Thanks."

I rolled up the window and put the car in gear. Macon pulled out first, waiting for me to do a U-turn so I could follow him. With the boys entrenched in their poker game inside, I was feeling safer than I had all day.

The parking lot at Tiny's was packed with cars, RVs, and pickup trucks with camper shells. I tucked the VW into a small gap at the end of the last row. Macon waited, watching me cross two aisles, passing through the shadowy spaces between vehicles. Once I was at the rear entrance, I turned and waved to him and he took off with a little toot of his horn. I checked my watch. 10:05. I had until 10:30 which should give me plenty of time.

Saturday night at Tiny's was a rowdy affair; two alternating live bands, line dancing, contests, whooping, hollering, and much thumping of cowboy boots on the wooden dance floor. There were six waitresses working in a steady progression from the bar to the crowded tables. I spotted Alice with her gaudy orange hair half a room away and I pushed my way through the jostling three-deep bystanders ringing the room. I had to yell to make myself heard. She got the message and pointed toward the ladies' room. I watched her deliver a sloshing pitcher of beer and six tequila shooters, then collect a fistful of bills that she folded and pushed down the front of her shirt. She angled in my direction, taking orders as she came. The two of us burst into the empty ladies' room and pushed the door shut. The quiet was remarkable, the noise in the tavern reduced by more than half.

"Sorry to drag you away," I said.

"Are you kidding? I'm thrilled. This is hell on earth. It's like this most weekends and the tips are shit." She opened the first stall door and stepped just inside. She took a pack of cigarettes out of her apron pocket. "Keep an eye out for me, would you? I'm not supposed to stop for a smoke, but I can't help myself." She shook a cigarette free and fired it up in no time. She inhaled deeply, with a moan of pleasure and relief. "Lord, that's good. What are you doing here? I thought you went home to wherever it is."

"I left. Now I'm back."

"That was quick."

"Yeah, well I know a lot more now than I did two days ago."

"That's good. More power to you. I hear you're investigating a murder. Margaret Brine's father, or that's the word."

"It's slightly more complicated, but that's about it. As a matter of fact, I was just at her place, asking about his last visit."

Alice snorted. "What a horse's ass he was. He hustled my butt off, the randy little shit. I pinned his ears back, but he was hard to shake."

"Who else did he hustle? Anyone in particular? Margaret tells me he was horny as all get out—"

Alice held up a hand. "Mind if I interrupt for a sec? Something I should mention before you go on."

I hesitated, alerted by something in her tone. "Sure."

Alice studied the tip of her lighted cigarette. "I don't know how to say this, but people around here seem to be concerned about you."

"Why? What'd I do?"

"That's what everybody's asking. Grapevine has it you're into drugs."

"I am not! How ridiculous. That's ludicrous," I said.

"Also, you shot a couple of fellows in cold blood a while back."

"*I* did?" I said, laughing in startlement. "Where'd you hear *that*?"

"You never killed anyone?"

I felt my smile start to fade. "Well, yes, but that was self-defense. Both were killers, coming after me—"

Alice cut in. "Look, I didn't get the details and I

don't really give a shit. I'm willing to believe you, but folks around here take a dim view of it. We don't like the idea of somebody coming in here starting trouble. We take care of our own."

"Alice, I promise. I've never shot anyone without provocation. The idea's repugnant. I swear. Where did this come from?"

"Who knows? This is something I picked up earlier. I overheard the fellows talking."

"This was tonight?"

"And yesterday some, too. This was shortly after you left. I guess someone did some digging and came up with the facts."

"*Facts?*"

"Yeah. One guy you killed was hiding in a garbage can—"

"That's bullshit. He wasn't hiding, *I* was."

"Well, maybe *that's* what I heard. You were lying in wait, which somebody pointed out was pretty cowardly. Word is, the most recent incident was three years back. It was in the Santa Teresa papers. Someone saw a copy of the article."

"I don't believe this. What article?"

Alice drew on her cigarette, regarding me with skepticism. "You weren't involved in a shoot-out in some lawyer's office?"

"The guy was trying to *kill* me. I just told you that. Talk to the cops if you don't want to take my word for it."

"Don't get so defensive. I'm telling you for your own good. I might've done the same thing if I'd been in your place, but this is redneck country. Folks here close ranks. You better watch your step is all I'm saying."

"Somebody's trying to discredit me. That's what this is about," I said, hotly.

"Hey, it's not up to me. I don't give a damn. You can whack anyone you want. There's times *I'd* do it myself, given half a chance," she said. "The point is, people are getting pissed. I thought I should warn you before it went too far."

"I appreciate that. I wish you could tell me where it's coming from."

Alice shrugged. "That's the way it is in small towns."

"If you remember where the story originated, will you let me know?"

"Sure thing. In the meantime, I'd avoid crossing paths with the cops if I were you."

I felt a pang of anxiety, like an icicle puncturing my chest wall. "What makes you say that?"

"Tom was a cop. They're mad as hell."

Alice dropped the lighted cigarette in the toilet with a spat and then she flushed the butt away, waving at the air as if she could clear the smoke with a swishing hand. "You want anything else?"

I shook my head, not trusting myself to speak.

I waited at the side exit, my hands in my pockets though the chill I felt was internally generated. I kept my mind on other things, defending against a mounting surge of uneasiness. Maybe this was why Macon was suddenly being so protective.

The night sky was overcast, and where the air should

have been crystalline, a ground fog began to drift across the darkened parking lot. Two couples left together. One of the women was blind-drunk, laughing boisterously as she staggered across the icy tarmac. Her date had his arm across her shoulders and she leaned against him for support. She stopped in her tracks, held her hand up like a traffic cop, and then turned away to be sick. The other woman leaped backward, shrieking in protest. The ill woman lingered, holding on to a parked car 'til she was done and could move on.

The foursome reached their vehicle and piled in, though the sick woman sat sideways with her head hanging out the door for a good five minutes before they were finally able to pull away. I searched the empty rows of cars, checking the dark. The music from the bar behind me was reduced to a series of dull, repetitive thumps. I caught a flash of light and saw a car pull in. I stepped back into the shadows until I was assured it was Macon in his black-and-white. He pulled up beside me and sat there with his engine running. I moved forward, walking around the front of the patrol car to the window on the driver's side. He rolled it down as I approached.

"How'd it go?" he asked. I could hear the racket of his car radio dispatcher talking to someone else. He turned the volume down.

I put a hand on the door. "Alice tells me there's a rumor going around that I'm some sort of dope-crazed vigilante."

He looked off to one side. He stirred restlessly, tapping the steering wheel with his gloved hand. "Don't worry about gossip. Everybody talks in this town."

"Then you heard it, too?"

"Nobody pays any attention to that stuff."

"Not true. Someone went to the trouble to do a background check."

"And got what? It's all bullshit. I don't believe a word of it."

Which meant he'd heard the same stories everyone else had been treated to. "I better see you home. I got a call to check out."

I got in my car and he followed me as far as Selma's driveway, his engine idling while I crossed the front lawn.

Selma had left the porch light on and my key turned easily in the lock. I waved from the doorway and he took off. I slipped out of my wet shoes and carried them down the hall to the guest room. The house was quiet, not even the murmur of a television set to suggest Selma was awake.

I slipped into the guest room and closed the door behind me. She'd turned on a bed table lamp and the room was washed in cheery pink. On the nightstand, she'd left me a plate of homemade chocolate chip cookies secured in plastic wrap. I ate two, savoring the flavors of butter and vanilla. I ate two more to be polite before I stripped off my jacket. Apparently, Selma was not in the habit of turning down the furnace at night and the room felt close with heat. I crossed to the window, pushed the curtains aside, and raised the sash. Frigid air poured through the gap left by the storm window, still resting against the bushes three feet down.

I stared out at the portion of the street that I could see. A car passed at a slow speed and I pulled back out of sight, wondering if the occupants had spotted me. I hated being in Nota Lake. I hated being an outsider, the target of local gossip that misrepresented my actions. I hated my suspicions. The thought of a uniform was beginning to make me salivate like a dog subjected to some odd form of Pavlovian conditioning. Where once the badge and the nightstick had been symbols of personal safety, I now found myself picturing them with trepidation, as if stung by electric shocks. If I was right about the guy's connection to law enforcement, then his was the badge of authority and what was I? Some little pipsqueak P.I. with a prissy sense of justice. Talk about a mismatch.

Why couldn't I just hop in my car and barrel home tonight? I needed to be in a place where people cared for me. For a moment, the pull was overpowering. If I left within the hour, I could be in Santa Teresa by four A.M. I pictured my snug platform bed with its blue-and-white quilt, stars visible through the Plexiglas dome overhead. Surely, the sky there would be clear and the air would smell like the Pacific thundering close by. I visualized the morning. Henry would bake cinnamon rolls and we'd have breakfast together. Later I could help him in the yard, where he'd kneel at his flower beds, the pale soles of his feet like something cast in plaster of Paris. I stepped away from the window, effectively breaking the spell. The only road home is through the forest, I thought.

Within minutes, I'd peeled off my clothes and pulled on the oversized T-shirt I was using as a gown. Usually I sleep nude, but in someone else's house, it pays to be prepared in case of fire. I washed my face and brushed my teeth with the usual difficulty. I returned to the bedroom and circled restlessly. The bookshelves were filled with knick-knacks. There was not so much as a magazine in view and I'd forgotten to bring a book this time. I was too wired for sleep. I took the file from the duffel and got into bed, adjusting the reading lamp so I could review the notes I'd typed. The only item that leaped out at me was James Tennyson's report of the woman walking down the road the night Tom died. According to his account, she was approaching from the direction of Tom's truck and she veered off into the woods when she caught sight of his patrol car. Was he lying about that? Had he invented the woman in an attempt to throw me off? He hadn't struck me as devious, but the touch would have been nice since it suggested Tom had been in the woman's company when he was stricken with his fatal heart attack. I wondered what kind of woman would have walked off and left him in the throes of death. Perhaps someone who couldn't afford to be seen with him. Knowing what I knew of him, I didn't believe he was having an affair, so if the woman existed, why conceal her presence? I knew he'd been at the Rainbow Cafe at some unaccustomed hour.

What was interesting was that James had told me about this alleged female as an addendum to his original comments. I tend to be suspicious of elaborations. Eyewitness reports are notoriously unreliable. The story changes each time it's told, modified for every passing audience; amplified, embellished, until the final version is a twisted variation of the truth. Certainly, the memory is capable of playing tricks. Images can be camouflaged by emotion, popping into view later when the mental film is rewound. Conversely, people sometimes swear to have seen things that were never there at all. For the second time, I wondered if Tom had gone to the Rainbow Cafe to meet someone. I'd asked Nancy about it once, but it might be time to press.

I set my notes aside and doused the lights. The mattress was soft and seemed to list to one side. The sheets had a satin finish that felt slick to the touch and generated little traction to offset my tendency to slide. The quilted spread was puffy, filled with down. I lay there and basted in my own body heat. In testimony to my constitution, I fell asleep at once.

I woke to the distant sound of the phone ringing in the kitchen. I thought the answering machine would pick up, but on the eighth persistent *ding-a-ling*, I flung off the covers and trotted down the hall in my T-shirt and underpants. There was no sign of Selma and the machine had been turned off. I lifted the receiver. "Newquists' residence."

Someone breathed in my ear and then hung up.

I replaced the receiver and stood there for a moment. Often, someone calling a wrong number will dial the same number twice, convinced the error is yours for not being who they wanted. The silence extended. I reactivated the answering machine, and then checked Selma's appointment calendar, posted on the refrigerator door. There was nothing marked, but this was Sunday and I remembered her mentioning a visit to a cousin down in Big Pine after church. The dish rack was empty. I opened the dishwasher. I could see that she'd eaten breakfast, rinsed her plate and coffee cup, and left them in the machine, which was otherwise empty. The interior walls of the dishwasher exuded a residual heat and I assumed she'd done a load of dishes first thing this morning before she'd left. The coffee machine was on. The glass carafe held four cups of coffee that smelled as if it had sat too long. I poured myself a mug, adding sufficient milk to offset the scorched flavor.

I padded back to the guest room, where I brushed my teeth, showered, and dressed, sipping coffee while I girded my loins. I didn't look forward to another day in this town, but there was nothing for it except to get the job done. Like a dutiful guest, I made my bed, ate the remaining three cookies to fortify myself, and returned the empty coffee mug and plate to the kitchen, where I tucked both in the dishwasher, following Selma's good example. I grabbed my leather jacket and my shoulder bag, locked the house behind me, and went out to the car. Phyllis was pulling into her driveway two doors down. I waved, convinced she'd spotted me, but she kept her eyes averted and I was left, feeling foolish, with the smile on my lips. I got in the car, forcing myself to focus on the job at hand. The gas gauge was close to E and since I was heading toward the Rainbow, I stopped for gas on my way out of town.

I pulled up to the full-serve pump and turned the engine off, reaching into my bag to find my wallet and gasoline credit card. I glanced over at the office windows where I could see two attendants in coveralls chatting together by the cash register. Both turned to look at my

VW and then resumed their conversation. There were no other cars at the pumps. I waited, but neither came forward to assist me. I turned on the engine and gave the car horn a sharp toot. I waited two minutes more. No action at all. This was annoying. I had places to go and didn't want to sit here all day, waiting for a lousy tank of gas. I opened the car door and stepped out, peering across the top of the car to the open bay. The two attendants were no longer visible. Irritated, I slammed the car door and moved toward the office, which had been deserted.

"Hello?"

Nothing.

"Could I get some service out here?"

No one.

I went back to the car where I waited another minute. Maybe the two lads had inexplicably quit work or had been devoured by extraterrestrials hiding in the gents'. I started the engine and honked sharply, a display of impatience that netted nothing in the way of help. Finally, I pulled out with a little chirp of my tires to demonstrate my agitation. I slid into the flow of traffic on the main street and drove six blocks before I spotted another station. Hahaha, thought I. So much for the competition. I had no credit card for this rival brand, but I could afford to pay cash. Filling a VW never amounts to that much. I pulled into the second station, doing much as I had before. I turned the engine off, checked my wallet for cash. There was a car at the adjacent pump and the attendant was in the process of removing the nozzle from the tank. He glanced at me briefly and then I saw the alteration in his gaze.

I said, "Hi. How're you?"

He took the other woman's credit card and disappeared into the office, returning moments later with her receipt on a tray. She signed and took her copy. The two chatted for a moment and then she pulled out. The attendant went back to the office and that was the last I saw of him. What was going on? I checked myself with care, wondering if I'd been rendered invisible in my sleep.

I stared at the office window and then checked for another service station within range. I could see an off-brand station three doors down. Even with my gauge showing empty, I knew my trusty VW could soldier on for many miles yet, given the mileage I got. Still, I was reluctant to squander the last of a tank of gas looking for a place to buy the next tank of gas. I started my engine, put the car in gear, drove out of that gas station, and into the one two hundred yards away.

This time I saw an attendant in the service bay and I pulled in there first. Let's get this out in the open, whatever it was. I leaned over and rolled down the window on the passenger side. Pleasantly, I said, "Hi. Are you open for business?"

His blank stare sparked a moment of uneasiness. What was wrong with him?

I tried a smile that didn't feel right, but was the best I could manage. "Do you speak English? *Habla Inglés?*" Or something to that effect.

His return smile was slow and malevolent. "Yeah, lady, I do. Now why don't you get the fuck out of here? You want service in this town, you're out of luck."

"Sorry," I said. I shifted my gaze, keeping my expression neutral as I drove out of the station and turned right at the first street. Under my jacket, the sweat was soaking through the back of my shirt.

TWENTY

Once out of sight, I pulled over and parked on a side street to assess my situation. The word had clearly gone out, but I wasn't sure whether these guys were cueing off my car or my personal description. I removed my leather bomber jacket and tossed it in the backseat, then rooted through the assorted garments I keep for just such emergencies. I donned a plain red sweatshirt, a pair of sunglasses, and a Dodgers baseball cap. I got out, opened the trunk, and took out the five-gallon gasoline can I keep in there. I locked the car and hiked over to the main street where I headed for a service station I hadn't tried so far.

I bypassed the office and went straight to the service bay, where a cursing mechanic was struggling to loosen a stubborn lug nut on a flat tire. I checked the sign posted by the door that said MECHANIC ON DUTY with the guy's name ED BOONE on a plastic plaque inserted in the slot. I moved out of the bay and sidled up to the office where I poked my head in the door. The attendant was maybe nineteen, with a bleach-blond crew cut and green-painted fingernails, his attentions focused on the glossy pages of a pornographic magazine.

"Uncle Eddy told me I could fill this. My pickup ran out of gas about a block from here. This is mine, by the way," I said, holding up the can. I didn't want the fellow claiming later that I'd stolen it. Given my current reputation as a stone-cold killer, the theft of a gasoline can would have been right in character. I fancied I saw a flicker of uncertainty cross his face, but I went about my business like I owned the place.

I walked to the self-serve pump, giving him a sidelong glance to see if he was on the telephone. He stared through the plate glass window, watching me without expression as I filled the container. The total was $7.45. I returned to the office and handed him a ten, which he tucked in his pocket without offering change. His gaze dropped to his magazine again as I walked off. Nice to know that regardless of how low you sink, someone's always willing to make a profit at your expense. I returned to my car, where I emptied the five gallons of gasoline into my tank. I returned the can to the trunk and took off with the gauge now sitting at the halfway mark.

My heart was beating as though I'd run a race and perhaps I had. Apparently, my actions would be observed and curtailed wherever possible from here on. Never had I felt quite so alienated from my surroundings. I was already on unfamiliar turf and in subtle and not-so-subtle ways, I depended on the ordinary day-to-day pleasantries for my sense of well-being. Now I was being shunned and the process was scaring the shit out of me. Scouring the moving traffic, I realized my pale blue VW was highly visible among all the pickups, campers, utility vehicles, horse vans, and 4×4s.

Six miles out of town, I pulled into the gravel apron of the Rainbow Cafe, angling around to the left where I backed into a parking spot on the far side of the big garbage bins. I sat for a moment, trying to get "centered," as Californians say. I've no idea what the term means, but in my present circumstance, it seemed applicable. If I was being banished from the tribe, I better make sure I had a grip on my "self" before I went any further. I took a couple of deep breaths and got out. The morning was overcast, the mountains looming in the distance like an accumulation of thunder clouds. Down here, where large tracts of land stretched out empty and desolate, the wind whistled along the surface, chilling everything in its path. Snow flurries, like dust motes, hung in the icy air.

Crossing the gravel parking area, I felt extraordinarily conspicuous. I glanced at the cafe windows and could have sworn I saw two customers stare at me and then avert their eyes. A chill went through me, all the ancient power of ostracism by the clan. I imagined church services in progress, the Catholics and the Baptists and the Lutherans all singing hymns and giving thanks, attentive to their respective sermons. Afterward, the Nota Lake devout would crowd into the local restaurants, still dressed in their Sunday best and eager for lunch. I said a little prayer of my own as I pushed through the door.

The cafe was sparsely occupied. I did a quick visual sweep. James Tennyson was sitting at the counter with a cup of coffee. He wore jeans, the newspaper open in front of him. Close at hand were an empty water glass and a crumpled blue-and-black Alka-Seltzer packet.

There was no sign of his wife, Jo, or his baby, whose name escaped me. Rafer's daughter, Barrett, with her back to me, was working the grill. She wore a big white apron over jeans and a T-shirt. A white chef's toque concealed her springy, fly-away hair. Deftly, she wielded her spatula, rolling sausage links, flipping a quartet of pancakes. While I watched, she moved the steaming food to a pair of waiting plates. Nancy picked up the order and delivered it to the couple sitting by the window. Rafer and Vicky LaMott sat in the booth midway down the line of empty tables. They'd finished eating and I could see that Vicky was in the process of collecting her handbag and overcoat. James looked baggy-eyed and drawn. He caught sight of me and nodded, his manner a perfect blend of good manners and restraint. His fair-skinned good looks were only slightly marred by what I imagined was a hangover. I headed for a booth in the far corner, murmuring a greeting to Rafer and Vicky as I breezed by. I was afraid to wait for a response lest they cut me dead. I sat down and positioned myself so I could keep an eye on the door.

Nancy caught my attention. She seemed distracted, but not unfriendly, crossing toward the counter to pick up a side of oatmeal. "I'll be with you in just a minute. You want coffee?"

"I'd love some." Apparently, she wasn't a party to the social boycott. Alice, the night before, had been friendly as well . . . at least to the point of warning me about the freeze coming up. Maybe it was just the guys who were shutting me out; not a comforting thought. It was a man, after all, who'd dislocated my fingers only three days earlier. I found myself rubbing the joints, noticing for the first time that the swelling and the bruises gave them the appearance of exotic, barely ripe bananas. I turned my crockery mug upright in antici- pation of the coffee, noting that the fingers still refused to bend properly. It felt like the skin had stiffened, preventing flexion.

While I waited for service, I studied James in profile, wondering about his contact with Pinkie Ritter and Alfie Toth. As a CHP officer, he would have been removed from any sheriff's department action, but he might have exploited his friendships with the deputies to glean information about the homicide investigation. He was certainly first at the scene the night Tom died, giving him the perfect opportunity to lift Tom's notes. I was still toying with the possibility that he invented the walking woman, though his motive remained opaque. It wasn't Colleen. She'd assured me she'd never visited the area, a claim I tended to believe. Tom had too much to lose if he were seen with her. Besides, if she'd been in the truck, she wouldn't have deserted him.

The LaMotts emerged from their booth, hunching into overcoats in preparation for their departure. Vicky crossed to the counter to chat with Barrett while Rafer moved to the register and paid the check. As usual, Nancy did double duty, setting her coffee pot aside to take his twenty and make change. James rose at the same time, leaving his money on the counter beside his plate. He and Rafer exchanged a few words and I saw Rafer glance my way. James pulled on his jacket and left the restaurant without a backward look. Vicky joined her husband, who must have told her to go out and wait for him in the car. She nodded and then busied herself with her gloves and knit cap. I wasn't sure if she was ignoring me or not.

Once she was gone, Rafer ambled in my direction, his hands in his coat pockets, a red cashmere scarf wrapped around his neck. The coat was beautifully cut, a dark chocolate brown setting off the color of his skin. The man did dress well.

"Hello, Detective LaMott," I said.

"Rafer," he corrected. "How's the hand?"

"Still attached to my arm." I held my fingers up, wiggling them as though the gesture didn't hurt.

"Mind if I sit down?"

I indicated the place across from me and he slid into the booth. He seemed ill-at-ease, but his expression was sympathetic and his hazel eyes showed disquiet, not the coldness or hostility I'd half-expected. "I had a long talk with some Santa Teresa fellows about you."

I felt my heart start to thump. "Really. Who?"

"Coroner, couple cops. Homicide detective named Jonah Robb," he said. He put one elbow on the table, tapping with his index finger while he stared out across the room.

"Ah. Tracking down the stories going around about me."

His gaze slid back to mine. "That's right. I might as well tell you, from the perspective of the sheriff's department, you're okay, but I've heard rumbles I don't like and I'm concerned."

"I'm not all that comfortable myself, but I don't see any way around it. Responding to rumors only makes

306

you look guilty and defensive. I know because I tried it and got nowhere."

He stirred restlessly. He turned in the seat until he was facing me squarely, his hands laced in front of him. His voice dropped a notch. "Listen, I know about your suspicions. Why don't you tell me what you have and I'll do what I can to help."

I said, "Great," wondering why I didn't sound more sincere and enthusiastic. I thought about it briefly, experiencing a frisson of uneasiness. "I'll tell you what concerns me at the moment. A plainclothes detective—or someone posing as one—showed up at a fleabag hotel in Santa Teresa with a warrant for Toth's arrest. The Santa Teresa Sheriff's Department has no record of an outstanding warrant anywhere in the system, so the paper was probably bogus, but I don't have a way to check that because I don't have access to the computer."

"I can run that," he said smoothly. "What else?"

I found myself choosing my words with care. "I think the guy was a phoney, too. He might have been a cop, but I think he misrepresented himself."

"What name did he give?"

"I asked about that, but the clerk I talked to wasn't on the desk that day and he claims the other fellow didn't get a name."

"You think it was someone in our department," he said, making it a statement, not a question.

"Possibly."

"Based on what?"

"Well, doesn't the timing seem a tiny bit coincidental?"

"How so?"

"Tom wanted to talk to Toth in connection with Pinkie Ritter's death. The other guy got there first and that was the end of poor old Alfie. Tom was a basket case starting in mid-January when Toth's body turned up, right?"

"That's Selma's claim." Rafer's manner was now guarded and he started tapping, the tip of his index finger drumming a rapid series of beats. Maybe he was sending me a message in Morse code.

"So isn't it possible this is what Tom was brooding about? I mean, what else could it be?"

"Tom was a consummate professional for thirty-five years. He was the investigating officer in a homicide matter that I would say, yes, captured his interest, but no, did not in any way cause him to lie awake at night and bite his nails. Of course he thought about his work, but it didn't cause his heart attack. The idea's absurd."

"If he was under a great deal of stress, couldn't that have been a contributing factor?"

"Why would Toth's death cause him any stress at all? This was his *job*. He never even met the man, as far as I know."

"He felt responsible."

"For what?"

"Toth's murder. Tom believed someone gained access to his notebook where he'd jotted down Toth's temporary address and the phone number at the Gramercy."

"How do you know what Tom *believed*?"

"Because that's what he confided to another sheriff's investigator."

"Colleen Sellers."

"That's right."

308

"And Tom told her this?"

"Well, not explicitly. But that's how the killer could have found Toth and murdered him," I said.

"You still haven't said why you suspect someone from our department."

"I'll broaden the claim. Let's say, someone in law enforcement."

"You're fishing."

"Who else had access to his notes?"

"Everyone," he said. "His wife, his son, Brant. Half the time, the house was unlocked. Add his cleaning lady, the yard man, his next-door neighbor, the guy across the street. None of them are involved in law enforcement, but any one of them could have opened his front door and walked right in. And what makes you so sure it wasn't someone in Santa Teresa? The leak didn't necessarily come from this end."

I stared at him. "You're right," I said. He had a point.

The tapping stopped and his manner softened. "Why don't you back off and let us handle this?"

"Handle what?"

"We haven't been entirely idle. We're developing a lead."

"I'm glad to hear that. About bloody time. I hate to think I'm the only one out here with my ass on the line."

"Cut the sarcasm and don't push. Not your job."

"Are you saying you have a line on Alfie's killer?"

"I'm saying you'd be smart to go home and let us take it from here."

"What about Selma?"

"She knows better than to interfere with an official investigation. So do you."

I tried Selma's line. "There's no law against asking questions."

"That depends on who you ask." He glanced at his watch. "I got Vick in the car and we're late for church," he said. He got up and adjusted his coat, taking his leather gloves from one pocket. I watched him smooth them into place and thought, inexplicably, of his early morning arrival at the emergency room; freshly showered and shaven, nattily dressed, wide awake. He looked down at me. "Did anyone ever fill you in on local history?"

"Cecilia did."

He went on talking as if I hadn't spoken. "Bunch of convicts were shipped to the colonies from England. These were hardened criminals, literally branded for the heinousness of their behavior."

"The 'nota' of Nota Lake," I supplied dutifully.

"That's right. The worst of 'em came west and settled in these mountains. What you're dealing with now are their descendants. You want to watch your step."

I laughed, uneasily. "What, this is like a Western? I'm being warned off? I have to be out of town by sundown?"

"Not a warning, a suggestion. For your own good," he said.

I watched him leave the restaurant and realized how dry my mouth had become. I had that feeling I used to get before the first day of school, a low-level dread that acted as an appetite suppressant. Breakfast didn't sound like such a hot idea. The place had cleared out. The couple by the window were getting up to leave. I saw them pay their check, Barrett taking over the cash register while Nancy hurried in my direction with a coffee pot and menu, all apologies. She handed me the menu. "Sorry it took me so long, but I was brewing a new pot and I could see you and Rafer had your heads together," she said. She filled my mug with hot coffee. "You have any idea what you want to eat? I don't mean to rush you. Take your time. I just don't want to hold you up, you've been so patient."

"I'm not hungry," I said. "Why don't I move to the counter so we can talk?"

"Sure thing."

I picked up my mug and reached for the silverware.

"I'll get that," she said. She took the menu and the flatware, moving to the counter where she set a place for me between the griddle and the cash register. Barrett was in the process of cleaning the grill with a flat-edged spatula. Bacon fat and browned particles of pancake and sausage were being pushed into the well. Nancy rinsed a rag and twisted out the excess water, wiping the counter clean. "Alice says you've been asking about Pinkie Ritter."

"You remember him?"

"Every woman in Nota Lake remembers him," she said, tartly.

"Did he ever bother you?"

"Meaning what, unwanted sexual advances? He attacked me one night when I got off work. He waited in the parking lot and grabbed me by the neck as I was getting in my car. I kicked his ass up between his shoulder blades and that was the last of that. He was convicted of rape twice and that's just the times he was caught."

"Did you report it?"

"What for? I took care of it myself. What's the law going to do, come along afterwards and smack his hand?"

Barrett had now come over to the small sink just below the counter in front of us and she was in the process of rinsing plates and arranging them in the rack for the industrial dishwasher I assumed was in the rear. She had her father's light eyes and she made no secret of the fact that she was listening to Nancy's tale and enjoying her attitude.

I caught her attention. "Did he ever come on to you?"

"Uhn-uhn. No way," she said, a blush creeping up her cheeks. "I was close to jailbait at that point, barely eighteen years old. He knew better than to mess with me."

I turned to Nancy. "What about other women? Anyone in particular? Earlene or Phyllis?"

Nancy shook her head. "Not that I heard, but that doesn't mean he didn't try. Guy like that goes after anyone who seems weak."

"Could I ask you about something else?"

"Sure."

"The night Tom Newquist died, he was in here earlier, wasn't he?"

"That's right. He came in about nine o'clock. Ordered a cheeseburger and fries, sat around and smoked cigarettes, like he was killing time. Occasionally he'd look at his watch. I couldn't figure it out. He never came in at that hour. I figured he was meeting someone, but she never showed up."

"Why do you say 'she'? Couldn't it have been a man?"

Nancy seemed surprised at the idea. "I never thought about that. I just assumed."

"Did he mention anyone by name?"

"No."

"Did he use the telephone?"

She shook her head with some uncertainty and then turned to Barrett with a quizzical look. "You remember if Tom Newquist used the phone that night?"

"Not that I saw."

Again, I directed a question to Barrett. "Did you get the impression he was here to meet someone?"

Barrett shrugged. "I guess."

Nancy spoke up again. "You know what I think it was? He was freshly shaved. I remember remarking about his cologne or his aftershave. He looked sharp, like he'd gussied himself up. He wouldn't do that if he were here to meet some guy."

"You agree with that?" I asked Barrett.

"He did look nice, now you mention it," she said. "I noticed that myself."

"Did he seem annoyed or upset, like he'd been stood up?"

"Not a bit of it," Nancy said. "Nine-thirty, got up, paid his check, and went out to his truck. I never saw him afterwards. I did closing that night so I was stuck in here. Did you see him out there?"

"In the parking lot? Not me."

"You must have. You took off shortly before he did."

Barrett thought about it, frowning slightly before she shook her head. "Maybe he was parked around back."

"Where were you parked that night?" I asked.

"Nowhere. I didn't have a car. My dad was picking me up."

"She lives just over there on the other side of that subdivision, but her folks don't like her walking home at night. They're real protective, especially her dad."

Barrett smiled, her dark skin underlined with the pink of her embarrassment. "I could be a preacher's daughter. That'd be worse."

We chatted on for a while. The place began to fill with the early church service crowd and I was clearly in the way. I was also hoping to avoid further confrontation with any irate citizens. I hunched into my jacket and went out to the car. Since the parking spot I'd found was around to the rear, I didn't think I was visible to passing vehicles. I didn't have the nerve to drive into town just yet. I couldn't bear the idea of wandering around on my own, risking rudeness and rejection on the basis of floating rumors. People in the cafe had been fine so maybe it was just the service station attendants who'd passed a vote of no confidence.

I saw Macon Newquist pull off the highway and into the parking lot in a pickup truck. He was dressed in a suit that looked as unnatural on him as a bunny costume. I knew if he saw me, he'd start pumping me for information. I torqued myself around, reaching for my briefcase as though otherwise occupied. Along with my case notes, I'd tucked in the packets of index cards. I waited until he disappeared into the cafe before I got out of the car and locked it. I took my briefcase with me as I crunched along the berm to the Nota Lake Cabins.

Out front, the red Vacancy sign was lighted. The office lobby was unlocked and there was a flat plastic clockface hanging on the doorknob with the hands pointing to 11:30. The sign said BACK IN A JIFFY. I went in, crossing to the half-door that opened onto the empty office. "Cecilia? Are you here?"

There was no answer.

I was tempted, as usual, by the sight of all those seductive-looking desk drawers. The Rolodex and the file cabinets fairly begged to be searched, but I couldn't for the life of me think what purpose it would serve. I sat down in the upholstered chair and opened a pack of index cards. I began to read through my notes, transferring one piece of information to each card with a borrowed ballpoint pen. In some ways, this was busy-work. I could feel productive and efficient while sheltered from public scrutiny. Transcribing my notes had the further advantage of diverting my attention from the state of discomfort in which I found myself. Whereas last night I longed for home, I couldn't picture turning tail and running on the basis of Rafer's veiled "suggestion" about my personal safety. So what was I doing? Trying to satisfy myself that I'd done what I could. The deal I made with myself was to keep following leads until the trail ran out. If I came up against a blank wall, then I could return home with a clear conscience. In the meantime, I had a job and I was intent on doing it. Yeah, right, you chickenshit, I thought.

I went through a pack and a half of index cards without any startling revelations. I shuffled them twice and laid them out like a hand of solitaire, scanning row after row for telling details. For instance, I'd made a note that Cecilia'd told me she got home around ten o'clock the night Tom died. She said she'd seen the ambulance, but had no idea it had been summoned for her brother. Could she have seen the woman walking down the road? It occurred to me the woman might have been staying at the Nota Lake Cabins, in which case her stroll might not have had anything to do with Tom. Worth asking, at any rate, just to eliminate the issue.

TWENTY-ONE

Cecilia was late getting back. Instead of returning at 11:30, it was closer to 12:15 when she finally walked in the door. She was dressed for church in a baggy blue tweed suit with bumble bee scatter pins on the lapel. The white blouse underneath featured a frothy burst of lace at the neck. She expressed no surprise when she saw me and in my paranoid state, I imagined my presence had been reported in advance. She opened the half-door to the office, closed it behind her, put her handbag on the desk, and turned to look at me. "Now. What can I do for you? I hear you're staying at Selma's so it can't be a room you've come to ask about."

"I'm still working on this business of Tom's death."

"Seven weeks ago tomorrow. Hard to take it in," she said.

"Do you happen to remember who was staying here that weekend?"

"At the motel? That's easy." She reached for the registration ledger, licked her index finger, and began to page back through the weeks. March became February as she reversed the days. The week of February 1 appeared. She ran a finger down the list of names. "A party of skiers, maybe six of 'em in two cabins. I gave 'em Hemlock and Spruce, as far away from the office as I could make it because I knew they'd get to partying. That type always do. I remember them toting in more cases of beer than they had luggage. Complained a lot, too. Water pressure, heat. Nothing suited them," she said, shooting me a look.

"Anyone else? Any single women?"

"Meaning what?"

"Not meaning anything, Cecilia," I said, patiently. "I'm following up on the CHP report. Tennyson says he saw a woman walking down the road. She may have been a figment of his imagination. It's possible she had nothing to do with Tom. It would be helpful to find her so I'm hoping against hope she was staying here that night. That way you could tell me how to get in touch with her."

She checked the register again. "Nope. Married couple from Los Angeles. Or so they claimed. Only saw that pair when they crawled out of bed to take meals. And one other family with a couple of kids. Wife was in a wheelchair so I doubt he saw her."

"What about you? When you came back from the movies, was there anyone on the road? This would have been between ten and ten-thirty."

Cecilia seemed to give it some thought and then shook her head. "The only thing I remember is someone using the phone out there. I try to discourage strangers stopping off to make calls; tromping up and down the porch stairs, ripping pages from the telephone book. Handset's been stolen twice. This is private property."

"I thought the pay phone was public."

"Not as far as I'm concerned. That's strictly for motel customers. One of the amenities," she said. "Anyway, I could see the Rainbow was closed and the outside lights were off. I poked my head out, but it was only Barrett calling her dad to pick her up. I offered her a lift, but she said he was already on his way."

"You have any idea if Rafer had picked up on the 9–1–1 dispatch?"

"You mean, the ambulance for Tom? Probably," she said. "Or James might have called him, knowing they were such good friends." She closed the ledger. "Now, I hope you'll excuse me. I have someone joining me for Sunday lunch."

"Sure. No problem. I appreciate your help."

I tucked my papers in the briefcase, gathered up the index cards, put a rubber band around them, and dropped them in there, too. I shrugged into my jacket, grabbed my handbag and the briefcase, and returned to my car at the Rainbow. So here's the question I asked myself: If Barrett left work at nine-thirty, why did it take her thirty to forty minutes to call her dad? I sat in the car, watching the clouds gather in a dark gray sky, watching the light dim down to a twilight state. It was only one o'clock in the afternoon, but the dark was so pervasive that the photosensor on Cecilia's exterior lights popped to life. Snow began to fall, big airy flakes settling on the windshield like a layer of soap suds. I waited, watching the rear of the Rainbow Cafe.

By two-thirty, the lunch crowd was all but gone. I sat with the inborn patience of the cat watching for a lizard to reappear from the crevice between two rocks. At 2:44, the back door opened and Barrett came out, wearing her apron and her chef's toque and carrying a large plastic garbage bag intended for the trash bin to my left. I rolled down the window. "Hi, Barrett. You have a minute?"

She dumped the garbage bag and moved closer. I leaned over and unlocked the passenger door, pushing it open a crack. "Hop in. You'll freeze to death out there."

She made no move. "I thought you were gone."

"I was visiting Cecilia. What time do you get off work?"

"Not for hours."

"Why don't you take a break? I'd like to talk to you."

She hesitated, looking toward the Rainbow. "I'm really not supposed to, but it's okay for just a minute." She got in the car, slammed the door, and crossed her bare arms against the cold. I'd have run the engine for the heat, but I didn't want to waste the gas and I was hoping her discomfort would motivate her to tell me what I wanted to know.

"Your dad says you're on your way to med school."

"I haven't been accepted yet," she said.

"Where're you thinking to go?"

"Did you want something in particular? Because Nancy doesn't know I'm out here and I really don't have a coffee break until closer to three."

"I should get to the point, now you mention it," I said. I could feel a fib start to form. For me, it's the same sensation as a sneeze in the making, that wonderful reaction of the autonomic nervous system when something tickles my nose. "I was curious about something." Please note, she didn't ask what. "Wasn't it you Tom Newquist was here to meet that night?"

"Why would he do that?"

"I have no idea. That's why I'm asking you," I said.

She must have done some acting at one point; maybe high school, the senior play, not the lead. She made a show of frowning, then shook her head in bafflement. "I don't think so," she said, as though racking her brain.

"I have to tell you, he made a note on his desk calendar. He wrote *Barrett* plain as day."

"He did?"

"I ran across it today, which is why I was asking earlier who he was here to meet. I was hoping you'd be honest, but you dropped the ball," I said. "I would have let it pass, but then the story was confirmed, so here I am. You want to tell me how it went?"

"Confirmed?"

"As in verified," I said.

"Who confirmed it?"

"Cecilia."

"It wasn't anything," she said.

"Well, great. Cough it up, in that case. I'd like to hear."

"We just talked a few minutes and then he started feeling bad."

"What'd you talk about?"

"Just stuff. We were chatting about my dad. I mean, it was nothing in particular. Just idle conversation. Me and Brant used to go steady and he was asking about the breakup. He always felt bad that we didn't hang in together. I knew he was leading up to something, but I didn't know what. Then, he started feeling sick. I could see the color drain from his face and he started sweating. I was scared."

"Did he say he was in pain?"

She nodded, her voice wavering when she spoke. "He was clutching his chest and his breathing was all raspy. I said I'd go back to the motel and get some help and he said, fine, do that. He told me to lock the truck door and not mention our meeting to anyone. He was real emphatic about that, made me *promise*. Otherwise, I might have told you when you asked the first time." She fumbled in her uniform pocket and found a tissue. She swiped at her eyes and blew her nose.

I waited until she was calmer before I went on. "Did he say anything else?"

She took a deep breath. "Stay off the road if any cars came along. He didn't want anyone to know I'd been talking to him."

"Why?"

"He didn't want to put me in any danger, was what he said."

"He didn't say from whom?"

"He didn't mention anyone by name," she said.

"What else?"

"That's everything."

"He didn't give you his notebook for safekeeping?"

She shook her head mutely.

"Are you sure?"

"Positive."

"I thought he gave you the little black book where he kept his field notes."

"Well, he didn't."

"Barrett, tell the truth. Please, please, please? Pretty

please with sugar on it? Trust me, I won't say a word to anyone about your having it."

"I'm telling you the truth."

I shook my head. "I hate to contradict you, but Tom always kept it with him and yet nobody's seen it since he died."

"So?"

"So everybody's been assuming he was by himself that night. Now it turns out you were in his truck. Where else could it be? He was anxious to protect the notebook so he must have given it to you. That's the only way it adds up. If you can think of another explanation, I'd love to hear it."

The silence was exquisite. I let it drag on a bit without breathing another word.

"I went for help."

"I'm sure you did," I said. "The CHP officer saw you on the road. What about the notebook?"

Barrett looked out the window. "You don't have any proof," she said, faintly.

"Well, yeah, I know. I mean, except for the fact that Cecilia saw you on the motel porch that night," I said. "She says your dad came and picked you up, which is what you said yourself. You just fudged a tiny bit about the sequence of events. I can't *prove* you have the notebook, but it stands to reason."

Nancy poked her head out of the Rainbow's back door. Barrett opened the door and leaned out, calling, "I'll be right there!" Nancy nodded and waved.

"So where's the notebook?"

"In my purse," she said, glumly.

"Could you give it to me?"

"What's so important about the notes?"

"He was investigating two murders so I'm assuming his notes are somehow relevant. Did you read them yourself?"

"Well, yeah, but it's just a bunch of interviews and stuff. Lots of dates and abbreviations. It's no big deal."

"Then why does it matter if you pass it on to me?"

"He told me to hide it 'til he could decide what to do with it."

"He didn't know he would die."

"What a bummer," she said.

"Look, if you'll give it to me now, I'll make a copy first thing tomorrow and give it back to you."

After an agonizing moment, she said, "All right."

She got out of the car on her side and I got out on mine, locking the doors quickly before I followed her in. She kept her handbag in the storage room to the left of the kitchen door. Barrett took the notebook out of her bag and passed it to me. She seemed irritated that I'd managed to outmaneuver her somehow. "The other thing he said was the key's on his desk," she said.

"The key's in his desk?"

"That's what he told me. He said it twice."

"In or on?"

"On, I think. I have to go."

"Thanks. You're a doll." I put my finger to my lips. "Top secret. Not a word to anyone."

"Shit. Then why did I tell you?"

Nancy stuck her head in the kitchen door. "Oh, Kinsey. You're here. Brant's on the phone," she said.

I went out into the cafe proper, which was virtually

deserted. The receiver was face down on the counter by the register. "Brant, is that you?"

He said, "Hi, Kinsey."

"Where are you? How'd you know I was here?"

"I'm at Mom's. I drove past the Rainbow a while ago and saw your car parked out back. I just wanted to check and make sure you're okay."

"I'm fine. Is your mother home yet?"

"She won't get back 'til close to nine," he said. "You need something?"

"Not really. If you have a way to call her, would you let her know I got it?"

"Got what?"

I curled my fingers around the mouthpiece, feeling like a character in a spy movie. "The notebook."

"How'd you manage that?"

"I'll explain later. I'll be home in a few minutes. Can you wait?"

"Not really. I just stopped by for some stuff I'll be taking to Sherry's later."

"You work weekends?"

"Not usually," he said. "I'm filling in for someone and hoping to run some errands first. We'll talk tomorrow."

"Right. I'll see you then," I said.

I let myself into Selma's house and headed out to the kitchen. The house was dim, silent, insufferably warm. Everything was much as I'd left it, except for a plastic-wrapped plate of brownies with chocolate frosting sitting on the counter with a note attached: HELP YOUR-SELF. The condensation on the wrap suggested it had been refrigerated or frozen until recently. Brant must have assumed the note was meant for him because a plate and fork, showing telltale traces of chocolate, were sitting on the table at the place he occupied. I was sorry I'd missed him. We could have put our heads together.

I went into Tom's study and sat down in his swivel chair. I turned on his desk light and started going through the notebook. The cover was a pebbly black leather, soft with wear, the corners bent. I took the obvious route, starting at the first page—dated June 1—and working through to the last, which was dated February 1, two days before he died. Here, at last, were the ten months' worth of missing notes. The scribbles, on thin-lined paper, covered all the miscellaneous cases he'd been working on during that period. Each was identified by a case number in the margin to the left, and included complaints, crime-scene investigations, names, addresses, and phone numbers of witnesses. In a series of nearly indecipherable abbreviations, I could trace the course of successive interviews on any given matter; Tom's notes to himself, his case references, the comments and questions that cropped up as he proceeded. There, in something close to hieroglyphics, I read about the discovery of Pinkie's body, the findings of the coroner, Trey Kirchner . . . whom Tom referred to as III. Any recurring name Tom generally reduced to its first letter. I found references to R and B, which I assumed were Rafer and Tom's boss, Sheriff Bob Staffer. By copious squints and leaps of imagination, I could see that he'd worked backward from Pinkie's death to his incarceration in Chino and his friendship with Alfie Toth, a fact confirmed by MB, Margaret Brine at NLSD,

Nota Lake Sheriff's Department. CS I took to refer to Colleen Sellers, sometimes referred to as C, who'd called to report Alfie Toth's jail time in ST. I found the summary of his trip to Santa Teresa in June, including dates, times, mileage, and expenditures for food and lodging. As I'd learned earlier, he'd talked to Dave Estes at the Gramercy on 6–5. Later, he'd talked to Olga Toth, her address and phone number neatly noted. By the time CS called again to report the discovery of Toth's remains, Tom's notes had become cursory. Where previously he'd been meticulous about detailing the contents of conversations, he was suddenly circumspect, reverting I suspected to a code of some kind. The last page of notes contained only some numbers—8, 12, 1, 11, and 26 writ large, and underlined with an exclamation point and question mark. Even the punctuation suggested a disbelief most emphatic. I sat and stared at the numbers until they danced on the page.

I got up and went to the kitchen, where I paced the floor. I poured myself some water from the tap and I drank it, making the most satisfactory gulping sounds. I put the glass in the dishwasher and then in a fit of tidiness, added Brant's fork and his plate. I let my brain off the hook, tending to idle occupations while I picked at the riddle. What the hell did the numbers 8, 12, 1, 11, and 26 signify? A date? The combination to a safe? I thought about Tom's telling Barrett about the "key" in or on his desk. I'd been working at his desk for a week and hadn't seen any key that I remembered. What kind of key? The key to what? It's not as though his notebook had a tiny lock like a teenager's diary.

I went back to the den and sat down at his desk,

immediately searching through his drawers again. Maybe he had a lock box. Maybe he had a home safe. Maybe he had a storage cupboard secured by a small combination lock. How many bags full of garbage had I thrown out this past week? How could I be sure I hadn't tossed the key he was referring to? I felt a wave of panic at the idea that I'd thrown out something crucial to his purposes and critical to mine.

One by one, I emptied the contents of each drawer, then removed the drawer itself, checking the back panel and the bottom. I got down on my hands and knees and peered at the underside of the desk, feeling along the sides in case a key had been taped in place. In the drawer with his handcuffs and nightstick, I came across his flashlight and used that as I felt along the drawer rails, tilted his swivel chair back to check the underside of the seat. Did he mean the key, as "a thing that explains or solves something else," or a literal key, as an instrument or device to open a lock? I put the drawers back together and moved everything off the top. I ran a finger across his blotter, looking for a repetition of the numbers among the notes he'd scribbled. The numbers were there—8, 12, 1, 11, 26—appearing in the center of a noose. They were written twice more, once with a pen line encircling it and once in a box with a shaded border done in pencil. What if I'd discarded the critical information? Had the trash been picked up? I was working hard to suppress the nagging worry I felt. I was in a white-hot sweat. The house, as usual, felt like an oven. I crossed to the window and lifted the sash. I loosened the catches on the storm window and pushed the glass out unceremoniously, watching with satisfaction as the window dropped to the ground below. I swallowed mouthfuls of fresh air, hoping to quell my anxiety.

I sat down at the desk again and shook my head. I cleared my mind of emotion, thinking back through the work I'd done earlier in the week. I didn't remember a key, but if I'd seen one I knew I would never have discarded it. If I hadn't found the key yet, there was still the chance that I'd uncover it somewhere. So. The point was to keep searching, as calmly and thoroughly as possible. Again, I went through each drawer, looking carefully at the contents. I checked each item in Tom's file folders, looked in envelopes, opened boxes of paper clips and staples, peered at pens, rulers, labels, tape. Maybe the key was a saying or a phrase that would make everything else clear. At the back of my mind, I kept returning to the notion that the numbers were a code of some kind. I'd never heard any mention of Tom's having worked in Intelligence so if I was right, the code was probably something simple and easily accessible.

On or in his desk.

I found a piece of paper and wrote out the alphabet in sequence, attaching the numbers 1 through 26 underneath. If the numbers 8, 12, 1, 11 and 26 were simple letter substitutions, then the name or initials would be *HLAKZ*. Which meant what? Nothing on the face of it. *Something-Los Angeles-Something-Something?* Didn't suggest anything to me. I tried the same sequence backward, letting *A* correspond with the number 26, *B* correspond with 25, and so forth until I reached the number 1, which I assumed represented *Z*. If this were the case, then the numbers 8, 12, 1, 11, 26 would spell out *SOZPA*. Another puzzlement. What the hell was this? A name? My frustration level mounted at a pace with my confusion.

8, 12, 1, 11, 26. Months of the year? August, December, January, November? Then what did the 26 denote? And why out of order? Was I supposed to add? Subtract? Sound out the words phonetically like a vanity license plate? I repeated them aloud. "Eight. Twelve. One. Eleven. Twenty-six." This meant nothing. If the numbers represented letters and this was a word, then all I knew for sure was that the five letters were different . . . with no repetitions. Someone's name? I thought about Nota Lake and how many people I'd met here who had five-letter first names. Brant, Macon, Hatch, Wayne. James Tennyson. Rafer. I looked at the exclamation point and the question mark. *!?* Which said what? Consternation? Dismay?

I realized I was famished . . . a manifestation of my anxiety no doubt. Waiting for Barrett in the cafe parking lot, I'd skipped lunch altogether and this was the price I paid. It was now four-fifteen. I went back to the kitchen in search of sustenance. I was so hungry and so befuddled, my brain cells felt like they'd quit holding hands. I looked in Selma's refrigerator, greeted by plastic-wrapped leftovers from last night's dinner. Not memorable to begin with and certainly not worth re-eating. I checked the bread drawer. No crackers. I checked the cupboards. No peanut butter. What kind of household did she run? I glanced at her note and in the absence of wholesome foodstuffs, I allowed myself to lift a corner of the plastic wrap and help myself to several brownies. The texture was off—a bit dry for my taste—but the icing was nice and gooey, only a faint chemical taste suggesting she'd used a boxed mix. Anyone who'd eat Miracle Whip would eat that shit, I thought. This was not Selma's best effort by a long stretch, but I figured my days consuming her cooking were just about over. I drank some milk from the carton, figuring to save a glass.

Thus fortified, I was prepared to tackle the problem. I went back to Tom's swivel chair and swiveled. What if 8, 12, 1, 11, and 26 were page numbers, referring to the notes themselves? I tried that approach, but the contents of the pages seemed in no way related, sharing no visible common elements and no designated page numbers. The afternoon was stretching toward evening and I was getting nowhere. I went back to the original premise. Selma had hired me to find out why Tom was distressed. I slouched down on my spine and leaned my head on the back of the chair. Why was Tom brooding, Kinsey asked herself? I rocked, allowing myself to ruminate at my leisure. If someone he knew had violated his privacy, reading his notes and using the information to get to Alfie Toth to kill him, that would certainly do the trick. But why would Hatch's involvement . . . or James's or Waynes's . . . have generated a moment's uneasiness or hesitation. Tom played by the rules. I'd been told over and over, he was strictly a law-and-order type. If he'd suspected any one of them, he'd have acted at once. Wouldn't he? Why would he not? It wouldn't have meant anything to him if Wayne had violated the sanctity of his field notes. My gaze dropped to the blotter. I pushed a stack of files aside. Down in the right-hand corner, Tom had drawn a grid, penning in the days of the month of February, the year unspecified. The First fell on a Sunday, the Twenty-eighth on a Saturday. The last two Saturdays of the month—the Twenty-first and the Twenty-eighth—were crossed out. Was the year 1908? 1912, 1901, 1911 or 1926? I got up and went to the bookshelf, where I took down a copy of his almanac. I thumbed to the index and found the page numbers for a perpetual calendar. In a table to the left the years between 1800 and 2063 were listed in order. Beside each year was a number corresponding to a numbered template, representing all the variations in the way the months could be laid out. Calendar number one was a year in which January 1 fell on a Sunday; February 1 fell on a Wednesday; and each month thereafter was depicted. Calendar number two represented any and all years in which January 1 fell on a Monday; February 1 fell on Thursday; and so forth. If you wanted to know the day of the month for a particular date—say, March 5, 1966—you simply checked the master list for the year 1966, beside which appeared the number seven. Moving to Calendar number seven, you could see that March 5 fell on a Saturday.

I flipped on the desk light and studied the series of calendar pages, looking at the Februaries laid out like the one he'd drawn. Calendar number five was like that. February 1 fell on a Sunday and the Twenty-eighth fell on the last Saturday of the month. Calendar number twelve was similar except there were twenty-nine days instead of twenty-eight. I checked the years that corresponded, starting with 1900. 1903 was such a year, but not 1908 and not 1912. In 1914, the First fell on a Sunday and the Twenty-eighth on the last Saturday, but the same wasn't true of 1926. 1925, 1931, 1942, 1953, 1959, 1970, 1981, 1987, 1998. Why were these particular Februaries important? The year couldn't be relevant, could it? And why had he crossed out the last two Saturdays of that month? I thought about it for a minute. Eliminating those two Saturdays cut the number of days from twenty-eight to twenty-six—the number of letters in the alphabet. I tried that approach, lining up the letters with the days of the month. The answer was still *HLAKZ*.

Still rocking in his desk chair, I swiveled toward the window. It was nearly five-thirty, fully dark outside. Cold air still spilled through the gap where I'd raised the window. I could almost discern the waves of household heat pouring out in exchange. The room was decidedly chilly. I leaned forward and closed the window, staring at my reflection in the smoke-clouded glass. What the hell did those numbers mean? I could feel a draft from somewhere. Was there a draft coming down the chimney? Curious, I got up and moved out of the den. I walked along the front hall to the living room where I turned on the table lamps. The drapes were wavering as though pushed by an unseen hand. I peered up the chimney and flipped the flue to the shut position. I checked the perimeter doors. The front door was closed and locked, as was the back door, and the door to the garage. That wasn't it. I poked my head into Selma's bedroom. All was undisturbed yet the draft was such that the curtains rippled in the windows. I proceeded down the hall. All the windows in Brant's old bedroom were closed.

I stopped where I was. The door to my room was ajar. Had I left it that way? I pushed it open with apprehension. Curtains flapped and fluttered. The room was a shambles. There were jagged shards of glass on the carpet. The window, which I'd oh-so-carefully locked, had been shattered by a hammer that someone had left on the floor. Pebbles of glass the size of rocksalt were spread out across the sill like discarded diamonds. The sash had been pushed up, probably from the outside. Someone had clearly entered. I moved to the bed and slid my hand between the box spring and mattress. My gun was missing.

TWENTY-TWO

I glanced at my watch. 5:36. I walked back to the kitchen prepared to dial 9–1–1. I hesitated, my hand on the receiver. Who was I going to call? Rafer? Brant? Tom's brother, Macon? I wasn't sure I trusted any one of them. I stood there, trying to determine whom I could confide in at this point. A chill went through me. Surely, there wasn't anybody in the house *with* me. I hadn't gone to the guest room since I'd returned to the house early in the afternoon so the intruder had probably been here and departed long before I showed up. Ordinarily, I'd have gone to my room to drop my jacket. After the day I'd had, I might have showered or napped—anything to perk myself up and restore my confidence—but I'd been intent on Tom's notes and I'd gone directly to his den. I felt disembodied, my mind having been separated from my flesh by the harrowing sensation of fear.

The phone shrilled with extraordinary loudness, setting off a surge of nausea. I jumped, nerves raw, my reflexes responding sharply, almost to the point of pain. I snatched up the receiver before it had ceased to ring. "Hello?"

335

"Hey, Kinsey. Brant here. Is my mom home yet?" He sounded young and carefree, relaxed, unconcerned.

My stomach churned in response. "You need to come home," I said. My voice seemed to be coming from a curious distance.

He must have been alerted by my tone because his shifted. "Why? What's going on?"

"Someone's broken in. There's glass on the bedroom floor and my gun is gone."

"Where's Mom?"

"I don't know. Yes. Wait. At your cousin's in Big Pine. I'm here alone," I said.

"Stay where you are. I'll be right there."

He hung up.

I replaced the receiver. I turned and leaned my back up against the wall, making little mewling sounds. A town full of cowboys and someone was coming after me. I held my hands out in front of me. I could see my fingers tremble, the recently dislocated digits looking all puffy and useless. My gun had been stolen. I had to have a weapon, some way to defend myself against the coming onslaught. I started opening the kitchen drawers, one after the other, in search of a knife. One drawer flew off its rails and banged against my thigh, spilling out its contents. Utensils jangled together, tumbling to the floor at my feet. I could feel the tears stinging my lids. I gathered a fistful of items and tossed them back in the drawer, but I couldn't seem to get it mounted on its track again. I banged it on the counter top so hard a metal spatula bounced and flew out. I left the drawer where it was. I found a steak knife, some generic brand that looked like a giveaway in a box of detergent. The overhead light glinted off its surface. I could see the bevel on the blade. What good would a serrated steak knife do against a speeding bullet?

Hours seemed to go by.

I could hear the second hand on the kitchen clock tick each passing second in turn.

Outside, I heard the squeal of brakes, and then a car door slammed shut. I turned and stared at the front door. What if it was someone else? What if it was them? The door flew open and I could see Brant in his civilian clothes. He moved toward me with all the comforting bulk of a battleship. I put a hand out and he took it.

"Jesus, you look awful. How'd the guy get in?"

I pointed to my room and then found myself following as he moved purposefully down the hall in that direction. His assessment was brief, the most cursory of glances. He turned away from the guest room and toured the rest of the house methodically, looking in every closet, every nook and cranny. He went down to the basement. I waited at the top of the stairs, one hand plucking at the other. My injured fingers held a particular fascination for me—clumsy and swollen. Where was my gun? How could I defend myself when I'd left the knife on the counter?

Brant returned to the kitchen. I followed him like a duckling. I could tell by his tone he was trying to control himself. Something in his manner conveyed the seriousness of the situation. "Did he get the notebook?"

I found myself grinding my teeth. "Who?"

"The guy who broke in," he said sharply.

"It was in my bag," I said. "Is that what he was after?"

"Of course," Brant said. "I can't think why else he'd risk it. Tell me exactly what you did today. What time did you leave and how long were you gone?"

I felt burbling and incoherent, spilling out the story of my rebuff, the refusal of the gas station attendants to do business with me, my subsequent stop at the Rainbow to talk to Nancy. I told him I'd run into Rafer and Vick, that I'd talked to Cecilia and Barrett. My brain was moving at twice the speed of my lips, making me feel sluggish and stupid. Brant, god bless him, seemed to follow the staccato pace of the narrative, filling in the blanks when an occasional word came up missing. What was wrong with me? I knew I'd felt like this before—this scared—this powerless—this out of it . . .

Brant was staring at me. "You actually talked to him?"

What was he talking about? "Who?" I sounded like an owl.

"Rafer."

What had I asked? What had he said before this? What did Rafer have to do with anything? "What?"

"Rafer. At the Rainbow."

"Yes. I ran into him at the Rainbow."

"I know that. You told me. I'm asking you if you talked to him," he said, with exaggerated patience.

"Sure."

"You *talked* to him?!" His voice had risen with alarm. I could see the question mark and the exclamation point hurtling through the air at me. "I brought him up to date," I said. My voice was delayed, like something in an echo chamber. Words in balloons bumped together above my head, images like projectiles flying off in all directions.

"I told you to wait 'til I could check it out. Who do you think started all the rumors?"

"Who?"

Brant took me by the shoulders and gave me a little shake. He seemed angry, his fingers biting into my shoulders. "Kinsey, wake up and pay attention. This is serious," he said.

"You're not saying it was him?"

"Of *course*, it was him. Who else could it be? Think about it, dummy."

"Think about what?" I asked, confused. The immediacy of his discomposure was contagious. I was relying on him for help, but his anxiety was pushing mine into the danger zone.

His voice pounded on, pleading and cajoling, wheedling. "You told Mom it was someone in law enforcement. Do you honestly think my father would have lost even one night's sleep if it was anyone but Rafer? Rafer was his best friend. The two of them had worked together for years and years. Dad thought Rafer was one of the finest cops who ever lived. Now he finds out he killed two guys? Jeez. He must have shit himself when he understood what was going on. Didn't he write this down? Isn't this in his notes?"

His words were like streamers, blowing above his head.

I heard snapping, like flags. "The notes are in code. I can't read them."

"Where? Can you show me? Maybe I can crack it."

"In there. You think he was on the verge of talking to Internal Affairs?"

"Of course! The decision couldn't have been easy, but even as loyal as he was to Rafer, the department came first. He must have been praying for a way out, hoping he was wrong."

My brain worked lickety-cut. It was my mouth that fumbled, thoughts crashing against my teeth like rocks. I had to clamp my jaw shut, barely moving my lips. "I talked to Barrett. She was with Tom in the truck just before he died," I said.

"What did they talk about? Why did he do that?"

"Something. I can't remember."

"Didn't you press her for answers? You had the girl right there in the palm of your hand," he said. His words appeared in the air, written in big capital letters.

"Quit yelling."

"I'm not yelling. What's the matter with you?"

"Barrett never said a word about Rafer." I remembered then. She did say Tom had asked about her father.

"Why would she? She doesn't know you from Adam. She's not going to confide. She wouldn't tell you something like that. Her own father? For god's sake, she'd have to be nuts," he shrilled.

"But why give me the notes? Wouldn't she assume they'd be incriminating?"

"Barrett doesn't have a clue. She has no idea."

"How do you know what he did?"

"Because I can add," he said, exasperated. "I put two and two together. Listen, Tom met with Barrett. He was probably trying to find out about Rafer's whereabouts when Pinkie was murdered. Same with Alfie Toth. He saw the connection. He was worried someone in the department would get wind of his suspicions, didn't you say that? Someone had already ripped him off for the information about Toth. Who do you think it was? *Rafer.*"

"Rafer," I said. I was nodding. I could see what he was saying. I'd been thinking the same thing. Tom's friendship with Rafer was such that he'd think long and hard before he turned him in to the authorities, betraying their friendship. A conflict of that magnitude would have caused him extreme distress. My brain was clicking and buzzing. *Click, click, click.* Rafer. It was like a pinball game. Thoughts ricocheted around, setting off bells, bouncing against the rails. I thought about the clerk at the Gramercy. Why didn't he tell me the phony plainclothes detective was black? You'd think he'd remember something so obvious. My mind kept veering. I couldn't hold a thought in one place and follow it to its conclusion. *Click, click.* Like pool balls. The cue ball would break and all the other balls on the table would fly off in separate directions. I wished I'd talked to Leland Peck before I left Santa Teresa. I was feeling very weird. So anxious. Sound fading in and out. I could see it undulate through space, sentences like surfers cresting on the waves of air.

Brant was still talking. He seemed to be speaking gibberish, but it all made a peculiar sense. "Pinkie went after Barrett. She was hiking in the mountains and stumbled across their fishing camp."

On and on he went, creating word pictures so vivid I thought it was happening to me.

"Barrett was assaulted. He put a gun to her head.

She was raped. She was attacked and sexually abused. Pinkie sodomized and hurt her. He forced her to perform unspeakable acts. Alfie did nothing—offered her no assistance—ran off, leaving her to Pinkie's mercy. Barrett came back hysterical, in a state of shock. Rafer went after Pinkie and took him down. He strung him up, hung him from the limb of a tree and let him die slowly for what he had done to her. He would have killed Alfie, too, but Alfie escaped and blew town. Rafer thought he was safe all these years and then Pinkie's body turned up and Dad found the link between the two men. He drove all the way to Santa Teresa to talk to him, but Rafer got there first. He hung Toth the same way he hung Pinkie." Brant was looking at me earnestly. "What's wrong with your eyes?"

"My eyes?" Once he mentioned it, I realized my field of vision had begun to oscillate, images sliding side to side, like bad camera work. I felt giddy, as if I was on the verge of fainting. I sat down. I put my head between my knees, a roaring in my ears.

"Are you okay?"

"Fine." Lights seemed to pulsate and sounds came and went. I couldn't keep it straight. I knew what he was saying, but I couldn't make the words stand still. I saw Rafer with the noose. I saw him tighten it on Pinkie's neck. I saw him hang Alfie in the wilderness. I felt his rage and his pain for what they'd done to his only daughter. I said, "How do you know all this?"

"Because Barrett told me when it happened. Jesus, Kinsey. That's why I broke up with her. I was twenty years old. I couldn't handle it," he said, anguished.

"I'm sorry. I'm sorry," I said, but immediately forgot

who was more deserving of my pity—Barrett for being raped, Brant for not having the maturity to deal with it.

Brant's tone became accusatory. "You're loaded. I don't believe it. What the hell are you high on?"

"I'm high?" Of course. Daniel playing the piano. My ex-husband. So beautiful. Eyes like an angel, a halo of golden curls and how I'd loved him. He'd given me acid once without telling me and I watched the floor recede into the mouth of hell.

Brant's head came up. "What's that?" he hissed.

"What?"

"I heard something." His agitation washed over me. His fear was infectious, as swift as an airborne virus. I could smell corruption and death. I'd been in situations like this before.

"Hang on." Brant strode down the hall. I saw him look out of the small ornamental window in the front door. He pulled back abruptly and then gestured urgently in my direction. "A car cruised by with its lights doused. He's parked across the street about six doors down. You have a gun?"

"I told you someone stole it. Whoever broke in. I don't have a gun. What's happening?"

"Rafer," he said, grimly. He crossed to the drawer in his mother's kitchen desk where she did her menu planning. He pulled out a gun and thrust it in my hand. "Here. Take this."

I stood and stared at it with bewilderment. "Thanks," I whispered. The gun was a basic police revolver, Smith & Wesson. I'd nearly bought one like it once, .357 Magnum, four-inch barrel, checkered walnut stocks. I studied the grooves in the stock. Some of them were so deep, I couldn't see to the bottom.

"Rafer will come in with guns blazing," Brant was saying. "No deals. He's told everyone that you're a killer, that you do drugs, and here you are stoned on something."

"I didn't do anything," I said, mouth dry. The brownies. I was higher than he knew. I racked back through my memory, classes at the police academy, my years in uniform on the street, trying to remember symptoms; phencyclidines, stimulants, hallucinogens, sedative-hypnotics, narcotics. What had I ingested? Confusion, paranoia, slurred speech, nystagmus. I could see the columns marching across the pages of the text. PCP vocabulary. Rocket Fuel, DOA, KJ, Super Joint, Mint Weed, Gorilla Biscuits. I was out of my brain on speed.

"You found him out. He'll have to kill you. We'll have to shoot it out," Brant said.

"Don't leave me. You talk to him. I can get away," I burbled.

"He's thought of that. He'll have help. Probably Macon and Hatch. They both hate you. We better get down to business."

When Brant peeled off his outer jacket, I smelled stress sweat, the scent as acrid and piercing as ammonia. I glanced at his hands. Given any visual field, the eye tends to stray to the one different item in a ground of like items. Even bombed, I caught sight of a blemish on his right wrist, a dark patch... a tattoo or a birthmark... shaped like the prow of a ship. The blot stood out like a brand on the clean white surface of his skin. Sizzling, my brain zapped through the possibilities: scar, hickey, smudge, scab. I was slow on the uptake. I looked back and then I saw it for what it was. The mark was a burn. The healing discoloration was a match for the tip of the ticking hot iron I'd pressed on him. Adrenaline rushed through me. Something close to euphoria filled my flesh and bones. My mind made an odd leap to something else altogether. I'd been struggling to break the code with logic and analysis when the answer was really one of spatial relationships. Vertical, not horizontal. That's how the numbers worked. Up and down instead of back and forth across the lines.

I put the gun on the kitchen table. "I'll be right back," I said. With extraordinary effort, I propelled myself into Tom's den, hand to the wall to steady my yawning gait. 8, 12, 1, 11, and 26. I sat down at his desk and looked at the calendar Tom had drawn. I could see the month of February, twenty-eight days penned in with the First falling on a Sunday and the last two Saturdays, the Twenty-first and the Twenty-eighth, crossed out, leaving twenty-six numbers. I'd suspected the code was simple. If Tom encrypted his notes, he had to have an uncomplicated means by which to convert letters to numbers.

I found a pencil. I turned to the calendar grid that he'd drawn on the corner of his blotter. I wrote the letters of the alphabet, inserting one letter per day, using vertical rows this time. If my theory was correct, then the code would confirm what I already knew: 8 would represent the letter *B*. The number 12 would stand in for the letter *R*. The number 1 would be *A*, and 11 would represent an *N*, and the 26 would be *T*.

B-R-A-N-T.

Brant.

I could feel a laugh billow up. I was stuck in the house with him. He would have had easy access to his father's notes. The search of the den—the broken window—both had been a cover, suggesting to the rest of us that someone from the outside had entered the house in hopes of finding the notes. It wasn't Barrett at all. Pinkie hadn't raped and sodomized Barrett. It was Brant he'd humiliated and degraded.

"What are you doing?"

I jumped. Brant was standing in the doorway. I was standing in horseshit up to my underpants. The sight of him wavered, shimmering, image moving side to side. I couldn't think of a way to answer. Nystagmus. Something in brownies, possibly PCP. Aggression, paranoia. I was smarter than him. Oh, much smarter. I was smarter than anyone that day.

"What are you looking at?"

"Tom's notes."

"Why?"

"I can't make heads or tails of them. The code."

He stared at me. I could tell he was trying to determine if what I'd said was true. I kept my mind empty. I don't think I'd ever seen him looking so lean and young and handsome. Death is like that, a lover whose embrace you sink into without warning. Instead of flight or resistance, voluptuous surrender. He held out his hand. "I'll take the notes."

I passed the notebook across to him, picturing the Smith & Wesson. Where had I heard about a gun like that before? I could feel my brain crackling, thoughts popping like kernels banging against the lid of a popcorn pan. There was no way in the world he would give me a gun unless he intended to see that I was killed with it. Rafer LaMott wasn't outside and neither was anybody else. This was a charade, setting me up in some way. I envisioned the scene—the two of us skulking through the house, ostensibly waiting for an attack that would never come. Brant could shoot me anytime he chose, claiming later he'd mistaken me for an intruder, claiming self-defense, claiming I was stoned out of my gourd, which I was. Even as the thought formed, I felt the drugs kick up a notch. I could feel myself expanding. I could outsmart him. He was strong, but I had more experience than he did. I knew more about him than he knew about me. I'd been a cop once. I knew everything he knew, plus some.

"Is the car still out there?" I asked.

Brant dropped back into his fantasy. He moved to the window and put his face close the the glass, peering off to the right. "Down half a block. You can barely see it from here."

"I think we should turn the lights out. I don't like standing here in plain view."

He studied me for a second, picturing the house black as pitch. "You're right. Hit the switch. I'll take care of all the other lights in the house."

"Good." I turned the den light out. I waited until I heard him moving down the hall toward the front. Then I eased to the window, flipped the lock, and pushed the sash up about six inches. I dropped down to the floor, felt my way across the room to the cabinet, and slid myself feet-first into the space beneath the bookshelves.

Birth in reverse. I was hidden from view. Moments went by, the house becoming darker by the minute as lamps were being switched off in every room Brant entered.

"Kinsey?" Brant was back.

Silence.

I heard him come to the den. He must have stood in the doorway, allowing his eyes to adjust to the black. He crossed to the window, bumping into cardboard boxes. I heard him force the window open and look out. I was gone. There was no sign of me running across the grass. "Shit!" He slammed the window shut and said, "Shit, shit, *shit!*" He must have had a gun because I heard him rack one into the chamber.

He left the den, hollering my name as he went. Now he was mad. Now he didn't care if I knew he was coming. I pulled myself out of the cabinet, hanging on to the shelf as I staggered to my feet. I crossed to the desk and opened the bottom drawer as quietly as possible. I took out Tom's handcuffs and tucked them in my back pocket. I could feel myself swell with power. I was suddenly larger than life, far beyond fear, luminous with fury. As I turned right out of the den into the darkness of the hallway, I could see him moving ahead of me, his body mass blacker than the charcoal light surrounding him. I began to run, picking up speed, my Reeboks making no sound on the carpet. Brant sensed my presence, turning as I lifted myself into the air. I snapped a hard front kick to his solar plexus, taking him down with one pop. I heard his gun thump dully against the wall, banging against wood as it flew out of his hand. I kicked him again, catching him squarely on the side of the head. I scrambled to my feet and stood over him. I could have crushed his skull, but as a *courtesy*, I refrained from doing so. I pulled the handcuffs from my pocket. I grabbed the fingers of his right hand and bent them backward, encouraging compliance. I lay the cuff on his right wrist and snapped downward, smiling grimly to myself as the swinging arm of the cuff locked in place. I put my left foot on the back of his neck while I yanked his right arm behind him and I grabbed for his left. I would have stomped down on his face, pulverizing his nose if he'd so much as whimpered. He was out cold. I double-locked both handcuffs in place. All of this without hesitation. All of this in the dark.

The light in the kitchen was snapped on. Selma appeared in the doorway, still wearing her fur coat. She stood as still as a soldier and took in the sight before her. Brant was now moaning. Blood was pouring from his nose and he was struggling for breath. "Mom, watch out. She's stoned," he croaked.

Selma backed into the kitchen. I was moving away from her down the corridor, looking for Brant's gun when she showed up again, this time with the Smith & Wesson in her right hand. I had no idea where Brant's gun had gone. I remembered the telltale thump at the end of its airborne journey.

"Stop right there," she said. She was now holding the gun with two hands, arms extended stiffly at shoulder height. I went about my business, ignoring her little drama. She had no way of knowing I'd been sanctified by Angel Dust. I was higher than a kite on PCP, methamphetamines, whatever it was—some amazing mix of excitation and immortality. The unpleasant side effects were now gone and I was detached from all feeling, secure in the sense that I would prevail over this bitch and anyone else who came after me.

"You're not going to take my son away from me."

As much as anything, I was annoyed with her. "I told you to forget it. You should have left well enough alone. Now you've not only lost Tom, you've lost Brant as well," I said, conversationally. I got down on my hands and knees and felt under the chair. Where the hell was Brant's gun?

"You are completely mistaken. I haven't lost Brant at all," she said. "Now get up right this minute! Do as I say!"

"Blow it out your ass, Selma. Do you see Brant's gun? I heard it bang against the wall. It's gotta be here somewhere."

"I'm warning you. I'll count to three and then I'm going to shoot you."

"You do that," I said. I moved into the dining room, convinced the gun had somehow become wedged under the hutch, the centerpiece in Selma's entire set of handsome, formal, glossy dark wood furniture. I placed my shoulder against the floor, reaching under the hutch as far as the length of my arm. It was in this awkward position—me spread-eagled on my stomach, Brant handcuffed and moaning in the hall, Selma angling herself into position to blow my head off if she could manage it—that I chanced to look up at her, watching in slow-motion amazement as she screwed up her face, closed her eyes, turned her head, and squeezed the trigger. There was a bright flash and a loud bang. The bullet exited the barrel at a lethal velocity. The normal football-shaped muzzle flash out the front of the gun and the vertical fan-shaped flashes at the cylinder gap seemed to be enhanced, a dazzling yellow. Brant had apparently packed the first cartridge with an overload of fast powder. I thought I knew now who Judy Gelson's lover was the night she blew a hole in her husband's chest. The chamber and the top strap ruptured. The blast unlatched the cylinder and drove it out to the left side of the gun. The brass cartridge case shredded and tiny bits of brass peppered Selma's hands, flakes of unburned powder peppering her face as well. Simultaneously, as though by magic, all the glass in the cabinet doors, including the crystal goblets and the bone china plates, exploded like fireworks and formed a glittering starburst of falling glass and debris.

"Fuck. That was great. You should try that again," I said.

Selma was weeping as I walked to the phone and dialed 9–1–1.

EPILOGUE

Later, the Nota County Sheriff gave me permission to read the file on the Ritter/Toth murders. Rafer and I sat down together and by comparing Tom's notes with other reports submitted in the case, we managed to piece together the course of Tom's investigation. The irony, of course, was that the evidence he'd collected was not only spotty, but entirely circumstantial. None of it was sufficient to result in an arrest, let alone a conviction. Tom realized Brant had committed double murder and he knew it was something he couldn't keep to himself for long. Revealing the truth would destroy his marriage. Concealing the truth would destroy everything else he valued. Tom had died in silence, and if Selma had been content to leave it there, the case might have died, too.

Brant is currently out on bail on a charge of attempted murder for what he did to me. Selma's hired a fancy-pants attorney who (naturally) advised him to plead not guilty. I suspect if we get to court this same attorney will find a way to blame the whole thing on me. That's the way justice seems to work these days.

In the meantime, Selma's house is on the market and

352

she's leaving Nota Lake. The town is unforgiving and the people there never liked her anyway. I guess what it all boils down to is a lesson in personal insecurity and low self-esteem. If I'd been clairvoyant—if I'd been capable of seeing all of these events in advance—I'd have told her to have her teeth capped instead of hiring me. She'd have been better off that way.

Respectfully submitted,
Kinsey Millhone

SUE GRAFTON

J is for Judgment

'On the face of it, you wouldn't think there was any connection between the murder of a dead man and the events
that changed my perceptions about my life . . .'

For Kinsey Millhone, the investigation started with a surprise visit from an ex-colleague at California Fidelity – the
company that had fired her nine months previously.

Five hours later she was on a plane to Mexico, hot on
the trail of a suicide who'd allegedly just come back to life.
After a five year wait, Wendell Jaffe's widow had finally
succeeded in having the real estate swindler declared dead,
collecting half a million dollars for her pains. Now it looks
more like 'pseudocide' – and Kinsey's ready to risk everything to get to the truth . . .

'Kinsey Millhone is up there with the giants of the private
eye genre, as magnetic as Marlowe, as insouciant as
Spenser . . . exhilarating stuff'
Time Literary Supplement

'Fiendishly clever . . . better than anything else that's
currently on offer'
Literary Review

'Human, humane, believable and engaging'
Daily Telegraph

SUE GRAFTON

K is for Killer

'In Santa Teresa, California, approximately eighty-five per cent of all criminal homicides are resolved. The victims of unresolved homicides I think of as the unruly dead; restless, dissatisfied, longing for release. In the hazy zone where wakefulness fades into sleep I can sometimes hear them whisper the names of their attackers. I lie awake, listening, hoping to catch a syllable, a phrase, straining to discern in that roll call of conspirators the name of one killer. Lorna Kepler's murder ended up affecting me that way.'

Lorna Kepler was beautiful and wilful, a loner who couldn't resist flirting with danger. She had also been found dead in mysterious circumstances and her death pulls Kinsey Millhone into a netherworld of deception, betrayal and unavenged murder.

'K is a wry, accomplished and entertaining addition to the series'
Patricia Craig, *Times Literary Supplement*

'*K is for Killer* is another exciting novel from the excellent Sue Grafton'
Maggie Pringle, *Daily Mirror*

'For characters and cunning, this may be Grafton's summit so far'
Sunday Times

SUE GRAFTON

L is for Lawless

'I don't mean to bitch, but in the future I intend to hesitate before I do a favor for a friend of a friend. Never have I taken on such a load of grief. At the outset, it all seemed so innocent . . .'

It was the week before Thanksgiving when Kinsey Millhone first heard the sad story of the late Johnny Lee, the World War II fighter pilot of whom, rather mysteriously, the military authorities have no record. His family are concerned – perhaps Kinsey could make a few calls, straighten things out?

Then Johnny's apartment is ransacked. In the debris a hidden safe is uncovered – and in that safe is a mysterious key marked LAWLESS.

That night Kinsey's on a plane to Dallas, at the start of a thrilling rollercoaster ride through Texas and Kentucky on the trail of long-buried treasure. Unfortunately there's a fire-raising psychopath on her tail . . .

And she's going to be late for a very important wedding . . .

'An alphabet of prime puzzles'
Sunday Times

SUE GRAFTON

M is for Malice

'M' is for Malice – and Malice kills . . .

'M' is for Malek Construction, the $40 million company
that grew out of modest soil to become one of the big three
in California.

'M' is for the Malek family: four sons now nearing
middle age who stand to inherit a fortune – four men
with very different temperaments and needs, linked only
by blood and money. Eighteen years ago, one of them –
angry, troubled and in trouble – went missing.

'M' is for Millhone, now hired to trace that missing black
sheep brother.

And, in brutal consequence, 'M' is for murder . . .

'An unusually compelling series of novels with a notably
convincing central character'
Guardian

'M is for marvellous, mesmerising and magnificent'
Val McDermid, *Manchester Evening News*